Rand flung a buffalo hide on the floor and pulled Kate to him.

They explored each other with eager hands, eyes, and lips as if they had never loved before. Shedding their skin garments to make soft puddles at their feet, they sank to their knees on the robe. They touched and tantalized, awestruck anew. They linked their bodies and their lives, moving in a rhythm so fierce, they moved the robe across the floor out of the sun into the chill shade. Yet they felt nothing but the heat between them. Finally, breathless, sweating, they collapsed but still held tight.

River of Sky

"Good writing, solid research, and a strong plot make this a hearty, stick-to-your-ribs romance that is guaranteed to satisfy." —*Kirkus Reviews*

"A satisfying romance set in a time and culture long vanished but still fascinating." —*Library Journal*

"Karen Harper brings the mighty river and the frontier people who inhabit the wilderness ... into clear perspective in this enthralling tale of a woman determined to make it on her own.... Readers will be drawn into *River of Sky* and will discover a memorable story and dynamic characters."
—*Romantic Times*

River of Sky

Karen Harper

A SIGNET BOOK

SIGNET
Published by the Penguin Group
Penguin Books USA Inc., 375 Hudson Street,
New York, New York 10014, U.S.A.
Penguin Books Ltd, 27 Wrights Lane,
London W8 5TZ, England
Penguin Books Australia Ltd, Ringwood,
Victoria, Australia
Penguin Books Canada Ltd, 10 Alcorn Avenue,
Toronto, Ontario, Canada M4V 3B2
Penguin Books (N.Z.) Ltd, 182–190 Wairau Road,
Auckland 10, New Zealand

Penguin Books Ltd, Registered Offices:
Harmondsworth, Middlesex, England

Published by Signet, an imprint of Dutton Signet,
a division of Penguin Books USA Inc.
Previously published in a Dutton edition.

First Signet Printing, August, 1995
10 9 8 7 6 5 4 3 2 1

As ever, to my husband, Don,
and
to the two Margarets in my life,
Margaret Kurtz,
mother and friend,
and
Margaret Ruley,
agent and friend

PART ONE

The Muddy Mississippi

Old Woman in the Moon hated mingled, muddy water. She must see her face to know she could control that might and power. So before a sacred song to her, she long ago decreed one must settle out the river clay from water in the hollow of a rock. Water over silt made a medicine mirror— *a-wa-sa-ta*, like the clear face of truth.

Chapter 1

St. Louis, Missouri, October 15, 1835

She could not believe that he was gone. Six years of marriage, two children, a booming business, this huge house—and he was gone.

To convince herself—to shake free of this stubborn, strange belief he must be coming back—Kate Craig forced herself to look at the narrow lines in today's newspaper again. From the black-banded heading titled simply "DEATHS," she read aloud, "Clive Craig, steamboat river captain and owner of Craig & Co., Fur & Indian Trade Goods, departed this life of a weak heart at his home, Winterhaven, on Spruce Street, 13th of October, aged 47 yrs., 5 mos., and 6 days. Formerly of Kentucky, Captain Craig leaves behind a grieving widow, Katherine, and a young son, James. Captain Craig was preceded in death by a daughter, Sally Katherine. . . ."

Kate's voice snagged on that, but she went on: "The deceased was admired by all for helping to build trade with the north Missouri tribes, especially the Mandans, to profit and benefit the commerce of our fair city. Calling hours at the home, at half past 11 of the morning, Saturday, the 16th of October. Interment immediately following at the new north cemetery, Fair Lawn."

There, Kate thought, she'd done it. Read the words aloud so she could believe and accept them. "Died of a weak heart," she whispered, clutching the newspaper to her. Her beloved Clive had suffered so with that at the end, and sometimes, these last years, both with and without him, Kate had wondered if that weren't her affliction too. Not a bodily ailment but one of the spirit—of not really doing things she longed to do, of not letting herself dare to feel things deeply anymore, at least since Sally's loss. And now this.

She rested her trembling hand on the edge of the polished oak coffin with its lifted lid. The big casket stretched between two tall-backed, upholstered armchairs. She gazed at Clive's face, pale and slack, so it hardly looked like him. Trembling, she reached out to stroke his brown hair. Yesterday Dr. Beaumont had been kind enough to help her wash and dress him. This morning Simon, their elderly carriage driver and gardener, and two neighbor men carried him downstairs and put him in. Poor Clive was ready for his callers, yet she dreaded bringing Jamie in to bid farewell to his father when the boy returned from his brief stay across the street.

But then she dreaded everything about losing Clive. This whole beautiful mansion might as well be a mausoleum without him ever coming back to it again. The mingled aromas of food, lemon wax, paint, oil lamps, perhaps the smell of death itself seemed to seal her in this home she loved so dearly.

"Madame, you are all right?" Even the familiar voice made her jump. It was Adele, one of her two housemaids, who were sisters. "I thought I did hear you speaking with someone," she went on, "but I did not hear the doorbell."

"No, I'm fine, Adele. There is . . . no one. Is the dusting done? It's just I want everything to be perfect tomorrow to honor the captain, so as soon as I finish painting the memorial plates, I'm going to assist you and Claire and help Maureen bake gâteaux for the funeral meal."

"Madame," the young woman said, fluttering her graceful hands as she spoke, "Claire and I, we think you drive yourself too hard when the captain was ill, but especially right now. Rest to greet your guests tomorrow. We will do the cleaning, help Maureen with the baking too, no?"

"But it *helps* me to keep occupied, Adele."

"We—all of us—are so afraid you will drop over."

"I might wilt like one of those flowers on my china plates, but I will not drop over . . . or break. You'll see."

Shaking her sleek head, Adele went out, evidently to

tell the others that Madame still insisted on overseeing everything, just as she had through the months of the captain's illness. For then Kate had felt more needed and important to him than when he was ordinarily away from home more than half the year.

Though Kate fought again for inward calm, rampaging emotions—grief, remorse, fear, even anger—crashed through her. So, again, she strode through the many rooms of the house, hoping its familiarity would soothe her.

Winterhaven was a wonder, surely a safe shelter to bring up her fatherless son. Now, she told herself, everything she did must be for little Jamie. At least Winterhaven's solid surroundings gave her some sustenance for this new ordeal.

Of local limestone, it shimmered white in summer sun, set like a massive pearl in its vibrant green velvet setting of lawns, trees, and gardens of flowers and herbs. In winter the facade glowed golden against the cloak of snow. At Christmas she loved to put lamps in every window to lend light to those who passed on the sparsely settled street at the northern edge of the growing city. So many happy family memories reflected in the windows, polished wood, and shiny, luxurious fabrics here.

With its sturdy stone exterior and high ceilings, the house was cool in the hot months; when winds whipped up from the river or in from the prairie, its heavy brocade curtains, Turkey carpets, and many hearths, each with its modern enclosed grate for coal, kept it warm. On its first floor Winterhaven had a central hall, huge parlor and dining room, morning room, library, and spacious kitchen and pantry. Up the sweeping staircase it boasted six bedrooms because they had been so certain they would have a big brood to fill them. Now the fact that Winterhaven, like her child, was hers to have and hold would have to get her through this crisis.

She drifted back into the parlor and stared up at the impressive oil portrait of Clive, which hung over the hearth behind the coffin. Though Kate would have loved to have painted it, it had been done by a visiting artist Clive had met down on the wharf. From its lofty vantage point,

Captain Clive Craig, in the ruddy glow of health, strong hand on the steamboat wheel with the wild Missouri beckoning him on to greater things, looked down on her. It was so realistic she almost felt she could talk to him, perhaps call him back from his river journey.

When the front doorbell clanged, she jumped again and went to open it herself. It was the butler from the Lautrec home across the street, where Jamie had been staying the morning until they had Clive properly laid out for the funeral. Kate leaned down to hug her son and asked the man to thank Mrs. Lautrec again for keeping him.

When Adele darted into the hall, Kate lifted her hand to indicate she had everything under control, however foolish a thought that was. When she and her towheaded son were alone, she knelt to hug him again.

Kate's heart twisted anew as she loosed him and gazed down into his angelic blue-eyed face. In his liveliness the child echoed his father's vitality, but his looks came more from her.

"Is Papa all right now?" the boy asked as he had yesterday outside the closed bedroom door.

"I told you, my darling, Papa has to go away for good to heaven, and we have to put him in the ground tomorrow. You know what I told you about your sister, Sally."

"Why in the ground if heaven's way up there?" the boy asked, and pointed, stiff-armed, toward the window and the sky.

"Because only his spirit—his soul—goes to heaven, but his body stays—stays buried," she said, floundering for an explanation that made sense. She took him into the parlor and sat on a chair to remove his coat and hat. She stroked his fine, straight hair, marveling how much its texture resembled Clive's.

"Jamie, I know this is hard to understand. It is hard for me too. I'm sorry if I cannot answer all your questions about Papa's having to leave us."

"He'll come back if he goes. He always does," he assured her, devastating her hard-won poise. "Is he sleeping in that box now? It's just a little boat, not the big one he likes. Can I look in it?"

Kate tugged Jamie to her and hugged him hard again,

though this time he wriggled free and stood on tiptoe. She was short, but the boy could not see up into the coffin at all. How touching, yet how tragic, that he thought of his father as being in a boat, sailing away for just a while . . .

She sniffed hard and, with the heels of her hands, swiped at tears before Jamie could see them. She rose and pulled the chair over to the coffin, then helped the boy climb on it. She stood just behind him, her hands on his thin shoulders, so she could speak quietly in his ear.

"You see, it doesn't quite look like Papa because he's sleeping forever now and won't wake up. It's called death. But his inside thoughts, his memories, his dreams, maybe even his laugh—what really made Papa the man he was to us—well, those things are his spirit, and that's flown away, something like a bird, clear up to heaven."

She thought of her own father, of how cruel he had been to her and Mama. How many times since he passed on she had tried to wish him in heaven, but she was so sure a man like Lester Warfield deserved to be in the other place. Besides, such memories made her miss her mother, who was remarried and lived a good ways upriver. At first Mama and her husband, Tom Barton, had come downriver once a year, but not lately, for Tom was a trading post blacksmith and always in demand there. It might be spring before they even knew Clive was gone.

Kate was somewhat comforted by the fact that her latest attempt at an explanation seemed temporarily to still Jamie's questions. She took him upstairs to entrust him to Adele's sister, Claire, for one of her lively French stories before a nap.

Kate went back downstairs to paint her memorial plates—fifty of them, for she had no idea how many might attend the funeral. Each plate bore a silhouette of Clive with the outline of a steamboat behind him. Her fingers cramped, her neck and back ached, her eyes strained as daylight fled. She lighted lamps and worked on, stopping only long enough to sit at the table while Jamie ate and then to tuck him in bed. She read him a story about George Washington as a boy and found in that another opportunity to talk about a child whose father had

died but who went on to do great things. How she wished
she could believe that of herself.

Later, after staring at her own plate of food, Kate went
back to her work again. Tomorrow was coming fast, and
everything must be in order to honor Clive. But her intense, forced concentration on her work could not keep
her mind from pacing back and forth, around and around.

Clive Craig had swept her off her feet in a whirlwind
courtship, and somehow their years together had blurred
by as fast—except for that painful period she tended her
ill daughter, then lost her to the whooping cough. And as
hard as she had tried to care for Clive, his convalescence,
which had ended so tragically with a second heart attack,
had dragged too. Even when she tried to keep calm and
controlled, she felt as if she were slogging upstream
through thick, muddy water only to founder in this deep
sinkhole of despair.

Kate knew she looked as grief-stricken as she felt.
Slight of frame anyway, she had lost weight during
Clive's illness; though she had once been shapely, her
gowns now hung on her, despite how much she cinched
in her ribboned belts. Sallow circles shadowed her wide-
set, large eyes that Clive had called china blue, but Mama
had described as cornflower blue. Lately, trying to stem
tears, she had squinted those eyes, pressed her lips together, and pinched her nostrils until she hardly looked
like her old self.

She had always thought her features were a bit too generous for her small, heart-shaped face. But with her
heavy, honey-hued hair parted in the center and pulled
back to a nape bun and a thick coil over each ear, the
frame for her face was widened. Clive had once said she
was as delicately exquisite as Sally's French porcelain
doll. Today she felt broken in body and spirit—shattered,
like that doll lost in a fall out the carriage window onto
cobbled, muddy Market Street.

As soon as the last painted plate was tilted on the windowsill to dry, she arranged, then rearranged chairs in the
parlor. She helped Maureen in the kitchen, even when,
she feared, the poor woman thought she loomed over her

like some haunting specter. She reexamined her artwork, looking for flawed brushstrokes, shutting out of her mind that Clive might not approve of the plates, for they displayed more than her usual sprigs of feminine flowers.

Keeping up conversation of things she recalled from happier days, she helped Claire and Adele arrange bowls of asters and mums and hang dried herb wreaths dangling black velvet ribbons. All the servants were dear to her, almost like friends, and she knew she would value them even more in the days to come. After she sent the staff to bed, as if she trod a relentlessly revolving steamboat paddle wheel, she returned to the dim parlor, where faithful, old Simon kept a nodding vigil over his master's lantern-lit coffin.

She quietly hung a black velvet swag across the top of Clive's portrait and one over the mirror; then she gazed out the parlor windows at the sweet autumn night, the sprinkle of stars, and the sliver of new moon.

"It's lovely out there tonight, Clive." She whispered so as not to wake Simon, but she wished, as Jamie said, she could wake her husband. "Maybe like from the deck of the steamer at night, hurrying back to Jamie and me after all that upriver trading, all the dangers. But soon, you'll sleep under the stars every night, and be able to—to look up at the heavens. . . ."

Forcing the tears back, she headed upstairs, rehearsing in her mind how she would greet their guests tomorrow. She could not stop her body or brain from moving, as she went, at last, into their room to pace there.

It was only when pink dawn feathered the eastern sky that she recalled the one thing that had slipped her mind and sank exhausted onto her bed, hers and Clive's: This day they were burying him was her twenty-ninth birthday.

For the first time since her husband had just keeled over his breakfast tray in this bed two days ago, she collapsed in tears.

In her bottle green brocade gown Kate welcomed funeral guests to the mansion Clive called Winterhaven. In the entryway overlooking the town and distant river, she stood with head high, although it hurt terribly from lack

of sleep and weeping. Each time Simon opened the door
for funeral guests, Kate inhaled the crisp tang of air to
steady herself and clear her head. Today even the coal
smoke that often lingered in the air of St. Louis seemed
swept away. She took in another deep breath as if that
could help as two familiar guests came up the flagstone
walk.

"Oh, Kate, what a dreadful loss to you, and just when
he seemed to be rallying a bit," Samantha Lautrec murmured, and patted her shoulder. "I hope the gâteaux our
cooks sent over help you out today."

At Samantha's side, her ribboned bonnet brim bobbing
as she nodded, Lilian de la Forest squeezed Kate's hand.
These two neighbors had been her closest companions
and only china-painting comrades until Clive took ill and
she chose to forgo her Wednesday afternoons with them.

"I can't thank you both enough for the gâteaux, and,
Samantha, for taking Jamie in for a while yesterday. He
loves playing with your pet dogs."

"A blessed way for a riverman to pass," Lilian said.
"In his own bed, I mean, when he used to deal with all
those wild Indians. And he always seemed so—mercy
me, you know—active and robust—before his troubles,
that is. At least he didn't have the numb palsy. Remember, Samantha, I told you my cousin Hector in Philadel-
phia had the numb palsy, and it's even worse."

"Lily," Samantha said, tapping her gloved fingers on
her friend's arm, "I daresay nothing could have been
worse than what happened to poor Captain Craig."

Kate motioned for the maids to take their capes. They
went in, still chattering. Next came Clive's lawyer, the
taciturn Jess Hartman, and his plump wife.

"You poor, little thing." Mrs. Hartman greeted Kate.
"At least he didn't suffer, not long compared with some,
did he? Just wouldn't do for an active riverman to be an
invalid, not for longer than he was anyway, would it?"

"That would have been hard for him," Kate admitted.
"As Dr. Beaumont can attest, Clive was in many ways a
very challenging patient. But these last few months we
shared while he was home were a strange blessing too—
with him being gone upriver so much of the year. It is as

if we got to know each other all over again, so the second, fatal attack came as such a shock."

The silver-haired Mr. Hartman cleared his throat. "It's a fact life's full of surprises. Indeed, one thinks one sees the way things are, and then, boom, reality intrudes." Frowning, he cleared his throat again. "Are you certain you'd like to come to my office for the reading of the deceased's last will and testament on Monday, instead of my calling on you here, Mrs. Craig?"

"Yes, to get out a bit," she told them as she ushered them on to the maids.

She welcomed the minister, the Reverend Mr. Compton, and his wife, who were friends of the Hartmans'. The Craigs had not had a minister per se, for when they attended church, Clive always found something about the service or the message he didn't like, and they went from place to place, except to the cathedral, of course. But Kate had been reared a Methodist and had a grandfather who was a Methodist preacher too, so perhaps she would try Mr. Compton's church on Fourth Street now.

She greeted several other business friends of Clive's including two upriver Indian agents home for the winter. Next came Sam Markwood, who oversaw Clive's fur warehouse.

"It's a clarion call to all of us he's gone, sure enough it is, Miz Craig," he said. Sam was thin as a fence post with a homely but kindly face. He drawled his words; it seemed to take forever for him to express a thought. "None of us all's gettin' any younger, no, ma'am. Captain's death's a warning to live each and ev'ry day best we can, and that's for certain."

"You're right, Mr. Markwood. I like to think Clive did that."

"You know, ma'am, maybe it'll help to think of Captain's loss as a blessin' for your little girl in heaven. Y'all know what I mean. Now she has her daddy back, like you've got the boy," he added as he joined the others.

With a tight throat, Kate fished her handkerchief from her sleeve to blow her nose and dab under her eyes. Sally had died at age three and one half, exactly Jamie's age

now, so she supposed that was why she fussed over him
so.

"Least Cap'n Craig's left you and yours well off without a care in the world," the next visitor, Captain
Wooster, one of the few steamboat pilots not working
down south out of New Orleans for the winter, told her.
Captain Wooster had been hired on to take Clive's newest
stern-wheeler, the *Sally Kate,* upriver when Clive fell ill,
but another man captained her this winter. "Built hisself
quite a little kingdom, the cap'n did, however much
Chouteau's big company controlled the trade. Always admired that about the cap'n, I did. A real rock of a fellow,
not afraid to stand up to the big man, always saying the
Injins deserved some competition from traders."

"Yes, he was a very idealistic man, a very fine man.
And I am grateful for our financial security," she added
as Captain Wooster moved on in the line of people.

Dr. Beaumont, the new doctor in town who had tended
Clive, arrived with his pretty wife on his arm. "I think we
both know it simply wouldn't do for a vital man like Captain Craig to be trapped in this house when he was used
to the massive realm of the Missouri," he said, trying to
console her.

"Again, I cannot thank you enough for your consider-
ation toward me and Jamie. You've gone above and beyond the call of duty, Doctor, and I shall not forget it."

"It's nothing, nothing," he told her, pressing her hand.
As soon as he and his wife were swallowed up by the rising buzz inside, Kate wished he had stayed. She felt suddenly light-headed and moved outside for a breath of air.

At that moment, from different carriages arriving at the
same time to swell the growing cortege of them before
the house, out stepped St. Louis's two most powerful
men: the wealthy Cadet Chouteau of the city's premier
founding family and General William Clark of Lewis and
Clark Expedition fame. Last year Mr. Chouteau had purchased the Western Division of the vast American Fur
Company from John Jacob Astor; General Clark was the
superintendent of Indian affairs for all tribes west of the
Mississippi.

The darkly handsome Chouteau approached first, looking every inch the concerned, bereaved gentleman. Despite the fact that he had been a formidable rival to Clive, the man's fine appearance, elegant demeanor, and soft French accent made him seem trustworthy and not intimidating. Besides, however adamant Chouteau was about stamping out independent opposition, Craig & Company's size could hardly have been much of a threat to Chouteau's near monopoly. But Kate felt fierce pride flare again that Clive's little David had been one of the few independent trade and steamboat companies to stand up to Astor's and then Chouteau's Goliath.

"I am honored you came, sir," she told him sincerely, "and my husband would have been too. Though he didn't see eye to eye with you on all things, he spoke highly of your abilities."

"Madame Craig, such a loss to the river trade, to the continued growth and might of our great city," he told her with a bow over her extended hand and a kiss on the back of it. "Please let me know if I or my family may be of any assistance in any way. And if you feel the need to sell anything, please be assured my company will be happy to pay the very best prices."

"It's too early to think about any of that, Monsieur Chouteau. My husband's business advisers—I'm certain they will still run the business for us—for me. As much as you control, surely one small independent company will be good for business. A bit of competition to keep things fair and square, you know."

He looked a bit surprised at that but said, "Certainly, but do not hesitate to call on me if it gets to be too much for you, a young woman with a child to care for above all else, eh?" Chouteau turned to greet General Clark. "*Mon ami,* General, so good to see you again, even in such sad circumstances. Imagine, a riverman like Craig dying in his bed tended by an earthly angel."

General Clark, a very tall, elderly man, stepped forward to clasp Kate's hand. She was deeply touched that this famous American hero, the man the Missouri tribes called the Great Red-Haired Father, had come to pay his respects. She had spoken with him only one other time, three years ago at a reception for Osage Indian chiefs at his mansion on the prairie, but of course, Clive had known him well.

Much of that grand, exotic event at General Clark's lived yet in her memory, the only night Katherine Warfield Craig had met St. Louis society and painted Indians face-to-face. It had been her debut and, evidently, her swan song, an emotional night for her for several reasons. And to her surprise and dismay, one of those reasons now galloped up right onto the fringe of the lawn, dismounted, tossed his horse's reins at the iron hitching post, and strode up the walk as Chouteau and Clark exchanged a few words and she stared past them.

Yes, she was certain it was the same man. That frown on a face much bronzer than Chouteau's and not a bit elegant or restrained, that glare—

"General. Mr. Chouteau. Mrs. Craig," he muttered, looking up at them from the first step as if he weren't certain he would be allowed on the porch or in the house.

It *was* Randal MacLeod, the man she had accidentally, publicly insulted that night at General Clark's. The man who had been most rude to her and ruined that precious evening. Still, that was three years ago, long past, surely for him as it should be for her. But why ever had he come here today?

He swept off his top hat, which looked totally out of place on him anyway. He wore a fringed buckskin jacket over his trousers and boots instead of shoes. Despite the proper head attire, his too-long hair was windblown; it was so dark it shone almost bluish in the autumn sun before he strode under the protective shade of the portico to the doorway where they stood. MacLeod's skin hue made him look as if he had been working outside all summer. He was a half-breed, son of a Scottish trapper father and Indian mother—"a country marriage," as polite company referred to it. But his beaked, crooked nose and scarred chin attested to the dominance of the Indian in him.

She hadn't seen him since that night at Clark's, but his name turned up now and then in the *Herald*. Clive had once mentioned that MacLeod could have lived in St. Louis, but he kept running into him upriver. She had read he was now working for Clark instead of Chouteau. If this man had been a friend of her husband's, he was welcome here, she told herself—and then told him so. He nodded curtly to her, then to Chouteau, but addressed Clark.

"Sorry, General, but that took longer than you thought," MacLeod said in a deep, quiet voice. It seemed his narrow lips hardly moved when he spoke.

"But task accomplished?" Clark asked.

"With difficulty." MacLeod's coal dark eyes narrowed as they met her nervous stare. She braced herself for what he would say; it was obvious he recalled their first meeting too. Neither of them had offered each other the proper grasp of greeting.

"I know, ma'am," he said, turning his hat in his big hands before him, "how bad it is to lose a loved one. But Captain Craig's loss is not your fault. I hope your suffering will soon pass."

It seemed such a strange thing to say; it surprised her— that and the fact those direct, simple words actually did comfort as nothing else had today. She said nothing for one moment, staring, standing between the tall Clark and slightly taller MacLeod, while Chouteau studied them. In the awkward silence she felt hot, even in the crisp breeze.

"Please, won't you come into the dining room, as the service will start soon, and I must see to my other guests," she managed to say, and led them in.

People ate, chatted, drank, commiserated, comforted. Comforted themselves, Kate thought, suddenly a bit bitter, that they weren't the one dead and life would go on. The yearly October horse races began today on the edge of the prairie, and she was certain most of these people would go directly there from the cemetery and have a roaring good time.

Guests began to file into the parlor so some Scripture could be read before Clive's final journey. Now Kate felt staggered by it all; she knew she could not bear up when they put his coffin in the ground next to Sally's little grave.

But she managed a stoic look at her husband's face and a soft "Good-bye, my love" before she sat down. She had

Jamie brought downstairs to sit beside her on the velvet
settee while others stood about in the hushed parlor. And
then, though people still whispered, waiting for the minister to begin, increasing noise in the kitchen permeated
her stunned state.

Whatever is the matter with the staff? she wondered as
she began to fidget worse than Jamie. The caterwauling
or altercation, whatever it was, grew so raucous she could
hardly ignore it. The minister obviously hesitated to begin; puzzled by the noise, he looked at Kate.

"You sit here and Mama will be right back," she told
the boy, and slipped out.

Could it be the cook crying like that? The staff had already said their good-byes. It did not sound like Maureen,
and Adele and Claire knew better. The service was ready
to begin, and she had wanted it to be solemn and respectful. She would not let anything go amiss in his memory
today, including some untoward ruckus in her own
kitchen!

She was barely into the hall when a stranger, an Indian woman, vaulted past her into the parlor. A frenzied
woman, a fright! From a gash in her forehead blood
smeared her face. Her hair both streamed long and was
hacked horribly short in other places on her scalp. A
deerskin dress of flying fringe and bouncing beads and
clamshells. A blur of motion and emotion.

Kate jumped back against the wall. Disheveled, wide-
eyed, all three women servants scrambled right behind,
trying to grab the running wraith. But when they saw
the assembled gathering, they drew back.

Heart pounding, Kate stepped to the parlor door. The
Indian screamed words Kate could not understand. She
heard another piercing shriek so close, then realized it
was her own. As Kate ran into the parlor, people in the
crowded room jumped, shifted, strained to see. Jamie
scrambled up to stand on the settee, his eyes and mouth
wide.

"*Miworo! Miworo!*" the woman wailed. "*Muhe!
Muhe!*"

Some guests jumped aside from the intruder as she
rushed toward the coffin. Kate lunged at the woman and

missed, toppling a china fern dish from a pedestal. It toppled and crashed. Someone else evidently shattered a memorial plate. General Clark and Randal MacLeod pushed their way through the crowd toward the woman.

She threw herself over the coffin, clinging to it, rocking it on its foundation of the chairs, still wailing, then, head down, lifted a hand in clawlike supplication toward the painting of Clive.

"Mi-wo-ro-ooo!"

General Clark bent toward the Indian, perhaps speaking to her, then said something to MacLeod, who had loosed the woman's grip on the coffin and held her firmly by her shoulders. He was speaking what seemed to Kate to be gibberish to the Indian, perhaps her own tongue, but she only thrashed and chanted. If this was a friend of MacLeod's, had he invited her? Had he come for retribution for Kate's inadvertently insulting him at General Clark's? The scene turned red and black in Kate's brain; screams pounded in her head.

"You know this woman?" she demanded of MacLeod, shouting to be heard over the hubbub.

He nodded; she did not let him answer.

"What is she saying? How dare you let this happen!"

MacLeod's face went even more stern and stony. "You think I planned this? And all because of something years ago?"

So he remembered too. Kate was beside herself with anger and grief. Her fingernails bit deep into her palms. She made fists at her sides to keep from slapping the raving woman to silence and dragging her outside. Over the hubbub she demanded MacLeod get out; the Indian spun on Kate and threw herself against her.

Kate squealed as she staggered back, bumping the coffin, which General Clark grabbed to steady. The lid slammed shut with a bang. Kate expected a thrust of knife, a blow, but the sturdy woman, just her height, clung to her amid that infernal, piercing wailing. And she smelled—of sweat, yes, but also of wet leather and some strange exotic perfume.

"Take her away! What is she saying?" Kate cried, and tried to thrust the Indian woman back at MacLeod.

"What's she saying?" His voice boomed out in the sudden rapt silence of the room. "All right, if you want to know. She's saying, 'Husband, my husband, here is your woman.' She's saying she's Captain Craig's country wife, and she's glad she's come in time to mourn with her dear sister, his city wife!"

Chapter 2

The next Monday afternoon, after returning from her meeting with Clive's lawyer at his office, Kate climbed down from the carriage before old Simon could help her and strode into Winterhaven before anyone could answer the door. At least Adele and Claire must still have Jamie out for some air or she would have had to face all of them right now, and she could not do that, not yet. She slammed the door behind her in a vain attempt to shut out Mr. Hartman's words of Clive's deceit and betrayal.

"First of all, I assure you, Mrs. Craig, there is absolutely no mention of the Mandan woman in his will. Anything left after debts goes solely to you and your son. But I thought you surely realized that your husband had built his business on speculation, on risks. He had no capital in the beginning and took none out but for the house, which, by the way, set him back more than he had expected, but he was enamored with the appearance, the brave show of the thing. Winterhaven was mortgaged to the hilt and, I'm afraid, will be almost immediately repossessed by the bank.

"Thanks to investors, your husband's fleet of steamboats operated on credit, as it were. That is, except for his original side-wheeler, *Red Dawn,* which is spending its last gasp hauling cane and cotton on the southern bayous to get something out of it before it's sold for scrap come spring. Mrs. Craig, are you quite all right? You look as if you're going to swoon. I assumed he had told you he had debts owed, which must, of necessity, now come due. . . ."

All that when she was still trying to explain the scene at the funeral to her son, explain it to herself. Jamie could

hardly grasp the import of what she told him—or, actually, didn't quite tell him—about the Indian woman he
thought was "so pretty and loud, Mama!" It turned out
that when the maids had convinced the woman at the
kitchen door that the man she sought was dead, she had
charged into the house, gone into a frenzy, hacking her
hair and cutting her forehead with a bread knife, holding
them at bay with it, and wailing.

And to make that heathen display even more disgust-
ing, Kate had heard that devil MacLeod tell General
Clark that they should give her a good watch so she
didn't cut off part of a finger in mourning, as "the Mandans *liked* to do!"

After General Clark and MacLeod had taken the
woman away, Kate had denied the Indian's claims. But
Captain Wooster and one of the Indian agents had quietly
confirmed the truth to Kate. "Other rivermen have done
the like for years." Captain Wooster had tried to comfort
her: "It's nothing you done, ma'am."

But she'd had her fill of false condolences by then. She
had composed herself and asked the minister to go on
with his final words. She had not heard one of them, as
stunned as she was. Suddenly she could not wait to get
Clive out of the house and in the ground. She sat like a
statue, holding Jamie's little hand so tightly he squirmed.
Then she had put one foot before the other to the carriage
and gone to the cemetery, watched them lower Clive in
the earth, hugged Jamie. And in her confused, wretched
heart, she had both grieved again and silently pronounced
"Good riddance!"

Now Kate stripped off her shoulder cape and threw it
toward the hat tree made of buffalo horns. For a few more
moments, but for the cook, she had Clive's sanctuary of
Winterhaven to herself. After ripping off her feathered
bonnet, she swept into the parlor and gathered from the
shelves above the carved mahogany sideboard her flower-
painted saucers and cups she had once so proudly displayed. She gathered up the six remaining memorial
plates of Clive and his steamship. Then she shattered
each of them on the floor, walls, or against Clive's portrait, just as Clive had shattered her trust and love, their

marriage, his son's future, her future, even this shrine of a home she had loved so dearly and he had evidently coveted for appearance's sake.

Everything was ruined. Clive might have been done in by a weak heart, but she was likely to be done in by a broken one! In life and from the grave he had destroyed everything, including his own son's secure future, her trust and love in him, their marriage. And to think she had felt remorse and regret about losing him! The liar had told her one reason he did not want to entertain or go out in society was that he wanted "to put family first." As a result, she knew little about how he ran his business, who his friends were. Except for Winterhaven, none of his earthly goods seemed real to her: not the four steamboats or the warehouse she'd visited only once, or the upriver fur and goods trade he'd no doubt loved because it let him be near his Indian woman.

To think she'd regretted that she hadn't told him often enough that she admired how he had built so much from nothing. Thanks to him, she and Jamie would soon have exactly that when just last week Clive had dared say that in a few years they would send Jamie to school in the exclusive children's division of St. Louis University. Now she would be lucky to be able to afford the books to teach him herself, even as Mama had taught her.

And so much for his supposed idealism she'd so revered. Clive had always said he believed people at both ends of the watery trading trail of the Missouri River were being overcharged by the monopoly of the Chouteau family and their massive empire, so he risked his life to help those who needed him. Damn the man! *She,* his legal, proper wife, not that wild Indian woman, who had her whole tribe around her off in the wilds somewhere, had needed him.

And poor, innocent Jamie. How ludicrous to think of her son as Clive's heir, for there was nothing for the boy to inherit save a few acres of land up in Free Indian Territory and one old, rickety steamboat Clive had evidently considered selling for scrap. Clive had thrown his family on the scrap heap! Who could live at the edge of the prairie in Indian Territory? They needed, if not this big place, at least a small house here in town. She could only pray that Jamie had not inherited his father's deceitful nature. Had she and Jamie—Sally too—been part of this horrid charade of his life? Were they all, like Winterhaven, just for show?

"How could you—could you?" she gasped out, glaring up at the looming portrait.

And she had thought she knew him, told others she knew him, especially after these last months, let alone six years. How they must have been laughing at her, pitying her. For she knew nothing of him. Total strangers at the funeral had known him better than she had. Captain Wooster, the Indian agents, Hartman, and, worse, that MacLeod wretch had no doubt known about Clive's other life and wife.

MacLeod had reveled in announcing who the woman was to everyone, while Kate, the bigamist's wife, knew nothing of her, of his other life upriver. She could not help thinking of it as his *real* life, that other woman as his *real* wife, a wife perhaps who had *really* known the *real* Captain Clive Craig. What a wretched, blind fool his "city wife" had been! And Winterhaven was the fool's paradise, a prison she had lived in so naively. But never, never again!

Her head spun. She wrapped her arms around herself and propped her knees against the settee for support. She heard the maids come in with Jamie and him run upstairs, no doubt looking for her. Sad to lose the servants, for in a way they were her only friends, now as good as gone, just like this house. But she would give them excellent characters and ask Mr. Hartman to help them get good situations.

Swiping at her wet cheeks, she shook out her wrinkled skirt and smoothed her hair. Soon she would be tending her own hair, their clothes, fixing their meals, just like the old days, she thought, but taking little things like that back into her own hands did not bother her. It was the big things that worried her: a shelter over their heads this winter, food on the table, some sort of livelihood to keep them.

She knew her thoughts ran wild; she had to rein them

in. She wasn't sure how long she stood just staring at the shattered mess she had made in the very parlor where the chaos had begun the day of the funeral.

Eventually Adele and Claire found her and helped her upstairs, but she would not let them send for the doctor. She could stomach nothing for supper but washed her face and went into Jamie's room to tuck him in. His trusting little face, his innocent comments tore at her. She wanted to wail as that savage Mandan had done. But she kept calm and tried to stay strong for her son, who would now be everything to her. For him she would find a way out of this. She kissed him good-night but stayed with him as he asked, then left the lamp glowing at his bedside when she tiptoed out.

In her room she just sat staring at her gray reflection in her framed mirror, wondering if she really knew herself any more than she had known Clive. She had always thought she was average-looking despite Clive's praise, but his love—she had thought his loyal dedication—had made her feel special and pretty. She felt low and plain—even ugly—now. She might be short, slim, and dainty, but in Clive's arms she had felt strong when she was weak. Now she must be strong in deed.

She let Adele help her undress and brush her hair. She donned her batiste cotton nightgown and said yes, she was fine alone. Thinking she would go to bed, Adele let the coal fire burn down in the grate in the hearth.

But Kate moved to her grandmother's pine rocking chair and rocked, though it squeaked, squeaked. The house went deathly silent but for the comforting sound of the chair and the tall clock on the lower landing bonging away the hours of the night. This old pine and cane-backed chair was the only thing her mother had of her own when she came to Father in marriage, and therefore, she had given it to Kate when she was wed. It had come west with Mama from Chillicothe, Ohio, after Grandmother Fencer—her name had been Katherine, too—died. Now it would go with Kate wherever she went. She had rocked Sally and then Jamie to sleep in this chair; she wished now she could be rocked to eternal sleep in it.

"How could you do this to Jamie and me, even to

Sally?" she whispered as if Clive lay in the big canopied bed yet or sat in his chair by the window.

She wondered if the Mandan had borne Clive children, half-breeds like that vile Randal MacLeod. But, she reasoned, Clive had left Blue Wing every year too. She had overheard General Clark tell Chouteau that was the Mandan's name. Thank God, Kate thought, she would never have to face the "other" wife again. She could have slapped, obliterated her face, Clive's too. . . .

And would do exactly that and with more than broken china!

She got up, lifted the lamp, and looked in on Jamie. She took his lamp too and went out into the hall and down the stairs to the parlor. Adele and Claire had cleaned up the broken china. She lit two more oil lamps to hold back the darkness of the room and her thoughts. She went to the morning room to fetch her oil paints for the china, then stood on a chair to lift down the portrait of Clive in its heavy frame. She lugged it across the room and leaned it against the wall.

Once she had spent hours "growing" flowers on plates, and for what? It was the only sort of painting Clive believed was proper for a woman in her position—but what position? A great lady of a powerful, rich steamboat captain and businessman, never. One of his wives, waiting stupidly for the bigamist's return, yes. At least Clive's gently discouraging her from painting people had been progress from Father's dictum years ago that "good women never do no fancy handwork 'cept sewing, else I'm gonna give you and your mama's s'posed to be rearing you proper what for!"

And since she'd agonized for years that Father might have gone to eternal damnation for the way he'd treated Mama and her, what of Clive? She had not been on speaking or praying terms with God since she lost Sally, but now she recalled Mama's muttering through bruised lips once after Father had struck her and stalked out, "Vengeance is mine, sayeth the Lord!"

She worked quickly, spreading bright paints across Clive's proud expression, obscuring his hand on the steamboat wheel, his brown eyes looking upriver—

toward Blue Wing, no doubt. Under the smear of her paints, he was no longer lord of all he surveyed. A few hollyhocks and roses now sprouted from where his ears had been; she almost laughed. Then, to obliterate his portrait, she rubbed the flowers out to create rolling hills beyond a distant blue prairie horizon.

She knew she had to stop this roiling fury that coursed in her swift and strong as the river in spring melt. This anger at a dead man, at MacLeod, at that Indian woman was giving her that same lump in the stomach that fear of Father had always given her, when she had vowed to herself and Mama she would never live that way again. She had to seize control of herself so she could find some way to salvage things for Jamie.

It wasn't the Mandan woman's fault, some strange little voice in her head insisted. Wouldn't she too have gone into a frenzy if she had just learned her husband was dead and had another wife? Kate wasn't sure how old the Mandan was, but she seemed young. And she had come some twelve hundred miles downriver looking for Clive when he didn't return to her. How brave and loyal; how she must have loved him.

And as General Clark had told the guests before the funeral procession, that wild scene wasn't MacLeod's fault at all. MacLeod had a Mandan mother; he had known this woman's family well, the general had said, that was all. Clark admitted he himself had known her parents when he lived near the Mandans the first winter of his western expedition. It was just chance he and MacLeod were here "to help."

Blue Wing—it was a pretty name, Kate thought, a color name suggesting the sweeping shapes of flight and freedom. . . .

She worked on and on, more clearly defining the long line of hills beyond the silver green of prairie grass, a copse of summer trees, a stream. It was a place she did not know, a place that somehow emerged full-blown from the depths of her yearning. And in the dramatic sky full of fierce clouds, flew bluebirds soaring, searching the vast, open sky with their blue wings—

She jumped at the knock on the door. For the first time

she noted it was a new day. Light sliced through the crack between the draperies.

"Come in," she called out, her voice so hoarse it startled her too. It must be Adele or Claire, as Jamie would just have run in. The door opened slowly, as if the person on the far side were afraid to see what chaos would greet her now.

"Madame, this note, it came for you at daylight, and when I did see your bed was not slept in last night . . ." Adele began. "Oh, such a *fantastique* painting, madame!"

The slender young woman extended a folded piece of paper to her, straight-armed, on a silver salver as if she were afraid to come closer. The poor thing, Kate thought: first an invasion by a screaming savage and now her mistress acting as if she had escaped from some lunatic asylum. And soon to be told she must leave. Kate knew then what she must do today. She would go through Clive's desk, his things, make a plan. She should even visit the office he kept at the warehouse down on the wharf. She must break the news about more changes in his life— some of it, at least—to Jamie, inform the servants. She must act.

She ripped open and unfolded the note, getting paint on it from her smeared hands. She was certain it was more bad news, perhaps one of Clive's creditors who smelled blood already. She thought the letter was scented ever so slightly with tobacco smoke and leather.

In strong slashes of bold handwriting, it read:

If it makes you feel better—Ahpcha-Toha—called Blue Wing—was coming to divorce Capt. Craig— She's living at Gen. Clark's till she can be sent home next spring— She holds no pious, selfish grudges against you— Mandan men often take more than one wife—the wives are either sisters or closer than sisters.

—R. MacLeod

Kate drove herself so hard the next two weeks that her fatigued body finally bestowed sporadic sleep on her. Each day she weeded through Clive's papers and possessions, visited or wrote creditors, and tried to grasp and untangle the web of obligations and debts that were his inheritance to her. She could not believe there was so much about Clive's business—about how the realm of economic realities worked in general—that she had not known. She signed documents, pleaded with the bank, met with lawyers and accountants, then, slowly, came to concede her financial fate. She paced through Winterhaven, trying to accept that it would be sold, deciding what she could sell, what she must keep, then realizing most—then all—of it must go. She cuddled Jamie, answered his painful questions, then night after night, stupefied by anguish and exhaustion, eventually staggered to bed.

Yet there was no solace in sleep. She dreamed endlessly of Clive leaving the house while she stood at the windows with Jamie—sometimes Sally too—and waved good-bye to him. Each time he walked across the wide, rolling river of cobbled street before their house, yes, as if he could walk on water. But the Lautrec house was not across familiar Spruce Street. Instead an Indian lodge stood in mist in a pretty place along the prairie where an Indian woman and two children, mirror images of her own, awaited him. Smiling, running now, Clive went to them, never looking back.

Sometimes Kate dreamed she broke out the window with her bare, bloodied hands and screamed at him to return; sometimes she shrieked in Mandan that she never wanted to see him again, that she wanted to divorce him. If the nightmare woke her up, she wandered the ghostly rooms torn between love and hate for this house of deceit, this place she had once called home. Torn between love and hate—yes, hate—for Clive for what he had done to her and his own flesh and blood.

The first week in November she walked the spacious rooms and halls of Winterhaven with Mr. and Mrs. Bartholomew Benetick, wealthy newcomers to the city, who, through Mr. Hartman, had agreed to buy the house. The first time they had come, she had taken Jamie for a walk; she could not bear to be in the house while they peeked and probed in each room, and she was heartily weary of Mr. Hartman. Now, as the couple peered into each corner, possessively patted upholstery, or fingered draperies, Kate felt they gaped at the private agony of her thoughts.

"Spacious, but I'd eventually want it redone," Mrs. Benetick murmured to her husband as they entered Clive's library. "Too dark."

Even that harmless comment hurt, but Kate said, "I'm sure you'll enjoy deciding how to make the house your own. I know we did—once."

Since Clive had died, Kate had seized upon so many hopes that had then been torn from her grasp. Even with Winterhaven sold and its goods to be auctioned in two weeks, with the warehouse loan assumed by Sam Markwood, Clive's overseer there, even with the three good boats purchased and the carriage and all but one horse gone already, there were still a few unsettled claims. If she sold most of her wardrobe and her pearls, if she sold her gold wedding band, the black sinkhole of debts would devour her profit, and she and Jamie would still be destitute.

She had been horrified when Mr. Hartman and Clive's accountant had pronounced Craig & Company absolutely bankrupt; there was not enough to salvage even basic sustenance for her and Jamie this winter. Mr. Hartman had suggested borrowing from him to get her through until spring, but she refused to accrue more debts, and what would she do to pay him back then? She would not take charity, though she supposed she could have pleaded for some place to live this winter, food to fill their bellies from the neighbors or even kindly Dr. Beaumont or the minister who had buried Clive. But she would not beg from those she had known; perhaps it would be easier to beg from these strangers.

"You know, this furniture was made especially for this house in New Orleans just three years ago," she told them, her voice trembling. She had first felt awed by the large-scale mahogany and black marble-topped pieces, towering four-poster beds, and huge wardrobes, and she saw the Beneticks were too. "If you would like to speak for any furniture pieces for a set price," she went on hurriedly, "I'd be willing to remove them from the auction list, and perhaps you could offer me a small favor in return."

"Perhaps," the portly Boston banker said hesitantly.

"You see, moving out so quickly puts me and my son at a bit of a disadvantage. Until I can get us permanently settled somewhere else next spring, I wonder if you wouldn't mind if the two of us wintered in the rooms over the carriage house."

"Dear me," the elegantly attired Mrs. Benetick put in, but Kate could tell she was relieved not to have been asked that they be allowed to stay in the house itself. "You mean, live in the groom's quarters out there?"

"Yes, there are two rooms and a little coal stove, so it could be made quite livable. We just need a small place until I can make—make other arrangements for us." She had decided how she would make a living for them. She would sell painted china to Main Street stores, perhaps even to the two big hotels in town. Later she would see her way clear to set up a portrait studio and attract clients, perhaps even patrons. She hadn't had time to ask the shopkeepers if they would take her goods yet, but they would just have to.

That would give her time to develop her real painting, as she had always longed to do. She was good at human likenesses; Mama and even a professional artist had told her so. Given time, she was determined she could make it work to support them. Besides, in the spring the *Red Dawn* would be back from down south, and she could surely get something for it. That boat alone had somehow escaped being part of this mountain of investment risks and debts.

"I'm afraid it's highly unorthodox," Mr. Benetick said, and wiped his forehead with his handkerchief on this cool early November day. "But we do agree charity begins at home, don't we, Mrs. Benetick?"

"Indeed, we do," she said, staring at Kate.

"If you hire a driver and groom, they could use one of the servants' rooms on the third floor until spring," Kate prompted. In truth, the small rooms above the stables were the only place she thought she could convince little

Jamie to be happy this winter, as if living there for a while could be a grand adventure. How much he had loved it when Simon had let him visit there, "where the horsies live." But how hard it would be for both of them to see their big house so close inhabited by another family and their brood of four happy children.

"I believe that would be a suitable arrangement for us then, don't you think so, Mrs. Benetick?" the man asked his wife.

"Till spring, to help you out of your predicament, Mrs. Craig," she said with a condescending nod. "After all, I understand perfectly how you feel. Having to pack up things and move is such a bother it can quite turn one's life upside down, and on top of everything else you've been through . . ."

"Yes. Thank you" was all Kate could manage to say as she escorted them to the front door. She was relieved this painful interview was over. And more relieved that however much these strangers who would take Winterhaven peered and probed here, they could not see or touch her shattered soul. No one could, she realized as she closed the door behind them, so she would have to pick up the pieces by herself.

Chapter 3

"Mama, can I have Papa's big Indian pipe if he's not coming back like you said?"

Kate looked up from cleaning out Clive's trunk to see her son standing in the door of her bedroom. She gasped. Blood on his face, just like Blue Wing! Then she realized her red paint streaked his forehead.

"Jamie, get in here. We've got to wash your face. And you're *not* to get in my paints. You know that."

"I forgot," he said, not budging. "But I can't reach the Indian pipe."

"They smoke it to make peace with the whites. We're not doing that, so we'll leave it where it is. Oh, Adele, there you are," she said as the breathless young woman appeared behind Jamie in the hall.

"Your paints, madame, I did clean them up. And now I will wash them off, good as new," she said, and tugged Jamie away.

Kate stared at the empty doorway, then down into Clive's trunk. How desperately she wished she could wash mistakes away and make everything good as new. For through the blur of work and worry, even when she was not having her recurrent nightmare, tormenting thoughts of Clive's "other wife" barged in.

Whatever Kate was doing, she wondered about Blue Wing, not only how she was faring out at General Clark's place on the prairie but what she was really like. Did the two of them have much in common, despite their obvious differences? Is that why Clive had wed them both? Or had he just been, well, hungry for any woman's touch, her bed, upriver half a year and found the Indian almost by accident?

In a way that was how she herself had met Clive, by
accident—she used to think by Providence—in an emporium on Main Street when she and Mama were shopping
for a gown for Mama's second wedding and Clive was
just back from upriver, looking for what he called "a civilized suit of clothes." It was that very set that became his
wedding garments which she now lifted from the trunk
and put in the pile to be sold. How Clive had charmed
her. Had he also swayed Blue Wing to his wishes so easily?

Kate had even wondered about the Mandan woman
when she signed over the steamship deeds, for those were
the very vessels that had taken Clive to Blue Wing. Again
and again Kate had read the brief note from Randal
MacLeod, marveling at the heathen belief that a man's
wives should be good friends, closer than the real sisters
one Indian man evidently married. Kate had always
wanted a sister. Still, she could not fathom Blue Wing's
home, where divorce, polygamy, and incest were de ri-
gueur. Why had Blue Wing, this Ahpcha-Toha, come to
divorce Clive? What had he done or not done? And such
power to be able to dissolve a marriage just by going to
one's mate and telling him of that desire. But why then,
if Blue Wing did not want Clive anymore, had she
mourned him so fiercely and publicly?

Now, as Kate delved deeper in the trunk, she wondered
if the Indian's hands had sewn this fringed buckskin shirt
with this skillful design of dyed porcupine quills. And
then, in the very bottom, Kate found a buffalo robe. Despite its bulk, she had never seen it before, so Clive must
have meant to hide it. Painted stick figures of Indians,
guns, horses, and long-handled hatchets cavorted across
it, surely telling some sort of story. Her legs crossed
under her grew numb, but she sat on the floor for a long
while, touching it, marveling at the artist's skill, wondering about its people. Then, suddenly, she knew what she
must do.

On a clear, brisk November day Kate made a sort of
necessary pilgrimage. She asked Adele and Claire—
whom fortunately she had obtained good positions for be-

ginning when the furniture went—to watch Jamie for the day. With the carriage at her beck and call she had not ridden much in years, but she cinched the sidesaddle on Calico herself, the only horse she had left. Calico would soon go too, but she had kept her for emergencies. And suddenly this seemed to be one.

She headed the dappled mare up Spruce Street, then north on Ninth, and down the rutted dirt road toward Normandy along Natural Bridge. Winterhaven stood on the outskirts of the burgeoning city; she was soon on the prairie, cantering toward General Clark's estate called Marais Castor "Beaver Pond." She did not want to have to face Randal MacLeod if he was about the place still "helping." She was not even certain she could bear to face the Mandan woman, but she would be comfortable enough speaking with General Clark about how the Indian was getting along.

It was wonderful on the spacious prairie, even though her long-unused muscles ached from riding and the wind was chill. She met and waved to a few riders and halloing teamsters, but she still felt blessedly alone out here. The wide, endless sky and open land, which had never felt the slash of a plow, eased the trapped feeling she'd had lately. Soon winter would come to cover all this rust-and-wine—hued grass with the weight of silent snow, but spring would return with the rebirth of silver green grass and rainbow wildflowers. Somehow she and Jamie would survive too.

Amazingly the distant scene reminded her of what she had painted that night of Clive's funeral. Grass swept and swayed in the wind as if she were riding the waves of the river or the sea. Trees, even leafless now, floated like dark, distant islands on the hazy bluish horizon. Wisps of patterned clouds Clive called fishbone sky were pierced by flying wedges of ducks and geese voyaging south. Their noise filled the sky and her soul, and she longed to escape with them. She'd been out here seldom, almost always staying in the town of her birth. Now this suited her more.

She did, however, recall one fine August day here shortly before Sally died as the carriage took her and

Clive to General Clark's for a formal dinner, the only time she had met the general before Clive's funeral. The prairie had been ablaze with wildflowers. In a pale gold satin gown, her partly bared shoulders covered only by a cashmere shawl, her beribboned bonnet blowing, how excited she had been to ride out to meet new people, including the general's exotic Indian guests.

Besides the Osage chiefs being honored—for signing over their upriver land or some such friendly gesture she could not recall—she had met the eastern artist George Catlin that day and watched him do an oil portrait of the stern-visaged Osages to commemorate the event. She had thought his capturing of their individual expressions wonderful, though as she stood and watched him, he admitted to her he had trouble doing hands and bodies, even landscapes. He was planning a trip up the Missouri to paint the tribes in their natural habitats, he told her.

His striking talent and vibrant personality had intrigued her. When she admitted to him she too loved to draw and paint people, but her father and husband thought it was not a suitable pastime for a lady, Catlin had pulled his intense gaze from his subjects at last. His brown eyes blazed as he turned to her.

"Do a little sketch of someone right now, and let me see it. I'll tell you honestly if you show promise."

She had been so excited; all at once the whole world showed promise. She saw Clive was busy speaking with the general and Cadet Chouteau. With shaky hands she took a piece of paper from Mr. Catlin's table and a charcoal pencil he indicated before avidly returning to his work. She thought of doing Catlin himself or daring to do the Osages he painted while others came and went to sneak a glance before drifting off to more food and drink. But the Indians seemed too unusual, and she could not hope to come close to capturing them as Catlin did.

She could see Clive across this large so-called council chamber where the general displayed Indian memorabilia from his historic western travels with Meriwether Lewis nearly thirty years ago. Yes, perhaps she should do the general—or Clive. Clive's face she knew so well; surely, she could do a good rendering of it.

But her attention was snared by the dynamic face of another man, who looked to be a compromise between the Indians and the whites. His skin was dark but not as coppery as the Osages'; his face looked carved from wood, austere yet compelling. It was not really a handsome face. She had not been introduced or seen him before. While others stood about with cups of punch or brew in earnest conversation, he stood a ways apart, watching—though not her.

She began to sketch him, doing him in angles and broken bits of straight lines, slashes, never curves, never smooth contours. This medium of black charcoal pencil seemed to suit him and his black hair; he wore dark trousers, a low waistcoat, and a cutaway coat over a stark white shirt that contrasted with his dusky coloring, but she did him only shoulders up. Her fingers flew. Breathless, she looked down again at her work to add the thatching of his hair, the hollows of his cheeks, to suggest the dark cloth stretched over his broad shoulders. She extended it to Catlin when he turned to her.

"Damn good, pardon my French, madam!" Catlin exploded. "With practice, training perhaps—listen, never let anyone make you forfeit your dreams if this is what you want. I've defied my parents and broken my good wife's heart to come west for this, and that's my credo: 'Never let anyone make you forfeit your dreams!' You've caught him, that brooding half-breed, what's his name."

"Oh, he's a half-breed? I don't know him either, but I thought he looked primitive and foreign. Thank you for your—"

But Catlin's enthusiastic outburst had drawn a crowd. Guests edged closer. Even the two Osage chiefs came quietly forward to frown at the little paper Catlin held. Worse, the object of her sketch approached. He snatched her work and glared at it. When he spoke, it was evident he had heard what she said.

"Shouldn't stare at *primitive, foreign* half-breeds, lady," he muttered, glaring at her.

"Oh, but—" she began to apologize as Clive, Chouteau, and General Clark came over.

"MacLeod, you look fit to be tied!" Chouteau exclaimed.

"I did some rather primitive sketches of artifacts and plants on our expedition to include in my journal, my dear Mrs. Craig. It's nothing—" The general's words floated to her, but Clive interrupted him.

"Kate, don't bother a man when he's working!"

The older of the Osage chiefs grunted as he squinted at the sketch she had done. He put his hand on the half-breed's stiff back. "Art man only make draw chiefs. Woman no make draw even half-breed or she catch your medicine there." He grunted and pointed an accusing finger first at her and then at the sketch MacLeod still held.

MacLeod glared at Kate again while everyone else stared; her stomach cartwheeled. Surely he did not believe that superstition! She had learned only tonight how the Indians feared, valued, and jealously guarded spirit power or strength, which they called medicine. She hadn't meant to insult or threaten anyone. She opened her mouth to make amends, but MacLeod crumpled her sketch in his big fist, turned, and stalked out.

And so she had never really had the chance to apologize for hurting MacLeod's feelings. She had insulted Indians when she had not meant to. But how, since Catlin had praised her art, she still treasured that one shining night on the prairie.

She jolted back to reality to see a pale, full moon had climbed into the eastern sky; she had forgotten the moon could rise in broad daylight. She shaded her eyes with her hands, even under her bonnet brim, to see the distant house and its cluster of outbuildings. Two ponds, which gave the estate its name, glinted at her in the midday sun. Though the trees stood bare now, she remembered the lush peach orchards edging the front drive, the tall walnut and catalpa trees standing sentinel in the front yard and around the fringe of the ponds. In their welcome shade that other day had stood the black majordomo and other slaves with trays of punch to greet the guests alighting from their carriages, while General Clark strode out to welcome them in person.

But now she only hoped the general would not be busy

so she could speak with him about Blue Wing to assure herself the young woman would be all right with him this winter. Strange that she cared about that when she had resented and detested her at first; she still did, but not as much. She urged her horse to a faster pace toward the house on the horizon under God's great, grand sky.

Behind the cookhouse of Red-Haired Father, Blue Wing sat cross-legged on blowing grass. She wore no robe or blanket over her dress, for she was hardy in any weather as were all The People. With buffalo sinew, she sewed a zigzag pattern of dyed porcupine quills on a pair of man's moccasins. In the month of Big River Breakup, when the robes of snow left the land, she would use these moccasins and other trade items to barter her way back up Big River. But in the months of cold, Red-Haired Father said she must live here.

Loneliness and longing for her people crushed her heart. One of the villagers of Mitutanka especially she yearned to see and say his name to his face. She scanned the sky, but surely it was not the same one over The People in their two villages on the cliffs above Big River. Then she gasped. The full moon, *mihnang-ga,* had risen in the same sky sun-god roamed. Somewhat rare, a special sign to her from Old Woman in the Moon.

Quickly she stuffed her things in her workbasket. She ran into the main house and up the twisting path of stairs. Her small room was on the top floor where the servants lived. This big, square house of many rooms was not spacious to her, not warm, fragrant, curved, and dim. Not like the great wood, earth, and clay lodges of her people. From these walls and ceiling hung no workbaskets, no baby boards. No shoulder blade hoes or snowshoes or quiver of arrows or extra clay pots. No drying turnips or baskets of buffalo berries to make pemmican. No smell of stewed elk, roasting buffalo ribs in hickory ashes. No marrow soup or white sage or fresh forest roots so the nose could fill the belly with hope.

If Red-Haired Father were here, he would understand her longing and her grief, for death had taken his wife. But he had gone to visit his family in villages called Vir-

ginia and Kentucky. Red-Haired Father had lived among
her people ten winters before she was born. He had
known her parents, Corn Basket and Long Hatchet, in the
days of their youth.

She missed Dark Water, too, called MacLeod, who had
brought her here with the Red-Haired Father. He was half
Mandan and the adopted son of Long Hatchet. Dark Water visited The People and knew their words and their
hearts. But Red-Haired Father had sent the half-breed to
the big village of Washington to smoke with the Great Father of all the Whites, called Chief President Jackson.

Here at the big house the black-skinned slaves of Red-
Haired Father stared at her. They nodded or smiled but
did not make talk with her. Only the cook, Big Bess, gave
to her many white man's words. Bess was big enough to
make two Mandan braves, but she smiled and laughed.
Besides, Bess was the first black woman she had ever
seen, and her darker-than-bark skin and curly hair peek-
ing from the bright red turban fascinated Blue Wing. So,
because of the comforting smells and a good heart toward
Bess, Blue Wing spent her days around the cookhouse behind the big house.

As for Kate Craig, River Walker's other wife, Blue
Wing regretted that woman had a very bad heart toward
her. But Blue Wing had never talked with a white woman
before to know she would be angry to see her. River
Walker had never wished to tell about that wife or her
ways, she so blessed with a son. But there was no time
now for dark thinking, not with Old Woman in the day-
time sky.

From Old Woman, Blue Wing could get the answer of
whether to obey Red-Haired Father and stay here or set
out on her own to speak with Kate Craig. Blue Wing had
come here to St. Louis to cut the cord that bound her to
her husband. But she knew his spirit would not travel
well to the spirit village if his two wives were at war during this sacred year of mourning.

Blue Wing dropped her workbasket on the floor, where
she kept her things. She always ignored the chair, table,
and bed. She did everything, including sleep, on her buffalo robe on the floor. Now she seized her rolled elkskin

and her robe and hurried back outside. In the skin were
her ritual goods, her fringed dress, and her precious personal medicine bundle. Its power had failed her in several
things, so she knew it lacked vital items. But it was the
best protection she had.

She hurried toward the small lake. With no river here,
it was the only place she had for the ceremony. She hoped
her plain mourning garment of soft, smoked deerskin
would not offend Old Woman. The Old One surely liked
her supplicants in fine fringed garments like her other
dress. Blue Wing finally slowed her feet at the beaver
lake, which touched the very edge of the prairie.

She had little good heart for this prairie. It had buffalo
grass but, Red-Haired Father had said, no buffalo. Here
the White Cow Society could never do the Buffalo Dance
and call Brother Buffalo with "Shorthorn, come here!"
Here no one could have the O-Kee-Pa ceremony to assure
the fertility of the buffalo bulls. The white man had killed
or driven them all away from this place. She knew Chief
Four Bears feared losing buffalo at home. And this lake
had few beaver. Red-Haired Father kept a few to show his
guests and let the rest be trapped for white man's hats.

She stood quietly, longing again for the vast prairie she
knew so well. It extended far—*tehansh*—from her lodge
village, Mitutanka, to the land of the Sioux and the Crow,
even to the Black Hills and Bighorn River. At least, she
thought, there were no marauding Sioux to fear on this
prairie the white man had tamed.

She unrolled her bundle at the edge of the water and
laid out her goods. With hands on her knees, she sat on
the buffalo robe. She stared up at Old Woman's face, seeing the sacred white band around her head, squinting to
see the places where her eyes and nose and mouth were.
Easier, much easier to see from the top of a curved clay
lodge in the depths of night, Blue Wing thought, feeling
again the knife of longing.

Despite her mourning, she decided she must fully
honor Old Woman to earn a sign. She stood and stripped
off her working garment, shed her leggings and moccasins, and stepped into the cold water. She swam out a
ways and ducked her head under to wash the world from

her skin and hair. She emerged naked, dripping, and donned her fringed dress, wide quilled girdle, leggings, glass beads, and clamshell necklace. She shoved her wet feet back into her moccasins and sat again. And then she sang the song she owned to Old Woman in the Moon:

Old Woman, mother of the corn, you who never die,
Brave to show your face when your dangerous son is in the sky,
May you smile upon The People and your earthly daughter.
May you send me sacred signs by stirring of the water.

But Blue Wing was not sure the chant had medicine here on white man's land, where the only water was this slightly ruffled lake. Old Woman might not bother to touch her hand to it. She loved Big River, where she stirred the water to foam, bathed, and became young and slender again. Old Woman loved Big River even though she could seldom find a calm stretch of it to admire her face.

But Blue Wing prepared herself to search for the Old One's sign here anyway. She rubbed on her head a sweet grass oil of her own making. Her hair had been long and heavy before she cut it four fingers wide to mourn River Walker. Still, she combed the essence through her ragged locks with her porcupine tail comb, set in a wooden handle. Because she was in mourning, she reddened her face with vermilion mixed with fragrant castoreum. She had used her own blood when she first heard River Walker was dead, but this was proper. She reddened the backs of her hands, then rubbed castoreum over her arms and throat. She found a flat, hollow-bellied rock and smeared it with silt, then poured on it a small puddle of water to make a sacred mirror, *a-wa-sa-ta*. She gazed long at her appearance. Only then did she remove her sacred items from the medicine bundle and, singing her song again, lay them out on the buffalo robe in a half circle before her.

A stone the shape of a goose, sacred messenger of Old Woman; sweet-smelling dried buffalo grass given her by her beloved grandmother of the same name, Buffalo Grass; dried chokeberries from the bush she had collapsed under the night she had the *xopini* dream of womanhood that gave her the guardian spirit of the goose; a broken piece of pot from the day she had purchased the right to make tribal pottery from her honored mother, Corn Basket; a piece of bark from the willow tree whose slender leaves always marked the return of summer moon. But surely, with her trials, some important thing was still missing from her bundle!

She rose and peered into the water of the lake, singing her song again, waiting for a sign from Old Woman's hand upon the water. Then she saw the duck feathers and down scattered on the grass at the very edge of the lake. A fox must have killed and dragged off a duck last night. But she had not seen these things when she bathed. It was as if they had just floated to earth. She bent to pick up two gray feathers with shimmering green stripes. She gasped upward in speechless joy as a crescent of honking geese flew directly overhead.

Yes! Her *xopini* guardian! The sign from Old Woman in the Moon! And then she knew what she must do.

Blue Wing strode farther along the water, still chanting her thanks to the Old One for this piece of wisdom. She found a tree with a long, straight branch as wide as a cornstalk. She broke and twisted it off, then trimmed twigs away with her skinning knife. Shaving bark from it, she worked quickly. Then she bent over it, binding the duck feathers to it with a vine, as was The People's way. She cut four ermine tails from the fringed hem of her dress and attached them, for four was the number of greatest medicine. She knew now she must remove the strip of quilling from the moccasins she had made to decorate this prayer pole. And of course, some sign of River Walker's personal medicine bundle she had made for him must be attached too.

Her hands ached, but she worked on. Her neck grew stiff, so she looked up now and then at Old Woman smiling down on her. Perhaps there was another good sign yet to come. Comforted, she worked on.

* * *

When Kate knocked on the door of General Clark's mansion, the old majordomo named Amos answered and informed her that the general had gone east with his son to visit family until spring. Crestfallen, she thought at first she'd made the trip for nothing, so she said, "Actually I came to ask how the Mandan girl is faring."

"That's kind of you, ma'am. Good 'nough, I guess, as the gal got a room of her own and three fine meals a day. Kind of mopes a bit now and again since the general and Mr. MacLeod's gone though."

"Oh, Mr. MacLeod went too?"

"On a mission from the general to the President hisself in the capital city of Washington," he announced importantly.

"Really? General Clark sent him to President Jackson?"

He nodded and invited her in for refreshments, but she refused. Since she'd heard the Mandan was fine, she'd just start back.

"Now, if'n you'd like to see the gal herself," Amos called after her, "spends her time out with Big Bess in the kitchen house most every day, out that way. I'd be happy to escort you."

"Oh, no, really that won't be necessary. I'm not staying."

"Big Bess, she could least give you a good meal to set you up real fine 'fore you start back. I could bring it to you. But if you'd like to talk to Bess or that Mandan gal yourself . . ."

"As long as I've come out, perhaps I will," she told the man with a smile. She did want to know the Indian was well. Besides, though she had not had an appetite since Clive died, she did feel hungry out here with all this fresh air and exercise. And now that she knew she could not possibly run into Randal MacLeod, she felt better too.

Pulling Calico behind her, she walked out past the stables, laundry house, and gardens. Big Bess was easy to spot and easy to talk to, as she bustled about to pack a meat pie and apple pie for Kate. Kate was willing to sit at her worktable to eat, but Bess wouldn't hear of her dining anywhere but the big house if she didn't pack her "a saddle picnic."

"Then a saddle picnic will be much appreciated," she told the kindly woman. "So Blue Wing seems happy enough here?" Kate asked, relieved the Indian was not anywhere about.

"Can't tell what's in her head much," Bess said shaking her own. "Does real strange things, but that's just 'cause she's Indian, the gen'ral says."

"Yes, of course. She's very different. Things like what?"

The woman's sleek eyebrows shot up the broad brow, and she lowered her rich voice. "Hear tell she don't use her bed nor no furniture but sleeps an' eats on the floor in the house like some of the general's dogs. Don't use the necessary out back with its perfectly good carved wood seats but does her business off in the back bushes, even in the dark of night, if you gets what I mean. Wears red face paint like she's on some warpath, but the gen'ral say it's 'cause she done lost her husband."

"Yes, I know," Kate said as she took the linen-wrapped bundle and a bottle of cider from Bess's big hands. She waited for Bess to say more, to give her that look of curiosity or disdain or even disgust she had seen on the faces of so many folks in town who knew that Clive had had two wives. But there was nothing but a conspiratorial wink from the massive woman.

"An' washes her whole body ev'ry morning in the pond, naked as a jaybird, I seen her!" Bess added. "She out there now, though least she got clothes on her brown backside again. Here, out here," she said, and stepped to the door to point in the direction of the closer of the two ponds.

Though Kate did not want to look, she did. Blue Wing sat on the ground at water's edge, hunched over something. Could she be crying?

"I—I'd speak with her, but I don't know a bit of Mandan," she told Bess as she took Calico's reins in her other hand. "But thank you so much for the food to eat on the way back."

"Oh, she talks middling to fair English, that gal does,"

Bess told her, standing in the doorway, wiping her hands on her apron. "Done said her husband learned her."

Kate's stomach twisted tighter as she looked toward the pond again. Something drew her feet in that direction, step by step. Raw curiosity? Bitter pity? Contrition? She had no idea why she pulled the horse toward Clive's country wife. But soon it was too late to turn back, for the woman heard her, jerked her head around, then stood with what appeared to be a long, decorated spear or lance in her hand. Kate jolted to a stop some twenty feet from her. At least the spear did not seem to have a sharp end, but she stood her ground here.

"Hello, Blue Wing," she called to her.

"Kate Craig, good," Blue Wing said.

They both stared. Blue Wing laid down the pole and walked toward her with easy strides. She looked wet-haired and windblown but not cold despite the lack of robe or blanket. Kate herself had felt chilled all day, right through her merino riding skirt and three-tiered shoulder cape.

Kate shuffled closer, studying her, without trying to seem as if she did. But for the dreadful chopped hair and red paint on the face, she looked, well . . . all right. Her attire was striking. She had a strong body and a nice enough face, with animated expression, not stern and stoic, as she had once expected all Indians to be. Her fine features included a thin, straight nose; long, narrow gray eyes fringed by thick dark lashes; and a shapely mouth with straight white teeth. When Kate was close enough to her, she noted that she seemed to have streaks of blond hair mingled with the dark. She moved gracefully, stepping quietly despite fallen leaves under her moccasined feet. Their eyes held.

"You see," Kate began again, "I did not know of you. Not even that Clive had a squ—another wife."

"I did know you, but he not talk much of that, River Walker."

"You called him River Walker?"

"For his big thunder canoe—steamboat," she said, and looked proud of herself for knowing that word.

"I do not speak Mandan. Your English is quite good. How long did you—did you know River Walker?"

"Married eight winters—how The People tell years. Really, eight summers, when River Walker visit The People. I twenty-four winters now," she said, and proudly held up a flurry of fingers, as if to assure Kate she could count.

So she was bright and willing to please. No wonder Clive had been intrigued. And Blue Wing had been his first wife, a bride at age sixteen. He'd had an Indian wife for two years when he courted her in St. Louis, curse him! She, not Blue Wing, was the second wife, the unlawful wife—if country marriages had been recognized. She almost did not want to know more, but she could not help her next question as Blue Wing came even closer and admiringly patted Calico's spotted flank.

"Do you have children?" Kate choked out.

"No. I want. I pray to sun and moon for children, but none." She lifted two empty hands as if in supplication to the sky. She used graceful hand signs as she talked, as if Kate could not grasp her stilted English. "But I give my life for to have them," Blue Wing went on. "For a son like yours and your daughter died! I care for my cousins' children, others' children, but it not enough. This is bad; this make me bitter in my heart!" Blue Wing cried, touching her breast as tears sprang to her eyes.

So Clive had trusted his Indian wife with knowledge of his white wife, but not the other way around. That ground the pain deeper. Or had General Clark or MacLeod explained things about Kate to Blue Wing? Either way, Blue Wing had evidently been the sort of woman one could confide in, and she was not. Despite churning confusion, Kate realized she was beginning to feel for the girl, not turn more against her.

"Then did you really come to divorce River Walker?" Kate asked.

"Divorce? See, my English talk not so good. Need you tell me that."

"Divorce, end the marriage. A woman of your people can do that? You came for that?"

"And to see why he not return to me, to the Mandans.

Why he not come back trade fair with The People. But yes, for that. I did not know your different path. I did think his other wife *manuka*, my friend, like sister wives among The People, give me a home for the winter. The general and Dark Water—you know, MacLeod—tell me too late it not this way with you," she said, and hung her head for one moment before lifting her chin to face Kate eye to eye again. "But now you come here, we mourn River Walker—your Clive—together?"

Suddenly that outrageous statement seemed much more civilized to Kate than enmity between them. This woman had expected hospitality and been thrown out of Kate's home. The kindly words and acts of a slave woman this morning seemed to shame the way others in town had treated Kate too, avoiding her once the funeral was over, looking askance or whispering if they passed her on the street. Kate would not be like those so-called civilized people if it was the last thing she did! Despite Blue Wing's heathen customs, she fascinated Kate. She understood her feelings, if not her ways.

Perhaps she should return later for another visit or even take Blue Wing into town for a visit before the house was gone. Surely she would like to see what Clive's other life had been like. The more the Indian woman talked, the more Kate's curiosity burned to know the Mandans. Why, if she had a lot of extra rooms, she might have even kept her for the winter, people's pious, proper opinions be damned!

"Bess gave me some food—enough for two—if you would like to eat here—a picnic," she told Blue Wing, and extended the wrapped package of pies and the cider she still held.

"A pic-nic? Yes, if we give some to Old Woman in the Moon first," Blue Wing said, and led Kate over to her robe. Blue Wing scrambled to pick up and pack away some old grass and stones in a little fur pouch.

"We say the Man in the Moon," Kate said.

Blue Wing frowned. "*Woman*, not man!" she declared, and shook her head vigorously as she unsaddled and unbridled Calico and gave her a quick rubdown with a handful of grass.

"Your name, Kate Craig," Blue Wing asked. "What it mean?"

"Mean?" Kate said as she gathered up her skirts and sat carefully but awkwardly on the ground. "It's just my name, like Clive Craig or William Clark, whom you call the Red-Haired Father."

Another frown creased Blue Wing's brow. "Names best tell something of *xopini* spirit or strength of person. Names like Runs Quickly, Dark Water—or Swift Raven," she said, her voice softening on the last name.

"I see what you mean. It is a useful custom; the names are pretty too."

Blue Wing nodded. "I call you Prairie Wind, for you came to me on the wind from Old Woman in the Moon," she declared with an impish smile that showed her white, even teeth.

"I came to the prairie when it was windy, but it is that horse that brought me," Kate insisted. "Still, I like the name."

"Good!" Blue Wing declared. " 'Good' is *shish* in Mandan."

"*Shish!*" Kate repeated.

"This thing," the young woman told Kate, nodding toward the mare's bridle in the grass, "some traders say cost two buffalo robes or six beaver pelts. River Walker say cost one robe or four pelts." Her fingers flew, as if Kate could not tell numbers just from her words for them. "River Walker have *shish* price!"

"I don't know any of the trading prices, but I know Cl—River Walker was fair to your people."

"*Shish* man!" Blue Wing declared as she sank gracefully to sit cross-legged next to Kate. "Makes Mandans want trade with him, but still have trade with big traders too."

Kate just nodded, but her mind raced. She had been cursing and hating Clive for days, wishing there were something good from him she could cling to, something to tell Jamie someday, besides the fact his father had never drunk to excess. And this young woman quite simply had given that something to her. Despite his many failings, Clive Craig had tried to bring fair prices to the

Mandans in the face of the almost overwhelming power of Chouteau's company. And Clive had been respected and admired for it. Perhaps this Indian woman would make her feel better in other ways too.

Her voice shaking, she told Blue Wing, "You may say Clive was a good man, but he had many bad debts; that means he owed people money, made promises to pay."

Blue Wing stared at her, waiting for more. Had she not understood? "So the big house, the steamboats you have seen—all but one that is nothing—had to be sold. Soon I will have no house, no money, nothing to trade. My son and I have just over two weeks, this many days"—she held up ten fingers and six more—"until we must leave our big house. But if you would like to ride back into town with me to visit just for those days, that would be fine."

"Fine," Blue Wing repeated. "See your son. In my heart, I want see the Mississippi again too. It not good as Big River Missouri, but this lake *no* good. Rivers *sinashush,* beautiful, like you."

Unshed tears burned behind Kate's eyes again at the young woman's exuberance and strange compliment. She was deeply touched that Blue Wing had immediately accepted her invitation. Though she could not explain it, she felt some tie to this very alien woman, and she trusted her to be around Jamie. Blue Wing might worship the moon, but at least she had sincere respectful feelings for a power bigger than herself, and that Kate would like to recapture.

After they ate, Kate explained things to Bess and Amos while Blue Wing fetched her things. But when it came time to ride back, the Mandan woman adamantly refused the loan of one of the general's horses.

"Blue Wing not be in debt to him for whole horse!" she exclaimed, and could not be persuaded even to borrow it. "Braves raid for horses." Blue Wing tried again to explain to the wide-eyed trio, looking earnestly from one to the other. "Men pay horses for brides. River Walker paid price of much horses for me. Cannot take—not even borrow horse now Red-Haired Father not here."

Kate stood agape, angry more at herself for thinking she could take on this woman than at the news Clive had

paid an Indian fortune for his pagan bride. She mounted
Calico from the stepstone block before the mansion and
carefully caught her feet in the sidesaddle stirrups. She
was not certain in that moment if she would ride off and
leave Blue Wing in her dust or go on with this lunatic
madness. The full moon, that was it.

"If you not ride that way, we both can sit this horse,"
Blue Wing told her with another pat on Calico's flank.

"Not ride sidesaddle?"

"Mandan woman never."

She dismounted and, with Blue Wing's help, mounted
astride, though she could use only one stirrup. Blue Wing
handed up her bundles, including things wrapped in a
buffalo robe that looked like the perfect mate to the one
Clive had hidden in the trunk. Then Blue Wing swung
easily up behind Kate and took a few of the bundles back
under one arm while she balanced her decorated pole in
the other.

"Now, if things don't work out for you," Amos told
Kate with a shake of his head, "you just get me word by
someone riding out this way, an' I'll send one of the general's men to fetch her."

Kate waved good-bye to Amos and Bess as they trotted
away. Blue Wing called out something in Mandan. For
the first time in weeks—in months—Kate almost
laughed. Did Old Woman in the Moon smile down on
them?

Her skirts ruffling calf-high in the wind felt good,
shish, more as if she were part of the horse, more in control instead of just being bounced along. But to have a
painted-faced heathen behind her who carried a decorated
lance, as if the two of them were riding into battle together! And maybe, just maybe, Kate thought, they were.

Chapter 4

The day after Kate brought Blue Wing to visit Winter-haven, she left her teaching Jamie an Indian game—under Adele's and Claire's close watch—and went out looking for a place to sell her painted china. She had broken much of her best stock but had gathered together a few other good pieces for samples. Roses and violets, lilies of the valley and daisies graced these cups and saucers, though she wished she had done some of prairie flowers. When she got her first orders, she would paint them and sign her new "Indian name," Prairie Wind.

On her way to an emporium on Main Street Kate walked down Walnut to the Catholic cathedral, called the Old Cathedral, although it had been restored just four years ago. On rare times when she was alone downtown, she slipped in to take a look at its interior, but she had not been here for months.

She loved the beautiful outside too, with its four Doric columns supporting a gabled portico and its steeple pointing heavenward. Its bells rang morning, noon, and sunset, as if to echo the steamboat bells that sounded down on the river. When the wind was right and the windows were open at Winterhaven, she could hear the clear music of the cathedral, a reminder of the possibilities of man-made but God-inspired beauty. Now she hoped, if she sat here a moment, it would give her strength to try to sell the woman-made beauty she had created on these plates.

The few other visitors or penitents in the vast cathedral knelt or sat close to the front. She slipped past the banked rows of flickering votive candles and slid into the back pew. The beauty of this building usually made her feel reverent and grateful, but today it hardly calmed her. For

the first time in her life, she had to use her own wits—
and china plates—to survive. Asking folks to buy would
be as bad as facing the Beneticks.

But she bowed her head in thanks that at least the
groom's quarters above the stables would shelter them
this winter. Then, awed anew by the beauty of the place,
she realized the Savior had been well acquainted with
poverty and a certain stable where He had first lived.
God's half-human, half-divine Son was a half-breed of
sorts, just like Randal MacLeod.

Kate held her basket handle tight as she turned onto
Main Street, which paralleled the Mississippi River just
down the bluff beyond the wharves and levee. There
stood the busy, smelly giant stone warehouses full of furs
waiting to be shipped to exotic-sounding places like New
York, Montreal, London, Leipsig, Lyons, St. Petersburg,
Canton, Athens, and Constantinople. And now that she
had met Blue Wing, she knew that the source of those
furs, the Mandan villages of Mitutanka and Ruptare and
the open plains beyond the Cannonball, Heart, and Knife
rivers, were exotic in their own way too.

Kate wrinkled her nose at the floating clouds of tart-
smelling coal smoke which hung heavy in the air to
speckle the snow with peppery ashes. Folks in carriages
or on foot crowded the slushy paved street and narrow
sidewalks; various languages—the liquid flow of French,
quick Spanish and lazy Caribbean dialects, the flat twang
of frontiersmen—swirled around her. Like the mongrel
national styles of city buildings, the ten thousand plus
populace of St. Louis was a mixed breed.

Main Street, where old mansions were slowly being
converted to mercantile establishments, was lined with a
potpourri of economic endeavors. The gray limestone
Union and Missouri hotels stood here. Several banks hovered nearby since coins and currency had taken the place
of fur as the item of exchange six years ago. Kate passed
her favorite dry goods store, then the shop at 10 North
Main, where fine beaver hats sold for ten dollars each, the
confectioner's, where Jamie got so excited over the tarts
and candies, the "Fine Imported Carpets" store, the "Fur-

niture and Undertaking" establishment, and her favorite
bookstore.

Though she had patronized most of these places in the
past, she now wished she could sell them the linens, hats,
carpets, furniture, and books that would be on the block
at Winterhaven soon. Unfortunately they all would go to
settle debts, not to provide security for her and Jamie's
future, so her selling her own goods would have to do
that.

But as she went from store to store on her list, her
vague fears began to harden to stone. No one wanted
painted china. At least, she realized, they didn't want it
from her. "Nice but not in demand," one shopkeeper told
her. Another man explained more kindly, "Now the
town's flush with fur money, folks here'bouts have their
hearts set on fineries like East Coast ware or British or
French imported porcelain, that's all, ma'am."

When she ran out of shops, she forced her chin up and
shoulders back and went on to the two hotels. She got her
hopes up when the man behind the polished counter in
the big, crowded lobby of the Missouri admitted, "Really
pretty stuff. Sure, I might be interested in four cups and
saucers for the missus."

"Just for your wife, you mean? I wasn't thinking of
single sales. I was hoping such china would bring a hint
of home but a touch of gentility to your entire set of dining room tableware here."

"Ma'am, I take it you never ate here? Thought not.
Quite a bunch of boys stops off here heading for parts
west or returning from the wilds—en route to the Santa
Fe Trail or up the two big rivers to Indian and fur country. Some of 'em come in just for a real bed one night and
a hot bath. But for a few exceptions, wouldn't give most
of the boys eating with us more 'n cheap china, what can
be easily replaced. But like I said, I got me a missus
would really love to have a tea set of four of that."

She wrote down what flowers he most liked and
thanked him, though she felt crushed. Four cups and saucers for four hours of walking and four years of painting
these? She forced her steps toward the last possibility, the
Union Hotel.

Its lobby too was full of noisy men. She gathered her skirts close to avoid getting them in firing range of the brass spittoons. Cigar and pipe smoke—and some of the language she overheard—turned the air blue. She smelled liquor and, as ever, shuddered as half-buried childhood memories assailed her. The faded flowered maroon carpet seemed endless as she wended her way toward the registration desk.

"Don't get us many ladyfolk," the stocky, balding man behind the desk told her, and spun the big registration book her way. "So where's the husband, little lady?" he asked, glancing behind her.

"Actually, sir, I am here to inquire if your establishment would care to purchase some fine painted bone china for teatime, even if you want cheaper china in the dining hall."

His brown eyebrows shot halfway up his forehead and lifted his lofty hairline even higher. He parted his hair low on one side of his head and attempted to comb it up and across his scalp to cover his baldness.

"These gents look to you like they have teatime, lady? A stiff belt of Old Monongahela or a snort of cherry bounce before victuals is more like it. 'Sides, the signboard out front says no solicitin'—'cept for the boys with newspapers. And speakin' of solicitin', no ladies unescorted on the premises neither. Gives upstandin' folks the wrong idea 'bout what kind of solicitin' it is, you know what I mean," he said, and dared wink at her.

She felt belittled and insulted. Her low spirits sank lower, but this was her last chance, for she would never go door to door in town. "But could I speak with the manager about possibly painting small portraits or silhouettes of hotel guests then?" She hardly knew where that desperate idea had come from. "You know, ones they could send home with letters to their people back East?" She plunged on. "Or paintings for your bare walls here in the lobby, perhaps of important city personages like General Clark or Cadet Chouteau or Mayor Derby?" Panic seized her now. She had to do something to earn her own way. Someone had to give her a chance to take care of her son!

"Look now, miss, ah—"

"Mrs. Craig. Katherine Craig."

His eyes widened again. "*The* Mrs. Craig? The one who took in her husband's upriver squaw and has to sell off everythin'? Say, that's it, ain't it?" he demanded, leaning forward on his elbows as if they were speaking intimately. "You know, there might be something in it for curiosity's sake—an oddity. Good gossip like this never lasts long, so we'd have to strike while the iron's hot. A few of those memorial plates you did been going for a good price here in the lobby. Could you paint some with maybe you and the squaw on them and we could peddle them as"—here he deepened his voice and held up his hands as if envisioning the plate—" 'Captain Craig's two wives, the civilized and savagized,' or some such? How many could you do in a hurry? Mrs. Craig?" he shouted as she started away.

Appalled but angry, she spun back to him, clinking her china together. She would have liked to have broken each one of them over his bare, empty head. "I do not appreciate or approve of your rude, crude implications, sir! And if there's any savagery involved here, it's in you— and all these gossiping people!"

She elbowed her way through the crowd that had begun to watch their interchange. She had no idea exactly what people she was accusing. These gawking men, everyone in St. Louis perhaps, French, Yankee New Englanders, the few Germans who had just come in, half-breeds. This last horrid experience made her feel more protective of Blue Wing, for their names were both being snickered over and bandied about to entertain pious, proper St. Louis. And the so-called Valley Queen City was hardly a pious, proper place at all. No, she was starting to see it was nothing but a big bully sitting on the fence of the frontier, taunting and threatening.

She started down the street toward home at a furious pace, but then her feet lagged, for she had achieved nothing. She was not certain she could even bear to begin the oil portrait of Blue Wing she had been so excited about. She stopped so fast her skirts swayed, her china clinked again, and the man behind bumped into her.

"*Pardon,* madame," he said, tipped his hat, and hurried on.

Stepping into a doorway near the corner of Main and Market, she noted her surroundings again. She stood across from the old French-style Chouteau mansion of Cadet's father; Cadet now had a much finer place out a ways, worthy of the grandson of the city's founder. She stood staring and thinking.

That wretch back at the Union Hotel had at least given her an idea. She would never paint plates with Blue Wing and sign her name so they both could be mocked, but perhaps people would pay for a portrait of a lovely anonymous Indian woman—one with long hair and without vermilion smeared on her face—done by a nameless painter. Unless she identified herself or even said she had done them, most people, especially perhaps those down on the waterfront, where folks came and went, would not know who she was. And if, like Father and Clive, they resented a woman artist, they could just assume it was done by a man. She felt desperate enough to consider it.

The trouble was, soon the river would freeze solid and there would be few "foreigners" in or out until the spring thaw. But then local people went out on the thick ice in a holiday mood. Sleighs came down from St. Charles. The French came in from their little village of Vide Poche with loads of cordwood to sell. Perhaps she could at least barter her Indian portraits for daily food and wood, for she recalled old Simon's grousing last winter that coal cost as much as twenty-nine cents a bushel.

Her mind raced as fast as her feet as she headed home. How wonderful to paint, even anonymously, to strike out on one's own. She had read that George Catlin had returned from upriver last year to great acclaim with hundreds of fine Indian portraits. If only she could really do as Catlin did, go upriver to paint more than just one Indian who had come to her. But she had hoped to return tonight in triumph with orders for china and enough money to put celebration food on the table! She hurried toward home—or toward what would be the Beneticks' home just fifteen days from now.

* * *

Late that afternoon, as if she had read Kate's mind about not having food, Blue Wing appeared with a freshly snared, plucked duck for dinner. But soon enough, Kate knew, the ducks would fly even farther south, and Blue Wing would be back on the prairie for the winter. And the Mandan woman's providing food for the table became a mixed blessing, just like everything else about her.

A few days later she appeared with a basketful of chicken eggs. Reluctantly Kate explained that other people's henhouses were not to be bothered. Mandan braves on the plains might raid for horses, but women in town did not raid for eggs. How Kate wished they had a garden. Clive had always disdained any sort of "farm chores" because of how hard his father had made him work their stony Kentucky farm before he ran away. They had always had Maureen buy eggs and other foodstuffs at the market. Except for jam from their Concord grape vines, Maureen had not even put up dried fruit or vegetable goods for the winter, for almost anything was—had been once—available for a price downtown. When Kate tried to explain all that to Blue Wing, she was aghast.

"No corn, nuts, and sunflower seeds buried? In the ground, a cache. That big garden all flowers and herbs? Nothing for time of cold?" Blue Wing demanded, eyes wide, as if her Prairie Wind were the most stupid of creatures.

"I said, we always just bought food at the store—like a trading post." Kate floundered, feeling fear coil in the pit of her stomach again.

"Not in time of cold." Blue Wing lectured her with a scornful shake of her head. Then she added, "You not use eggs I find, you use nuts I find?"

"Nuts? Of course. But it's too late to gather them. What hasn't been taken by people or squirrels has already rotted on the ground."

But after that they had baskets of walnuts and chestnuts, most of which Kate divided into three equal amounts. She saved most of hers and Jamie's for Christmas treats, for there would be few enough of those this year. Blue Wing's share could go back with her to General Clark's. How Blue Wing found this bounty so late she could not fathom, until glancing out the back window one day, she saw the young woman shoo away a digging squirrel and dig in his place to uncover a whole cache of them.

From the edge of the prairie, dried roots began to appear too; wild turnips and wild onions and something Blue Wing called breadroot, which she declared River Walker had loved roasted. Jamie, after hanging on Blue Wing's every word and action, insisted to Kate he did love them too, "just like Papa when he visited Blue Wing, whose real name is Ahpcha-Toha!"

Even as the Mandan squirreled away her treasures by hanging them from the ceiling of the carriage house rooms for Kate or by laboring to dig a hole in the frozen garden soil, Kate still felt torn between gratitude and resentment toward her. She kept indirectly reminding Blue Wing that in such and such many days she must return to Red-Haired Father's house. Blue Wing listened without an apparent flicker of emotion, never responding.

Then one day, when Kate was working in the kitchen, Blue Wing came home through a foot-deep snowfall and, with a flash of white smile, held out her day's catch by its tail: a dead skunk! Kate smelled it even before she saw it.

"Blue Wing, that's a skunk!"

"Schochta," she said proudly.

"But we can't eat that. It smells—it stinks—bad!" Kate cried, and reverted to pinching her nose and fanning the air to be certain she understood.

"Smell not bad. Go away when cooked!" she declared.

"Not in this house. Not on the first day we're without Maureen!" Kate insisted, and shooed her out. It was one thing, Kate fretted, that the Indians rubbed their skin and oiled their hair with Indian castoreum perfume, made from the hind end of female beavers, no less. Castoreum had a pungent smell, but it was bearable. This skunk stink was too much!

"It not bad. The People eat sometimes," Blue Wing threw back over her shoulder as she went, unwillingly, shaking her head in disbelief, to take it back outside.

"Better than that—what you say—French toilette water stink you try put on my hair!" she shouted before the door slammed.

Kate stood staring, then burst into laughter. Touché. So Blue Wing detested what Kate thought fragrant. Blue Wing's ways were not—at least some of the minor things—better or worse, just different. Holding her French perfume–scented handkerchief to her nose, Kate went to tell her so.

When she could, Kate tried to teach Blue Wing more about the white man's world. Perhaps then she would be more content to spend the winter at General Clark's big house when she went back next week. The Mandan was very teachable when she wanted to be: She sat on chairs, ate at the table using the proper utensils by mimicking Kate. At least Kate had convinced her to use the necessary out back or the chamber pot in the room at night instead of the bushes as Bess had reported.

Blue Wing was willing—actually thrilled—to dress in Kate's clothes, so people did not stare or even harass her when she went out. But because of Kate's size and the high, tight waists in vogue, Blue Wing was unable to fit into any gowns but some Kate had worn in her pregnancies. She had saved them only for sentimental reasons and now planned to sell them; however, she was starting to realize she'd best give them to Blue Wing as a farewell gift.

The Mandan woman spent hours each evening, changing her clothes, preening before the pier glass in Kate's bedroom, rather than stay in her own room, where she still would not sleep in the bed but rolled up in her buffalo robe on the floor. And all this pirouetting and peering with her chopped hair sticking out from a bonnet brim and that red-painted face amid ruffles and ribbons! Kate had at least talked her out of wearing her garish cosmetics when she went outside.

"Blue Wing, by the way, Adele and Claire say they cannot find my hairbrush," Kate remarked one evening as she boxed all of Clive's and most of her clothes to sell. "It's a silver-backed one—shiny like a gun barrel." Clive had given Kate the monogrammed set of brush and hand mirror for their first anniversary, though why that mattered to her since she had emotionally renounced him, she wasn't sure. But she didn't need to have Blue Wing stealing from her the way she did from squirrels. And the basic hint she was the culprit was that her own beaver tail and wood comb lay in place of the silver one on Kate's dressing table.

"A gift. A trade," Blue Wing said, momentarily stopping her swirling before the mirror. "Long Hatchet made for Corn Basket. She give me, I give you."

Kate knew quite well the names of Blue Wing's parents and brothers and her sister, Clam Necklace, married to Wolf Trap. Sometimes she longed to meet these people, but Blue Wing seemed not to want to discuss them much, and Kate realized something was amiss in the family. She wondered about the widower whom Blue Wing declared she loved, but she seemed reluctant to speak of him too. Since Randal MacLeod's note to her had said sisters sometimes wed the same man, she asked why Blue Wing had not wed Wolf Trap too. At that the Mandan's expression hardened, but she gave her a brief glimpse into her world.

"Very bad heart to me, Clam Necklace. And my dear— what is that word with loved?" She interrupted herself.

"What I just called Jamie? Beloved?"

"And my beloved family that I love have bad heart to me I not marry Wolf Trap too."

"But from my point of view, you see, you did the right thing. So it's a falling-out with your family because you would not marry your sister's husband?"

"If falling-out mean much bad heart, yes."

"I'm sorry about your family problems. I know how hard that can be, like . . . buried nuts and roots in the ground of your mind. Sometimes you dig them up, but you'd like to keep them hidden."

"Yes," Blue Wing said as their eyes met. "And we can share hairbrushes," she announced, and went to fetch Kate's. In that moment, like a few scattered others, they seemed almost friends, Kate thought. Like those times Blue Wing sat to have her portrait painted but kept getting up to look. She would smile proudly at the emergence of Kate's rendition of her quilled and fringed dress, the café au lait–hued face, and long, luxurious hair Kate created from her imagination.

"Very *shish*," Blue Wing declared. "*Sinashush*, beautiful."

"Then you won't mind if I do other small paintings of you after you're gone? I won't put your name on them or mine either."

"But The People own what they make, painted robes, pottery, stories, sacred songs," Blue Wing protested, making Kate realize how weak she had become to be willing to paint anonymously. "My father, Long Hatchet, very proud of buffalo robes he paint of the battles of braves!" she declared, answering Kate's unasked question about where Clive had gotten his buffalo robe. Yet Blue Wing evidently sensed her desperation and nodded permission. She put her hand on Kate's shoulder as Kate darted another brushstroke on the clear gray eyes.

"You make me look good in my heart too," Blue Wing said with a strange little catch in her voice. "Good in heart, like you."

Following in Maureen's and Simon's footsteps, Claire and Adele departed the evening before the auction. Kate wished she could give them a handsome parting gift of money, but she knew they understood. At least the Creole sisters would be staying together at their new position, working for a relative of the Chouteaus no less, so they could use their native French. Kate gave both of them finely woven Scotch shawls she had bought just last year and bonnets of bright hues to echo the blues and greens in the shawls. The parting was difficult, for they had been loyal—yes, really, her best friends—and they knew what she faced. And Jamie cried almost as hard as he had when Calico, the last "horsie," had been claimed by its new owner.

Now Kate walked through rooms of tagged and rearranged furniture, of rolled carpets, piled linens, mirrors and paintings stacked against the walls, saying farewell in her mind to them too. She did not want to be here tomor-

row, when people came to paw through the remnants of
Clive's dreams, the tattered remains of their marriage, the
broken promise of her and Jamie's futures. She had taken
her grandmother's rocking chair and two narrow servants'
beds out to the rooms above the stables. The other plain
pine furniture there would have to do. A few of the servants' dishes the Beneticks would surely not miss, all her
painting things, a small mirror, a commode. And just
those few things made the two small rooms that would
soon be her home seem so crowded. She and Blue Wing
carried out the twenty jars of grape jam Maureen had put
up. How would jam taste on dried, roasted roots sprinkled
with chopped nuts all winter? Kate wondered.

At least Blue Wing had boundless energy to amuse
Jamie. She had taught him a game in which five pebbles
were tossed and caught in a basket and one in which a
ball was bounced endlessly between foot and knee. She
had made him a small sled from a discarded window
shutter and—before she got in trouble with the Lautrecs
across the street—harnessed two of their pet dogs to pull
it. She had taken the boy for walks, even without the
maids, for Kate trusted her. Besides, she was so weary, so
disheartened, so busy, and Blue Wing kept Jamie's spirits
up. The boy adored her, and she him. But that opened a
whole new Pandora's box for Kate.

Blue Wing's admiring attention to the boy made Kate
feel guilty. Jamie went about quoting Blue Wing, chattering in Mandan, and telling Kate about Old Woman in the
Moon. Kate realized then she had let her own disillusion-
ment stop her from teaching him what he should know
about his own religion. Her mother, who could quote Bi-
ble chapter and verse, would disown her, and her Methodist minister grandfather was probably thundering curses
on her head. Nor lately had Kate been giving Jamie the
attention he needed and deserved with all he'd been
through. She knew she had herself, not Blue Wing, to
blame for that.

The week before the auction the Beneticks requested
Kate call upon them at their temporary residence, as their
note said, to "discuss the young heathen woman currently

residing at Winterhaven." Feeling she was being summoned before a firing squad, she went to face them in the
lobby of the Union Hotel, which she dreaded reentering
after her wretched experience with the man at the desk
two weeks before.

"I assure you both," she had said, still standing, since
they made no offer they be seated when they met her just
inside the lobby door, "Blue Wing's presence in the house
is causing no problems."

Mr. Benetick's eyebrows humped together, and Mrs.
Benetick's mouth puckered to a pout. "I'm afraid," Mr.
Benetick said, "we must rescind our charitable offer that
you and your son live in the carriage house *if* the Indian
squaw remains any longer about the premises. And until
we take formal possession of the house, we must hold
you fiscally responsible for any damage done to wood-
work or the furniture pieces we have chosen. We have it
on the best authority that the Indian has been seen about
town with knife in hand, and we all know how savages
like to carve and cut up things."

"And I am the best authority to tell you she has not
harmed a thing in the house!" Kate protested. "With the
knife she only gathers food or occasionally skins a tree
limb for a new prayer pole—"

"Really!" Mrs. Benetick declared. "I'm afraid we simply cannot have it . . . or you staying anywhere about if
that—that person is not . . . dispensed with immediately!"

Suddenly Kate had a vision of herself and Jamie out in
the cold, going door to door in blowing snow, begging
bread to put on their painted plates. Her stomach seemed
to drop clear to the carpet. Those two rooms borrowed on
the sufferance of the Beneticks were all she and Jamie
had this winter.

"Actually," she began, fighting to control her voice,
"Blue Wing is to return to General Clark's home outside
town soon, Mrs. Benetick, if you'll just give me a few
more days until the general's men come to escort her.
But," she added, her anger roiling again, "if it weren't for
the fact she's departing—and for my son's welfare—I tell
you, I'd be tempted to carve a few things on trees or
houses in this town myself, to tell folks—other folks, of

course—how wrong and cruel they can be. Good day to you!"

Before she was even out of earshot, she heard Mrs. Benetick's hissing whisper. "She's actually come unhinged. That savage is rubbing off on her!"

Once Kate had herself dressed the morning of the auction, she was surprised to see Jamie was still asleep. Usually he got up at first light with Blue Wing, but then their romps outside had no doubt worn him out. Assuming Blue Wing had gone out to the necessary—for the cold weather never seemed to faze her—Kate got Jamie dressed and began to heat him porridge in the kitchen. She wanted them all out in the carriage house or on a walk when the auctioneers arrived. It was starting to snow again, but perhaps they could go out in it anyway. She could not imagine the three of them cooped up in those two small rooms above the stables all day while her family's past was carted out of Winterhaven by strangers.

And though one part of her hated to do it, she had sent a note to Amos at General Clark's estate, telling him that next time the estate workers came to town for supplies, they could also return Blue Wing to Marais Castor. Despite everything, she regretted their parting. Now perhaps this snow would delay things, but it made her really worry about where Blue Wing had gone.

Glancing out the window through heavier falling snow, she could see that the fading prints of the snowshoes— Blue Wing had adapted Clive's big ones to fit her small feet—went out the back door, around the front, and down the street. Perhaps she had gone to snare meat again, as she did when the larder got low, as it was now.

Kate checked to be certain she had packed all the food in the kitchen to go with them and discovered the butt end of the ham, some bread, and—oh, no—even the rest of the bacon she'd bought by trading a pair of jet earrings were gone! Her stomach cartwheeled. Could Blue Wing have stolen that food and set out for General Clark's across the snowy prairie? Clever Indian or not, if she got lost or frozen out there, Kate would never forgive herself.

The front door bell clanged in the row of bells mounted

high on the wall in the kitchen. For one moment she almost waited for Adele or Claire to answer it, but she jumped up and went herself. Surely the auctioneers weren't here already! But Samantha Lautrec, wrapped tightly in a fur-lined cape, stood at the door, shivering and stamping snow from her sharp-toed, polished boots.

"Samantha, come in. Whatever is it?" She had not seen her neighbors in weeks, but for the day Mr. Lautrec yelled at Blue Wing to loose their dogs from Jamie's sled. "May I fix you some tea?"

"No, nothing, Kate. Sorry to pop in like this, but before you leave today, there are some things you should know. *She* hasn't come back, has she?"

"Blue Wing? No. Do you know where she went?"

"Hardly. It was barely light when I happened to notice her trudging down the street like some sort of trapper carrying a decorated war lance with feathers and who knows what else dangling from it. But, Kate, for Jamie's sake, I had to come. I'm sure—I pray—you don't know all that's been going on, as I'm sure you've been distracted, and—"

"What are you trying to say? Blue Wing's been a—like a kindly nursemaid to Jamie."

"I assume you don't want your son turned into a savage!" Samantha declared. She shook her head so hard her hood dropped to her shoulders. "Over on Poplar, Mrs. Winstock saw the two of them coming down the street one day, and that Indian let—Kate, I don't know how to put this delicately—she let Jamie relieve himself into a bush right in the Winstocks' front yard!"

"He's just a boy, Samantha. Or do you mean she did too?"

"I certainly hope not! Did she? Does she? I can't believe you took her in—after everything."

"If that's all you have to say, then—"

"I'm afraid not. Jamie was outside on your lawn running buck naked through the snow the other day! Naked! And *she* was there, running with him. Oh, he had a pair of heathen moccasins on, and she was dressed, but they were running in little paths chasing each other."

"Fox and geese," Kate said.

"What? I only know he could have caught his death of cold."

"Strangely, he has never been healthier or—yes, even happier—Samantha. I'm sure Jamie did that only once, and no, I didn't know. The Mandan boys do it all the time, even in the snow or on the ice, so I hear. It strengthens them for manhood. Their ways are different, that's all."

"Well, I never . . . You *have* changed! Have you taken leave of your senses?"

"I've taken leave of a lot of things, including most of my possessions, my husband—and maybe my old, patient, quiet self, Samantha. I appreciate your concern, I really do. But Blue Wing is going back to General Clark's soon. Jamie and I will be living in the groom's quarters until spring and then . . . be moving on."

"The servants' quarters? Then that's true? I couldn't—couldn't believe it. If I can help . . ."

"How kind of you, but I'm getting used to being independent now and don't want to be beholden or in debt to anyone again if I can help it. But if you would take Jamie home with you just for a bit this morning and not let him get upset when things start to be carted out of Winterhaven, I would appreciate that. And if I could have the use of one of your horses, just for an hour or so, as she couldn't have gotten far."

"She? The Indian? You're demented if you're going after her. If she's left, let her go."

"Will you take Jamie and lend me the horse?"

"Yes, of course, but for Jamie's sake, Kate, as well as your own," Samantha pleaded, "don't bring that Indian back here."

"I said she's going," Kate said, her voice breaking. "I'm so sorry, but it's time for her to go."

Kate felt she was on some great adventure in the wilds as she began to track Blue Wing by the disappearing imprints of her snowshoes down the familiar street. If poor Samantha had been watching out the window, she would be newly shocked, for Kate rode astride. The snow was getting heavier, and the wind was picking up; she had to hurry, or she would lose even these large tracks. How far could she have gone in this amount of time? A terrible day for a public auction; a worse one for traversing the prairie.

As Kate feared, the tracks did go north, although not out Ninth Street toward Normandy. But perhaps Indians disdained following streets and went their own straight way, as Old Woman in the Moon's geese would fly. The snowshoe imprints seemed to plunge into the treed grounds surrounding Chouteau's Pond, so carefully Kate urged her horse off Seventh Street to follow.

In clement weather St. Louisans enjoyed picnics, boating, and fishing for bass here; the pond froze long before the river, and then people would skate or sleigh on these grounds, but not in a heavy snowfall. The pond was the shape of a half-moon, Blue Wing had told her. Kate had never thought to describe its shape one way or the other before. It was large—two miles long and a quarter mile wide with a stone flour mill at one end.

Kate glimpsed a bulky figure ahead through side-sifting snow and urged her horse on. At least it was just over fetlock deep so far. But she was to be disappointed; the person was an elderly man, bent into the wind, apparently just taking a stroll.

"Hello!" she called to him to make him look up. "Have you seen an Indian woman hereabouts?"

His head and face were wrapped in a tweed scarf; only his narrowed eyes peered out from a wrinkled but evidently hardy face. He had wrapped a blanket around his coat like a shawl.

"The one who comes most mornings to bathe in the water?" he asked in a high-pitched voice. "Saw her even break the ice to wash one morning. Reminded me of the good old days, steaming up the Missouri to trade with them Osages."

"She's Mandan. Have you seen her today?"

He pointed east. "Went into that new burying ground thataway, just two doors from my daughter's house," he told her.

The cemetery where they had buried Clive! Blue Wing had asked to see where he was. Kate had vaguely told her but had not offered to take her to see it. No, she could not have stood with Blue Wing over his grave.

At first she felt relief to think perhaps Blue Wing had not set out over the trackless prairie. But now . . . surely she could not be planning to harm herself in the cemetery. Just the other day she had explained to Kate that mourning relatives cut off digits of a finger to show respect for the dead, a perpetual reminder of their loss. She explained that Randal MacLeod and General Clark had stopped her from that. But she had adamantly declared it was better to place the honored dead on a scaffold lifted toward the sky until their bones fell to the ground. Surely Blue Wing could not be meaning to use that lance to dig Clive up as she had nuts and caches in the ground. . . .

Without thanks or farewell to the old man, she urged the horse away from Chouteau's Pond and back on the street.

Clive was buried not in the old town cemetery but in a newer one, in a plot next to where Sally lay. It had been closer to the house, and the other one seemed crowded—cluttered, even—with its many French names and ornate monuments. Now black iron gates and the scripted words "Fair Lawn" swam at her from the swirl of snow.

She dismounted to unlatch and shove one tall gate open. Its creak was lost in the wail of wind. Had Blue Wing really come here and reclosed the gate? She was forever leaving doors open in the house.

Pulling the horse's reins, Kate trudged through drifting snow that showed no respect for where lanes or paths should be. As she approached the Craig family plot, she did not see Blue Wing at all and panicked again. Must she set out onto the prairie after all? And then the silhouette of a kneeling, huddled form emerged from around the two headstones up the familiar little rise under a bare catalpa tree. Relief that she had found Blue Wing flooded her, but she felt anger it was here. She prayed she had not harmed herself or Clive's grave.

Kate did not call to Blue Wing but crunched on through the snow. She did not know if she could speak; her throat felt tight with jumbled emotions she could not name. She noted that the tall, wind-buffeted lance was stuck in the ground of Clive's grave. Blue Wing had explained the stick was a prayer pole, and now Kate saw it was adorned with bobbing feathers, ermine tails, and slices of bacon! As ever, Blue Wing's keen hearing served her well. The dark head jerked in Kate's direction.

Blue Wing looked as if she had fully expected Clive's ghost. Her face was painted again; her eyes wide. But she composed her startled expression and rose in one slow, graceful movement. Apparently she did not deem it unusual that Kate had found her here. Kate spoke first.

"You should have told me where you were going. I worried."

"That I did steal things again?" she said, and gestured toward the bacon—and to the snow she had scraped off Clive's grave to lay out the other food in a neat circle.

"No—not after all you've done to help me and Jamie. I feared you would set out on the prairie by yourself to return to Red-Haired Father's house."

"You want me go," she said matter-of-factly. "But before I go, on this day River Walker's house and goods be sold, when his spirit be restless, I bring him a feast and prayer pole for his journey."

Tears blurred Kate's view of Blue Wing. Her past pressed in on her: the happy days with Clive at Winterhaven, the love and loyalty she thought only they had shared. She sniffed and wiped her nose with the back of her glove. She shuffled closer to see Blue Wing did not have her buffalo robe over her ceremonial attire to keep her warm. This was not unusual, but it did not lie discarded on the ground beside her. It was carefully arranged, hair side up, on Sally's grave as if it were a coverlet to warm a little bed.

"Your daughter," Blue Wing said when she saw where Kate stared. "I honor her with my robe."

When Kate's voice would not come, she went on. "I like this place, this little hill. *Sinashush.* I did go to Baby Hill to ask for a son—a son strong like Jamie, a daughter too, like this one lost," she said, and pointed to Sally's grave.

"Baby Hill?" Kate asked, thinking she must mean the section of the graveyard where babies were buried.

"By hills near the Heart River, onetime home of my people. Near spirit village," she explained. "I pray, I hope a baby spirit choose me for mother and come to me here." She put both hands on her stomach, and Kate wrapped her arms around herself almost to mirror the stance, remembering carrying Sally within her there, her first child. She missed her yet and always would. But how much sadder it would have been if like Blue Wing, she had never known a daughter at all. She had not thought of it that way before; it was not cold comfort, for suddenly she felt warm.

She could not have fathomed such strange things as baby hills and prayer poles just weeks ago—or standing here with Clive's other wife. But now she nodded in the silence of the snow.

"I pray hard," Blue Wing went on, "for a child with River Walker, even if half-breed. Now I even pray hard for one with another, who is not mine and not to be named."

"I'm sorry," Kate said. "I hope he can be yours someday."

Blue Wing's distant stare focused on her again. "You will take back these things?" she asked with a nod toward the food.

"Blue Wing, I don't believe the dead need food or blankets for their journey, but your heart is good. No, I—we shall both sacrifice this food together and trust the Lord God will help us find more. And despite my different beliefs, I cannot tell you how many nights when the wind howled and it rained or snowed that I wanted to hold my daughter in my arms to warm her again. . . ."

Her shoulders began to shake. She had not sobbed since the night of Clive's funeral, but she did now, yet without tears, standing straight, shoulders heaving. Blue Wing came to touch her arm; then suddenly they were hugging hard. Their cheeks brushed; their chins rested on each other's shoulders.

Chapter 5

Kate and Blue Wing left the food and prayer pole at the cemetery, but Kate insisted Blue Wing take her buffalo robe. She held her snowshoes as they rode the borrowed horse back. When they turned onto Spruce Street, they saw that the weather had not stopped townspeople from coming to the auction. Carriages, wagons, and carts crammed both sides of the street.

"Like turkey buzzards. *Ruh-hah-deh!*" Blue Wing said, and spit into the snow.

"As if Winterhaven were a big warehouse they could unload," Kate muttered. Grim-faced, she turned the horse toward the Lautrecs', where Jamie waited. But in that moment, in her own words, she glimpsed a possibility to save the three of them—together—this winter.

"I don't really want you to have to live out there at General Clark's," Kate admitted, swiping at her wet cheeks before they glazed with ice. She saw she had gotten Blue Wing's mourning paint on her face, but she did not mind. "I want you with Jamie and me—like a friend or visiting aunt to Jamie. You've been such a big help. But the people who own Winterhaven now won't let all three of us stay in the little house . . . too many."

"They not want me, like you before." Blue Wing corrected her. "Why not we build a winter lodge in forest by half-moon lake, part under the ground, like Mandans do? The People live through many cold days and years, still go on."

"We can't do that, Blue Wing. Unlike where you live, people own the land here in town, and we'd never survive out on the open prairie. But I have an idea that just might help."

"*Shish,*" the Indian replied. It bucked Kate up that Blue Wing trusted her without another question or doubt. Now, whatever happened, she had to deserve the trust Blue Wing and Jamie had in her.

They returned the horse, retrieved Jamie, and with him riding Blue Wing's back to "play horsie," they trudged toward Winterhaven's stables. As they walked by the mansion, people peered out the windows at them, talking, pointing; these called a few more over to gawk; the outcasts could hear the shrill voice of the auctioneer as bidding mounted. Kate shushed Jamie's questions as they climbed the narrow stable stairs to the tiny, slant-ceilinged rooms under the eaves. She put a hand on Jamie's head and touched Blue Wing's arm as they both stood, looking at her, waiting for her to speak.

"For several reasons," Kate began, "we cannot stay here as I had hoped. But I think I know a place. Let's get bundled up and take Jamie out for a ride on that little sled."

They plodded back out through snowy streets toward downtown. "Can we get some candy at the 'fectioner's?" the boy asked. "Where we going, Mama?"

"To Papa's old warehouse to see his friend Mr. Markwood," Kate explained. The snow had almost ceased, but wind yanked the puffy clouds of their breaths away.

"Down on the river?" Blue Wing said, a hint of challenge in her voice. "I did see that place when I came on keelboat. Not good place for you and boy down there," she quietly protested.

"I know," Kate said, meeting Blue Wing's concerned gray eyes. "But we *cannot* stay near Winterhaven. We will have to make our own winter haven someplace else, so that come next spring, you can go home—and Jamie and I can find a new home too."

"You come upriver with me, live at Mitutanka or Fort Clark," Blue Wing proposed.

"You know white women don't go way up the Missouri," Kate insisted. But then, as Blue Wing had said, they didn't come down here to the man's world of the wharves either.

On the crest of hill above the partially frozen gray-brown Mississippi, they stopped to rest. St. Louis sat haughtily on this limestone bluff as if it were a royal dais from which to reign over the river. The muddy Mississippi flowed fast and free below until it finally froze solid each winter in silent tribute. But the two annual river rises sometimes wet the feet of the Queen Valley City, so it hardly ruled the rivers. Clive had said that nothing did, not even a sturdy steamboat, which could only hope for tolerance and compromise.

Just twenty-three miles upriver the Mississippi was joined by the wide Missouri, Blue Wing's Big River, the longest one on the continent. The Missouri could be followed westward across the state, then climbed north like a twisting, turbulent staircase to fur and Indian country.

They walked downhill to the levee with its vast warehouses and jumbled assortment of buildings; on the snowy slant of Market Street the women held to Jamie's sled rope to keep him from slipping down past them. Surefooted Blue Wing lost her balance and slid a ways on her bottom, laughing and hooting as if it were the wildest fun. But Kate felt very solemn and still. This had to work. It was absolutely their last chance without begging to keep from being homeless and hungry this winter.

On the levee near Laclede's Landing, memories bombarded Kate again. The other once-a-year times she had been briefly down here—seated in the carriage to flutter her handkerchief out the window at Clive when he cast off—she had seen keelboats and steamboats three or four deep along the wharf. Tandem-drive drays had rattled over the cobblestones at all hours. Teams of six to eight oxen pulled wagons narrow enough to get through the original French-built streets. Three seasons of the year the moving and storing of cotton, hemp, sugar, molasses, and mountains of furs—as well as the manning and servicing of the boats that imported or exported these treasures—took precedence over everything.

And everywhere had been swarthy French *engagés*

waiting to go back upriver to trap and trade, American roustabouts called roosters, and black slaves lifting, toting, and pulling. St. Louisans had long argued conflicting opinions of slavery. Kate's Methodist family had been staunchly against it; Clive's were proslavery but too dirt-poor to own them. Kate had convinced him they must have only free, salaried house servants, though she knew he employed slaves in the warehouse and on the boats. How she wished now she had argued against slavery—and other things—with him.

When he said she should not be down here, she had not even told him how much she had loved the purposeful bustle, however raucous and rowdy. Blessedly things were quiet today but for the crunch of their feet on snow and the pounding of her heart.

They walked close to the buildings along the levee, hoping to dull the bite of wind, but it only whistled more shrilly and colder. They passed dram and billiard parlors, saloons, and chandlers set among the larger warehouses. Men's voices and loud laughter boomed even through closed doors and shutters now and then.

Kate squinted up at the swinging, creaking sign that had once said, CRAIG & CO. FUR & INDIAN TRADE GOODS. Now, newly painted over, it simply read, S. MARKWOOD. FURS.

"Mama, why does it smell so bad?" Jamie cried as Kate knocked loudly on the narrow front door. The big double doors for wagons were barred and bolted this time of year.

"Just animal and fur smell," Blue Wing told the boy. "I think I give to you name Much Questions."

Determinedly Kate pounded harder on the door, then tried to open it. It pushed inward at her touch. She stepped in, holding Jamie's hand, then entrusted him to Blue Wing. They followed as she advanced into the vast, dim room with its narrow alleys between piles of pressed, crated furs. She had been here only once before on the grand tour with Clive after they were first wed. How she had changed since that day. Then she was protected, coddled—and blind. Now she must do the protecting and coddling with both eyes wide open.

"Mr. Markwood! Sam Markwood, are you here?" she called.

A distant door banged. The lanky man thudded partway down the narrow stairs from his office, then descended more slowly, smoothing his hair and tucking in his shirt. "Why, that y'all, Miz Craig? I was goin' up to Winterhaven today, hoping to buy me some small 'membrance of the captain, but guess I overslept, with this weather and all. What are y'all doin' here with the boy—and I heard you was keeping that—that there Indian lady too."

Kate smiled at him as he came closer. No one had referred to Blue Wing as a lady, and Kate liked him immensely for that. But then she had initially liked some of the men in the shops and hotels uptown who had turned her down. She curled her toes in her boots; right through her gloves she gripped her fingers tightly together.

"Mr. Markwood, I'll come directly to the point. Mr. Hartman said you were pleased that I wanted you to keep this warehouse when there was some other big buyer who could have paid more."

"Oh, yes, ma'am, Cadet Chouteau hisself."

"Was it Chouteau? Then I'm doubly glad you got it because Mr. Chouteau was not really a friend of Captain Craig's and you were. And Mr. Hartman said the fact you could assume the loan without paying more meant you could finish the new front office and not have to use the back two rooms upstairs where Captain Craig started out years ago."

"You got a good head, Miz Craig, remembering that with what y'all been through. Believe it or not, the new office is done, and I even built me a room to live in up there."

"Then may I be so bold as to ask what you are doing with those old back rooms upstairs? You see, the three of us need a place to stay this winter, and I recall they had an outside entrance from the back alley too."

His blue eyes widened in his homely, concerned face. "Y'all mean to *live* there? You?"

"I do. If you would be so kind. Just until spring when the *Red Dawn* returns and she can be sold for scrap to give us a little nest egg. And I promise, one way or the other, I will pay you back for your kindness to us if you agree."

"Well, I'll be. There's only an old potbellied wood burner up there, but we could sweep the rooms out and fetch your goods with the wagon. Wish I could do more, but you know, ma'am, a bachelor living by the seat of his pants, pardon me saying it that way, with taking nearly all my savings to assume Captain's loan and all, I just can't do more. But sure enough, y'all are real welcome to them."

Kate's lips trembled. She hadn't felt really welcome to anyplace or anything in this town for what seemed like eternity. She managed to control her emotions and her actions, but she wanted to shout and to hug the man. Relieved and proud, she thrust out her hand to seal the first successful business deal she had ever made.

To her travois made of tree limbs, Ahpcha-Toha loaded another piece of driftwood, which had been caught in the brush along the river just north of town. She shook her head that the whites did not use dogs to pull burdens as the Plains tribes did. Prairie Wind's people used horses, slaves, even steamboats to do their work, but here dogs were treated like hunting companions or spoiled extra children.

She'd had a good day foraging for wood. And she had dug a hole in the ice and caught two fish. Even if Prairie Wind had not sold any small paintings on the wharves today, there would be something to eat.

But then, when she put the rope to her shoulders and began to tug the travois toward the city, she saw a thick tree limb wedged in river ice about three man lengths out from the bank. It would make her load almost too heavy, but it was worth it. Much Questions had watery eyes and nose this month of the Little Cold, which Prairie Wind called December. This burning log would warm them for a long time. It would give them light and heat for Prairie Wind to work at night, for she complained the cold weather stopped her paints and pencils.

Blue Wing shuffled carefully out from the bank. Mandans were adept at judging the thickness of river ice. In the winter months they migrated back and forth across the northern Missouri to their winter villages. They would also walk the ice to hunt if Buffalo Brother came to the river forests for protection from snows on the plains. But here, farther south, she had seen the ice was not so thick this early or so predictable. Intent on hacking out just enough ice around the piece of wood to free it, she jumped when a man's voice shouted close, "Hey, red gal, want to build a fire with a riverman?"

Knife raised, Blue Wing whirled. From the way the bearded white man stood, legs spread, arms crossed, booted feet firm on the bank, she judged he would not come out on the ice.

"Real feisty with that knife, ain't you?" he said, and laughed. "Wal, that's fine with me!"

He wore stained fringed buckskins. He had four dead white rabbits on a string he now dropped in the snow. His eyes were narrow and narrow-set. Rat's eyes, she thought. His nose was flat and as crooked as his teeth—and words. He had a long, jagged scar that puckered his left eyebrow and cheek. Even his black beard and hanging scalp hair could not conceal it. If he tried to touch her, she'd give him another cut to match that one!

But she had judged wrong that he would just taunt her and move on to his trapline. He slowly edged out onto the ice after her.

"You Hidatsa, Mandan, or Ree tribe, gal? I can tell you ain't Sioux. Speakee English? *Parlez-vous française?* See, even those white clothes don't hide that face—nor that ripe body you got neither. Known a few squaws in my day upriver, and they were *real* friendly, but don't re-call seeing you 'round here."

The man spoke his words calmly and quietly, as if she were a wild animal he could tame or lure. But she backed farther out, away from the piece of wood now bobbing free in the hole in the ice. She felt the ice bend and heard it creak under her. The river looked frozen clear to the other bank, the place the whites called Illinois Town. But even they knew not to walk it yet or ride horses and carts on it as Prairie Wind had said they would.

"Got a name, gal?" Scarface was asking. He too skirted

the hole in the ice. When he was out nearly to her, she leaped aside and tried to skid past him toward the bank. But she had underestimated his guile and agility. He kept his feet to lunge at her.

If only she were not wearing this full dress now. If only she had left her deep bonnet on to hide her face. She jumped back, slipped, slid to her knees, and scrambled away. He grabbed one ankle and yanked her flat on the ice. He slammed the knife from her grip, but she cut his wrist first. Blood spurted, staining the ice and her skin and hair. He straddled her writhing body. He banged her head once, twice, against the hard ice right on the edge of the hole. She could feel it widen, wetting her hair and shoulders. And then she heard the crisp cracking.

Cursing, holding his wrist, the man rolled sideways off her and scuttled toward the bank. Too late for her. She half slid, half broke through into the freezing water. She kicked the hole wider, fighting to right herself, to keep her head up. When she looked, he was on the bank, gasping, bleeding, glaring at her while she thrashed in her heavy, sodden clothes. She refused to scream to him for help. She had not given to him one word and would not now.

She was a strong swimmer, as were all The People. But not with these skirts. Her head hurt where she had hit the ice. Treading water in the jagged hole, she looked up at blue sky and bare bank. Had someone been there, or had she just fallen in? She was so dizzy, so cold, so confused.

Ahde! She saw blood in the snow. Yes, she remembered now. She hoped Scarface bled to death. She preferred this icy, heavy death to his touching her when she wanted only Swift Raven always, only him. Swift Raven could swim strongly. He would pull her out. The People would come running to help if one fell in. It happened when they jumped from ice piece to ice piece to snag driftwood or floating dead buffalo.

Strong, her people were strong. Never cold in winter, never cold like this, like the way she felt now . . . and Much Questions had a running nose and what would Prairie Wind say, she who had worried so when Blue Wing went out alone to bring back the wood for warmth . . . for

like a small winter lodge of The People was their place
above the alley in the fur warehouse ... furs, so many
furs from her people piled there ... furs to keep The People from freezing when they did not sell them to buy
tools and goods from the white man who looked down on
The People ...

Looked down ... Old Woman in the Moon looked
down but not today. ... Today the sun-god and his evil
sister who caused misfortunes looked down from the sky.
Ahde! Why had she left her medicine bundle on her buffalo robe in their winter lodge? Is that why this had happened? Blue Wing kicked her strangled feet and moved
her numbing arms slowly, even more slowly.

She scraped her hand on the tree limb, which shared
her hole in the ice. It had caused her misery but now
jolted her alert. She grasped it. Would it be enough to
float her if she tried to roll it under her? Her fingers were
so cold, but yes. Yes, it let her lift herself to roll out on
the ice, if it would just hold her.

She broke through twice again, then clawed herself out
and rolled a sodden mass of sopping skirts across the ice
to the bank. She lay there, panting, wanting to sleep forever, to cuddle deep into her buffalo robe and hope Swift
Raven came to her bed to warm her. She rolled to her
knees and staggered to her feet. Where had these dead
rabbits come from to spread their blood across the snow?
Who had left them here on this line next to her firewood?

Wood and rabbits, warmth and food. Her hands were
numb, but she reached for the rabbits, dragged them on
the wood, dragged her feet she could not feel toward
home.

"Miz Craig!" Sam Markwood's shout from outside in
the alley stopped Kate's pacing while she waited long after dark for the missing Blue Wing. "Your Indian friend
fell in the river, and she's real bad!"

Jamie waited on the landing as Kate rushed down to
help. Blue Wing's hair had iced; her skirts were stiff; her
brown skin looked purple in places in the light of Sam's
lantern. "Oh, no, I was so afraid of this along that partly

iced river! She's half frozen. Sam, can you carry her up-stairs for me?"

"Sure, Miz Craig, and I'll bring the other stuff up too. Don't know how far she walked like that, but she brought back some food and wood. You know how to fight frost-bite, don't you?" he gritted out as he carried the uncon-scious Indian upstairs. "Rub the funny-looking patches with snow and hope for the best."

Kate did hope and pray for the best. She rubbed Blue Wing's hands and feet and face with snow, then tepid wa-ter, and wrapped her in the two buffalo robes and all three blankets she had. There were many furs in the warehouse Sam said they could use this winter, but they still reeked, and Blue Wing had not cured any yet. Now, even as Blue Wing's skin began to warm, she quivered with ague. Be-cause she was using Jamie's blanket, Kate put him to bed fully dressed under a pile of clothes and, for hours, fed the stove the wood Blue Wing had brought back. It smoked, but it warmed and lit the stone-walled place.

She cleaned the two fish, though she hated to do it. Fighting to keep from vomiting, she skinned the rabbits the way she had seen Blue Wing do other meat, but the Mandan must have dropped her skinning knife, and Kate's was not as good. She made stew and broth, hoping it would help both Jamie and Blue Wing.

But Blue Wing was worse by morning. Sometimes she was unconscious, sometimes delirious. Kate's stomach twisted tighter. "Please, Blue Wing, come back to us," she whispered to the feverish young woman as the first hint of dawn lit the room. "You're strong. Mandans are strong and don't catch cold, remember?"

But the only reply from Blue Wing was broken ravings in her own language.

Sam was kind enough to take a bundled-up Jamie for a walk after he came up the back stairs to inquire how Blue Wing was faring. And though Kate had no money to spare and didn't know if the doctor would come for a sick Indian, she asked Sam please to tell Dr. Beaumont, who had tended Clive, what had happened. She tried to ladle hot broth down Blue Wing's throat, though the Mandan sometimes fought her. She could not bear to tie her hands.

It looked like a clear day out, but Kate would not leave her patient's side to try to sell her miniatures and silhouettes along the wharf today. Sam and Jamie returned. Dr. Beaumont, Sam said, was off delivering a baby, but his wife would give him the message.

When Jamie fell asleep early that night, Kate hovered over Blue Wing in the wan light of their single oil lamp. No wonder the boy slept well, she thought, for she had burned the bounty of Blue Wing's driftwood all day, hoping the warmth would help revive her. She had barely enough for another night and day left. She was so tired herself; sometimes when she almost nodded off, she thought she was back tending Clive. Dr. Beaumont had evidently abandoned them as others had. At least the frostbitten places on Blue Wing's skin looked better, but she had not awakened; she still muttered in Mandan, with occasional words of broken English, including a little chant about a swift-flying raven. More of her nature gods, Kate supposed, but though floating in exhaustion, she prayed hard to her own God for Blue Wing's deliverance.

She might have wanted Blue Wing's death at first, but not now, not ever. To see the sturdy, stubborn young woman helpless like this was to realize how much she had come to mean to Kate.

Kate jerked from dozing, sitting straight up, at a sharp sound. Blue Wing slept so quietly that she felt her neck for the pulse there. Yes, alive. Then she realized the sound had been a knock at her door in the other room, the one that went directly into the warehouse. She stepped over Jamie and opened the door. Sam stood there with the cloaked and top-hatted Dr. Beaumont.

"I came when I could, Mrs. Craig," the bleary-eyed man told her, with a quick glance around the dim, small rooms as he entered and gave her his hat. Kate was so relieved to see him she did not even feel shamed by the pitiful place she had summoned him to.

She explained Blue Wing's plight. "I will be glad to pay you to dose her," she added.

He said nothing but stooped over the girl, touching her wrist and neck, listening to her heart, lifting her eyelids, feeling her head, checking her limbs, fingers, and toes for frostbite. "Ah, perhaps here's another culprit, besides that dousing in the river," he said. "A large contusion—a bump on her head. And of course, in this case, her fever could turn to lung fever or pneumonia. You are doing well to keep her warm and try to get broth down her. We will just have to hope that fever breaks soon and make her sit up to keep her lungs clear. Is there no bed for her?" he added with a disparaging look at the pallet she lay on.

"I could put her in mine, but she hates beds," Kate explained. "Are you sure there is no medicine, nothing like you gave Clive?"

"Mrs. Craig," he said, his weary voice a monotone, "digitalis is not for this, for it's not her heart. But I will give you some distilled oil of peppermint to make her some tea. The Indians trust herbs to heal them, I've heard. Here, I'll help you lift her up into this bed."

They laid her there and propped her up with both pillows they owned. Kate got out her money box and escorted the doctor to the back door.

"Your house calls are a dollar, if I remember right," she said, "so if I could pay you some now, and—"

"I don't expect you to recall with all you went through when your husband died, but you were paid ahead for several visits then. I have it on my books. And I believe little James was due for his smallpox—or cowpox, as it were—inoculation just before Captain Craig died, so bring him in sometime soon, won't you? I'll check in tomorrow on the girl, and promise me you will take some of that peppermint tea yourself and get some sleep."

Kate nodded. Gratitude and exhaustion swamped the last of her self-control. She had no idea if Clive had really paid the doctor ahead or this was old-fashioned Christian charity, but she felt too beaten to argue. "I can't thank you enough, Doctor!" she called after him as he started down the worn wooden steps with his black bag in hand.

She brewed the tea on the single plate on the stove, got some down Blue Wing, drank some herself. Though the doctor had not taken their last fifty cents, she sat staring into the burning belly of the stove, telling herself she should go out and try to sell something when the sun came up tomorrow, some paintings of dear Blue Wing, who would not wake up.

Kate slept beside the single bed, next to Jamie on his pallet that night and the next morning. She slept fitfully, and dreams haunted her: Blue Wing in the cemetery flat and dead on Clive's grave. Blue Wing snuggled under the buffalo robe on top of Sally's grave until all was covered by white, endless, cloaking snow. She herself felt like the walking dead when she got up and fed Jamie.

But near nightfall the second day Blue Wing sat straight up and said, "I need medicine bath and swim in river."

Kate jumped up from her rocking chair so fast she fell. The foot curled under her had gone numb. She limped to the bed and perched on the edge of it. "Do you know where you are? What happened?"

"I fell in river. So cold, need steam and river bath, need Mandan shaman, not this bed!"

Kate touched her forehead. Still hot, but at least she had returned to the living. But to have almost died from falling in the river and then to say she needed a river bath—Kate would not allow it! Her patient coughed then, raspy and wheezy, deep in her throat. Did pneumonia sound like that? Kate wondered.

"Frog chest need white sage burned," Blue Wing diagnosed herself again. "Need medicine bath, steam, swim in river, sacred singing, with deer hoof rattles. My spirit wandered far away . . ." she said, and wilted into the pillow with a rasping sigh as if that much had taken all her strength. Despite that, Kate was so thrilled words tumbled from her.

"Blue Wing, there will be no swim in river! But if we try to do these other things for you—I mean, we don't know the sacred songs or how to give a medicine bath— but if we do the best we can, will you try to get better? Your Old Woman in the Moon will understand. With her help and that of my powerful God, who I told you has much more medicine than the moon or sun"—she wished now she had taken the time to show Blue Wing the im-

pressive cathedral—"you will have to rest and get well.
And don't worry about getting wood or food. I can do
that, just as I cleaned the fish and skinned those rabbits
you snared."

Blue Wing furrowed her brow. "Rabbits? I did not
catch rabbits. I fell in ice to get some wood out. I hit my
head, I think that all. . . ." Her thoughts muted to a mur-
mur as she fell asleep again.

Under Blue Wing's directions, Kate heated four large
cobblestones in the stove, while she and Jamie erected a
small buffaloskin tent on the floor for her to lie under,
propped up with driftwood. With water sprinkled on the
stones set on piles of pebbles, they made a little steam
bath. Then Kate and Blue Wing compromised on another
dip in the river by letting her wash in tepid water from
the painted china basin. As for sacred songs, dear little
Jamie sang one Blue Wing had taught him about a boy
who won a dart game—at least it was in Mandan—and a
French lullaby Adele had sung to him. Kate, though she
knew her voice could not keep a tune, went through every
Charles Wesley hymn she could recall from her mother
and tried to convince Blue Wing that these were "white
medicine songs." The sick woman especially liked
"Hark! the Herald Angels Sing" and "Soldiers of Christ
Arise and Put Your Armor On."

"Mandans have singers—good, *shish,* singers—and
soldiers. Braves wear armor of painted hides in battle,"
Blue Wing said. "I get better with your medicine, Prairie
Wind and Much Questions. I will arise and sing, like your
songs, so I can go home when river ice melts, home to
my people at Mitutanka."

Home to my people, Kate's brain echoed those words.
Blue Wing had a home and family. But where was her
and Jamie's home? Drained but relieved when Blue Wing
slept quietly this time, Kate was calmer when she greeted
the doctor that evening. "Your care—and ours—has
worked wonders for her," she whispered to him, and explained what they had done.

"Now, don't expect her to get her strength back soon,
especially with that hacking cough even in her sleep," he

cautioned. "And don't forget to bring the boy by next week for that inoculation. Smallpox is more deadly than a spill in the winter river, you know, and this vaccine is certain prevention, whereas there is no real cure. That reminds me: As soon as the Indian is strong enough to walk, you bring her by too for a smallpox inoculation. It's swept through many a tribe, though some have been immunized."

"All right, yes, I will," Kate said.

"Oh, almost forgot," he added. "My wife said she'd like you and the boy to stay for noon dinner when you bring him in. I hear you've been selling your artwork in these parts, so bring us one of those miniatures to buy, won't you? Wednesday, then," he said over his shoulder in that half-whispered voice. "And we'll just send something back with you for the Indian as she shouldn't be up and about for a week, I don't care how stubborn or hardy she is. Barely two weeks till Christmas, you know . . ." he added as he went downstairs.

Kate stood above him on the dilapidated balcony, holding to the shaky handrail. She wanted to thank him again, to tell him how deeply she appreciated his care and concern. Dr. Beaumont had not been able to heal Clive's heart, but his kindness—along with Blue Wing's and Sam's—had helped heal hers.

Evidently surprised she still stood looking down at him, Dr. Beaumont glanced up and tipped his hat to her. She smiled for the first time in days. Guests and good luck come in threes, Mama used to say—the only superstition Kate could recall that she ever had. But if Dr. Beaumont was their first guest here, there were two more to go.

The next day Kate took Jamie out with her so Blue Wing could sleep, but they hurried back upstairs at noon to check on her.

"Much Questions help you sell paintings?" Blue Wing asked Kate with a sleepy smile at the boy.

"One, and Dr. Beaumont wants one tomorrow, though I intend it to be a gift to him."

"I want rise up, go get wood, but my head make room

go around, and my legs like new cornstalks," Blue Wing said, and sank back on her pillow. "I think this bed make me weak. I get down on my robe again."

"Not until tomorrow!" Kate insisted. "Jamie's going to be with Sam for a while this afternoon, so you can sleep again right where you are as soon as I heat some stew. I will just sell one more painting this afternoon, collect some driftwood, and get us a nice loaf of bread. Promise me you will sleep again."

Blue Wing frowned and lifted a hand to her head. "Maybe I dream where I did get those rabbits," she said.

Outside on this chill December afternoon Kate could not sell one more tiny painting. When the river froze, however, people from the outlying districts, who did not own boats, would ride the ice in. She just knew she could interest outsiders in these charming oil miniatures of an Indian maid—if the three of them could last until then. And today, to make things worse, a fur-coated Frenchman kept staring at her and swigging something from a bottle. So she went over to sit on a piling along the wharf next to the kindly cross-eyed whittler named Gabe Taylor she had spoken to several times before.

"I wish that one would choke on his bottle," she told him, and nodded toward her ogler without looking up. "If he doesn't want to buy, he doesn't need to stare."

"Even with one good eye, I can see why he does, though," the rusty-haired and bearded man told her. "Now don't you get your dander up over that, ma'am, but there's not the likes of you 'round here. You're like a fish out of water."

"I know," she said, and sighed. She realized how much she appreciated Gabe's honest camaraderie. If he knew her story, he hadn't let on or probed. Perhaps he had his own story and respected her privacy.

"Now you just keep on sitting here, like I'm your big watchdog," Gabe told her, and lifted thickly thatched eyebrows over crinkly blue eyes—only one of which looked right at her while the other stared toward the river. "See, I don't look like a big bruiser for nothing, even if I can hardly stand to kill a merskeeter."

"Thank you, Gabe. Oh, you're carving a harlequin clown," she noted, looking at the delicate wooden piece cradled in his big hands. "My daughter had a little stuffed doll like that once. It's excellent work, especially for a keelboater whose hands are used to the steering pole."

"Gonna be a jumping jack on a string," he told her, beaming at her compliment. She had noticed he also carved tops, skeleton ladders that clack-clacked, turning end over end when the pieces were joined by woven canvas webs, and penny banks shaped like steamboats. He spoke softly and smiled a lot. Still, it seemed most folks had little to do with the man.

Perhaps it was because he occasionally broke up fights so swiftly and furiously that even the loud river roosters were afraid of him. When anyone argued or jostled, Gabe was quick to step in with a bellowed "There is no peace for the wicked!" or some such thundering judgment to make the contenders jump apart. Folks evidently thought he was simpleminded or fearsome. Besides, she surmised, they couldn't quite tell whether Gabe was looking their way or not and, therefore, what he was thinking or going to do next.

This winter, he'd told her and Jamie, he was living in the Last Chance Saloon, where he swept the floor and generally kept order among the patrons. But come the ice breakup, he'd said, "Gonna hire myself out as a keelboat captain again and go up the Missouri I love!"

"I'd never thought about loving a river," Kate had admitted to him, "though I suppose I've known a few who have loved where the Missouri led."

"A trip on that river's like living life itself!" he'd explained. "You think you see the lay of the land, but there's something new 'round the next turn that can thrill you or do you in."

"*Any* next turn on the river could do you in, you old cross-eyed coot!" A mouthy, rum-reeking troublemaker had interrupted Gabe's philosophizing. "And you been boastin' for years you could pilot a steamboat upriver, *Captain* Gabe," the man taunted, "instead of just pullin' on a keelboat steerin' pole!"

"Why, you can't see straight yourself from drinking

that rotgut all the time, you egg-sucking snake of a polecat!" Gabe had retorted, and shoved the drunk on his way.
Kate had really come to admire him after that and especially today, when he walked her upriver to find some
driftwood so that staring man wouldn't dare bother her.

After that she jokingly called the big gentle bear of a
man Gabriel, her guardian angel. And both of them reveled in their fellowship of standing and selling their
goods together. He bought a miniature of Blue Wing that
allowed Kate to take home a fresh-smelling baguette that
night. And she told him that come Christmas, she would
have enough saved to buy one of his wooden steamboat
banks for Jamie.

The second visitor to Kate's new winter haven was the
last one she would ever have expected. As she sat one
early evening rocking and darning Jamie's socks by the
wan light of the stove while Blue Wing and Jamie played
a game she had taught him with a pole and small rolling
hoop, a knock rattled the back door.

"Who is it, please?" Kate called out, and motioned
Blue Wing to sit back down when she jumped, instantly
alert.

"It is Monsieur Chouteau, Madame Craig," a deep
voice responded.

Chouteau! She could not believe it. She shook out her
skirts and opened the door before realizing her hair was
down and looked as wild as Blue Wing's did as it grew
back.

"However did you find us, sir?"

"It is a bit brisk out here. May I step in?" He entered
before she indicated he could and peeled off his elegant
gray kid gloves, though he kept his tall hat in place. "You
know, dear lady, I have many people who work for me in
this area of the city, who report to me things they see on
the river, eh."

That man just drinking and watching her on the ice, she
thought, could have worked for Chouteau. He had been a
French *engagé,* and she heard that Chouteau hired many
of them to trap for his company.

"But I was shocked," he was saying, "when I had once

offered you Chouteau hospitality, no strings attached, I assure you, to hear of your sorry plight here."

"I chose to live here this winter, monsieur, and the three of us are doing quite well enough."

"Ah, quite well enough, the three of you." Sarcasm laced his voice. His eyes skimmed the dim interior, challenging Blue Wing's sullen stare and studying the boy's wide-eyed face. "I am afraid, for your own good, as a concerned citizen, I must assert myself, madame. I really think you should move in with my family. The Indian will have to return to General Clark's, where she should be anyway." He went on as if Blue Wing were a stick of wood that could discern nothing he said. "And that cough of hers sounds horrendous. You'll all die of garret fever in this hovel, and I'd never forgive myself. Please, madame, come along now."

"I thank you for your concern, sir, but to repeat, the three of us have decided—*I* have decided we shall stay together here. You see, Blue Wing is spending the winter with my son and me, for General Clark isn't home to entertain her anyway."

"Entertain *her*? Really, madame . . ."

"Besides, sir, Blue Wing is my friend, and I will not be in debt or beholden to anyone, especially not those would separate us."

"Us? In these dire straits you choose to befriend your husband's upriver paramour? Let's be reasonable—and ethical—now. Surely you do not mean to make your son remain here this winter when he could sit at a bounteous table with my children, even share their tutor, eh? And if it worries you that you will be beholden, then I shall buy from you that last little ruin of a Craig steamship—what is its name? *Red Dawn,* I think—and you may consider that payment for your room and board. One of my men is waiting outside to take the Mandan girl with him, so he can get her to Marais Castor first thing in the morning. After all, the general—who is, you know, still superintendent of Indian affairs—decided she should stay out there for her own protection and good health. You should not have absconded with her by merely telling his darkies."

Here, unfortunately, Blue Wing went into a frenzy of coughing that made them just stand staring at each other until she quieted. Kate's distrust of the man began to harden to dislike. Of course, he was used to giving orders and having them obeyed. But she had the strongest instinct there was something cold and calculating behind his supposedly sincere concern. Besides, she did not like his subtly couched assumption of right and his superior attitude toward Blue Wing and General Clark's slaves, let alone toward her and Jamie.

"I am sorry, Monsieur Chouteau, but I must decline your thoughtful offer."

His expression did not change but for the tightening of one corner of his mouth. For one moment she was not certain he took in her refusal.

"Little boy," he said, and hitched up his trousers slightly at the knee before squatting to look Jamie in the eye, "you would like to live at a place that had lots of food and games to play with other boys and buffalo fenced in to pretend to shoot, wouldn't you?"

Jamie, suddenly shy, nodded and, as he hadn't done for months, thrust his thumb in his mouth. "There, you see?" Chouteau said, and looked up at Kate with a triumphant smile while he ruffled Jamie's hair. "Children know whom to trust!"

His using Jamie this way further annoyed her, but there was something she really wanted to know before she asked him to leave. Perhaps it was all Gabe's chattering about being anxious to get upriver come spring; perhaps it was Blue Wing's longing to return to her people. It was definitely that she wanted to salvage something from the many things she once thought Clive had owned so Jamie had some heritage of fortune and pride. But mostly she wanted to keep alive Clive's worthy goal to trade fairly with the Indians and find some way to feed her family; those were *her* goals now.

"Monsieur, would you answer a question for me?" she asked Chouteau as he stood, looking quite pleased with himself.

"But of course, madame."

"How much would you pay me for the *Red Dawn* for

scrap, or would you still use her on the river if she were yours?"

He seemed surprised; their eyes met and held. The small ebony pupils in his eyes widened ever so slightly. "I hear she's an old boat, and a side-wheeler to boot, that catches every bank sandbar and submerged snag in the water," he began, speaking tentatively. "But if you come to the Chouteaus, I will pay you handsomely, perhaps put someone good on her and try to eke one more trip out of her at least to Fort Pierre before the scrap heap. I could give you a small percentage of that run, you know. I'll really have to see her condition when she returns this spring to decide, madame. Now, get your things together, if there's anything here," he added, looking around with a frown, "worth taking."

His presumption that he could control her with carefully couched orders and subtle bribery made her even more wary. "Monsieur Chouteau, I am afraid I must still refuse," she told him, pleased her voice sounded steady and strong. "We prefer not be at your mercy, like—like those buffalo fenced in on your estate. As for Blue Wing, she has chosen to stay with us."

"This is entirely ridiculous," he said, his smooth tone roughening. He smacked his gloves into the palm of one hand. "You are making yourself, your dead husband, this child, even this runaway Mandan laughingstocks far and wide. Now gather your things before I call my men up here to—"

He gasped as Blue Wing flashed the long kitchen knife with which she had replaced her little one. "Blue Wing!" Kate said. "The man is leaving. I am certain he will go as calmly—and cleverly—as he has offered us his kindnesses."

Kate preceded him and opened the door. He gave Blue Wing a wide berth and pushed past Kate. For one moment Kate feared his stepping to the door was a signal to the men he had mentioned, for a big form loomed on the top step.

"Kate"—the twang of Gabe's voice surprised her—"just stopped by with a wooden top I'd like the boy to try out for me."

"Please, won't you step in, Gabriel?" she said, and stood aside so he could squeeze past Chouteau.

"You're being very silly and stupid," Chouteau whispered to her. "At least your husband never was that." Then he went, tugging on his gray kid gloves, down the steps into the darkness. Seeing Chouteau did indeed have four men and a carriage waiting for him below, Kate realized Gabe had probably seen them down the alley from the saloon and come with the excuse about the top.

Jamie darted to Gabe to see it. Gabe knelt to show the boy how to wrap the string around its neck, then give it a good yank to free it. Kate's thoughts were whirling like that top. Suddenly she felt ecstatic. For Cadet Chouteau, without realizing it, had helped her loose a daring idea that had been snagged inside her for weeks.

That night she could not sleep. Not because Mama's superstition of three guests arriving had been true or because she had dared defy the powerful Chouteau. She could not sleep with sheer excitement because she now glimpsed a way to accomplish much she would do, however formidable the obstacles, however impossible the task and risks.

She would build on the only part of Clive's legacy worth bequeathing to Jamie. She could help Blue Wing's people as Blue Wing had helped her. She would earn her way in this world. See her mother. Become independent and free and—and, like her hero, George Catlin—have a blessed opportunity to paint the people and places along the beautiful Big River. Besides, if she didn't seize this chance, they would be destitute and forced perhaps to give in to Chouteau. It was a fervent hope for all this as well as survival that drove her now.

She tiptoed out of bed at dawn, but her thoughts had kept her so warm she did not even stoke the stove at first. She cracked the drapes made from linen towels and peered out at the eastern sky. Yes! Listening to Blue Wing with her belief in signs from nature was perhaps changing her, but there it was as clear as anything.

The rising sun painted the eastern sky crimson. She would hold to it as a promise from the heavens that she could make her *Red Dawn* dream come true.

Chapter 6

It took many days for the frog croaking to leave Blue Wing's chest. As soon as it did, she had a journey to make to the lodge of Chouteau. She did not let Prairie Wind know where she was going or why. If this became bad, her *manuka*, Prairie Wind, must not be blamed.

Blue Wing went at nightfall the day before the white man's Christmas, when there would be sacred ceremonies, feasting, and gifts. Even before Prairie Wind told her how a holy child came to earth while beings with bird wings sang in the sky, Blue Wing had known of this great medicine day of the whites. At Fort Clark on Christmas, Blue Wing recalled, white men sometimes gave The People tobacco or gunpowder to hunt buffalo. So she would have gifts for Prairie Wind and Much Questions.

But today Blue Wing was surprised how quickly she became tired carrying the rifle. Like the snowshoes on her feet, it had belonged to River Walker. She had found the rifle in the room with all his books and had buried it in its otterskin case in the garden behind Winterhaven. Evidently Prairie Wind had not thought to look for it during her days of work and worry in the big house. Blue Wing had never shot a rifle, but today she must.

She did not want to walk at night, but it was safer and wiser. The people who bought River Walker's house must not see her digging up a rifle in their garden. No one must stop her on the street with the gun. Most of all, she did not want Chouteau or his men to see her and stop her when she arrived, even though the stars looked down and Old Woman's face was full. She had told Prairie Wind she must go out this night to thank Old Woman in the Moon for the return of her strength, and that was true.

But mostly she wanted Old Woman to guide her steps to what she must do.

Despite legs gone as weak as grass, Blue Wing set up a steady pace, moving easily on the wooden and webbed shoes through the soft snow. Her thoughts also made steps back to the edge of another prairie.

How angry the Mandan chief Mato-Tope, called by the whites Chief Four Bears, had been at the Indian agent at Fort Clark, John Sanford. For from Chouteau's steamboat Sanford took the Mandans' yearly gifts from the Great White Father in Washington directly into Fort Clark, not to the village. Only a few blankets and axes did he give The People. Did he think they had blind eyes and had forgotten promises with the smoking of the pipe? Then that man and the traders of Chouteau did tell The People they must trade furs for what they knew was theirs in the fort. The Indian agent Sanford and the traders were all the hands and mouth of Chouteau's company! Sanford even married Chouteau's daughter.

Dark Water, called MacLeod among the whites, knew these things and, even as Blue Wing, did tell them to Red-Haired Father. Dark Water also told that the prices of Chouteau were more than River Walker asked—and now he lay in his white man's grave. Dark Water said he would also tell to the Great White Father in Washington that The People did not get their yearly gifts but must trade furs for what was already theirs.

But now Blue Wing had new hope that her white sister, Prairie Wind, would make openhanded trade with The People. Prairie Wind saw Chouteau's bad heart. Like many Mandans, Kate Craig would not let Chouteau pull a blanket over her eyes. But that was not enough. Someone would have to kill Chouteau to stop his crooked ways!

The wrapped rifle was heavy on her back. But the bullets jingled merrily in her pouch like the bells on sleighs in which the white people of St. Louis had sailed across the ice of the frozen river these last days. Tomorrow, Prairie Wind had said, they would go out on the river for the day. And, Blue Wing thought with a tight smile as the lights of Chouteau's big house came in view just where

Sam Markwood said it would be, she hoped to have something to give her friend Prairie Wind to lift her heart even more.

Just as Sam had said, Chouteau made fences here to close off what he thought was his part of the prairie. Did the whites not know this was wrong? Blue Wing followed the three wooden rails toward the lights of the big house, glad the wind was not so bitter this night. Yet it meant when she left, she must find the branch of a bush to cover her tracks. Now where was that man?

She climbed on the lowest rail to get a better view into the lighted house. Inside, many laughing people, smiling, drinking people. Yes, there was Chouteau. And the Mandan Indian agent John Sanford, for he visited The People only in the warm months. She also glimpsed white-haired people of many years, those in the spring of youth, and young ones. All in bright garments, some women with winking stones in their hair as well as on necklaces. Under hanging lanterns of glass icicles, people had plates of food—much food.

And then she saw among them a man she thought she must surely know, but she did not: an ugly man with black beard and scarred face. He was dressed well, perhaps a son of Chouteau or one of his men. Had she seen him on the keelboat or at Fort Clark? She shook her head to throw off her confusion and jumped down. The cloak of moonlight was so bright across the snow someone might look out and see her. But it was even brighter in there, so she thought not. Along the rail fence she hacked off a piece of thornbush with dried leaves and frozen buds, then edged her way farther along, dragging the limb back and forth behind her, retracing her steps.

And then she heard what she sought. She squinted into the gray distance. Yes, they were here, snorting their welcome, Brother Buffalo of The People, penned in like prisoners on what had once been their prairie. The small herd of them—perhaps ten or twelve—huddled in the corner of the rails. They shuffled and cowered, these great, curly-haired shorthorns that should stand proud and bold and tall as a man. Did they fear they would be run about their pen again or tormented like a half-dead beaver thrashing in a trap?

She recalled how Chouteau had boasted he would let his boys, even Much Questions, chase and pretend to shoot them. Sam had said that now and then Chouteau strolled out his front door and shot one just for fun. Blue Wing knew that was bad, for these could not run far, did not have a chance to fight back or choose their fate. Even when surrounded by many Mandan braves, Brother Buffalo had a chance and a choice. The People always danced and sang to him first, asking him to choose to come to them. Many times in the hunt buffalo gored horses, maimed and killed their attackers, and ran away. And always, when slain, their bodies went for many honored, necessary uses among The People, lives given to give life.

As Blue Wing slowly approached the nervous beasts, she began to chant low in her throat to call them. It was not the sacred song owned by the White Buffalo Cow Society, for she could never use that without payment or punishment. It was a song of her own making, one Old Woman in the Moon would understand.

The animals clustered tighter together under the watchful eyes of Old Woman high above. They did not bolt. Perhaps they knew she had come to help them. When she stepped closer, she saw how still and dull now looked those dark, shiny-pebble eyes.

"Shorthorn, Brother Buffalo," she whispered in her singsong chant, "never be afraid again."

She saw that some places on their thick winter coats so valued for robes, they had rubbed themselves bare on the rails. *Ahde!* They did not look well fed for being fenced, not like penned horses of the whites. She saw a shallow wallow in the corner they had tried to make to replace the big, deep ones they loved to hew from clay creek beds or the bottoms of Big River when they ran free.

Her hand touched the metal piece of gate; it was so cold, like the gun barrel even under its otterskin robe. But it meant their freedom.

"Shorthorn, Brother Buffalo, I will free you to the prairie. No more bad man will keep you here, as he wants to keep The People penned to do his will. I ask but one favor. If I free you, will not one of you give to me his meat and hide for those who have good hearts to you? A boy and a woman. Then they may eat and live this cold, bare winter. I too, Ahpcha-Toha of Mitutanka. And if you run free to the north, will you not visit the forests near the winter village of my people to give them food, and warmth, and hope?"

With one last glance toward the golden glow of the house, she turned back again to the buffalo, silvered by Old Woman and stars. She lifted the latch on the gate and swung it wide. It creaked, but with all the noise inside the house, no one heard.

Brother Buffalo did not stir. Must she walk in to force them out? Had Chouteau broken their great spirits? Still dragging the branch behind her footsteps, she started away, hoping they would find the open gate and flee. She chanted low in her throat, then stopped, unwrapped, and loaded the rifle. She had loaded many a gun for men but had never shot one. Would one of the buffalo be willing to answer her request? She could never just shoot one penned in by Chouteau like that, and this close, the gun might call the whites.

She was a good walk away when she heard the sound her people loved: the muffled thudding of hooves, the snorted breaths, the rush of wind as buffalo ran free. She stood behind a tree so they would not trample her, but they did not come so close. A blur of shadow beyond the streambed, they ran toward town and then, behind one big bull, veered off toward open prairie.

But a middle-size one lagged behind. Perhaps it was a cripple, perhaps too old to run. It came close and put its head down as if in obedience. It turned the left heart side to her and pawed the ground as if to say, "I am here a sacrifice for our great freedom."

Blinking back tears of gratitude and awe, Blue Wing raised the heavy rifle. As she had seen the men do on many hunts, she fired.

Though Kate had been dreading Christmas this year, she was not as sad as she had thought. Jamie seemed happy enough and that was all, she told herself, that really mattered. He was thrilled to have a penny bank carved like "Papa's very best steamboat, *Red Dawn!*" He made engine sounds and ran it endlessly that Christmas morning across Blue Wing's old buffalo robe as if the fur were a wide, wavy, muddy river. And to have three pennies of his own to drop in it just like cargo that could clink about inside when shaken—boy's heaven, indeed!

Kate gave Blue Wing a new skinning knife to replace the one she'd lost in the river; it was an old carving one Gabe had traded for upriver and said he seldom used. With a smile, Blue Wing announced, "I belove it!" Kate was glad she no longer went about with the big kitchen knife stuck through her belt, the one she had pulled on Chouteau.

Blue Wing gave both Kate and Jamie moccasins beautifully adorned with porcupine quills. *"Shish, sinashush!"* Kate praised them, for she was determined to learn Mandan so she could trade directly with the Indians from the deck of the *Red Dawn* upriver next summer. But she had asked Blue Wing not to promise Jamie he could visit her people. Gabe had told Kate that above the trading post of Bellevue the river and land got much more treacherous, and she was determined to leave Jamie for a few weeks with her mother at Bellevue.

But best of all today, last night Blue Wing had brought buffalo meat back from her walk to speak with Old Woman at the edge of the prairie. Buffalo had not been spotted there for years. They had not had a roast of any kind in weeks! A Christmas miracle! Blue Wing had shot the bison with Clive's rifle she had hidden in case they needed it, and they just might need it next spring to provide meat on their way upriver to Mitutanka. Blue Wing said she had more meat frozen in a cache on the prairie she could fetch from time to time and a hide she would cure this winter. This was turning out to be a lovely day after all, Kate thought.

In the early afternoon, when church services were long over, Kate took Jamie and Blue Wing to see the cathedral. Blue Wing was awed by its size and the colored transparencies—and, therefore, the "big medicine of this

Lord God, He Who Lives Above." Again Kate told them both the Christmas story, pointing out several scenes in the windows.

"Why did not the Son of He Who Lives Above come be born among our dogs and horses in a winter lodge?" Blue Wing asked on the way out. "Mandans not have inns or mangers but always make room, always take strangers in. Besides, I like to see those angels singing in the sky near stars and Old Woman in the Moon."

With a sigh and shake of her head at the mingled message she must have conveyed, Kate led them down to the busy river. Although she knew it was a fine opportunity to sell her goods, she was determined just to enjoy the day.

In the clear, crisp air many people were out to have fun or to work off hearty dinners. People waved and shouted, "Merry Christmas, everyone!" each time private sleighs with their jingling harness bells or the public sleigh ferry made its path back and forth across the ice between the rows of food and drink tents. Small sleds too were decked with greens or holly boughs.

Strollers and skaters dodged wagon teams crossing from the Illinois to the Missouri shore with coal. Jamie scrambled with some other boys to pick up precious pieces that dropped. The bigger boys made a sort of shooting game with the lumps. Kate caught snatches of their outrageous stories told to scare their wide-eyed younger siblings, tales of terror about the exploits on the old dueling grounds of Bloody Island, just offshore. She laughed and shook her head as she pulled Jamie on.

Kate steered them around the whiskey tents set up every half mile on the ice. They did not have coins for the pickled pigs' feet or roasted nuts at other stalls, but Kate told them they would roast their own chestnuts later. She wished she could have bought them all tarts and candies at the tent that sold them, but she didn't have enough for that.

And the thought came to her again, though she had tried to shut it out today, that she had no idea in her grand scheme of running the old steamboat upriver how she would ever pay for trade goods unless they could sell pas-

sages way ahead. Or when the boat returned from southern waters, would it have made some profit? She certainly had no intention of getting things on credit, as
Clive had done, to pile up a mountain of new debts.

Her attention was soon pulled back by Jamie's begging
to join the children's sliding games on the ice. Blue Wing
and Kate joined long lines of parents clapping and laughing as their youngsters of different sizes ran, then slid as
far as they could. Kate waved to Samantha Lautrec,
whose husband hurried her on before they could speak.

A deep voice called Kate's name, and Gabe Taylor
walked toward them. She was surprised he had picked
them out from way over there, but then she really wasn't
certain how well he could see.

"Happy Christmas, ladies! Where's the boy?" he called
to them.

"In that sliding race with the little ones," Kate said,
and pointed him out. "He loved your carved steamboat."

"Soon as your *Red Dawn* comes in this spring, I'll do
an actual carving of her for you," he promised as Blue
Wing walked closer to the race.

"And you'll help me assess what repairs she might
need to go upriver? You're the only one I know I can
trust on that, as Sam's always kept the warehouse. You
said you've longed for the chance to work on a steamer,
to captain one, Gabriel," she told him.

"True, but I'm just a hired keelboat captain."

"But you know the river, and that's the most of it, you
said."

"I'll get a fellow I know to give me a little help looking at the engine and boiler parts of her before you hire
someone on for captain or pilot. Say, I was thinking, you
gonna change her name, Kate?"

"No, why should I?" she asked as they walked closer
to the crowd.

"Thought maybe you'd heard that silly rhyme about
the weather: 'Red sky at night, sailor's delight. Red sky
at morning, sailor take warning.' "

"It's not Red Sky, it's *Red Dawn*, Gabriel! It has a special meaning to me, and that's its name. Besides, I'm not
a bit superstitious."

"Then it's a miracle you and the Mandan gal's getting along so good. Say, I was wondering if I mightn't buy the three of you some candy or a pastry for your Christmas dinner today," he offered.

"On one condition," she insisted. "Blue Wing actually shot a buffalo last night! Come home and have what she calls back beef with us. Gabriel, whatever is it? You don't like buffalo roast?"

"Fancy it real fine, Kate. But I take it you ain't heard the word going 'round 'bout what happened out at Chouteau's estate last night."

"No, what?" she asked as Blue Wing came over laughing with an out-of-breath Jamie.

"Seems," Gabe said, speaking slowly and deliberately now, "someone let Chouteau's little bison herd loose last night and not a one of them's been found."

Kate stared at Blue Wing. For one moment she thought the girl would say something, confess, or laugh, or act defiant. "All this Christmas make me hungry!" was all she said as they headed back toward shore.

That evening the five of them—Sam included—sat on small boxes around an empty crate Sam and Gabe carried in from the warehouse for their Christmas dinner. Kate felt almost guilty at her good fortune these last two weeks: dining at Dr. Beaumont's the day Jamie had his inoculation and now this! Today Sam had given them a pound cake full of citron and raisins for supper and a keg of lantern oil; Gabe made good his offer of crusty apple-filled pastries that smelled enticingly of cinnamon and a big piece of nougat he and Jamie had fun pounding into bite-size pieces; Blue Wing's buffalo hump roast and turnips joined roasted chestnuts and Kate's treat—Christmas omelets in the tradition of her family. Gabe, asking Kate's permission first, produced a bottle of brandy for him and Sam and even poured a bit of it into the omelet pan.

"I know you don't 'low no drinking, Kate," Gabe said solemnly, then winked at her. " 'Cept for holidays, I take it. Actually I have a quick nip myself every day—just for medicinal purposes—and so's I might give a toast to my hero, Andrew Jackson, Old Hick'ry, now our esteemed

President! To the gen'ral!" he cried, and with a flourish tipped the bottle smartly to his lips, then handed it to Sam, who gladly followed his lead.

"It's not I don't approve of a little bit of social drinking, Gabriel, but I cannot abide a man who cannot hold his liquor and then turns mean-spirited. My father did that, I'm afraid, and made others suffer for his weakness."

Gabe nodded. "All of us got things dear to our heart we 'low or don't 'low," he said. "Like I'll bet there's Mandans don't like buffalo penned up by whites, right, Blue Wing?" Warm and sated with food, she only smiled at him across the table, so he plunged on.

"And Kate don't like no undisciplined drinking 'cause of her father, and I can't abide folks who fight, no, sir. That's one reason this is my favorite day of the year with peace on earth and all that."

"Why y'all drinking to Jackson, who was a soldier above all else, then, Gabe?" Sam asked.

"That's a clever question, Sam, very clever. It's 'cause of my parents or, that is, the folks what took me in. See, when my real folks died of cholera in Cincinnati, my two older brothers didn't want me hanging 'round, no matter what they'd promised Ma 'bout taking care of me. You know, couldn't have a funny-eyed six-year-old to watch out for when you took to the river for your livelihood. Jeremy and Dan, their names was—well ... I guess they meant to leave me with someone, but I got lost on the docks in New Orleans—like you say it, N'Awlins, Sam."

Everyone sat entranced as Gabe told the tale of how a drover named Jake Taylor had taken him home to his childless wife, Mary. "Mary—real nice name for a mother on Christmas, ain't it?" Gabe went on. "That rough-and-tumble drover Jake wasn't what he seemed, no, sir. On the wharf he was a gimcracker, though he and Mary were Quakers, see, gentle folk who didn't believe in fighting nor no kind of violence. Mary Taylor, the most wonderful second mother a man could ever have, God rest her soul. So"—he sniffed hard once and went on— "when she upped and died, Jake and me set out north to

St. Louis right up the muddy Mississippi. I was twelve then, in eighteen and eleven, it was."

As he went on, he drew a faded, folded letter from the inner pocket of his coat and just fingered it. "But the very next year, Daddy Jake was real tormented 'bout being true to Mary's Quakerism or being true to the country he loved. That's when the second war for independence 'gainst England commenced, see, in eighteen and twelve. And after much wrestling with his soul—that's the only good kind of fighting, boy," he said to Jamie, "you remember that!—Jake decided there was some things worth fighting for even for a lapsed Quaker. So he 'listed in the war. That man was father, brother, friend to me."

"Did he come back from the war, Gabriel?" Kate asked quietly when he just sat silent a moment, holding the creased piece of paper.

"No, only this did," he said, and put the letter back in his pocket. "He wrote me how he was glad he went into the Army under General Andrew Jackson, who took real good care of his men. Jake was proud he got to fight to defend his home city of New Orleans on January 18, 1815; that's the exact date he wrote me. He died there soon after, see, of battle wounds. Mary prob'ly would have been disappointed in him. Daddy Jake, I know he promised Mary, just like I did, the day she died that he wouldn't ever do nothing violent, but he done it and made peace with himself, and that's the best kind. But me, unlike my brothers and Daddy Jake, I'm gonna keep the promise I made to a good woman on her deathbed!"

He patted his pocket as if to be sure the letter was still there. "So now I try my best, big as I am—and mean-spirited too sometimes, like you just mentioned, Kate—not to fight and to stop others from it. That's really why I would hesitate to be at your side if you decided to go upriver, not 'cause I'd rather be running a keelboat. No, it's my dream too to take a steamer upriver. But the wide Missouri can be real dangerous even for the likes of me, and if something happened to you, I'd not be able to pick up a gun nor fight for you, and I'd never forgive myself."

"But there are some men, Gabriel, a woman would like to have at her side no matter what!" she said.

The big bear of a man had almost looked as if he were about to cry through his whole story, and now tears shimmered in his eyes. "Saying that's the best Christmas gift you could of given me," he choked out, and looked down at his plate.

"Better than this candy?" Jamie asked.

"Almost," Gabe whispered, "almost."

It was almost a perfect day for Kate. She felt she almost had a family. It was more than she had hoped or dreamed or prayed for in the long nights she had worried and feared since Clive died.

"Then let's have one more toast," she said, lifting her piece of nougat. "To the spring and summer success of the *Red Dawn!*"

Kate almost gave up on the return of the steamboat. She should have known, she fretted silently, that her last hope would fall through after the way everything had gone last autumn. How she had prayed the new year would change her and Jamie's fortunes! And the more she asked Blue Wing about her people, the more dedicated she became to picking up the mantle of her fallen husband. His purpose had been noble, however deceitful he had been in other things, she told herself. By taking trading goods upriver in the *Red Dawn,* she would build on that and have a proud legacy—as well as a firm financial future—to bequeath their son.

She hated to think of letting her friends down too if the boat never returned. Sam had offered free warehouse space for the furs she brought back and told her she could have the remnants of some trade goods—fishhooks, knives, bolts of flannel and calico, bridle parts, axes, buckets, bracelets, glass pendants, and earbobs—he had left from Clive's last haul. The other half he would have to sell to make ends meet until he took on other clients. But that cache of items would be his investment in the future of her new venture.

And dear Gabe had insisted on giving her "a good piece of what I been saving for my own keelboat someday, even if I can't be going with you as your boat's captain or pilot." But she could sell lots of passages to *engagés* and travelers. Then she could see her way clear to hire a good crew, fill the hold, and be able, as Gabe put it, "to buy wood to feed that big belly of a steamboat, let alone feed those folks going upriver with you." But none of these good things could happen if something horrible had happened to the boat down south.

In the first week of April, other steamers, big and small, new and old, stern- and side-wheeler chugged back to St. Louis from southern waters. None of the captains she questioned had seen her boat, but one of them said, "Don't mean a thing, as most of 'em works the back bayous and private levees bringin' in plantation cotton."

Kate was excited when the *Sally Kate,* once Clive's newest vessel, steamed in the second week of April. How she wished that had been the boat he had not encumbered in the muddy morass of debts. Its captain had heard Clive had died and the boat had changed hands. He offered her condolences but no word of the *Red Dawn.* Later Kate was saddened to see the boat repainted and renamed *Platte Warrior.* And she was most annoyed to hear it was now owned by Chouteau and Company!

"Sometimes I think that slippery eel owns the whole blasted country," Gabe muttered, "least east to the Appalachians."

"He didn't own Clive, and he'll never own me or my boat, Gabriel, you'll see!"

But no one, she agonized, would ever see such a thing if they never so much as laid eyes on the *Red Dawn*: crossed eyes, Mandan eyes, sore eyes—for it would be a sight for those, she told herself as another sun sank behind Illinois Town across the river. Would her ship never come in?

"Kate! Kate, get on down to the wharf! She's back! She's back and acoming in!" Gabe's voice shouted up her steps on April 14 near dusk.

Her sewing basket scattered. She tripped over the rocker as she made for the door and clattered down the stairs. Jamie and Blue Wing were with Sam in the warehouse. Had they heard? She shouted for them as she ran by but did not stop. She had to see for herself!

She held up her skirts to run. She skidded around the corner of the alley, nearly losing her footing in the rutted mud. She tore down the cobbled wharf, trying not to turn her ankle, past people, around wagons, squinting into the setting sun across the river. Her hopes, her dreams, their future—where was it?

And then, above the buzz of men's voices and loading of other boats, above the snort of oxen and rattle of horse harnesses, she heard the sporadic chug, chug of a single steamer. She saw two tails of smoke in the orchid sky before she shoved her way to the edge of the river. She clasped her hands and bit her lower lip as she stood by Gabe, waiting, looking.

"Small, compared with most," he pronounced, pointing, "but ain't she pretty? And, goldarn it, if that little gimcracker ain't still afloat! I was starting to wonder but didn't want to worry you none by admitting it."

She nodded. She could not speak. Pretty? Even with its typical wedding-cake silhouette of three stacked decks topped by a boxy pilothouse, it looked forlorn and ragged compared with the giants already tied up. Its peeling white and yellow paint and touch of tattered gingerbread gave the vessel a faint air of faded glory. It seemed to heave and cough itself forward to the edge of the wharf, but it ran. It looked absolutely beautiful to her; she loved it instantly.

The rush of its paddles made a hissing, mesmerizing sound before its bell clanged out. Two tin lanterns lit aboard sent bright shafts of gold across the darkening water, and the frayed American flag flapped boldly at its stern. The boat bumped, then shuddered against the wharf at their feet. Four roosters leaped off and tied it securely. As the roar of engines died and the stench of smoke and engine oil blew away, Kate waved up to Captain Marcus in the glassed-in pilothouse. He nodded, but she wasn't sure he recognized her or if he knew she was the owner now.

Sam, Blue Wing, and Jamie joined them, cheering, then standing there, silent, staring. The roosters plunked the gangplank down on the dock. Shaking with excitement, Kate strode aboard her ship.

The next day Kate learned both the good and the bad of her boat. Its small size meant it would, as Captain Marcus put it, "practically walk over sandbars or run miles on suds if you tapped a keg of beer in the ornery river up yonder." However, its old shallow-draft hold would not take much cargo. It had had repairs recently but needed others. It had made a bit of money this winter, but what hadn't gone for a rebuilt boiler and patched chimney—"a chimney, ma'am, not a smokestack!" Kate learned—would barely be enough to pay the crew and keep them in wood when they could not cut their own.

Its paddles, covered by a big wooden cylinder above the waterline, dipped in but a few inches—great for shallow going—but it was a side-wheeler and the paddles, unprotected by the hull, broke a lot. The boat was insured until the end of April, but after that the renewal cost for the aged, ramshackle boat would be exorbitant. And Captain Marcus knew how to "nurse this old baby along through anything," but he was definitely not willing to take her up to Mandan country and would soon be a captain for Chouteau.

Gabe told Kate not to fret, as he had someone he thought could help her. She prayed so, because every other potential captain-pilot she asked on the waterfront either had a contract or would charge too much "on that risky crate," as one man put it, for her to afford.

At noon the day after the *Red Dawn*'s arrival, Blue Wing was washing windows in the pilothouse with Jamie "helping" her. Kate had just finished scrubbing out the four tiny private compartments on the boiler deck. She was sweeping around the Franklin stove in the small adjoining common room when she saw Gabe come slowly up the gangplank with an old man. She dried her hands on her apron and met them down on the open-sided main deck. She thought the white-haired gentleman with Gabe looked familiar, but she could not place him.

"Kate Craig, like you to meet Captain Zeke Pickens,

one of the best and longest-running pilots on the Missouri, lately retired."

"I'm pleased to meet you, sir," she said, and shook his hand. It was cold and trembling. But if Gabe thought this man could give a sound assessment of the equipment or knew someone she could hire for a pilot or captain, she would be very grateful and told him so.

"How many years on the river, sir?" she asked.

"Since eighteen and nineteen, the year steam first come to these parts," he told her proudly. "Hear this vessel's only six years old, but on these rivers that's enough for her to show her age." His voice seemed strong and steady at least, but Kate saw he was only too glad to lean both hands on the rail as he looked around. "I captained many a boat to St. Charles, Jefferson City, Independence, Fort Leavenworth, even Fort Pierre till the big blow."

"A big storm?" she asked before Gabe's warning shake of a head behind her.

"The big explosion when my ship's boiler blew up and almost kilt me. Did kill thirty-four," he said, and shook his head. "Been a bit of an outcast, I have, to some on the river since then, but my friend Gabe here picked me out of the bushes that fateful day and saved many another soul when he come along on his keelboat."

Kate's eyes met Gabe's double stare. "I can believe Gabriel would do a fine, heroic thing like that," she said. "I've been trying to get him to pilot this boat upriver for me, but he has his reasons for refusing. And I realize now, Captain, where I have seen you before. Do you remember a day last December when you were walking in the snow by Chouteau's Pond and I asked if you'd seen a Mandan woman? You said you lived with your daughter near the north cemetery, I believe."

"Why, sure, I remember you!" Captain Pickens said with a flash of partly missing teeth. "I've lived with my girl a bit too long, and Gabe's convinced me I ought to take another trip up the wide Missouri. And if I don't have to steer but could just be his eyes—"

"My brains *and* eyes, Captain," Gabe put in. "And I'd just be first mate, but steering most of the way, learning from you."

"Why, yes. There's a stretch I haven't been on from Fort Pierre to Fort Clark, but I can read that river and teach you to, Gabe. Then, you see, Mrs. Craig, under those conditions, I'd take just one more trip upriver, for I miss those old days much as I miss my dear, departed wife."

Kate's stare slammed into Gabe's. This was the answer to her prayers, but could she risk it? To have for a captain an old man whose hands trembled, whose ship had blown up and killed dozens? A cross-eyed, peace-loving keel-boater as first mate? A past-its-prime, ramshackle unpainted soft pine soon-to-be uninsured boat? And a green-as-grass owner who had determination but no knowledge of what she was getting into and was evidently prepared to commit an outrageous act of being the managing owner of a steamboat, let alone the first white woman up the river? "You mean," Captain Marcus had shouted at her, "you're going farther up on her than just overnight to St. Charles? *All* the *ladies* get off at St. Charles and take a carriage back!"

But old Zeke Pickens was hardy and sharp-witted; she had seen that for herself. He had years of experience with steamers on the river. Besides, the fact he was an outcast in this town put her on his side. She trusted Gabe, and that meant everything in a world run by Chouteau and his ilk. And she believed with all her heart the *Red Dawn* could make it to Mandan country and back to give her and Jamie a new beginning. But then she had believed with all her heart in Clive once too, and that had blown to bits like—like Captain Pickens's steamer.

"If you sign on, Captain Pickens, at the rate we're offering, I can promise you a bonus at the end when we safely tie up here again," she said. "And now I'd like you to meet the rest of the *Red Dawn* family, and then we can get down to really hiring the crew. We are going to be the last boat upriver as is if we don't hurry."

"Mrs. Craig, you know that could give one a little worry. I mean, if we go aground or some unforeseen mishap occurs, there will be no one coming up behind to help. Not when we get up on that rainwater stream above Fort Pierre, for most boats don't go that high up anyway."

"Then we must leave as soon as we can load and hire folks on. Gabe, you said we could put up posters advertising a departure date as soon as we knew. What do the *Red Dawn*'s captain and first mate think about setting out next Monday? Let's see, that would be April eighteenth, a momentous day."

"Nothing could be finer!" Captain Pickens said, and Gabe nodded his agreement.

That blasted Cadet Chouteau had once told Kate she would be the laughingstock of St. Louis, and she guessed she was—of the riverfront now as well as uptown. But determined she was doing the right thing, she ignored people who lollygagged on the wharf, laughing, calling out jokes or insults, watching the frenzied preparations of a woman, a cross-eyed keelboater, an Indian woman, a four-year-old boy, and old "Fireworks Pickens."

They hired on a crew: a second mate, an Irishman named Fynn Winston, to oversee the eighteen roosters; Bill Blake, a blacksmith, a freedman, who had been a slave in Kentucky; Pete Marburn, a carpenter, who also would hunt meat; and a cook named William Nill, who went by the name Willy Nilly, which Jamie kept repeating until it drove Kate to distraction.

They stowed their trade goods in the hold and took on more with each bit of money that came their way. When Kate and Jamie were the only ones aboard early Sunday morning, a man named Jacques Marbois visited to ask if they would take twenty barrels of medicinal wines to Fort Clark. He offered her a good price for transport. He was a rather rough-looking man with a long scar, whom she told, quite frankly, that if his goods were lost, they were not insured.

"I'll chance it," he told her, fingering his black beard. "These goods came in late, and most of the other boats is gone. Need this medicine delivered to Mr. Kellen Blackwell, the new Mandan Indian agent at the fort—for dosing both the whites and maybe Indians too."

"Then the *Red Dawn* will do its best to fulfill your trust, Mr. Marbois. I'm pleased to be able to help our government agents and promote better care for the Indians."

But when she told Gabe what was newly nestled in the hold, he got angry with her for the first time. "Don't you know the soldiers at Fort Leavenworth will search the hold and prob'bly take that stuff?" he demanded. "There's new laws on the books about liquor going into Free Indian Territory! And I thought you were against drinking."

"I *am* against drinking, and no, I didn't know they'd take it. Mr. Marbois must be aware of that law, and he evidently thinks it will go through. It's medicinal, Gabriel, just like your daily drink!"

"Sorry, I exploded, Kate," he said, shaking his head. "Course, you don't know how some folks try to use liquor against the tribes, though the Mandans seem too smart for that. Guess it won't do no harm to try to get the stuff past Leavenworth and hope it's just for Fort Clark and none of the tribes who like firewater. Who knows, maybe that's why this Marbois fellow put the stuff in our hold, thinking the Leavenworth boys won't fuss much with a little boat."

"And with a stupid, little lady owner, you mean. I may have a lot to learn, Gabriel, but I *am* learning."

She was surprised that the roosters, most of whom were rowdy runaway farmboys or unruly Irishmen, had foul mouths and believed they could "take a leak" over the side into the river when there was a toilet on the stern, but Gabe and thick-fisted Fynn declared they'd talk to them about that. Kate lectured herself to stay calm, even accepting. She was entering a man's world and must learn to adapt, at least to some things.

Kate took the largest cabin for herself, Jamie, and Blue Wing. That compartment had straw-filled ticks on four narrow bunks attached to the wall and room for little else, though she wedged her rocking chair in. She insisted Gabe and Zeke share another compartment with two bunks since there were no officers' quarters. That left the two smallest cabins with one bunk to fill at a five-dollar fee each.

Deck passage space went to far fewer trappers than they had hoped, but it was late. Some would-be travelers, when they heard Fireworks Pickens was to captain the voyage, claimed he was a curse and booked themselves aboard the cruder keelboats. Still, Kate refused to take on several *engagés* who admitted they were employed by Chouteau's company and had missed his other boats upriver.

"As Blue Wing says, that man will not pull a blanket over our eyes again," Kate told Gabe. "I don't trust those Chouteau employees not to—to try to sabotage us somehow. We need the extra two dollars each deck passage brings, but I'll swim and shove this boat upriver before I'll help Chouteau earn one more penny off the poor people of this world!"

And then, the day before they left, good fortune came calling in the guise of General Clark. They welcomed him aboard and gave him a quick tour of the boat.

"I had to see it myself," he told them. "Young lady, *you* are the talk of the town."

"I suppose so, but necessity rules, sir," Kate admitted. "Besides, it's my opportunity to see Blue Wing gets home safely and to trade fairly with the Mandans. I'm happy to see you have returned hale and hearty from your visit east."

He later spent time speaking to Blue Wing in private, then told Kate he was pleased her English had improved and Kate had given her such a "fine home" this winter. Touched, Kate just nodded.

"I'm always looking for excellent Indian representatives to send to Washington as goodwill ambassadors, you see," he confided to Kate when they were alone in the common room again.

"You might send Blue Wing to Washington?"

"Someday, with others of her tribe, of course. Besides, it does the native red man good to see the power and might—the big medicine, as it were—of the President and our capital city. But to business, Mrs. Craig. I would like to book your last two vacant passenger compartments, if I may."

"For you, General?" she asked as Gabe and Captain Zeke came back in from duties.

"Alas, no. Perhaps if I were forty years younger and beginning my western journey all over again . . ." he said with a distant look in his pale blue eyes. "But that brings me to the two men of whom I speak. One is a recent acquaintance of mine, Stirling Mount, a young man highly recommended from the East, who will become my new bookkeeper next autumn. I want him to see the tribes first and how things are, so his new position is not all just columns of numbers to him. By the way, I will be sending a man around with five barrels of brandy for him to preserve his specimens. He's an amateur scientist of sorts, so he will be bringing back preserved samples of fauna and sketches of flora, et cetera."

"Is he an artist, General?"

"Not really, my dear. Just a bright, exuberant, hardworking young man a bit wet behind the ears who needs to see the real West before he settles into the offices of the superintendent. And the other man is my newly appointed subagent to the Mandans, actually the son of a friend of mine from the old expedition west with Meriwether Lewis and all . . ."

Blue Wing had come in and, as General Clark's words seemed to trail off, she put in, "That good you give The People new head and subagents, Red-Haired Father. Not that Sanford anymore."

"I recalled and replaced John Sanford for not spending enough time at his post, Blue Wing," General Clark said with a shake of his head. "He has a wife and life here he dearly loves, and summer visits seemed to be all he could spare." Again, his blue eyes glazed over as his thoughts seemed to drift. "Then, if these arrangements are suitable, Mrs. Craig, I shall leave you the ten dollars your first mate mentioned for the two cabins and bid you the best. You're making history here in your own way, just as Meriwether Lewis and I did three decades ago."

He shook hands with them all, then kissed Blue Wing and Kate's cheeks. "Godspeed," he said, his voice a mere whisper. When Gabe walked him out to his carriage, Blue

Wing followed after, still chattering away to him, half in Mandan.

"Ten dollars more, Captain Zeke!" Kate cried triumphantly as she picked up the heavy silver coins. "It will get us more trade goods, and we'll save some for wood!"

"Two very important passengers!" Captain Zeke said with a shake of his head that worried Kate. "What did he say the new subagent's name was?"

"He didn't, but it doesn't matter. In taking him to Fort Clark and Mitutanka, we're evidently helping Blue Wing's people even more than our fair trading will do. She told me that last agent really cheated them."

"If Chouteau's fleet won't have beat us to the trading there," she heard Captain Zeke mutter as he went slowly back out and up to his lofty realm of the pilothouse again.

As the roosters were preparing to loose the mooring lines the morning of departure, Kate was sick with worry they would have to hold up for General Clark's passengers, who had not yet appeared. She was standing on the hurricane deck just under the pilothouse with Blue Wing and Jamie, watching the bustle of departure. Sam had bidden them all farewell. He stood now on the edge of the wharf, waving already, standing next to Captain Zeke's daughter and her two sons, who had pleased the old man immensely by coming down to see him off. Kate's great venture—her *Red Dawn* dream—was about to come true.

When the first visitor arrived and hallooed up at her, she went down to the main deck to greet him, stepping over several roosters and independent trappers sleeping off their last noisy night of freedom and fun. The visitor came up the gangplank carrying a stack of books, a rifle, and a bulging portmanteau.

"The name is Stirling Mount, ma'am. I am pleased to make your acquaintance, and if there is anything I can do to help on board, I would be honored," he said, dropping his portmanteau and extending a firm, warm hand. He was tall, blond, and, she saw as he swept off his top hat, very good-looking.

"I was afraid you wouldn't make it, Mr. Mount. Where's your friend?"

"The new subagent? I have not made his acquaintance. I spent last night at the Union Hotel and hear he has an elderly aunt in town with whom he stays."

"Please, bring your things, and let me show you to your cabin, small as it is. I understand you will be sketching plants along the way, so perhaps I can help you too, as I love to draw and have painted flowers for years."

The rising sun lit his blue-gray eyes and wide smile. She couldn't quite guess his age: perhaps twenty-four or five. He parted his hair in the middle and combed it smoothly down just over his ears, a style that looked affected on most men but only served to highlight his regular features. He spoke with a very clipped eastern accent and seemed polite and friendly as they chatted on the way to the common room.

And then, just before the roosters hauled the gangplank up behind him, the other stranger boarded. Kate excused herself from Mr. Mount and went back down to greet the new arrival. And came face-to-face with Randal MacLeod.

"Oh!" she said. "What is it? Did something happen to General Clark's new subagent to the Mandans?"

"At your service," he said, and took off his squirrelskin hat. His face looked older than she remembered, his skin stretched tauter over his angular cheekbones but not so dark after the long winter. His hair was trimmed, and he was clean-shaven. He studied her as intensely as she did him. He dropped his goods, bundled inside a buffalo hide, to the deck, put his rifle butt between his spread feet, but rested both big hands on the barrel.

"You?" she said. "I thought you were sent to Washington."

"It was not, thank God, a life sentence. And I never expected you to do this," he added with a narrow glance that seemed to encompass the small ship.

"I don't care what you think."

"That's obvious. But you ended up caring for Blue Wing, didn't you? Besides, I didn't say I disapproved, as long as this thing gets me where I'm going. I'm the first half-breed Clark has dared appoint an agent, and everyone's talking about me too. And I'm proud to say, I have

Chouteau nearly as riled as you do. He doesn't want a Mandan agent who really cares about the tribe any more than he wants you taking an independent steamer up-river."

He paused, seeming to study her intently for a moment, then plunged on: "Whatever Chouteau thinks of us, at least we'll make interesting company for twelve hundred miles. And I applaud your motherly instincts, but you shouldn't have brought your boy on board or go yourself up into Sioux and rough-water country. You have no idea what you're getting into."

"Frankly, Mr. MacLeod, how I rear my son or live my life is none of your concern, nor is the operation of my steamboat. You may get off right now if you don't approve."

As ever, they ended up just glaring at each other. She could think of nothing else to say. His expression had gone as still and hard as carved oak. The deck began to vibrate as the engines leaped to life. At first she thought it was her own churning fury at seeing MacLeod again. Why, on the most important day of her new beginning, had this—this bugaboo dared barge back into her life? He made her feel not as much in charge of things as she wanted and needed to be.

She turned to grip the rail as the bell clanged, clanged overhead. Her stomach seemed to drop away as the boat lurched once. Although their first stop would only be the Illinois bank across the river to take on a load of wood, she suddenly felt she was sailing to the farthest reaches of the earth. Jamie and Blue Wing—she wanted to be with them at this moment, not standing here with this man staring at her.

As she hurried up the steps to the hurricane deck, she heard Gabe's deep voice singing: "Adieu to St. Louis, I bid you adieu, likewise to the Frenchies and merskeeters too!" The crated chickens on the main deck started to protest. A tenor voice among the trappers replaced Gabe's tune with the more mournful "Shenandoah": ". . . away, I'm goin' away, 'cross the wide Missouri . . ."

Her emotions a jumble of regrets and possibilities, anger and awe, Kate hefted her excited, squirming son into her arms and stood next to Blue Wing at the rail. They waved and called farewell to Sam, even to the small crowd on the wharf. As morning sun etched the hills of St. Louis, the *Red Dawn* jerked away from the wharf and took the current of the muddy Mississippi.

PART TWO

The Wide Missouri

Once Old Woman in the Moon watched Big River twisting past homes of The People, many buffalo, and beaver. Even then the Old One could seldom see her face in the mirror of wild water. But now she cursed the thunder canoes of the whites churning the river, pushing The People and animals away.

Chapter 7

Randal MacLeod sat cross-legged on the prow of the *Red Dawn* as it churned through the current. His thoughts churned as fast, for he was both leaving home and going home. A new beginning beckoned, and he was ready. He reveled in the wind in his face and the pushing stride of the vessel as it swung westward into the mouth of the Missouri.

Both big rivers were the same width at their juncture, pouring their many mingled waters south toward the sea. He liked the power of the place, the contesting currents, for now his life had come to this. Half-breed or not, he had been named subagent to the Mandans and hoped someday to become head agent. He had a chance to help his mother's people—*his* people—and he must not fail.

He bit into an apple, what was left of a huge breakfast which Aunt Alice had packed for him when he left the guesthouse she oversaw this morning. He shook his head to cast off memories of sad partings with others in his life as his eyes took in the newly budded trees speckled by blossoms of red bud and white plum. That sight calmed him, but soon again the river made his thoughts race. He heaved the apple core far out into the coffee-colored river and saw it ripped away.

Unfortunately, to help the Mandans, he would have to take orders from and please a man he did not respect or trust, Kellen Blackwell, the new Mandan head agent. Blackwell followed Cadet Chouteau's bidding, often at the tribe's expense. And Blackwell was tight with Chouteau's fur factor at the fort, Jacques Marbois, who had ties to the Sioux, deadly enemies of the Mandans. But Rand had promised Clark he would keep peace with

Blackwell and Marbois, and somehow, point of honor, he must be true to that vow.

Over the years Rand had learned that Chouteau was more deceitful than a thieving wolverine. The wily bastard always changed to fit his circumstances. When he saw that John Jacob Astor was criticized for ruthlessly crushing "independent opposition" in the fur trade, Chouteau had decided to appear to do the opposite when he bought the Western Division from Astor.

Chouteau had covertly funded Captain Craig's "independent" trading company—but with Craig's knowledge. Chouteau had Craig underbid him for furs, then pointed him out to all as an example of free competition. When Craig died, Chouteau pulled back his funding and the boats he'd "loaned" Craig, leaving only this sorry little steamer.

Would Chouteau now prop up another independent company built on sand? As far as Rand knew, the Frenchy wolverine could even be financing the *Red Dawn* and Kate Craig's sudden emergence from financial ruin. Rand was going to see if he could tie any cargo aboard to Chouteau or his lackeys, but even getting away with an inventory of the hold presented problems in this small world he now shared with nearly fifty inhabitants. A candle down there at night could be dangerous if there was gunpowder, but during the day someone might see him and tell Mrs. Craig. He needed no more confrontations with her until it was absolutely necessary.

Already, when he first came aboard, he'd tried to bait her about Chouteau. But he'd seen nothing amiss in her expression when he praised her for riling the man. With what he had heard about her dire circumstances last winter, perhaps she was not on Chouteau's string. When the time was right, Rand would tell her the truth about her husband to assess if she had known of it. Meanwhile, he'd keep a close watch on her. Now *that,* he admitted to himself with a grin, despite her tart tongue, would be a pleasure.

Rand leaned back against the jack staff flagpole and stretched his long legs so his booted feet extended over the prow. Above him in the fresh western breeze flapped the obviously new pennant which identified Kate Craig's old ship in this frontier world where many could not read the name on the pilothouse. And you might know, on both sides of the piece of stout cloth she had *painted* a rising yellow sun with red rays—no domestic sewing here. The bright crimson-gold banner exemplified for him the transformation of the petite, pretty city lady into a stubborn, bold woman on the river.

"Hey there, mister, you looking for Indians?" jolted him from his thoughts. He turned, annoyed his usual sharp hearing had not warned him someone had sidled up behind him. It was the towheaded Craig boy.

"Not many Indians for a while, son."

"I gotta see some before Bellevue, I hope. We're not there yet, are we? I'm going to visit my grandmama there, and Mama will come back for me soon."

At least Kate Craig had more sense than he'd given her credit for, Rand thought. So she had a mother at Bellevue and was going upriver to see her? A sharp, hurtful memory thrust at him, but he forced it away. He supposed he should apologize to her for lecturing her about her son, but something about her always vexed him. As if his thoughts had drawn her, here she came, blue skirt swishing and tendrils of loose honey-hued hair blowing in her hurry to pull the boy back from so much as speaking to him.

"Jamie, please don't bother the man—or get so near the edge. It isn't that I mind you talking to him, Mr. MacLeod, but he needs to learn safety on the ship and not wander off."

Rand stood, one hand on the jack staff. "He wasn't bothering me a bit. But that's real sensible, ma'am. First chance you get you should teach him to swim—yourself included, if you don't know how. On the river things do happen."

Their eyes met and held before she looked back down at Jamie. "I know they do. Now if you'll excuse us."

"And, Mrs. Craig, you'll find white folks upriver call me Rand Cloud. My—my mother's name was Rain Cloud. So I kind of have her name and my father's, since MacLeod is said like 'mac-cloud.' "

"I see. But Blue Wing calls you by another name."

"The Mandans call me Runs Quickly or Dark Water."

"It always sounds as if you are two people. Well, I didn't mean that like it sounded—half and half—you know."

"I know," he said, trying desperately not to have this meeting, like their others, end poorly. He squinted into the afternoon sun to study her face as he said, "Besides, most of us have two sides, things we're trying to hide."

"Obviously, I have learned that the hard way, Mr. . . . Cloud. Come along now, Jamie," she said, and pulled the boy away.

Rand sighed, realizing regretfully she thought he was criticizing her husband or even her when he was only fishing for information about her ties to Chouteau. It seemed there was no way they could speak without bad, unintended feelings between them. Damn, but he was as much of a bumbler at this underhanded stuff as he had always been about grasping what women were thinking and feeling. Best to go right at things. When the time was right, he'd just confront her about her husband's working for Chouteau.

He stared again upriver at a fenced-in farm floating by on a wavy green meadow. Kate Craig seemed in her element here on her ship in the stretch of river still cradled by civilization. But how would it be for her when forests deepened and fields became endless prairie, and low river rocks climbed to cliffs and buttes, and friendly, waving white people turned to Hidatsas, Rees, and deadly Sioux? He shook his head and went to find Blue Wing to practice his rusty Mandan.

On the second morning out, Kate stood in the back of the pilothouse and, from Gabe and Zeke, learned to "read the river." The day before she had overseen on-board procedures, established a schedule for meals, gotten to know Stirling Mount a bit better, and given Jamie a reading lesson. Today she was getting one.

"See, Kate, the current's only 'bout five miles per hour here on the lower Missouri," Gabe said. "And luck'ly we got us plenty of river under the hull in this April rise. But between this and the later one in June, when the Rockies dump their snowmelt in the river, we're gonna see some pretty shallow, shoal-filled water."

"At least everything's calm so far," she observed, peering around their shoulders at the bucolic scenes ahead.

She noted that the picturesque islands had a pattern to them. The sandy point was thick with timber of young willows, then poplars, trembling their young lime green leaves in the breeze, then hard timber, and finally high rushes. Pretty houses peered down from eminences in this section well populated by people, if not by game. For several weeks they must eat the river catfish, smoked meat, and chickens, until fresh meat could be found upriver.

She had thought St. Charles a charming old French settlement on the east shore. One properly said it was on the left side of the river, because right and left were always designated as if one were looking downstream, not up. Although the *Red Dawn* was late setting out, this part of the river had traffic too: other steamers, ferries, an occasional dugout canoe, and flat-bottomed mackinaws, which only hauled loads downstream and then were dismantled for their wood. Keelboats, with which Gabe often exchanged quick, shouted information, had sprouted sails to fight the current or were "roped upriver" by their crews clambering along the muddy banks. If Kate had not been so busy, she would have sketched several scenes.

"Enjoy the peace and quiet while you can," Captain Zeke told her from his tall three-legged stool next to Gabe at the wheel. Zeke had an old ship's log on his lap, and she saw he often diagrammed and labeled new river landmarks in it.

"Soon enough," he told her, "we'll see rock reefs and rapids, maybe worse, when we're not scraping off sandbars. Now just another mile here, there's a whirlpool called Ramrod Eddy needs a good watch and steady hand, eh, First Mate Gabe?"

"I know that one. Aye, aye, Captain!"

Kate learned that rivermen had named each twist and landmark of the river. They passed Tavern Rock with its shady cavern marking danger on both banks where swirls and ripples concealed sandbars, rocks, even snagged trees. The wind could help by uncovering submerged dangers, but rain could dapple the water to hide things. Near the village of Pickney, as they passed the Isle of Beef with its rocky ravines and tangled foliage, Captain Zeke explained to both her and Gabe—for Gabe had to accustom himself to this lofty position above the river—that surface glare was deadly when the sun sank lower than forty-five degrees above the horizon.

Kate discovered that sandbars drifted. But there were "good" bars too, where racks of driftwood collected which could be gathered for fuel. Wood was power on the river, for the steamer's hungry fireboxes burned ten cords a day. It was the duty of the ship's master, be he captain or pilot, to judge where to find wood ahead either cut or live and never to run out on a barren stretch.

"Thank heaven for landmarks on shore," Kate observed.

"Even the banks themselves can change where landmarks wash away," Captain Zeke said. "This river's fickle as a woman!"

"I'd say as untrustworthy as a man," she put in.

"Maybe for some," Captain Zeke admitted, "not me. Keep her steady as she goes while I take a moment to myself," he told Gabe, and went slowly down the ladder.

"Is he miffed I sassed him, Gabriel?"

"I think you just touched a tender spot without meaning to. See, when he says his wife departed, he don't mean she's dead. She lit out when Zeke got the bad name in the boat tragedy. She's gone all right, but still of this earth."

"Oh. Sad, she didn't stick by him when tragedy struck. At least his daughter did."

"Not 'xactly. She just had no choice but to take him in when he fell from top of the heap to bottom of the barrel."

Kate shook her head. "Tragedy does strange things to families. You and I both know that, Gabriel. But I'm coming to see that learning to read this shifty dark river water is probably easier than learning to read people."

* * *

Later that day Kate swept the living quarters and put her exhausted son down for a nap. He had hardly slept while they cruised all last night, as they would do the first few days when the river was well marked and safe at night. Then she went out on deck to stand, finally alone, at the rail, watching the lush scenery and thinking.

She had not been really able to "read" Clive during their marriage. She and Mama had never been able to read when her father would start drinking and explode. It was still often hard to tell what Blue Wing was thinking because her past was so different. Sometimes, Kate feared, she hardly knew herself, setting out boldly into the unknown of the frontier when she had once been such a hothouse flower. How far away Winterhaven—even her sweet Sally—seemed out here.

And she wondered what "Rand Cloud" was really thinking. He had said one of his tribal names was Dark Water, and it suited him, like this seething river water one could not see into. It was worse than the muddy Mississippi. Why, even the wash and drinking water was murky, and they kept prickly pears in the barrels to settle out the silt.

Kate had overheard Fynn Winston say the water wasn't bad to drink—with a quick chaser of whiskey. And at the end of each twelve hours or so of steaming, the fires had to be extinguished, and the boilers opened and drained. Several poor roosters, designated firemen for the day, went inside to shovel out the steaming mud sucked in with the water.

On the other hand, Blue Wing loved Big River because at night its load of silt reflected Old Woman in the Moon's face better than did the Mississippi—even though it was not yet a quarter moon this time of the month. Like Blue Wing's loving the smell of skunk and hating the fragrance of French toilette water, Kate thought, a dirty river was all in the eye of the beholder.

Stirling Mount watched Kate standing at the rail, apparently lost in thought. In profile, her brow puckered and her lips pursed as if something worried her. She looked so fetching, all windblown and disheveled from some task, that he stood stock-still and just took her in at first. When he had been assigned to this ship, he had never dared hope that the female owner of the new trading company and its ramshackle boat would be so lovely and so delicate-looking. Surely, any man would find it easy to desire and court such a woman, who no doubt needed a strong man in her life to be helpmeet, lover, and father to her son.

"I hope I am not bothering you," he said, not to startle her, before he walked closer. He swept off his top hat and held it in one hand, while he rested the other on the rail beside hers.

"Oh, not at all. Consider the ship at your disposal."

"You are very kind. And forgive me for my forwardness, but you are looking very lovely today all windblown out here."

She turned to him with tears in her eyes, then looked out over the river again. Had his merest compliment so moved her? he wondered. He reveled in a sense of surging power, in the awareness he was an attractive man. Sometimes he did not care about that weapon he possessed with the ladies, but now it whetted his sense of masculinity. He shifted one step over, sliding his hand closer to hers on the rail.

"Thank you for the nice compliment, Mr. Mount. It's been awhile since anyone has said anything like that."

"More fool they. Perhaps they have all seen you only as a very strong woman—to do all this," he said, annoyed that he was floundering for words. What an amazing effect this woman had on him. She jangled his poise and made his pulse pound. When he was hoping to assert an influence over her, she lured him without apparently trying.

It sobered him how much he wanted to touch her, protect her, possess her. He'd had no notion getting to know her would have this immediate, devastating effect on his emotions—on his body too, he thought, as he pressed his hips into the railing as if to contain his desire. He had always prided himself in keeping his head. Yet it seemed this journey and new assignment were going to be much more enjoyable and exciting than he had been led to believe.

"But"—he tried again when she said nothing more—"you also seem as if you could use a friend out here. Please, Mrs. Craig—"

"Kate."

"Yes, thank you. Kate. And you will call me Stirling. What I am trying to say is that if you need any assistance out here with anything—any task, the crew, the other passenger ..."

"I am sure Mr. MacLeod will be no problem."

"Of course not, but you never quite know what the brooding, silent type is thinking."

"I must admit that is true. And I'm pleased to have a new friend in you, someone to talk to. Later we could draw together—I mean, with our charcoal pencils, sketch," she said, and blushed at her unintended pun.

"I would love for us to draw together, Kate," he said, and could not help just staring into her clear blue eyes before she looked away. He moved his hand even closer on the rail, and together they watched the river run.

The next morning Rand stretched his big frame at the rail of the open-sided main deck where deck passengers slept. Some of them were still wrapped in blankets or buffalo robes and would not come to life until the steamer did. It had run all night, but they had stopped to douse the fires and shovel out the boilers. He saw a few men on this deck were already gobbling bowls of their lye hominy, fat pork, and biscuits they carried or prepared themselves. He knew a few of these trappers and backwater traders and planned to know them all by the time they departed ship near their various posts and ports. They could be his additional eyes and ears and feet in both Mandan and Sioux country up north.

Rand had already eaten and was clean-shaven, though he had taken time this morning to begin to pluck his beard with shells the way the Mandans did. It beat any razor-strop close shave the whites could give. It was time to ease himself back into living among The People again, even if his quarters were to be in Fort Clark. But he knew his body, like his heart, would always be more Mandan than white when he lived near Mitutanka.

He jerked his head around when he thought he heard a woman's giggle, but he knew it would not be Kate Craig's. She had been all starchy business at breakfast, helping carry to the common room table for officers and cabin passengers the fried ham and eggs and redeye gravy on beaten biscuits from the cook's adjoining kitchen. She had poured Rand a second cup of coffee. Though she had not said more than "Good morning, Mr. Cloud," and given him a curt nod, he was touched to have her serve him. Now he craned his neck and did not see her or Blue Wing anywhere when he had definitely heard a feminine giggle.

Although he had been a bachelor for all his thirty-four years, he had enjoyed glimpses of domesticity among both the Mandans and the whites. From his sixteenth year on, when he had begun to make trips to the tribe after his father's death and his years with his aunt in St. Louis, he had lived with a series of Indian girls, all of whom had since wed. Relations were like that in the tribe: easy to bind and easy to break, and mutually understood as such.

He knew his adopted tribal "medicine father," Long Hatchet, was disappointed he had never married a Mandan, but he could not accept the tribe's lack of dedicated loyalty to a mate for life. At least that was what he told himself each time he considered commitment and decided against it. His father had loved his mother until—until he . . . lost her. And Aunt Alice, widowed at twenty en route to America, had never wed again, not even to have a child of her own, whom she had dearly wanted.

For Rand it just didn't work to get too close to women. They clung; they needed more; they were so damned concerned with feelings when they should just stick to ideas and actions. Besides, the pain of partings wasn't worth the risk of deep dependence.

Though he knew he could get a white woman if he chose to, she'd want a stable home even more than a Mandan would. In his wanderings he could never provide either. Still, he mused as another muted laugh tickled his interest again, he sometimes longed for womanly companionship in bed and out and a hearth and home of his own.

This time he realized the laugh had come from down the few steps into the shallow hold. He walked over just as the steamer began to vibrate and chugged out into the channel. With the noise he didn't hear the sound again but went down into the dimness.

He was a practical man without much fancy or fantasy in his life, but the laughter had lured him. The hair on the nape of his neck prickled. A shiver slid up his spine. He would like to find Kate Craig down here, hair loosed, smiling in the dim depths, just waiting for him, beckoning to him. . . .

"Did you come down to play hide-and-seek with me and Blue Wing?" The unmistakable boy's voice sliced through his reverie.

"Blue Wing!" Rand called out, then went on in Mandan not to alarm the boy. "Don't you know once this boat gets under way these barrels and boxes might slide around? And if the boy is playing hide-and-seek, he could be under something when it rolls!"

She came out looking shamefaced. "My mind was in the mud," she told him in Mandan. "We go up now or else trouble."

"Does she get angry with you too?" Rand asked.

"Who is you too?" she countered with a little smile. "Prairie Wind angry with you? I did see her very, very angry at a man only one time since I live with her. When she throw Chouteau away."

"What do you mean? What happened?"

She told him, dramatically recounting the night Chouteau came calling. With words, grand gestures, body and facial expressions, she even showed him the expression Chouteau had when "a whipped dog, he did run away with his tail between his legs."

As Blue Wing and the boy went upstairs ahead of him, Rand had to smile at how Blue Wing had unknowingly answered his question. There was no way Kate Craig could be in with Chouteau as her husband had been. If she and Chouteau were going to stage a falling-out, it would not have been merely for the benefit of a Mandan girl—would it?

Yet on a whim, now that he was down here and enough light seeped in to see, he walked the narrow passageways between stacked boxes and barrels, clear to the end of the farthest row. It hit him like a fist to his face as he squinted to read what was stamped on barrel after barrel after barrel stowed here: "MED. SPIRITS ONLY. MARBOIS TO K. BLACKWELL, FT. C."

The third night out, it rained, and they tied up instead of running in the dark. At Otter Island near the Gasconade River the next morning, the skies cleared, but they put in again to take on wood. Kate fretted at the frequent stops, but Captain Zeke told her to expect worse delays. She didn't mention to him she was worried that the ship was insured only for the rest of April well before the most difficult part of the river began.

At this stop Gabe announced a two-hour stay for them to stretch their legs ashore while the roosters hauled wood. It was a spot with sandbanks and hills and forests painted in a palette of greens. Cut white and yellow pine used in St. Louis for building timber was soon being carted onto the main deck and stacked by the firebox.

Though the rain had doused and drooped the foliage and left a mist, Kate went ashore with Blue Wing and Jamie only to discover solid land made her feel as if she were still moving. Blue Wing and Jamie went off with Willy Nilly to catch soft-shelled tortoises in the Gasconade for supper. Kate strolled slowly up and looked over Stirling's shoulder as he perched on a big rock to sketch the *Red Dawn*. Like several of his other efforts she had seen, this one was crude. She had thought the others to be just rough drawings made with the movement aboard ship, but now she wasn't sure.

"That's not exactly the flora and fauna you came to draw," she observed.

"Oh, Kate," he said, jumping to his feet. "You are as quiet as that Indian of yours."

"She's not mine, not a servant, Stirling. Just a friend—an adopted aunt to Jamie," she explained as they settled side by side on the boulder. They exchanged smiles as he closed his sketch pad.

"You are so good at drawing I am nervous doing it around you," he told her. "I admit this is not one of my strengths, but I thought it would be another way, besides collecting wildlife, to preserve memories of this voyage. This whole adventure is really a thrill for someone who is used to mathematics and ledger books."

"It is for me too, Stirling. My great—if necessary—adventure."

"You know, Kate, even though the East has many lovely spots, out here one just says, 'This is raw, untouched beauty as it was meant to be.' "

When he looked at her like that, she felt warm to the tips of her toes. His gaze touched her, sliding quickly down, then up to linger. She felt very at ease with him yet disturbed by his nearness in the most pleasant way.

"I suppose," she said to break their silent spell, "it's only untouched here because the settlers aren't on this stretch of river yet. But this land has been touched by the Indians, trappers, and rivermen who came before."

"You are always as practical as you are artistic, and that is unusual, I would think, for one so young."

Again his gray-blue gaze held hers. She had not realized how hungry she was to be appreciated, to be looked at the way a man does a woman he admires. He made her feel so vital again, with so many things possible in life—and between them.

"You know, Kate, I would love to have a big piece of beautiful land like this to build a home on someday."

"My husband left me sixty acres upriver a ways, along the Missouri near the Sky River. I've been worrying so much about the boat, I haven't thought much about it. I'd have sold it in a moment, but my lawyer says it's out in the middle of nowhere in Free Indian Territory, and who would want it? As for me, I've always lived in St. Louis."

"Lucky you, though, to have some place to call your own. I would like my land to be near St. Louis, maybe on the prairie like General Clark's estate. Have you seen it?"

"It's lovely there. He's carved out a little piece of paradise, but I think he's very lonely."

"Yes, so I gather. But I would have a home *and* family on my piece of land. I would want a devoted wife and a fine boy like your Jamie. And I admit I would like to be wealthy but for the right reasons."

"And what would those be?"

"To help bring civilization to a place like St. Louis. I know it has a theater and university, but more could be done to help people live worthwhile lives. You know, appreciation of the finer things, art, music, understanding other cultures. I know I'm a dreamer, Kate, but I am willing to do whatever I must to make those dreams come true. I would like to be able to stand up to those who think they can control other people not as fortunate or powerful as they. My father lost his bookkeeper's job in Richmond just because he talked back once. It crushed him, and that is not fair, not in America! I admit there are good wealthy men—like General Clark and like I want to be—but there are the other kind too."

"There surely are, and St. Louis—even the farthest reaches of this river—have not escaped one I could name!"

"Who?"

"Cadet Chouteau and his father, Pierre, before him—all of his ilk."

"Did I hear a familiar name?" Rand Cloud's deep voice interrupted them. Kate and Stirling both jumped up as if they'd been caught at something. The man seemed to have materialized from the bushes. She resented his barging in on their heartfelt talk.

"No one called *your* name," she replied. "Have you been eavesdropping?"

"No eaves for miles around. But about Chouteau—"

"I believe you used to work for him."

"So did half of the state if they don't still," he said, glaring at her. "I just happened to see you have booze in the hold."

"Booze?"

"Liquor, barrels of it. Haven't you heard it called that? It's not an Indian word, though I apologize if it's a bit rough for your ears. The liquor I'm referring to is marked from Marbois, who is Chouteau's factor at Fort Clark. It's going to Kellen Blackwell, the new head Indian agent there."

"Wherever it's going, why were you in the hold?" she demanded, more loudly than she had intended.

"Your son and Blue Wing were playing hide-and-seek down there. I suggested the boy hide other places as the barrels might roll around and crush him! Will you scold me for that?"

"No, but I repeat, our cargo is none of your concern."

"As new subagent to the Mandans I don't want alcohol going up there. I don't care if Blackwell is expecting it or not. More likely it's for bribes and mischief, even if it is marked as medicine. Besides, the government can legally confiscate it at Fort Leavenworth, or were you planning some guise or diversion to sneak it through? Chouteau's lackeys have managed that before."

His narrow stare challenged hers. The impact on her was far different from that of Stirling's glance; it was like comparing light with lightning. This man was annoying, not alluring.

"I am not Chouteau's lackey or his anything," she insisted. "I didn't know this Marbois worked for him. I turned down passage to every *engagé* who'd admit he was on Chouteau's pay. Besides, my first mate said the Mandans do not drink firewater, and I suppose that's an Indian word. I assure you, I am dead set against drinking to excess," she said, trying to calm herself. "And as you noted, Marbois said it's medicinal."

"The Mandans don't drink firewater, but there are some who would like them to start," Rand said, also quieter now. "Drunken Indians are easier to pull things over on. And it's something else they have to trade for, as well as goods they're becoming more and more dependent on, some of which are already embezzled from them. And how well do you know Marbois?"

"Now, look," Stirling put in, "Mr. MacLeod, or Cloud, whatever your name is. Like me, you are only a passenger on Mrs. Craig's boat. She is not some criminal on the stand to be questioned or harangued. You have no right to make crude insinuations."

"Concerned inquiries, Mr. Mount," Rand said, pointing

a finger nearly in Stirling's face. "And a warning to the lady who knows just a bit more about what she's getting into than you do." With that he spun away and walked deeper into the forest.

Rand knew he was sulking at dinner the next noon, though he wasn't the only one who ate without talking at the table. Captain Zeke just shoveled food in as if he were feeding the boilers, and Blue Wing always fretted over eating with the men. Kate Craig did not understand a lot about the Mandan woman yet. It was unheard of for one to eat before the men were done, let alone with them and be expected to keep up her usual chatter. She responded in near grunts at Kate's prompts for conversation.

Stirling Mount, of course, and First Mate Gabe were only too happy to jabber to Kate. Both of them were smitten by her in different ways, Rand noted. It would probably lead to trouble. Suddenly he realized Gabe was speaking to him.

"Hear you been to Washington, Mr. MacLeod. Andrew Jackson's a partic'lar hero of mine. You get to see him there?"

"I'm afraid so, after going through every contact I knew. There's no way to speak to him without using what everyone there calls proper channels."

"Heard he always did have an aide-de-camp," Gabe said.

"Maybe once. That aide-de-camp has mushroomed to a series of secretaries at the Bureau of Indian Affairs, subcommittee chairmen, senators, Cabinet chairmen, the secretary of war. But I'll admit I was still excited when I finally got my chance to speak my piece, even though I knew he'd made his reputation as an Indian fighter."

Gabe leaned forward across the table. "Don't forget he fought the English too. Well," he prompted, "so what was it like to meet the great man hisself?"

"A great disappointment," Rand said. He hated to burst a man's bubble, but Gabe had picked the wrong hero, and once he started in, he couldn't stop himself. "I could not believe the man could speak out for democracy in one breath and for Indian subjection in the next. His idea of 'all men are endowed by their Creator with certain inalienable rights,' at least for Indians, is that the red man should be shoved west. He should be resettled on reserves 'protected' by the Army—unless, of course, that new land is wanted by the whites too. The President admitted he'd made and broken many treaties but claimed the promises were dated because times had changed now."

Gabe shook his head and frowned. Stirling Mount asked, "Don't you admit, MacLeod, if progress is to be made, things have to change?"

His stare slammed into Mount's. "I hope, since you're going to be working closely with General Clark, you'll learn to adopt his attitude that the Indians have rights too."

"Of course, they do, but no one's moving your tribe out, are they?"

"Not yet. But President Jackson also said there's such an abundance of national wilderness and wildlife— evidently the red men were included as wildlife—that dwindling species or tribes are of no immediate concern. On this trip, Mount, I hope you—*all* of you—learn that animals, and certain tribes, are in danger of eventually being hunted or shoved on to oblivion."

"I can see why you left your important interview with the President very disillusioned," Kate said. At first he was annoyed she was putting words in his mouth, but sincere concern stamped her face.

"Frustrated and furious," he admitted, tearing his gaze away from her, not looking at any of their white faces now, just staring at the opposite wall. "When I told him that the Mandans had never been vaccinated against smallpox by government doctors four years ago, when other Missouri tribes were protected, you know what he said? Go tell the War Department about it, and they'd take care of it when they got further funding. The Indian Bureau, you see, always comes under the War Department and can wait forever for help—"

He clipped off the further tirade he felt coming. He stood at the table, forcing them to all look up at him. "At least one good thing came of my trip to Washington. It taught me that I can't trust the government to get things done, and I've got to pitch in myself." He shoved his chair back from the table and strode from the room.

That evening, when the two women stood at the rail of the hurricane deck in the dark, Rand, hoping to mend bridges, went over and asked, "Mind if I join you, Blue Wing and Prairie Wind?"

He saw Kate's head turn and hoped she would not have some sharp retort. If she had, he supposed he might deserve it.

"My name is Oh-karachtah Scha in Mandan," she told him proudly. Her voice caught on the *ach* guttural, but her pronunciation was good otherwise.

"I know," he said. "Not an easy language to learn. I admire your dedication. Traders and trappers, even Indian agents to the tribe try to get by with just a few cheap phrases. Please let me know if I can help you with it. Blue Wing's the best tutor here, but since I know more English words, maybe I can help too."

"Yes. Fine, thank you."

He could tell she was staring at him through the darkness, obviously surprised at this new tack he had taken. Her lower lip dropped open before she thought to close it. The tin lantern down the way and perhaps the thin slice of moon overhead etched her profile and gilded her hair. Looking at her from this close range, he could not bring himself to believe now that she could be either working for Chouteau or aware that her husband had done so.

"The portrait of Blue Wing in the common room is much better than common," he told her, and saw she appreciated his compliment and little play on words. "Mrs. Craig, you have captured her expression and the clever woman inside."

"Thank you," she said again while Blue Wing beamed, even in the dark. "It is nice to be encouraged for my art, especially from you after—after that time before."

"That was different. And unfortunate."

"Yes. Well, you see, my father and my husband had both been adamant against my doing portraits, and what happened that night just brought all that back."

He wanted to say he was sorry about that night, but he could not get the words out. He nodded and cleared his throat.

"And please call me Kate, like Stirling, Gabriel, and the captain do. I'm hoping to paint other Indians on the way," she added, and looked up at the moon as if she finally realized she had been staring at him.

He moved next to her along the rail, with Blue Wing on her other side. His big fists made her hand look so small. "Be sure," he said, "to ask Indians you paint if they would mind. Some of them believe you are capturing their spirit—stealing their essence or power medicine—if you draw or paint them. It could cause trouble for you. And some braves and chiefs will see you as a woman who has no right to draw or paint men."

"I understand. Through my friendship with Blue Wing, I'm learning their ways are very different. I believe one of those Osage chiefs the first night we met said something about my trying to catch your spirit too. Mr. Cloud—Rand—I have long regretted that I embarrassed you that night, but I didn't know they thought it wrong I draw you. You just looked . . . interesting."

"I'll take that as a compliment. I also regret that evening and the day of your husband's funeral turned out to be so chaotic. It seems we're always at odds, and now here we are penned in, more or less, on this little boat for several months."

"I'm sure we can make the best of it."

"I was going to mention something that might interest you when we go by it tomorrow morning. I see you're always very busy, but past Jefferson City there's a place called the Manito Rocks, two isolated blocks about fifty feet high."

"Sounds as if I can't miss them."

"But the thing is, the beauty there can distract you: ravines, towers, tall trees with osprey building nests. Then you can miss some overhanging rocks where the Indians in these parts once drew stick figures in red paint. There's one man rendered with uplifted arms like this," he said, and demonstrated as if he, like Blue Wing, were worshiping the moon.

"What Indians were hereabouts?" she asked, and he caught the note of alarm in her voice. "They aren't still, are they?"

"Now I know where your boy learns to ask all his questions," he said, and was rewarded with the first smile he had ever seen from her. It was fleeting as a rainbow, but he caught it. Lantern light and wan moonlight silvered her teeth and hair as she pushed back a stray tress from her face and hooked it behind her ear.

For one moment he almost forgot what she had asked him. "The Indians here were also Osage, just thirty years ago," he said. "And you know, unlike many other tribes that have been pushed out, the Osages actually tried *not* to adopt white ways. Their chief thought it would weaken them. And now there is nothing left nearby to remind us of them. Nothing but ruined villages and old drawings on rocks."

"And tumbled towers the whites built to fire rifles to drive them out," Kate said with a shake of her head. "Like the ones at St. Charles or even the fortifications overlooking St. Louis. I understood what you were saying at the table about the dangers to the Indians. It's wretchedly unfair of the powers-that-be, from Chouteau up to the President, to think and act that way."

"Yes" was all he could manage. He was stunned not only that she criticized Chouteau but that she sympathized with him about the Indians. That warmed something cold and black inside him. "I hear you're going to leave the boy with your people at Bellevue," he said. "I regret accusing you of not thinking of his safety the other day. But you see, there are hostile tribes north of there just waiting their turn to be driven off, and boats on the river risk an attack."

"My son," she said, looking up at Rand as if she had been miles away. "Yes, at Bellevue. My mother remarried after my father's death and lives there now. I can't say I grieve my father's gone, but I miss my mother terribly. I cannot wait to get upriver for a reunion with her."

He tried to shield his mind and heart from the stab of those words. He had let down his guard. He bled anger when those red-black scenes in his brain came pouring back to drown him.

"A grown woman longing for her—her mother?" he said. His hard-won control slipped away. It didn't sound like his voice now. It went bitter and hard; despite his earlier intentions, he could not help it. "All of that is past, gone, especially out here!"

He turned away and strode through the common room into his tiny cell of a cabin and slammed the door.

"What is wrong with that man?" Kate asked Blue Wing through gritted teeth. "He's a half-breed all right. Half nice, half rude, half man, half monster, practically in alternate breaths."

"Those last words maybe because his mother did die and you soon be with yours," Blue Wing said, returning her gaze to the new sliver of moon in the sky.

"Many men have lost their mothers and don't carry on like that," Kate insisted. "And what's wrong with my missing her? You say you miss Corn Basket."

Blue Wing's eyes glowed in reflected skylight before she turned to Kate. "When that man you call him was four summers, the age of Much Questions, he called Runs Quickly because he one of fastest two boys at Mitutanka. He had Mandan mother, trapper white father who did go over mountains with Red-Haired Father and his men and one Indian woman, Sacajawea."

"Rand's father went west with Lewis and Clark?"

"To shoot meat. And while he gone, Runs Quickly did find a pistol of his father. He shoot his mother, Rain Cloud, dead."

"What? He killed his own mother? That . . . can't be. Why didn't you tell me before?"

"You know you never want talk of him, hear of him. You not have good heart to Dark Water."

"That's not true! He killed his own mother when he was four?" she repeated, her voice strangling on the words.

"Didn't mean to, did. Chiefs say it accident, no can blame boy. But after some months Runs Quickly still not speak. For years he not remember killing Rain Cloud.

Sometimes he wander, looking for her among other women at Mitutanka. But because this thing well knowed in tribe, his sad father did take him to St. Louis live with father's sister."

"So he really grew up in St. Louis," Kate whispered, still trying to accept the horror of Blue Wing's tale.

"But he come back sometimes be with The People when he a man. Some still knowed this terrible thing, but no one speak it now. Runs Quickly's father died, foot caught in trap, eaten by bear—"

"Blue Wing, his father, like that—"

"But boy not see father die. A hunting party find his father, tell boy later. My father, Long Hatchet, did change Runs Quickly's name to Dark Water when he become his medicine son—what you say?—adopted. Somehow Dark Water did talk again. Now he speak too much, you thinking."

"I am only thinking of the terror of it: to kill his own mother, to shut it out, and then to recall it. He named himself for her, he mourns her doubly, and I just carried on about my own—"

Kate hunched over the rail. She ached with agony. She thought she might be ill. As if it were a nightmare painting in her mind, she saw that scene of the boy blasting his own mother. The dead woman, the stares of the tribe, the blame and guilt of the boy, even of his father. And then to lose him so brutally too.

"Prairie Wind, you not make sick in the river?" Blue Wing asked, and put her hand on Kate's trembling shoulder.

"No."

Beside her Blue Wing heaved a huge sigh and looked down into the depths. Kate kept staring at the dark, rushing current. They both knew, she thought, Old Woman did not see her slender face in the river on this night.

Chapter 8

The fourth day out, near where the Grand River flowed into the Missouri, the water got even wider and a bit cleaner. But it turned more shallow too, and for the first time Fynn Winston oversaw the roosters taking continued soundings for snags and sandbars. They proceeded slowly, for huge pieces of driftwood protruded from caved-in banks. The wedged trees called sawyers, with their roots sticking up, clawed at the *Red Dawn*'s paddles and hull from beneath the surface.

Kate had been sitting in her rocking chair on the boiler deck outside the common room until things got so dangerous she stood up to watch. Most of the other passengers now seemed subdued; Stirling had been making small talk, evidently to calm her, but she was too nervous to respond to it.

"I was about to tell you that you are much too young for a rocking chair anyway," Stirling went on as she peered over the rail. "Despite the danger in the river, aren't these banks beautiful with all this thick willow and poplar?"

Kate startled when Rand responded close behind her. "Indians used to hide there, waiting for unsuspecting souls towing vessels upriver by long ropes. Which, if you ask me, is what we should do here."

"They haven't asked you or me," Kate told him. "Things are well in hand. And I guess what you said just goes to show the Indians were not only violently wronged but sometimes violent and wrong themselves," she added pointedly.

She had so wanted to be conciliatory when she spoke with him next, but the man made it impossible. He had no right to criticize her crew. And all she needed right now was to have him and Stirling sniping at each other or for her to be arguing with Rand herself. Still, she had been doing so much thinking about him. Every time she looked at Jamie, she thought he was just Rand's age when he had lost his mother . . . that way.

"All right," Gabe bellowed down to the roosters, "we're gonna run her right over that sandbar! Brace yourself, everybody!"

"Where are Jamie and Blue Wing?" Kate asked, and started up the steps until she saw them holding to a deck pole. She grabbed the one Stirling held. Below on the main deck, firemen fed more wood to the fireboxes; the boilers rumbled; the engine boomed like cannonade; smoke hissed from the chimneys to cloud the blue sky. The *Red Dawn* jerked, stopped, jerked, stopped. On both sides of the boat, paddles stirred sand. The pressure in the boilers built to make the decks shudder more than usual.

Gabe had explained to Kate that there was no way to tell if the boiler pressure was too much; captains and crews had to rely on instinct for that. And she thought that was exactly what Captain Zeke had not done right the day his ship blew up.

As the ship strained and jolted, she started up to the pilothouse, clinging to the wooden rail. Bells dinged commands to the engine room; Gabe shouted down to Fynn to tell the roosters what to do. The boat heaved, hung, surged, struggled. Kate wasn't sure why she was going up there: to learn more herself, to tell them to be careful, or—curse it—to make them stop before they all blew up!

"I think we're free!" she heard Gabe cry. Then a grinding, tearing sound rent the air. But even that did not drown the shouted profanity that assailed her ears from the pilothouse. Finally, that too quieted as the engines hissed to a steaming stop.

"Bet we got the port paddle tore up on one of those son-of-a-bitching sawyers," she heard Captain Zeke say. "I swear, I'll never get used to this old side-wheeler after those stern-wheelers I had."

"I just knew," Gabe told Zeke, "we should of poled or pulled her past those snags in this narrow channel. Can't

believe that upriver rise just disappeared out a the blue
today."

"*Ahde!*" Kate spit out Blue Wing's favorite Mandan
expletive as she stood on the steps just below the pilothouse. In their first real trial for the ship the *Red Dawn*
was stuck and broken, and neither Captain Zeke nor Gabe
had done the correct thing. Worse, Rand Cloud had been
right to criticize them. Somehow this did not bode well.

Gabe tore down from the pilothouse so fast he nearly
knocked her off the steps. "Gotta put the blacksmith and
carpenter to work, Kate," he said, reaching out to steady
her. "But it'll give us a chance to get the roosters cutting
wood. 'Cause to pull ourselves offa here, we'll burn so
much we might not make Webb's warehouse up the way
for a new load.

"Three hours, maybe four!" he bellowed down at the
upturned faces below. "And it would help if all of you
that's not crew lighten the boat by getting off till we
move her. You can wade right over that sandbar to the
bank the short spell."

Deeply disappointed, Kate tried to look at the good
side of things. At least the Grand River a short distance
back had cleaner water to do laundry and wash her hair.
Only four days out, and everything was dirty from smoke
or river water. And she was very grateful they had not
had a serious wreck or been blown to bits. Sometimes,
when she tried to look at her life objectively now, she
could not believe she had gotten herself and Jamie into all
this.

"Come on, Jamie and Blue Wing," she called down,
trying to sound calm and cheerful when she wanted to
scream. "I'm going to get some things to wash, we'll take
our rifle, and walk back to the other river."

They found a little sandy shore cove along the Grand
River where Kate washed her hair, her son, and their
clothes. She and Blue Wing spread laundry across the
bushes to dry while Jamie waded, looking for turtles.
They dangled their bare feet in the water and munched on
fried chicken wings and butter biscuits Willy Nilly had
sent with them, but Kate worried. This was starting to

seem like a picnic when they should be under way. Stirling had strolled by awhile ago, in leisurely pursuit of flora and fauna, though he too carried a gun. And across the narrow stretch of shallow river sat Rand, wearing only his trousers, just lolling about in the river. *That* too annoyed her, though he had as much right to the river as she.

"He could walk a little farther on," she muttered to Blue Wing. "It's indecent he's that close with my underthings hanging here."

"Maybe he guarding us," she said, and yawned. "Like when Mandan women work in cornfields, braves sit on scaffolds with guns, guard from Sioux."

"We are not working in the cornfields, and I certainly hope there are no Sioux in these parts," Kate said low enough that Jamie could not hear. "But before we get too far north, you should teach me how to shoot."

"Mandan women not shoot. I only kill Brother Buffalo at Chouteau's lodge because Old Woman bring him to me."

Kate decided not to argue all that today. The breeze felt cool on her damp hair, but the sun was warm on her back. The idea of getting in the water for a sort of bath like Rand across the way did seem inviting. But in just a little while she was going to march back to the boat and see how things were coming there.

"Want me to give you and the boy a swimming lesson?" Rand called over, splashing water as if he were a boy himself.

"I don't think so, thanks!"

"Ah, Mama, why not?" Jamie asked loudly.

"Maybe later," she said. "Blue Wing said she'd show us how to swim. If Mr. Cloud goes back to the ship, then may—" she had got out before her angelic-faced four-year-old turned the air blue with cursing.

"Son-of-a bitching bastard, goldarned polecat rock! I just stubbed my toe!" the boy shouted.

"Jamie!" Kate sloshed through the water to grab him. He jumped away from her and slipped. She pulled him up, soaking wet, by one arm. "I told you the next time you talked like the roosters I'd wash your mouth out with

soap, and I just happen to have some here! Your grandmama will be appalled!"

"Aw, Mama, I forgot!" he protested like a shrieking Indian, and tried to pull back from her. Across the river she
could hear Rand laughing—actually laughing at them!
She hauled Jamie toward the bank, across a mossy rock,
stumbled, and went in herself with a big splash. She
sprawled sideways; her head went under; she spit and
sputtered. When she sat up, Jamie was soaked, Blue Wing
was laughing, and Rand had crossed the river to help her
up. She was furious.

"Looks like you're wet anyway," Rand said. "Or is that
madder than a wet mother hen? Might as well let Blue
Wing and me show you a thing or two about staying
afloat if you fall in."

Still holding Jamie's arm, with Rand lifting her from
behind by her elbows, Kate stood, dripping wet. She
shoved her heavy hair from her face; her sopping clothes
made a second skin, but at least she was dressed. Rand
stood there half naked with water clinging to his curly
black chest hair and gleaming from his brown, hard arms
and belly. His soaked trousers flaunted his narrow hips
and big thighs; it was completely indecent, if entrancing.
Worse, he was still grinning and looking her over as if
she were a newly hooked fish he could buy at market.
Her first instinct was to use some language of her own, to
douse him too in a good scolding or cursing.

But he looked eager to help—like a boy. His hair was
so flat to his head that it made his ears seem to stick out;
droplets of water clung to his chin and nose and lashes.
Yet the assessing, challenging way he looked at her, deep
into her eyes, made her realize she was very foolish ever
to think of him as a boy at all. No, this person in a powerful body who had accidentally shot his mother years
ago was a full-grown man and not one to be pitied. He
could take care of himself. She just wished he would
keep to himself instead of evoking this distressing mixture of sympathy and fury and longing in her. Besides,
there was still something frightening and forbidding in
those eyes as hot on her now as the sun. Despite herself,
she shuddered.

"Come on, Prairie Wind," Blue Wing said to her in Mandan.

"*Hu-ta,* come here." Jamie chimed in with one of his Indian phrases and walked knee-deep into the river, obviously hoping his punishment would be forgotten.

She darted another glance at Rand to see what he would add to their pleas. She saw his lips bend to form words, but she did not want to seem to follow his bidding.

"All right," she said, "since Blue Wing and Jamie want to. A quick swimming lesson, as long as we're all wet anyway."

When Rand showed them what to do, Jamie took to the water, blowing bubbles, ducking his head, paddling, kicking. Kate thought how Clive had said he would teach him to swim this summer at Chouteau's pond, but that, like many things, was not to be. She could only hope and pray that those things which were to be would be good and keep them safe.

She did all right herself, though she realized it was silly with these sopping skirts and petticoats clinging to her legs and these sleeves tight to her elbows. Rand put his arm around Jamie's waist and leaned close to let him kick, but fortunately he did not suggest the same for her.

"At Mitutanka," Blue Wing put in, "no one wear clothes swim."

"We are not at Mitutanka," Kate said.

"When we there, you do like Mandans," Blue Wing insisted as if that were settled.

Kate's eyes met Rand's again before she looked away. She had been following his instructions but trying not to make the mistake of staring him down again. Now the water had relaxed and calmed her; she'd floated languidly with it, felt caressed by it, carried away from herself at times. It was cold but invigorating. Now, after one more stare from him, she felt fluttery and warm in her belly though her teeth chattered when she got out.

She was grateful when Stirling came back and insisted she wear his coat, however wet she got it. He had not shot anything, but he carried a few samples of lavender columbine and blue phlox, which he offered to her.

" 'With sweet flowers a true love showers,' " he whispered to her.

"What pretty blossoms, Stirling, and a prettier poem." She felt herself blush, though the sun had already tinged her nose and cheeks pink.

"From Shakespeare's *Hamlet*," he told her, looking quite proud of himself. "But here's one from Stirling Mount: 'from my favorite play for my favorite lady.' I saw *Hamlet* acted at home just before I came west."

Though she did not say so, that impressed her. Stirling's intriguing world was obviously a far cry from hers. Clive had known nothing about book learning and cared less. She had at least cared, though she'd been to none of the theatricals which played occasionally in St. Louis. She realized now, far too late, that if she wanted to attend, she should have. When Rand came up beside them, she was glad he had not heard Stirling spouting either Shakespeare or compliments to her, for the two men were already stiff and silent with each other. Walking between them on the way back to the boat, she almost felt as if she were under arrest, for they both carried rifles.

"Leavenworth is about a week away," Rand finally said to her. "What have you decided to do about Marbois's liquor in the hold, let alone Mr. Mount's?"

"You mean they might take Stirling's too?" Kate asked. "But his is just to preserve biological specimens!"

"And Marbois's is just medicinal," Rand countered. "I need to know if you will try to hide those barrels. Will you tell the soldiers there you have a good supply of spirituous liquors?"

She felt hurt he had ruined the day. But it seemed, somehow, he always did. And she was annoyed he had become his old, domineering self again. After living with her father, then Clive, she was finally learning to recognize the type and wanted nothing to do with it.

"I'm going to obey the *government*'s orders totally," she told him, hoping he would get the point. "You believe in that, don't you, Rand Cloud, alias Dark Water?"

"Until that law breaks higher laws," he said, shouldering his rifle. "I'm going to try to shoot some meat before that bell rings."

And he was gone into the thick trees along the river before she could say one more word or take any satisfaction in having bested him.

From that day on it seemed to Kate the surroundings got wilder. They passed a place called Fire Prairie where some Indians had died in a fast-sweeping inferno; though some of the fields were cultivated here, they now promised wide-open prairie. After the boat was stuck again, they "lightered their load"—unloaded people and some goods to float free before reloading—then passed the site of old Fort Osage. Under an earlier treaty between General Clark and the tribe, the Osages had been forced to leave. They passed the small but booming town of Independence, from which the Santa Fe Trail took traders and settlers to the southwest, a dangerous trek. They passed the Konzas River and, shortly after, the invisible boundary separating the United States from Free Indian Territory.

Beyond the Konzas, the riverbanks became yellow clay. In the forests, Captain Zeke said, lived the remnants of tribes shoved west of the Mississippi River: Delawares, Shawnees, and Miamis. Though they saw not a soul now, Kate felt them there. Islands narrowed the channel, and she recalled Rand's warning that Indians used to lurk in heavy foliage waiting to grab the unwary. She made Jamie stay by her side; she counted off the last thirty miles to Cantonment Leavenworth, where there would be American troops. And she rehearsed in her mind what she would say about Marbois's barrels of liquor and worried that she would never be able to pay him back for their loss.

"It's so barren here," she observed to Rand as they approached the fort, where fields and hillsides stood naked in a stubble of stumps. "Someone's made a wasteland of it, cutting down all those trees."

"They used them for the stockade and buildings, but the idea is that no one sneaks up who's not welcome. The Army's supposedly here to guard the Indians' boundaries, but it's the whites they're really protecting from the Indians. You have noticed, haven't you, that a confrontation the whites win is called a battle and one the Indians win is a massacre? There it is," he said, pointing at the stockade with American flag flying.

A sentinel was rowed aboard to tell them where to tie up. He was shocked to see a white woman "up this far beyond them few woman what's westered on the Santa Fe." Keelboats and two other steamers were tied along the crude wooden wharf as they put in. Three officers and four soldiers came aboard and spoke with Captain Zeke, Gabe, her, then Rand.

"I hear you're Major MacLeod now, Rand Cloud," the youthful-looking sergeant said, and saluted him. "If you can't beat them, join them, eh?"

"I didn't know you were in the Army," Kate whispered to Rand before she and Captain Zeke escorted the soldiers down into the hold.

"I'm not," he told her. "All Indian agents are called by the honorary title of major."

At least he hadn't reminded her again there was so much she didn't know, she thought, as she went down the steps. And she had no idea how to protect Marbois's goods as she had promised him but still not break the law or harm the Mandans if this liquor went upriver.

"Anything to declare down here before we look around, ma'am?" the officer in charge asked. He was obviously amazed to see a woman too. He had fallen over his own feet to offer his arm yet let her precede him. She supposed she could try to wheedle a favor from him, but she was determined to tell the truth, then trust the government to do what was right. Surely, Major MacLeod's being part Indian had somewhat slanted his view of how the U.S. government handled the Indians.

"We have twenty-five barrels of spirits in the hold, sir, not counting a few kegs of beer brought for the passengers and crew. But I was told twenty barrels of cargo were medicine for Fort Clark, and I can attest that five barrels of brandy were approved by General Clark himself, strictly for preserving biological specimens which Mr. Mount will be taking back."

They asked her other questions, whispered among

themselves, walked the narrow isles with a lantern, counted barrels. "Twenty seems too large a number, so we'll have to confiscate five of those barrels, ma'am. But since they are going to General Clark's new agent there, Major Blackwell, we'll allow the others to pass. Mr. Mount, being he's in General Clark's employ, will not have his scientific allotment touched. Men, pull out the five barrels I indicated."

Kate went up on deck and explained to Rand what had happened. She saw his jaw muscles tighten as if he gritted his teeth. "They must be on Chouteau's take too," he muttered. "Confiscating one fourth is not what the law says, but no doubt Marbois knows something I don't about its getting by."

"You won't protest?" she asked. "I told them the truth, and the decision was theirs."

"I'm *assuming* it's not your fault," he said so menacingly she didn't know whether to feel relieved or not. Without another word, Rand disembarked and wandered down to the far end of the wharf, where soldiers were unplugging the barrels and pouring the liquor in the river. She saw him bend over close once, as if to speak to the soldiers. When Stirling joined her at the rail, he seemed nearly as pleased as she that his barrels had passed unscathed.

Later that evening Major Ryley, the fort commander, invited her, the crew, and the cabin passengers to dinner in the officers' quarters—the center of the cluster of neat buildings surrounded by a veranda within the stockade. Blue Wing said she'd rather stay aboard with Jamie. Kate was feted and toasted and escorted back to the steamer after dark by Major Ryley himself, who gallantly kissed her hand and made her promise a return visit on her way back to St. Louis. She'd had a wonderful evening, but she noted that neither Stirling nor Rand, unfortunately seated together down the long table, had said much before disappearing early.

She went in to kiss Jamie and whispered good-night to Blue Wing. Then, with a light shawl around the scoop shoulders of her only good gown, she strolled the hurricane deck, reliving the evening. How much she enjoyed the company of other people; how heady it was to be entertained and amused by a group of men wanting to please and not to criticize her.

She smelled tobacco and spun around. Rand sat cross-legged on the deck behind her, his rough features gilded by the glow of his pipe. He rose to his feet in one quick, quiet motion.

"I didn't know you smoked."

"All Mandan men do."

"You do see yourself as Mandan then?"

"I could have said some white men do. But I'm not waiting up for you to get into all that. Nor do I intend to give you my usual lecture about all you do not know."

"I guess I'm to be grateful for small favors."

"Never mind. I just thought you should realize that those five barrels the officers took were all marked with a special slash under Marbois's name and they all contained water."

"Water!"

"Keep your voice down. Water colored and flavored with molasses, I guess. I tasted only a little of it. So Chouteau, through Marbois, did set you up as a carrier of this liquor and arranged with someone here to remove the five harmless barrels for the record. They can always change their books to say they took it all. Of course, you didn't know a thing about this," he said in his tautly controlled voice, and leaned closer to peer down into her face. "Did you?"

"I most certainly did not."

"I don't know why, but I believe you."

"Why shouldn't you believe me? That's terrible that Marbois thinks I'm so—curse him—so darned stupid."

"I brought you the piece from one of the barrels to show you," he said, and held up a broken, curved stave of wood to catch the light of the distant, single lantern on deck. "Under his name, see? None of the barrels they didn't touch have that."

"Should I complain to Major Ryley?"

"Hardly. Who knows how high up the bribe money goes? Chouteau has a very long arm."

"I'd like to dump every one of those barrels in the river and let the fish get dosed with medicine."

"I like your sentiments and spirit," he said, and stepped closer.

"Clive was so brave to face up to Chouteau, and I must be too! I'm carrying on for him so Jamie will know what a good man his father was—despite, you know, some other things— What? What else were you going to say just then?" she demanded as he stepped back and looked away disgustedly.

"Nothing. Just that when we get our first storm on the river, the barrels should accidently be staved in or washed overboard. Do I have your word you will let me care for that?"

"Yes, but don't bother Stirling's allotment. You won't get caught?"

"I appreciate your concern, as I'm sure Stirling does. I won't get caught if you don't tell anyone, and I do mean anyone, including Stirling. Do we have a bargain?"

"A peace treaty, you mean?"

"Most treaties are sealed with lies," he said, and knocked his pipe on the rail. The ashes cascaded into the river. "But let's seal this agreement with the truth and a handshake."

He extended his big hand, and she thrust hers to meet it. His hand was warm, encompassing, strong. When they shook, it seemed her whole body did too. She believed that despite her being taken in by Chouteau again, she had won a small victory with this man. It made her almost giddy; either that or the wine served at the officers' table tonight did.

"And what do the Mandans do to seal an agreement?" she asked.

"Among men, smoke the pipe. Among women, exchange a gift. Between the sexes, it depends on what the agreement is for." His deep, quiet voice seemed to catch in his throat as he finally loosed her hand. "Sometimes," he added, "a deal between different tribes is sealed not by shaking hands but the person's shoulders—like this."

Before she could step back, he gripped her shoulders; her shawl lay there, but his calloused palms seemed to brand her bare skin. Though he grasped her tightly, he shook her gently, barely pulling her toward him. She looked up into his face, feeling dizzy. His eyes, narrowed to ebony slits, seemed to study her, to penetrate her thoughts. He stepped back, shook his head, and went down the passageway. She heard his cabin door close with a muffled thud. Then a second door, perhaps Stirling's or Gabe's, closed quietly too.

Inside her cabin she undressed in the dark so as not to disturb Blue Wing and Jamie, but she could tell by Blue Wing's breathing she was awake. Still, her friend said nothing.

Kate leaned against the wood wall and looked out toward the big shadow of the fort—the protection of the United States government they would leave behind tomorrow. Those men she had relied on here—at least some of them—had betrayed her and their people they were sworn to defend, not to mention the Indians. The people of the "red race" were supposed to be protected, weren't they? They were often portrayed in newspaper cartoons as President Jackson's or General Clark's children, sitting on their knees and begging for gifts.

Betrayal in life was to be expected, she thought sadly. She had seen it before and would see it again. It made her more anxious to see her mother again, for mothers at least could be trusted. And she had dependable friends in Gabe, Zeke, and Stirling—and now Rand too. He had even shown her the evidence and told her what he'd learned, not gone behind her back, not accused her. She had trusted him, at least on this. Surely—fuzzy-brained or not—she should have. She didn't fully trust him the way she did Stirling, nor did he attract her the same—well, the same good way.

She got onto her narrow, hard bed and pulled the blanket up over her shoulders. She curled her legs up nearly to her chest despite how it bumped her bottom into the wall and made her knees stick out over the side. Exhaustion flowed through her limbs. She could just picture it now, Marbois and Chouteau's molasses-colored water pouring down the wide Missouri clear back to St. Louis.

* * *

During wood stops, Rand and the boat's official hunter, Pete Marburn, began to bring in wild turkey for the table. For the first time so few whites inhabited the area that animals abounded, though there were still no buffalo or beaver. On Cow Island they saw where stags had made paths and lick spots on the saline clay banks. At times they could have walked across the river on sitting wood ducks, until the approaching noise and smoke of the steamer sent them flapping skyward. Bald eagles wheeled overhead, and flocks of Carolina parakeets or loud sandhill cranes occasionally darkened the sky. Blue Wing was excited to see Old Woman in the Moon's sacred geese thick along the banks, tending their woolly young.

"The Old One's geese teach loyalty to little ones," Blue Wing told Kate. "They never desert young, even if someone shoot arrows or bullets at them. Same way children honored and beloved among The People."

"And that is one reason you have prayed for children," Kate said. She knew she was broaching a tender subject with her friend. The woman's love for Jamie seemed as fierce and true as her own. And more than once, though Kate told her she did not believe it and didn't want to hear it, Blue Wing had assured her that little Sally could choose to return to her again as another child if Kate would ask this at the Baby Hill and find a man to father Sally's return.

"But if you had a child, who would be the father?" Kate asked. The unnamed man Blue Wing loved was another subject that was avoided between them, though they had shared so much.

But today, as they stood watching the geese protect their young, which could not fly from the noise and wake of the boat, Blue Wing said quietly, "He would be Kattuscho Kahka, Swift Raven of The People."

"Oh. You said his name over and over when you were ill that night after you fell through the ice, but I didn't know what you meant. Will you tell me about him?"

Solemnly she nodded. "Because you will see him, know him. Always I did belove him when young, like those little geese. Later he did look at me with eyes of wanting. But he belonging to family with much medicine, with great tribal medicine bundle."

"Like the personal medicine bundle all Mandans have," Kate asked, "only bigger?"

"Much bigger," she said, gesturing. "To bring all power of life and death to tribe in corn and buffalo and battles. So children of tribal medicine bundles marry children with other tribal medicine bundles, get more power. The way of The People, a good way."

"I guess it's like the wealthy and landed folks marrying their own kind among the whites to get more prestige and power," Kate said. "So Swift Raven had to marry someone else—and you married River Walker?"

Blue Wing nodded. "But before Swift Raven say he take a wife, my sister, Clam Necklace, marry Wolf Trap. The People know I must go to lodge of Wolf Trap, marry him too. But I say no to my beloved parents, hoping, praying Swift Raven still take me for his woman. Besides," she added, her voice now hard instead of wistful, "I not can honor Wolf Trap, not can live in lodge under Clam Necklace, ever!"

"And so bad family feelings."

"Bad hearts in tribe and bad in family lodge. I did run away on river, go toward Hidatsa village, but found River Walker put in with his boat for wood. He—he take me; then he pay my father much trade goods to buy horses for me wife to him. This the want of every Mandan girl."

"What happened then with Swift Raven?"

"He take wife to honor his family. They have two children, she die. So I want separate River Walker because Swift Raven look at me the old way again when River Walker in St. Louis with you."

"Will you marry Swift Raven when you return to Mitutanka?"

"It my first and always prayer to Old Woman all this time; besides, I want become your sister. My own sister hate me, say I have bad heart to her and family, also Wolf Trap. Clam Necklace not want Blue Wing ever come back to Mitutanka. Wolf Trap, like Swift Raven, maybe next chief, have much medicine."

"Swift Raven and Wolf Trap are powerful tribal rivals

with you caught in the middle? As for children, you want
to bear them for Swift Raven, but Wolf Trap would want
a child by you—to prove his power and make things right
in the tribe?"

"But if I have no child with Swift Raven before marriage, no child with our River Walker, and you have two
... then I maybe no deserve any. ..." Her voice faded.
She looked away from the geese at last, down at her
hands clasped on the rail. Kate put her hand over Blue
Wing's and leaned close to comfort her.

"If things are bad," Kate said, "with your sister and
your family, you have me and Jamie now. And I shall tell
Swift Raven myself what a blessing you have been to
me."

"A blessing," Blue Wing whispered. "Just like a baby
from Baby Hill when Prairie Wind, Blue Wing go there,
pray together for our children be born."

Not only wild game was more abundant now, as were
Indians, though supposedly not hostile ones. They passed
an old trading post, once independent, but now part of
Chouteau's web of empire. There Jamie got to see his
first Indians in the wild as Ioways, from their village a
few miles from the river, stood about to trade. The *Red
Dawn* passed Indian huts, seasonal dwellings deserted
only until the next hunt. And they entered what Captain
Zeke called "half-breed territory," land sparsely settled by
whites intermarried with the Omaha, Ioway, and Yankton
Sioux, who were forced to live in this no-man's-land between the whites and their tribes.

"A cruel fate if no one accepts them," Kate said at
dinner when Zeke explained.

"Outcasts on both sides," Rand put in. "Usually half-
breeds are just rejected by the whites." Kate looked at
him, then back down at her plate.

"It seems to me," Stirling said, "they should be given
a fair chance to choose where to live."

"Half-breeds should but not full-blooded Indians?"
Rand asked. Kate had been aware for weeks that the two
men did not get along. She mostly blamed Rand. Stirling
was always charming and accommodating and obviously

wanted to please; Rand could be abrupt and rude. Stirling's sunny nature just didn't mix well with Rand's frequent stormy moods, she thought.

"I did not say a thing about full-blooded Indians, Major MacLeod," Stirling countered, his fork halfway to his lips, his usual calm voice tightening. "I suppose you see yourself as caught between the two peoples too."

"I am placing myself between the two," he said. "I hope to be a bridge—what's that fancy French word?—a liaison, Mr. Mount. I don't think the Indians and the whites can live together peacefully, not in this day and age, maybe never. But I want to be blasted certain that the Mandans and their tribal neighbors don't suffer the same fate these others have—to be, like the beaver and buffalo, which once flourished on this river, driven off by greedy whites pretending to be their friends."

"That was quite a speech," Stirling said, but he added hastily, "and I agree. I really do not believe we have a thing we can argue here. And I certainly wish game were better here too, as I am having a devil of a time finding specimens for my brandy barrels."

"Then perhaps next time Pete Marburn and I go off to shoot, you will want to come with us," Rand said, too obviously dripping charm and politeness. He excused himself from the table and went out on deck to smoke. He was still there, alone at the rail, after Kate had helped Willy Nilly clear the table, so she went out to him, wiping her hands on her apron.

"I'm sorry you and Stirling don't get along."

He studied her quickly, blown hair to shoe tips, looking slowly down, up, then out at the river again. It was strange, but she almost felt as if he had touched her everywhere he looked. Yet she was not offended, only—curse him—intrigued and determined to stand her ground.

"Stirling gets along with you at least," he said. "Not to change such a fine subject, but did you see those clouds? Perhaps we're going to get our first big storm, raining buckets—and barrels."

"Barrels of molasses-colored rain?"

"Something like that."

Though they had jokingly hinted at their common desire to get rid of Marbois's illicit barrels, they did not share a laugh or another look. One glance at the sky immediately sobered and transfixed Kate. Beyond the vegetation-choked bottomlands fringing the river here rose a chain of bare hills, and from those hills raced low clots of boiling black clouds directly at them. And behind and above those loomed a giant cloud of such density it looked like a solid body stabbing forks of lightning at the ground.

They were near the mouth of the Grand Nemahaw River with its freshening water, but the river itself soon turned inky black like a mirror to the sky, as if the river and heavens were seething as one. Kate hurried off to help the crew stow things, as Gabe and Zeke headed for shore to tie the *Red Dawn* up for the blow.

Kate did not even take time to put her rocking chair back in the cabin but lashed it to the rail of the hurricane deck where it sat. The roosters threw out lines to snag trees to secure the boat. The wind alone rocked it as if they were at sea.

When rain began, it seemed a solid sheet of gray, closing out the bank, the trees, the sky, the world. Water cascaded off each deck to the next below it. Kate stood in the window of the common room, watching the river rise. It took the shallow-bottomed hull with it, yanking at the ropes, twisting the prow as if the *Red Dawn* wanted to plunge downriver.

"All those creeks and rivers above us rising too danged fast!" she heard Gabe shout up to Captain Zeke, who still manned the pilothouse, lost up there in darkness in the middle of the afternoon. "If she pulls loose, let's try to run her aground on that big sandbar above the Nemahaw!"

"You'd intentionally run her aground?" she asked Gabe, and grabbed his arm as he hurried by.

" 'Less the water goes higher. It beats a rough, rudderless ride downriver!"

"What can I do to help?"

"Now you get on in your cabin and let us handle this."

For Jamie's sake, she did as she was told. They huddled with Blue Wing on the floor of their cabin, wedging themselves between the bunks, so they wouldn't slide. Still, they felt tossed and turned. Blue Wing looked ashen. Even sitting there, Kate could picture what was happening outside.

The wind howled as it ripped in over open prairie from the southwest. It tried to drive the boat out to the deep central channel. The *Red Dawn* thrashed and heaved, then yanked free of its bonds, turned, and bounded off downstream. They heard a thudding sound that was not thunder, a deafening crash, a ripping tear. A huge tree limb plunged through the outside wall and rammed their door off its hinges on the inner wall. Smaller leaves and twigs scraped over them as they cowered even lower. If they had been standing in the room, they could have been crushed.

But just as quickly as it came, with a groaning shudder, the tree twisted back out, tearing a larger opening. Rainwater poured in after it. Kate jumped to her feet. They could not stay here now. But Rand suddenly stood where the door had been. Even in the dusky light and roaring wet, he looked relieved to see them.

"Up on the hurricane deck!" he shouted. "Thank God that tree limb missed you!"

He took Jamie under one arm; Kate and Blue Wing scrambled after him. The boat stayed upright but turned and tipped. Despite the downpour and occasional crack of thunder, Kate was glad to be out of the cabin. But through a slit in the sky she could see lightning whips cracking trees close by. The wind almost yanked her words away, so she screamed at Rand, "What about the lightning?"

"It will hit the metal chimneys if anything!"

"I want to help! What can I do?"

"Just take care of Blue Wing and Jamie. I'll tie you here, but if it tips over—"

"Tips? Over?"

"From this wind. If it tips, keep tied to it, hold to it, unless you can reach the bank. They're trying to put her aground to stop it, to snag trees with ropes again."

He leaned close to her and wrapped the rope twice around her and Jamie. He grasped her waist, her hips to keep himself at his task. She held to him to help him; his arms and back were rock-hard and slick. Their skin slid together, wrist to wrist, cheek to cheek, as he fastened Jamie to her by another loop of rope. For one moment in the sliding storm of dark and wind, his breath heated her throat. Their eyes met, lit by distant lightning. She wasn't sure as he lunged away, but she thought he squeezed her waist as if to comfort her.

He secured Blue Wing within arm's reach to the next post, where she had almost fastened herself. Down just a ways Kate's rocking chair, which she had tied, tilted madly back and forth. But before Rand went below, he came back to hand Kate his knife.

"Cut the ropes and get ashore if you have to."

"Where's Stirling?" she screamed above the shriek of wind, but Rand half slid, half climbed back down to the main deck.

The maelstrom moaned and worsened. A slatted chicken coop flew from the deck to the far bank, then bobbed away in the black current. With a horrid crack, then crash, the back chimney toppled, crushed the aft rail, and wedged them in the bank by its fall. With that, Zeke and Gabe got the prow thrust on the same big sandbar they had so carefully avoided hours earlier.

At least the falling iron stack had not hit anyone scrambling on the deck below. The women could see the roosters two decks down, heaving ropes, trying to hook a bankside tree, even trees lying in the foaming river to be sure they stayed put this time in the constantly rising water. Gabe, Fynn, and Rand—the ones who could swim, she supposed—were leaping out onto the toppled chimney to tie the boat to it. They walked its slippery surface, then lunged back for the deck to avoid the turbulent current below. Through all this, Kate spoke soothingly to Jamie, who clung tightly to her, his arms like iron bands around her hips, his face thrust against her stomach: "It's all right, it's going to be all right, I promise."

Everyone shouted when a rooster, then another tied to him fell in and were sucked away. Kate gasped; surely the men could grab something downstream and they could recover them soon. The sky darkened and shouted; the rain pounded again, stinging their skin.

She tried to squint through the streaming wet. One fewer man just below. Gabe? Had Gabe gone in? And then she saw him bending over the side, reaching out with a sounding pole to a man in the water between the hull and fallen chimney. She saw Stirling for the first time, leaning over with Gabe, helping the men. She was relieved that once she spotted him, she saw he occasionally looked up and waved his arm as if to comfort her. Then she saw that all the other men clustered there with Stirling were short, shorter than Rand. Where was he?

She realized he must be the one in the water. But he could swim; he was strong.

"Dark Water go in!" Blue Wing shouted to her. "Holding to a rope!"

Kate touched the knife he had given her, grasped the rope with which he had tied her and Jamie. She sawed through the sodden bonds and shifted Jamie to Blue Wing. "Hold him! Hold him!" she screamed.

On the slippery hurricane deck, she scrambled toward her rocking chair. It meant so much: her past; her grandmother, whose namesake she was; her mother; civilization, all she had left of the onetime dream of Winterhaven, now replaced by this drowning nightmare of going up the wide, wild Missouri. But she had to hurry and did not hesitate.

She cut the chair loose with the knife. Grasping the post of rail between her knees, leaning over, she shouted to the men below, "Look out! He can grab this chair to float. If you can't get him back, he can swim with it—look out!"

Stirling looked up, startled in a flash of lightning. His face, streaming water, looked shocked. She heaved, let go. The chair bounced once below somewhere, then splashed just downstream from the thrashing man. She saw him swim for it, seize it, but as he did, he and the chair bobbed and twisted off together into the howling storm.

As soon as daylight came, despite the continued, though quieter, rain, Kate belted her skirt to her hips to free her legs, and insisted on walking the riverbank with the others, looking for the three lost men. She turned her back on the destruction of the boat; there would be time enough to assess that damage later. Zeke and Fynn stayed behind with the remaining roosters to oversee and repair what they could. She had given them a heartfelt talk about how they must now all pull together more than ever.

She felt exhausted and stunned, yet determined. She plunged on behind their blacksmith, Bill Blake, the tough, muscular onetime slave whose skin was as dark as the river. Stirling came right behind her; both men had rifles at the ready. On the other side of the river, staying in sight, Pete Marburn searched with Willy Nilly, both armed.

"You think you can fix that chimney while Pete patches broken walls, Bill?" she asked the big man ahead of her.

"Fix it but not hoist it proper and solder it down, ma'am. Not without a second smithy."

"After a rest stop near Sky River, temporary repairs will let us make it to Bellevue on half steam. My step-father is a blacksmith there," she told him. "He'll help you—after we find the three lost men." She only prayed her brave words of help from her mother's husband would come true; she had learned now what it meant when someone worked for Cadet Chouteau, and everyone at the Bellevue trading post did.

And this was half-breed territory again now, but they had decided to risk the half Indians being hostile, hostile the way she and Rand had been at first. Her thoughts poured on as she trudged through clay and mud and clung to saplings to avoid little landslides into the foaming river. They had decided to chance calling for the men even if they attracted someone unfriendly. Unfriendly, she thought as she went on, drenched with sweat but shuddering with shivers. How she had distrusted and disliked Rand from the first, Blue Wing too. Sad that her affinity for them had never been as swift and sure as her bond to Stirling.

"Parsons, Faubert, MacLeod!" Bill bellowed as he had

before. Birds flew; his cry echoed from the depths of dark trees.

"Major MacLeod likes to go by Rand Cloud out here on the river," Kate told Bill. She was suddenly utterly convinced they would find him and the others unharmed. "His mother's name was Rain Cloud and he took her . . . part of her name," she heard herself say, though she really felt too tired to form words.

"Kate, save your strength," Stirling said, his voice weary too.

"I can't," she told him. "Parsons! Faubert! Rand Cloud!"

Dizzily she put foot ahead of foot. She felt she had to talk, had to encourage the others, to urge them on to find the men, fix the ship, shove on, succeed. But first they had to find Rand. This voyage, this venture, their very survival were on her head—and firmly stuck in her heart, never to wash or yank away. Gabe's investment, Sam's goods, General Clark's trust, Clive's true legacy and Jamie's heritage, their whole future—so much was at stake.

She gasped when they found her rocking chair snagged on a big piece of driftwood wedged in the bank. Actually she saw it was only part of the chair. One rocker and one leg and arm hung there, swaying in the wind. Kate felt grateful such ruination was not the fate of the steamboat itself, but what if that was the fate of the lost men?

They beat the bushes, calling their names. No other broken limbs, no Rand, not even footprints among thick green-black sodden foliage.

"He could have just been swept farther on," Stirling said, leaning against a tree to squint downriver. "I am sure we will find him in better shape than your chair, Kate."

She turned away from him and plodded on, though she shook deep inside now as well as out. "Parsons!" she called, cupping her muddy hands to her mouth. "Faubert! Rand Cloud! Ra-and!"

Chapter 9

In late afternoon, along both sides of the river, the weary searchers sat down to eat cold corn bread and slices of venison to keep up their strength. They would have to turn back soon if they did not want to spend the night out there.

Kate had a leaden weight in the pit of her stomach to think the men could be hurt or ... even dead. She kept picturing Rand: speaking in kindness or stalking off in anger, Rand tying her to the ship, Rand swept away from it. Swept away: She felt her hopes, her belief in success had gone with him, yet she would go on.

But they could not push on without finding the missing men, without knowing their fate. They were just a few days from a repair stop at Sky River and a reunion with her mother at Bellevue, but all that would have to wait. Tomorrow, Kate thought, they would leave the heavy chimney where it fell and backtrack in the damaged steamer. They must go miles back they had struggled to cover. Her *Red Dawn* dream was as broken as her boat.

But then, across the river, Willy Nilly started screeching and pointing. Stirling leaped up; Kate leaned out to look down this side of the river. Two mud-caked men, one leaning heavily on the other, both limping! And one of them was Rand!

Kate darted around trees, skidded down a muddy gully, and scrambled up the other side of it. Stirling and Bill thrashed through the brush behind her. Across the river Pete and Willy Nilly cheered, but the current was too deep and fast for them to come over to help.

"Rand, thank God!" she cried. She felt so relieved and

joyous she could have hugged them both. But she stopped.

She saw no third man. Parsons's face was contorted in pain; he grasped his side. Rand's smile at seeing them was a grimace; his eyes were stark white in his blackened face. His tattered trousers displayed a huge blood-caked gash on his left thigh. Purple circles edged both eyes as if he had been beaten.

Kate helped the men sit while Stirling and Bill fed them. "Have you seen Faubert?" she asked.

"We buried him this morning," Rand said. "Drowned."

"Oh, no! No! At least you two—how are you really?"

"Bruised or broken ribs," Rand said through a mouthful of corn bread with a nod at Parsons, who sipped water from Bill's canteen. "Pains him to walk or talk. I broke my nose and caught a sharp rock here, you can see."

"Better there than a bit higher, Major," Bill said, and the two men exchanged nods.

When Kate realized what he meant, she interrupted. "I have salve for the cut. Your leg's not broken?"

"Not if I can walk. It needs stitches, keeps opening."

"But at least I can bind it closed now," she said, and went off a ways to rip a strip from the bottom of her petticoat for a bandage.

They slowly retraced their steps with Bill helping Parsons and Stirling giving Rand support. Kate, too short to lend even a shoulder to either of them, came behind carrying the rifles. She grieved for the lost Faubert but could not help rejoicing in the two who had been found. And this calamity might be a blessing in disguise, for Rand would surely feel more kindly toward Stirling for his help today.

When they passed the ruin of her rocking chair, Rand called back, "That saved me, Kate. I was exhausted fighting the current. Even when it broke apart, I held on to some of it until I snagged some driftwood. I just might have you to thank for my life. In the tribe, if someone saves someone else's life," he went on through gritted teeth as he stepped down on his bad leg again, "you get to have the exploit painted on your buffalo robe by Blue Wing's father—Long Hatchet, the tribal artist."

"I'll remember that when we get to Mitutanka. Now don't talk, just save your strength." For the first time ever he did as she ordered.

It was long after dark when they sighted the steamer's tin lanterns lit to guide their way. Kate had never been so glad to see anything in her life. After the injured men told their story to the hovering crew and ate again, they washed and went to their respective beds. Kate insisted Gabe give a prayer for the lost man and the deliverance of the others; she saw the French roosters make the sign of the cross on their big, heaving chests and shake their heads. Afterwards she knocked on Rand's door with her sewing kit.

"Yes?"

"You said you needed that sewn up."

"Come in."

She opened the door slowly. "I'll try to help."

"You said you were never good at sewing," he reminded her. "And Blue Wing is. I was going to call for her."

"I *am* good at darning."

"This is not darning. It's damned delicate embroidery. Blue Wing has probably sewed up her share of her brothers or other braves. But I do appreciate the intent."

"I'll fetch her then," she said, more relieved than annoyed. She was also pleased that they could discuss differences now without arguing. Besides, one quick glance into his little room had told her he was probably not even dressed under that buffalo robe draped across his middle from waist to knees as he sat on the bunk with his legs spread.

But Kate did hold the lamp for Blue Wing as she skillfully stitched his long gash with buffalo sinew. Though his pain must have been intense, he made not one sound beyond an initial grunt. He tipped his head back against the wall and seemed to press it there. Kate saw his fists and jaw clench; the powerful cords at the side of his throat tightened; sweat broke out across his forehead above his swollen nose and blackened eyes.

Even when he looked his best, she thought, Rand Cloud was not a handsome man, but even in his worst moments there was something utterly compelling about his rugged features and the fierce intensity that burned behind his eyes. And now, instead of pinching them closed, as she would have done, he stared at her as if challenging her to go through this agony with him, not to look away, to know he was strong and steady through it all.

She did not flinch from his gaze but stared back to tell him she admired his might, his "medicine." She only looked away from his consuming stare at last when she went out to find some alcohol to wash the wound a second time. She had used Gabe's rum before the stitching, but now she carried the lantern and a pitcher down in the hold to put some of Marbois's blasted medicinal spirits to good use.

But there she found she would have to take a bit from Stirling's yet untapped supply, for the "storm" had somehow managed to stave in every one of Marbois's fifteen remaining barrels of booze.

Kate never wanted to forget the day the limping *Red Dawn* put in for repairs along her piece of land abutting the Sky River. Even as the stretch of bank just past the confluence with that little tributary came in view, she whispered to herself, "I must remember this day, May 22, 1836."

For she had never owned a piece of land before; she realized now that Winterhaven had never really been hers. You might know, she mused, this property was hundreds of miles from home in Free Indian Territory. But Rand had said this was a seldom-used hunting preserve of various "subdued" tribes, who seemed not to bother whites at trading posts clinging to the river through here. It didn't matter, she supposed. She'd never live here, but it was so lovely, and it was hers. Unlike the steamer, it seemed solid and safe.

No wonder Clive had purchased this before it became designated Indian land and managed to hang on to it later, she thought, glad to be able to cling to one more good thing he had done. Had he planned a grand house here on the grassy brow above the river? A trading post? He had never mentioned this land, at least to her. Or had he meant to bring Blue Wing here, perhaps to have her closer to St. Louis? Kate did not intend to ask her friend. No good to dredge up those memories on this sunny day.

She could tell from her lofty position on the hurricane deck that each boundary of the sixty-acre property was different. On the east, a grassy, gradual slope edged the Missouri River, where they tied up to willows drooping slender new leaves in the current, still high from the rains. On the north side, richly wooded hills plunged to deep-shaded ravines. The western perimeter, though she couldn't tell where it ended from here, was rolling prairie. And the Sky River marked the south boundary where she wanted to begin her circuit of the land.

"You just go on ashore today and enjoy yourself," Gabe called down from the pilothouse. "You and Blue Wing got things as swept up as possible here till we do more repairs. The crew's gonna be busy, but you and the passengers can have a dry land day."

She pulled her eager gaze away from the view to squint up at him in the early morning sun. "A day without rain or snags or sandbars? That sounds as wonderful as it looks here, Gabriel."

With a basket of food and her painting supplies—the first time she had unpacked them—she went ashore with Blue Wing and Jamie. First they walked the meandering Sky River as it burbled over mossy rocks between which silver slips of minnows darted.

"Can I go fishing here, Mama?" Jamie asked.

"Maybe later, but first we want to look around," she told him, bending down to ripple the river with her hand. "I love this place already," she told Blue Wing.

The girl nodded and smiled. "It very good place. Old Woman in the Moon must love this river too. It have peace in its heart. She can see her face in its clear mirror. And when she do that, she give her blessing."

"Sky River, a *sinashush* place that reflects the sky. What would its name be in Mandan, my *manuka*, Ahpcha-Toha?" Kate asked.

"Passachta char-tosch," she whispered, her voice almost reverent. "River of Heavens. River of Sky."

* * *

The place did indeed seem heaven to Kate. They walked the boundary as best they could discern it. They ate lunch on the spot which Kate knew would be perfect for a trading post or house overlooking both the river and the prairie. She set up her little easel and got out her brushes and palette while Blue Wing and Jamie went back to the boat for a fishing pole, then dangled it in the ribbon of river below. Their laughter floated to her on the breeze from time to time.

Kate took off her bonnet and shook her hair free to enjoy the warm sun and cool breeze. When she stood on the big rock here, she could see the *Red Dawn* below, for this spot commanded a view of the whole area. She leaned back against the rock and began to paint.

As she outlined the spring prairie with the chain of blue hills beyond and puffs of clouds above, she realized that this was very like the scene she had done from the depths of her yearning the night of Clive's funeral. She had thought then the place must be the prairie outside St. Louis or a flight of fancy—or even a way to escape her fury. But it had been here, this place in her mind's eye, the very core of her dreams before she ever saw it. Although she had just arrived today and had not yet left her River of Sky land, she still missed it desperately already.

Wild strawberry blossoms visited by droning, besotted bees speckled the early bluestem grass she painted. Pale pink petals of shooting stars, blue lychnis, and early-budded prairie wild roses scattered themselves across the still-short grass to make a painter's palette to match her own. Both horned larks and meadowlarks serenaded her with their lilting songs while they darted here and there. She was breathless at the beauty.

"Kate!" Stirling's voice floated to her as he approached from the north forest glen in long strides. But for his wrinkled broadcloth coat, his top hat and garb made him seem to be out for a city stroll. "Mind if I join you for a moment?" He put down his sack, evidently bulging with specimens. When she acquiesced, he tossed his hat with his things and sat close to her on the rock. "This place of yours suits you," he said. "It is as lovely as you are."

She smiled and put her brush down to wipe her hands. Everything was perfect today; Stirling only enhanced the sunny scene. "I'm glad you like it," she told him. She was surprised her voice sounded as if she were about to cry. "Where would you put a cabin or trading post here?"

"You don't mean it?"

"No, I don't mean it. Just dreaming."

"It is a day for dreams," he said, and shifted even closer, leaning forward on his hand propped behind her hips. He brushed her blowing hair back from her face before she could. "I told you I am a dreamer, Kate."

"And that you would do anything to make those dreams come true. I met an artist once who told me, 'Never let anything make you forfeit your dreams.' "

"Exactly. And for me, you are fast becoming part of those dreams. Now don't protest, as I know we have not known each other long. And this rough ride upriver is not the place for proper courting. But surely you must know how I feel. You must feel it too!"

"Yes, but my responsibilities . . ."

"I know. Jamie, the ship, the need to get back on your feet financially. But I could help you more with Jamie and decisions, certainly with money. After this trip perhaps we could even go into a partnership, just the two of us, or with Gabe too. I am not a rich man, but I will have a steady job with a very influential mentor. Business partners could also be partners of another more intimate, familial kind, dearest, beautiful Kate. . . ."

He leaned closer, covering her hands with his free hand. She parted her lips; his kiss was warm and beseeching. His touch complemented the rich flow of her emotions here. Love and possibly marriage with Stirling? A father for Jamie, a sturdy shoulder to share the burdens? And this—this sweeping, sweet kiss . . .

Their lips parted, yet they hung suspended, inches apart, gazes locked, eyelashes almost brushing. "I don't mean to rush you, Kate," he whispered, "but will you not consider it?"

"Yes, I—of course, I will consider all of it."

"Then I am the happiest man alive. I will leave you

now to think. And," he added with a low laugh, "I must go put this squirrel and this snake in brandy."

"A snake?"

"Dead, so don't fret. I am certain it is a rattler."

"But no serpents are allowed in this Eden!" she told him, smiling shakily up at him as he stood. His eyes darted to her lips again. He reached down to cup her chin in his big hand, to stroke her cheek with his thumb. He darted a quick kiss to her pursed lips again, retrieved his hat, hefted his sack, and walked toward the river. He stopped and turned back to wave at her, before going jauntily on. Finally Kate remembered to breathe.

Her thoughts buzzed like the nearby bees. A suitor out here when she had thought it would be all business on the river. How long it had been since she had been courted and caressed. And the things he had said, promised, vowed—could she learn to trust again? He was younger, but so open and honest. He would not leave her alone in St. Louis if he worked for his mentor, General Clark. He came upriver only this once to see things before he settled down. It all seemed too good to be true, but it had fallen right in her lap.

She sat, not painting for how long she did not know. And then she heard a voice other than the distant voices of Jamie and Blue Wing. It was so close she jumped.

"Kate, I know I said it's pretty safe, but you shouldn't be sitting here alone in the middle of nowhere," said Rand, bareheaded and clad in his fringed buckskins as he came up, carrying his rifle. He limped from his leg wound, but it hadn't slowed him down. And though his broken nose was not so swollen now, it still looked a bit crooked.

"I'm not in the middle of nowhere. I feel like I'm home," she told him. She was very relieved he had not come upon her and Stirling earlier.

"It's a special spot," he admitted, and surprised her by perching on the same piece of rock Stirling had vacated. He laid his gun across his splayed knees.

"Your leg must be better."

"Believe it or not, I've had worse wounds than that."

"I believe it. I—I understand wounds of the heart as

well as the body." There, she thought, she'd said it. She had wanted him to realize she knew his past and therefore understood—even forgave—his volatile temperament.

"Blue Wing told you about my childhood at Mitutanka?" he asked, his voice taking on a too-familiar hard edge. "That woman talks too blasted much sometimes."

"I was glad she told me, so I could understand you."

"And you think you do?"

"Now I know why you were so distressed when I carried on about the reunion with my mother. I just want you to know that my mother and I . . . the reason we are close in heart, if not in miles, even as adults . . . is that my father . . . he used to drink and then . . . beat both of us, but her worse than me. At least you had two fathers, while I never really had one, not one who acted like a father."

He said nothing, so she turned to stare at him. He was listening intently, his eyes steady on her. They were such dark, beguiling pools she could almost swim in them. This close, she saw her reflection there. That is all she had meant to tell him, but now words kept pouring out with long-buried feelings of terror, the deepest buried memory of pain.

"I tried to shoot him once, you see, when he was . . . on her, hitting her. But his big rifle misfired. I had no idea how to aim it anyway. I was twelve. He screamed at me, broke the gun against the wall, just missing me, shattered windows, and the glass cut me. That's when Mama took me and went to her minister and finally left him, though she thought it was a sin, and . . . and Father fell down a flight of stairs in a brawl of some kind and broke his back and was paralyzed and died soon after. But you see, I could have shot him . . . too."

"And he would have deserved it, but my mother did not," he said.

"But I would have meant to do it, and you did not."

He nodded, his lips pressed tight together. Suddenly she was surprised to feel the wind cooling tears on her cheeks, and she swiped at them with the heels of her hands.

"Still," he said, his voice rough, "I can see why you

thought you could understand me. But no one can really, nor can I fully grasp your feelings, even when you share them. Not really."

"That's a sad, lonely philosophy of life, Rand Cloud."

"But it doesn't mean," he said, "a man or woman can't reach out for things they can share, to touch in other ways. . . ."

He reached for her wrists. His hands were warm, heavy bracelets. He turned her to him. She meant to protest what he obviously intended, but she was so surprised at his move, at this happening again so soon here, at the raw flicker of emotion in his eyes even his stoic face could not hide . . . and at her desire that he kiss her.

Yet she was not ready for this, unlike Stirling's kiss and caress. It came anyway, a torrent roaring over her, through her. No sweetness, no sunlight, no control. As in the storm she was swept away with awe and fear at his strength and the power of her own reaction.

He let his gun slide to the ground and half lifted, half hauled her into his lap. His kiss was devouring and hot, but she responded to match his demands, wrapping her arms around his neck, pressing to him. His thighs, wound and all, cradled her bottom; his chest crushed her breasts, hard to soft, angles to curves. His powder horn pressed hard against her hip where it was trapped between them. His hands molded her back and bottom as if she were soft clay; her fingers clasped solid shoulder muscles. Slanted, open mouths tasted more fully. She had never been kissed like this, for she could feel it down into the very bottom of her belly. They breathed as one, holding tight as if their rock were the only steady thing in the whole shifting world.

And then he set her back. He stood slowly, helping her stand.

"I don't know . . . how . . . that started," he said when he loosed her. "I didn't mean it to."

"But you did. We did," she managed to say, and shook out her skirts.

"Strange," he said, his voice so quiet, "but every time we argue I want to do that, and we were not arguing."

"It's just this place." She was floundering as she leaned

down to hand him his gun and hide her flushed face. She realized that her legs still shook, that he had changed this placid place for her forever, and this frightened her. And yet how much she had reveled in the burning power of his kiss, which reduced Stirling's warmth and sweetness to muted memory.

"If you were going hunting," she added, "you'd best head out before you lose the light."

"I wasn't going hunting. I came to tell you something important, to clear the air between us. But I guess I fogged it up more than ever."

"Came to tell me what?"

"Maybe it should wait until another time." At last he looked away from studying her. "All right, since we started this today," he said as if he'd just made some new decision, "I guess I'd better get it out before it festers any longer. You have a right to know, and I don't want you to hear it from someone else at Bellevue or Fort Clark."

"Hear *what*?"

"Kate, I realize you have no hint that your husband's biggest backer was Cadet Chouteau himself."

"What? That can't be! They were rivals, though Chouteau bought some of Clive's ships when they went on the block."

"Those were Chouteau's steamers from the beginning, as well as a lot of Clive's other investments and backing. Evidently, but for the *Red Dawn* and this piece of land, Chouteau owned Clive lock, stock, and barrels of liquor."

"But Clive would surely have told me—" she got out before the stupidity of that argument hit her hard. Surely this could not be something *else* Clive had not told her. It resurrected everything he had not shared.

"That's impossible," she insisted. "Clive was proud to be Chouteau's competition. Those ships weren't Chouteau's because he even asked if he could buy them back or help me financially at the funeral."

"And you're believing Chouteau now."

"No, but I'm not believing you either! You have no right to speak ill of a dead man who can't defend himself."

"Think about it," he said, and leaned his gun against the rock to grasp her shoulders hard. She tried to shake loose, but he did not budge. "Chouteau was wily to have a 'free' competitor to point to, one to prove he did not have a monopoly to give him a bad name with the Indians, General Clark, and the government in Washington. And Clive was wily to let Chouteau finance the business he could have had no other way. I was worried at first that Chouteau was now paying for the *Red Dawn,* but I see now that was crazy."

"Yes, crazy . . ." she echoed as her mind ticked off all the other things she knew about Clive's company that had suddenly turned up under Chouteau's control—the *Sally Kate,* even Captain Marcus—and Chouteau had almost reclaimed Sam's warehouse.

"But Clive was proud to trade fair with the Mandans!" she protested, fighting her own fears now as well as Rand's accusations. If she wasn't loyal to Clive on this last thing, Jamie would have nothing from his father. "I am carrying on for him, for Jamie! Just let go of me and get off my land! Back to the steamboat—my steamboat— let me go. . . ."

He loosed her then, stepped back, picked up his gun again. "I am sorry I told you here but not sorry I told you," he said. "I should have known you'd react emotionally and not rationally, not at first anyway. I'll be just over there waiting until you are ready to return to the boat."

"Don't bother! Just keep on going . . . for good!" she shouted, and then felt heartily ashamed. Just a few days ago she was desperate he had been lost along the river. Curse the man!

She spun her back to him as he walked away. She stared out over prairie stretching to the hills. Why did it always have to be that this man ruined things for her? Clive's dedication to help the Mandans in the face of Chouteau's might and this land now were all she had left to honor of Clive from her past. Her own words that she was "carrying on for Clive, for Jamie" echoed through her brain.

And then a new thought came to her as if it were a gift bestowed by this beautiful place.

As she had seen Blue Wing do so many times, she crossed her ankles and sank gracefully to the ground. She put her elbows on her knees, her head in her hands. She was hiding herself from Rand's view if he stayed near like a watchdog, but she could not hide from herself anymore. She put her arms behind her and leaned back on them, looking up at the sky above this place that felt so right to her.

"I'm *not* doing this *just* for Jamie," she said aloud as the revelation shook her. "Not just for money or Blue Wing or for the Mandans. And *not* for Clive's memory. I am following the river to a new life because it is what *I* want to do for *me*."

It seemed an utterly radical, revolutionary thought. To be in control of and responsible for her own life. No father, no mother, no husband, no lawyer, no smug society to tell her what she must do. She could barely conceive of what it meant, yet she held to this new realization of her power—her spirit "medicine"—as she knew she would always cling to this piece of land, however far away from it she was. Her River of Sky would always mark for her not only the heart of the frontier but the frontier of her heart, a new, bold beginning.

And just as Blue Wing had told her an Indian must find a sign of a sacred, protective *xopini* spirit when he or she became an adult, she picked up a concave piece of smooth stone that must have fallen off the big rock. She grasped it in her hands, turning it around, feeling how real it was.

She sat there a very long time. She sensed Rand nearby, but he did not disturb her. Nothing did for these moments in the flow of her life, however long or short it would be. She heard Blue Wing and Jamie come looking for her and Rand's deep voice telling them she wanted to be alone but would be back to the boat soon. She felt grateful to him, even thankful he had cut her last cords to Clive. She felt strangely free and whole.

The blue arc of sky began to deepen to dusk; swallows flitted and a few fireflies blinked their tiny gold lanterns.

The sun slanted lower, and the heavens turned to hues of orchid, violet, and pink as if to make this whole place one grand painting. At last she stood, gathered her things, and started back. But as she walked down the hill, back to the life she had chosen—no matter what events had pushed her to it—she stopped on the brow of the hill where Rand awaited. She nodded to him, and he to her. Below, she saw two things.

Stirling walked up toward her with Jamie. And the mighty Missouri had taken on the muted pinks and blues hanging above her land, River of Sky.

Sitting cross-legged on the hurricane deck with his back against the steamer's yawl, Rand watched steam pour from the glowing hot escapement pipe in front of him. It hissed so loud even on half steam it almost drowned the boat's huffing to make it to Bellevue before nightfall. The crew had sealed off the hole for the fallen chimney and floated it with logs alongside the boat. With that extra burden, even on part power, the *Red Dawn* tilted and dragged and forced its firemen to work harder to feed the fireboxes to shove them upriver.

In a way he felt like that too. Ever since this voyage—since Kate Craig—had come along this summer, he had been on half steam, fighting a huge current, dragging an added burden. He had promised General Clark and himself he would be solely dedicated to his new position to help his mother's people, but too often he thought about Kate—wanted Kate, damn her. And though it distracted him, he worried about her safety, for she was still what his father used to call a babe in the woods out here. As far as he knew, no white woman had ever been above Bellevue, certainly not up to Sioux and Mandan country. At least she would leave the boy behind, but he wished she would stay herself.

He feared that his single-minded desire to destroy Marbois's barrels of booze might have endangered her even more. He'd also promised General Clark he would get along with Blackwell and Marbois, then set himself, and possibly her, up for confrontation with them. But just as when it came to Kate, he had acted and then considered the consequences later. Why did it have to be like that when a woman began to cling?

But now he'd just steer clear of her. Let Stirling Mount worry about her! They made silly cow eyes at each other all the time; when Kate looked at Rand, she either narrowed her gaze or glanced quickly away. He could read her reluctance to repeat or even to recall what had happened between them at what she was now calling River of Sky. Let Stirling Sweetness-and-Light have her and good riddance!

At least—Rand tried to buck himself up—he and Kate did not fight anymore, and that was one thing, the *only* good thing, that had happened so far. As a matter of fact, more and more she seemed to trust him. As they got farther into hostile territory, that could be helpful. Besides, the emotional steam they had blown off had just been a product of the moment and the place. He felt calmer now; yes, he definitely did. He was even glad she would get to see her mother.

But when Bellevue emerged from around the next bend, and the crew and passengers cheered to see the little cluster of fenced wooden buildings clinging to the hills, he felt his heart harden again. As the steamboat bell clanged, he heard Kate shout from the deck below, "Tell Mrs. Barton her daughter's here! Her grandson too! Tell Miriam Barton!"

Traders, trappers, and workers gathered along the wooded banks. Steamboat arrivals were always an event this far upriver. Folks popped out of cottage doors and the few fields of new corn beyond. Broad-faced Omahas, wrapped in blankets, materialized from everywhere with dogs yapping at their feet. And one petite white woman emerged from a cabin door, waving her apron and crying, "Katie? My Katie!" as she ran down to the river.

Rand tried to stop the emotions, but they blew him apart anyway. His own mother, running from the lodge toward him, waving, calling his name, her arms outstretched, her black hair flying, her eyes alight with love after he was lost in the woods that day just before he lost her for good. He sniffed hard as Kate tore down the gangplank the minute it dropped and flew into her mother's arms. Jamie ran after her, squealing in excitement. Stirling got off more slowly and just stood there, evidently waiting to be presented, but the crying, hugging women ignored him.

Tears and emotion were always traps! Rand thought. He stood and went down to the main deck. In all this chaos he didn't even want to go looking for Major Dougherty or Major Beauchamp, the Omaha, Oto, and Pawnee Indian agent and subagent who were stationed here. He'd talk to them later. Like many places along the river, Bellevue had once been an independent post that was now in the government and Chouteau's hands, and all of a sudden that annoyed him more than ever.

"Pete!" he called to the ship's carpenter. "They won't put you to work for a while. Let's get some game, as there will probably be some sort of welcome home feast."

Without waiting to see if Pete followed, Rand grabbed his gun, disembarked, skirted the noisy reunion, and strode up the single twisting dirt street of Bellevue toward the upland forest.

Kate, Jamie, and Miriam sat in the Bartons' small cabin that afternoon, talking and talking. Tom Barton, Kate's stepfather, sandy-haired and big-shouldered, joined them and made Kate even happier by saying he'd be glad to help the ship's blacksmith repair the fallen chimney and they could get the other "boys" to help hoist it back in place.

"Chouteau might not like it when he hears, but he's one who's got to understand blood's thicker 'n water," Tom told her with a nod at Miriam. "The big man's always pulling trading post folks into his family through marriage, so no wonder they're loyal to him, and I am too, but when family's concerned, that comes first!"

Later Tom pried the squirming Jamie from Miriam's embrace and took him outside to "whoop it up a bit." Blue Wing came to help as they prepared dinner. It was not Blue Wing who got in the way, but the curious Omaha women toting wide-eyed infants on back-strapped baby boards. Strings of wampum dangled from the women's ears; smallpox scars pitted many of their broad faces.

And they wanted to touch Kate's face. "I don't think you've been wearing a proper bonnet lately, Katie girl." Mama scolded her lightly. "It's those golden freckles on your nose and cheeks that fascinate them." They also wanted a handout of the food, but Mama said they would never be satisfied with just a taste and shooed them out with a broom, even when Kate was all for feeding them. But through it all Kate and Mama exchanged news and sometimes stopped their busy hands just to stare and smile at each other.

Miriam Fencer Warfield Barton was a faded portrait of her daughter. She was delicate-looking but with the same sturdy constitution she had bequeathed Kate. Her hair, once Kate's rich honey hue, was now silvering in her forty-ninth year. Her life, first with an abusive husband and now on the frontier, had etched permanent frown lines on her once-fine skin, but she smiled frequently today. She was a strong woman, in convictions too, and it showed in the cast of her brow and steely blue eyes.

"And you're happy here, really happy, Mama, I can tell."

"Yes, with my Tom, Katie. Oh, there has been a valley or two, but none that has been really his doing, and that's the difference, praise God. If it wasn't for being away from you and yours—especially now that Clive's gone—I'd be perfectly content. But to have this gift from heaven—you to visit now and then and Jamie to stay with us a spell—oh, my Katie, I'm so blessed to see you, and you've been through so many things without me to help!"

They hugged for the hundredth time despite floury hands and the return onslaught of curious Omaha women. "So much still to say, so much to get caught up on," Mama said as she once more urged her unwanted visitors out the door and this time latched it.

Using some of the boat supplies, some from the post, that night, they fed three women, Jamie, and seven men: Tom, Stirling, Captain Zeke, Gabe, Bill, Pete—and Rand. Rand had brought in venison but ate quickly, thanked them, and went off to see the other Indian agents. Stirling stayed on to charm her mother until Tom coaxed him out for another walk with him and Jamie.

"I can see how much Tom loves you, Mama," Kate said as they finally sat on the wooden settle before the low-burning hearth. "He seems so mindful of your feelings. The valleys of marriage you mentioned before—nothing like with Father?"

"Mercy, no, sweetheart. And with Tom's love—and that of the good Lord God—I've forgiven, if not quite forgotten, all of that. You know, I married your father too quickly and for the wrong reasons because I was afraid to be alone after my mama's death and losing my father heading west. Your father vowed to give me protection and a home when we got to St. Louie. But I didn't have to marry Tom Barton—married him for love. He's a brawny man who deals with iron and flame, but he's kind-spirited. And, Katie, what a kindly suitor you have too in Mr. Mount. And he's asked you to marry him?"

"Yes, later, when we return to St. Louis. I've no definite plans until this run can be made, so I haven't exactly accepted."

"He'd be a fine man for you, I can tell. Calm-tempered, trustworthy, ambitious, and only drank one mug of beer. He's dashing too, and he'd be a good provider for you and Jamie. And with those blond good looks, folks will think he's Jamie's father anyway. And he'd be a homebody, unlike Clive."

"Yes, all that—I know."

"And if you try to build some kind of trade business, he could run it for you with his bookkeeping talents and all. Sweetheart, what is it?"

"It's just I never really meant to be looking for another man so soon after Clive. I've just realized I've been enjoying leading my own life, I guess."

"But that's what I was saying earlier. You'd wed Stirling Mount not because you have to but because you want to. I married your father after I'd known him but two weeks, and you got swept off your feet pretty fast by Clive with all his big ideas. But, Katie, a woman was meant to be wed, to be a helpmeet to a man—as long as he's a good man. 'Wives, be in obedience to your husbands and husbands, love your wives,' as the Good Book says."

"That works out fine, depending on the man's definition of love and obedience. But I've made one mistake in picking a man—just like you, Mama—and don't mean to make another."

Miriam reached over and took Kate's hand. "I know. You and I learned the hard way, didn't we? But we've got your grandmama Fencer's blood in us too, and she loved her man with everything she had till she died of fever in Chillicothe, sitting in that rocking chair of hers, the week before we were all to head west, as if she couldn't bear to leave her home behind."

"I know, Mama. I'm so sorry that I lost the chair, but like I said, it saved a man's life."

"Now just listen, as I'm not arguing that. Your grandmama loved that fire-and-brimstone man of hers, however hard he was to live with at times. He was stern, strict, but she stuck by him through thick and thin, through traveling and all sorts of his crazy ideas about the end of the world coming and all that. She didn't want to leave Ohio, but my father heard the unsaved souls of St. Louie calling. Sometimes I think the only way she could keep a home for once was in her grave. Katie, that's why I still regret not going to nurse your father when he fell down those stairs and couldn't walk. Lester Warfield was a hard, bad man, but I should have forgiven him there and then to stick with him, help him, and I didn't. But like I was saying, though you and I've each had a bad misstep in marriage, I've got a good man now, and you could too. You just listen to your mama."

Though she had sworn to live her own life now, Kate did listen. And she was so glad to tell Mama everything—or almost everything. For she had said next to nothing of Rand Cloud beyond how she had lost the rocking chair in the storm. From now on, Kate decided, she must respond only to Stirling's love rather than to what, for Rand, must be only lust.

Three days later—more time than they should have spent, but Kate told herself the big repairs excused it—they were almost ready to cast off. She had even repainted large, rebuilt portions of the ship with bright white and yellow paint that had been sitting forgotten in a Bellevue storehouse. They had laid in fresh meat and dried wood. Today she had hugged Jamie good-bye ten times, given him all the advice she could think of, stroked the stubborn little cowlick on his blond head, and said, "I love you, and I will be back before the leaves turn their bright colors."

She left Mama the sketch she had done of herself by looking in a mirror and took the drawings of Mama and Tom with her to make a marriage portrait for them. But just before they began the final loading of the boat, her mother said, "Katie, do you have just a moment more? That valley in my marriage I mentioned—I wasn't going to say a word, as Tom and I decided we'd never speak of it, but I told him I wanted to tell you, and maybe we were wrong."

"Whatever is it?"

"Just come on up here with me and leave the boy to watch the loading, won't you?"

Kate thought she had explored thoroughly all three levels of the little "village" of Bellevue. But today Mama led her higher, up a twisting path to a small opening above the trees hidden beside a big field of newly planted corn. And there under a single oak tree stood a small fenced area with four wooden tombstones, one of which Mama pulled her to and pointed out.

"I—Tom and I—had a change of life baby, Katie, a sister to you. Smallpox took her when it was plaguing the Omahas and Poncas—I guess some Omahas brought it in, though they'd supposedly been immunized—and she died in three days, barely two months old. When Clive came through twice that year, I never mentioned it, first when I was breeding at my age, after because of all the pain we had to lose her."

"And now you have to look at those Omaha squaws with their smallpox markings and their babies all the time."

"Mercy, it really wasn't their fault. You'll find the red man doesn't understand some things and won't be convinced. Some in the tribes, even when white doctors came through here, refused to be vaccinated because they weren't sick yet and no amount of explaining helped. One of the doctors tried to tell them it was just cowpox disease, an illness in a milder form to protect them from a worse one to come, and then they really thought the whites were crazy. No, it just wasn't God's plan that my little one should live, and I don't blame those poor Omaha heathens."

"That's just like you to be so forgiving, Mama."

"I told you, Katie, I never forgave your father in time. And I do blame myself about losing the baby too, because if we still lived in St. Louie, I could have had her inoculated and she would have been saved. I had a few bitter words to Tom about us living out here, which I regretted later."

"But she was so young, Mama. The doctor didn't do Jamie's immunization until this year. Just terrible luck."

"When you believe in the hand of God, nothing's really luck, Katie. It's all lessons for living."

"Losing her—Leah Miriam—" she added as she read the carefully carved headstone, "was not just some lesson any more than my losing Sally. They were really important individuals, important to God and to us! Just think," she said as she sank to her knees by the little mound as Mama knelt beside her, "this is my sister. I always wanted a sister, and strange as it seems, Mama, Blue Wing's come closest to being that. I'm so sorry you lost Leah but so glad you told me. One thing Blue Wing taught me is that it's better to have had the child to love and remember than not to have had her at all."

She was momentarily tempted to tell Mama all about Blue Wing's beliefs about the Baby Hill, but she knew better. If she herself thought that sort of talk was absurd, what would Mama think of it?

"I guess," Mama said, "it makes it better to bear that I told you at least. I wouldn't have wanted you to hold back about Clive or about losing any of the things you did this last year."

"I have lost a lot, but I've found things too, Mama," she said, and put her arm around the older woman's shoulders. "I feel like I've found you again and . . . kind of found myself."

"And a man to love," Mama put in, and Kate nodded.

Until they heard the distant bell aboard the ship, calling them to cast off, they sat there, the two of them, Kate thought, like silent living monuments to what was gone and would never be again. But they had shared their love and memories, and there was strength in that.

Chapter 10

"Kate, you've seemed different since our stops at River of Sky and Bellevue," Stirling observed one evening as they strolled the deck, her arm linked in his. He was relieved to find a night when MacLeod was spending time with the *engagés* belowdecks instead of smoking that damned pipe of his nearby. It had really bothered him lately that Kate was so busy it seemed he hardly ever got her off alone anymore, even with Jamie out from underfoot.

"Changed how?" she asked.

"You are more subdued, sadder. Please, dear, if there is anything I can do . . ."

"Fly back to Bellevue and fetch Jamie to see me," she told him with a rueful laugh and shake of her head. "I've been missing him something awful, Stirling. And now that I've seen the might of the river, I worry more that I've risked so much to take it on."

"You sound ready to head back now."

"No, we didn't come over five hundred miles to Bellevue and beyond to go back. For many reasons, I can't go back again. . . . But sometimes I feel my worries are reaching out to grab at me like the huge snags in the river, like those right out there," she added, and pointed an accusing finger at the now-ghostly branches which looked like giant, protruding elk horns in the inky water. Stirling had even helped Gabe laboriously saw away a massive snag one branch at a time before they could proceed today, but Kate's gratitude had been worth the effort.

"And then I tell myself," she went on as he clasped her arm even closer to his ribs, "I'm a lucky woman who should not complain or get downcast. Lucky that I have Jamie, Blue Wing, the ship, my piece of land, lucky—blessed, as she would put it, that my mother's happy—and really I am too."

"I would dare to hope so," he put in, trying to keep his voice light but wanting to press his advantage. "After all, you have me at your eternal beck and call. And you could be happier yet if you would but say the word—or maybe three of them, Kate." He turned her to face him and dropped his hands to her waist to draw her closer. She placed her palms flat on his chest but did not resist.

"And what words are those?" she asked. A wisp of smile lifted her lips; the tease in her tone tingled from the nape of his neck to his loins when he realized she could play the coquette. And how dreary he had once thought his task aboard this old ship would be!

"How about 'I love you'?" he whispered. "Or how about 'Stirling, my love,' or 'Yes, I will!' "

"Marry you, you mean? I thought we decided we can't think of such things now. But I must admit you know how to lift a lady's spirits out here, Stirling."

He grabbed the chance, even though he steeled himself not to grab her as he wanted. He lowered his mouth to hers and took a long, deep kiss. She seemed merely welcoming at first, then eager. At her response he could have soared high enough to fly back to Bellevue to fetch Jamie—or better yet, all the way back to St. Louis, triumphant, with her held captive in his arms.

Other difficulties abounded during the next days, but Kate tried to face each new challenge with a stout heart. Besides the fact that prairie fires had encroached to destroy some stands of trees, good wood began to thin. They made frequent stops where everyone but Captain Zeke combed the shore for dry wood. The hearty burners like oak, ash, and hickory disappeared. They took sandbar willow, cottonwood, as well as random pieces racked up along the shore, including those "elk horns" they sawed off. Wet wood burned poorly without handfuls of rosin thrown into the fireboxes, and none of them had thought to bring along buckets of that.

The soft banks along the river here were like sucking quicksand if one stepped on them. Sandbars and shallows were trickier and more frequent. They had to zigzag their way through the section called the Devil's Raceground. Repeatedly they were forced to "grasshopper" the boat over barriers of sand with the sturdy wooden spars that could be lowered and used like giant crutches to "walk the boat" to deeper water.

"See what I mean, Kate?" Gabe said one day when he saw her leaning on the rail and frowning out over the river. "The wide Missouri's a lot like life with its problems, but somehow, we keep steaming on. And you just wait, 'cause we're gonna hit us a good spell soon. The snowmelt from the Rockies is due to give us some real good water, however much we're gonna have to fight the faster current."

Gabe was right. On the last day of May the so-called June rise rushed at them to give them good water. But no one had mentioned the new threat of dead buffalo carcasses roaring downriver to get wedged under and tangled in the paddles.

"You might know," Kate remarked to Rand as they stood on the prow one day, "I've been wanting to see a beautiful buffalo in the wild, and these are all dead and bloated."

"Sometimes I'm afraid if the U.S. government and some whites have their way, they're all going to be dead."

"You can't mean that," she said. "I heard there are thousands in the northern herds. You are very bitter about the government, yet you work for it."

"I see myself as working *for* the Indians and working *toward* the government's being fair to them. When you have been with the Mandans awhile, you'll see what I mean. How long are you planning to trade at Mitutanka and Ruptare?"

"I don't know. Probably not as long as I had hoped, as I'm still missing Jamie so much my arms and heart feel empty."

"Lucky Jamie," he said, and strolled off downwind to light his pipe.

* * *

The next day, as they approached the spot on the river where Lewis and Clark had named several landmarks after a Mr. Floyd, a man who died on their expedition, Kate was able to repay some of the kindnesses Gabe had shown her. Something had not set well on his usually cast-iron stomach, and he was vomiting over the aft rail back by the toilet. Soon he was as weak as a baby. She and Stirling helped him to his cabin.

"You just lie there and don't worry about a thing," she told the queasy man. "I'll go up and help Captain Zeke spot landmarks and he can steer for a while, or I can do that at his bidding, like you do, Gabriel."

"It's too hard a pull," Gabe whispered, his complexion chalky white. "Take Stirling or Rand."

"Now don't you worry. And just knock on the wall for Stirling if you need anything else," she told him as they went out and closed the door.

"Stirling, I hope you don't mind staying in your cabin for a spell, in case he needs you."

"Anything," Stirling said, and tugged her closer in the corner of the deserted common room, "to help a friend of yours. But please remember *I* need you. And I would rather help you in the pilothouse."

"I'll call down if that's necessary. I've spent a lot of time up there with the two of them, so I'm good for a few hours of steering with Captain Zeke's help."

"I am glad to see you determined instead of melancholy. And I'm glad it isn't over my asking for your hand—and actually asking for the *very* lovely rest of you."

She smiled at his banter as he squeezed her waist. She had managed to put on weight and regain her more shapely form on the river, despite the work and worries. But how brave Stirling was to always be so light-hearted—especially when Rand could be so dour.

She kissed Stirling before he could kiss her this time and climbed the narrow stairs to the hurricane deck. Rand sat there, staring out at the passing banks as if looking for something or someone, but he did not see her. She went up the iron steps to the pilothouse. Captain Zeke sat on his high stool, his hands clutching the wheel, which he didn't like to steer. But he wasn't looking where he was going; his head was drooped as if he peered straight down. Surely he had not fallen asleep!

"Captain Zeke, if you just tell me what to do, I'm here to help you."

He didn't speak or turn.

"Captain Zeke?"

She touched his shoulder, and he toppled off the stool against her. He was not heavy, but the shock took her down to her knees.

"Annie, thank God, you came back!" he whispered. His eyes were glazed; his body was limp. He shuddered and went still.

"Rand!" she screamed toward the open door. "Rand!"

He came thudding up the steps, rifle in his hand. "Have you spotted some—" he said before he saw what had happened. He grabbed the ship's wheel.

"Is he dead?" he asked.

"I think so. There's no neck pulse. But he was fine at dinner! What could have taken him so fast—like this?"

"Kate, the man told me he was seventy-two. Too much living. Old age took him—or a bad heart."

"It's just that he seemed still strong and . . . two deaths in two weeks! Rand, we can't go on without Captain Zeke!"

"We have to! I'll hold the wheel, but you go down and get Gabe, even if he's ill. Kate, I said, put the captain down right there and go get Gabe to tie this thing up or whatever we have to do. Go on!"

She felt as if she were moving through thick water, like the ship itself. She went for Gabe, told him. Despite his weakness and shock, he hurried upstairs and took the wheel from Rand.

"Did he say anything 'fore he went?" he asked Kate.

"Only, 'Annie, thank God, you came back.' "

"His wife. I hope he thought so. I hope it made him happy."

"Gabriel, we should never have let him come upriver!"

"Talk about making him happy! That's what you did for him by putting him in charge, Kate. Remember he said he loved being a captain almost as much as he'd loved his wife?"

"Yes. He felt wanted and needed even after he was deserted."

"That's right. I learned that helps the hard way when my brothers deserted me all those years ago," Gabe said, and dashed out to retch over the rail again.

Rand and Kate grabbed for the wheel together. "Thank you for helping me," she told him, her voice shaky.

"You have helped me too," he said. "Gabe and I will get the boat against the bank, and we'll bury the old man. You go fetch some roosters to carry him down."

"All right. Oh, Rand, I'm so afraid without him."

He seized her upper arm as Gabe came back in to take the wheel. Gabe looked at them, then away at the river. "Don't be afraid," Rand told her, his voice hard and his face angry. "It's the worst thing you can do in these parts. If you're afraid, you make mistakes, and no one can afford that, especially you."

"Yes ... I ... you're right. I'm going to have to help take Captain Zeke's place somehow. Rand, you have been upriver all those times; could you help too? Captain Zeke and Gabe have been only as far as Fort Pierre, but you've been all the way and more than once."

"If I can, but I'm no boatman. I watch what's along the river, not the river itself."

She nodded and bent down to cover the dead man's face with her handkerchief. Strangely, in this new loss she felt strong again, stronger than she had since River of Sky. "Ezekiel Pickens was a fine captain and even a better man," she said. "He could have died of a broken heart or a tired one, but never a bad one."

Gabe nodded at the wheel, and Rand's eyes met hers. As the boat bumped the bank, she hurried out and down the steps.

Kate and Gabe said more good things about Captain Ezekiel Pickens when they buried him that evening just before dusk beside Floyd's grave near Floyd's River under Floyd's Hills. It was starkly pretty here. Gabe gave a speech about "blessed are the peacemakers" and ended,

"The Lord giveth and the Lord taketh away." After snatching a few caps off roosters' heads to make them show proper respect, Kate recited the Twenty-third Psalm, thinking all the time about the green pastures and still water of her beautiful River of Sky. But the words about fearing no evil and being comforted further calmed her heart, even as Rand had helped do earlier, even as Stirling had lifted her spirits. Now she walked between them back to the ship, her hands on their arms.

After that Rand and Kate took turns in the pilothouse with Gabe, who put in almost every hour of daylight there. The June rise was a blessing now as they passed Cedar Island with the first live buffalo and elk they had seen. Rand told them when they reached the Dry River, that would mark the southern border of Sioux territory. But Kate recalled his words not to be afraid or she would make mistakes. No, as he had said, she could not afford those now.

As they put into the Sioux Indian agency at Fort Lookout, where some of the tribe camped in the summer to trade, she breathed a sigh of temporary relief for a day off the river. The fort had been built over ten years before by the once-independent Columbia Fur Company but had passed into Chouteau's hands. That fact, as well as their many delays, was one reason they were pushing on early tomorrow morning.

Kate stood with her passengers at the upper deck rail, scanning the tanned-hide tepees which encircled the walled fort. Even crew members had come up on deck to catch a glimpse of their first Sioux, and several of the *engagés* and trappers would be getting off here until the *Red Dawn* or some other steamer or keelboats headed south at the end of the summer.

To welcome every steamer here, ceremonial cannon were shot off from the blockhouse and the American flag was lowered and raised again. During that, at least fifty braves and a few curious women and children spilled down to the waterfront to stare and gesture—at her! No, even though Rand seemed to fear and mistrust the Sioux, she would not be afraid, Kate vowed, and she gripped the rail tighter.

"I'll bring the Sioux agent, Major Bean, on board to meet you later," Rand said as he stood by her on one side, with Stirling on the other. "It's probably smart not to go ashore if you don't want to be pawed."

"It's my freckles, isn't it?"

Rand's lips tilted to a tight grin. "It's fair skin and fair hair on the fair sex," he said. "I doubt if any of these Sioux have seen a white woman. One of them asked me once, 'Why is it white men are so interested in our Indian women? Do they not have women of their own?' Now they know for sure."

"Not only do whites have women of their own," Stirling put in with a possessive arm around her and a frown at Rand, "but you are my woman, Kate. And Rand is right: You must not go ashore."

"It's nice to hear you two agreeing, but I am not here to take orders from my passengers or cower—even before the Sioux. I believe someone told me not to be afraid, not to show fear. So, if you two gentlemen will excuse me, I will greet just a few of these people. Blue Wing, you said you would come with me," she called to her.

But Kate's bravado did not keep her knees from knocking or her lower lip from trembling as she and Blue Wing disembarked. The Sioux, she thought, looked to be a better lot than the Ioways and Omahas she had seen: handsomer, cleaner, and better attired. Rand, no doubt, would say it was because the whites had not corrupted or corralled them yet. They looked tall and strong, with dark brown well-featured faces. The men wore their hair long over the shoulders, some with feathers stuck in it. Beads and silver medals, painted leather leggings, tomahawks in hand—she would love to paint them. But now she held her head as erect as they and walked the gangplank.

A communal gasp went up as they surged toward her. She grasped Blue Wing's wrist and stood her ground. Suddenly Stirling and Rand were beside her. But the crowd parted and passed by her as if she were an island in the current. The four of them spun around to see what had happened.

Though a few threw a backward glance at Kate, the Sioux had surrounded poor Bill Blake, where he stood at the top of the gangplank, just watching. Braves patted his short, curly hair; squaws touched his black face, trying to rub the "color" off. Some held their children up to see. Bill's eyes were as big and white as saucers in his dark face as they pressed in on him.

"They might never have seen a white woman, but they have seen white skin," Rand said, and started to laugh. "But they've never seen a black man before, not one who is not painted. And since black paint on the face means a man is on the warpath, who knows what they're thinking about poor Bill? Mrs. Katherine Craig, I'm afraid your debut as the belle of the ball will have to come later."

"That isn't funny," she told him. But they were all laughing, and she joined in. "Maybe we'd better rescue Bill."

"No," Rand said, "it looks like they're going to give him gifts, though what a steamship blacksmith will do with beads and tomahawks is beyond me."

A high-pitched voice spoke behind them. "Probably start his own trading company, just like Mrs. Craig. All Craigs think they can trade on their own, Major MacLeod, ain't you heard?"

Everyone spun to face a bearded man with a livid scar marring his left brow and cheek. Kate recognized him at once as Jacques Marbois, and her heart began to pound. She had not expected to have to explain to him about his lost barrels before Fort Clark. Rand, who looked anything but pleased to see the man too, took care of introductions when she had expected him to curse the man. But Marbois himself was staring at Blue Wing, his eyes narrowed as if to study her; Blue Wing returned the stare.

"Now this fine-looking Mandan gal," Marbois said to Rand as if he could not address Blue Wing directly, "you say she's the one General Clark took in? Ask her if we ain't met before—at Fort Clark, I mean," he ordered Rand.

"Ask her yourself, Marbois. Her English is much better than your Mandan," Rand countered.

"That right?" Marbois asked Blue Wing. "You know me, gal?"

"I not think so, but if you Chouteau's chief trader, not want to," she said, then turned and walked away, giving a wide berth to the crowd of Sioux still surrounding Bill Blake.

"How are my barrels faring—medicine for the fort?" Marbois asked Kate, evidently only too glad to ignore Blue Wing's snub.

Kate did not blanch. She stared the man straight in the eye. "You should have warned me that the soldiers at Fort Leavenworth would confiscate some, but at least I warned you that we didn't have insurance," she said. "When I went down into the hold to check on those barrels remaining after a horrible storm nearly capsized us and killed one of our men, every barrel the soldiers had chosen to leave us was broken, evidently from being bounced around."

"Hellfire, you don't mean it?"

"I'm afraid she does, Marbois," Rand put in. "I saw it myself. But at least all that medicine won't fall into the wrong hands, someone unscrupulous, who might misuse it for something else. Besides, it's smallpox medicine we need to bring to the Mandans, not some molasses-colored rum, don't you think so?"

"Why, you . . ." he said so menacingly before his high voice trailed off that Kate shuddered. Besides, she could smell whiskey on his breath even in the fresh river breeze. But rather than explode, as she expected, Marbois merely shrugged. Perhaps she had misjudged the man if he was going to let the loss of his barrels pass so magnanimously.

"Wal, that's a shame, 'cause it will be another long winter up there, especially since General Clark thinks we'll all just be sitting tight and cozy there this year, eh, MacLeod? And sure, if you want to get on your high horse again about smallpox problems, I'll back you. Don't want no plague stopping the tribe from coming in with furs and robes to trade."

Kate listened intently. If all the Missouri tribes had been inoculated for pox, why had the Mandans been skipped? She thought about the scarred Omaha women, about her dead baby sister, and about how Dr. Beaumont had insisted Jamie be immunized when it slipped her mind when Clive died. Fortunately he had vaccinated Blue Wing too. Now Marbois turned to her again.

"Ma'am, let me put a proposition to you, since them barrels been lost. I was just visiting some friends here and need a ride back upriver to Fort Clark. If I could have a piece of deck for my blanket, I'd call us even on the loss of all them medicinal spirits."

Kate could tell that idea riled Rand, and she knew Marbois was in Chouteau's employ. But as Rand had put it once, most people on the river were. Rand had also said he wanted to get along with both Major Blackwell and Marbois so he could convince them to treat the Mandans better. Marbois had just said he would help Rand with the smallpox protection problem. Besides, she would tell everyone to keep a good eye on the man. She was just grateful he hadn't claimed she owed him for the ruined barrels.

"All right then," she said, "as long as you obey the steamer and company rules of Craig Independent Shipping and Transport all the way to Fort Clark. I hope you won't mind taking orders from an independent and a woman, Mr. Marbois."

"You know, ma'am, I think I could get right used to it for a spell," he said, smiling to display crooked teeth. "And that way, I'd return whatever courtesies you feel fit to extend when you reach Fort Clark."

"Why, thank you, sir. I just hope you will convey to Monsieur Chouteau that Craig Independent will offer the Mandans fair prices, and if he wants to be at all competitive, he must too." On Stirling's arm, she skirted the slowly dwindling crowd around Bill Blake and went back aboard.

"What a hell of a woman!" she heard Marbois's sharp voice behind her, but if Rand replied, his deep voice was lost in the babble of the Sioux.

During an afternoon repair and wood stop two days later, the *Red Dawn*'s roosters cut off dead limbs and sawed up fallen trees in a cedar stand. This land along the river was flat with sporadic overgrown ravines. A dark forest of red cedars edged the river and reached to the hem of the prairie about a fourth of a mile from the bank. The closer one got to the prairie through the trees, the more stunted and withered-looking they became.

Kate hated to see the beautiful, violet-hued, white-veined cedarwood go into the fire, but she helped by harvesting the bark, which hung down like old skin on the tree. Blue Wing gathered early blackberries that clung to low brush and brambles.

About two hours before dusk Kate sat on a stump to rest. Despite the strangeness of the place, she liked it here and saw that animals did too. Elks and stags had rubbed the bark off with their antlers, and red-eyed finches, which Stirling tried unsuccessfully to net, darted through the trees.

She saw Rand and Pete emerging from the direction of the prairie, empty-handed for once. "No game today?" she called to them, realizing Willy Nilly would have to serve catfish again.

"With all this thrashing around here?" Pete said as he headed toward the boat and Rand lagged behind. "We'd have to hike miles to find some that ain't been spooked. Unless you crave some prairie dog pie, and those critters got no good meat a-tall."

"Prairie dogs!" Kate said to Rand. "I'd love to see some, and I'm sure Stirling would too. He's trying to get unique specimens."

"It's more obvious every day he's caught one," Rand replied, and gave her that teasing up-and-down look that always heated her face. "Bring him along if you want. I think that stretch of prairie dog town is as good a spot as any to teach you how to shoot before we meet some Sioux who fancy your hair for another reason than its light color. Why don't you go get your gun?"

"If shooting won't spook the prairie dogs too," she said as she jumped up and brushed her dark blue skirt off. "But I could never shoot a dog, and I certainly don't want to rile their whole town." Rand grinned at something she had just said, but she was not sure what.

She was quickly back with Stirling, his gun, and Clive's rifle, powder, and shot. They followed Rand, who carried long pieces of bark, out of the narrow strip of cedar forest to the edge of the prairie and strode through knee-high bluestem grass.

"Quiet now. Don't move," Rand whispered, and pointed. And there, outside their sandy holes, sat many yellowish brown, short-eared animals squatting on their hind legs, looking around and uttering sharp, twittering sounds. Kate thought they looked as much like cats as dogs and sounded more like birds. But when Stirling sneezed, there was a fierce barking cry, a wagging of short tails, and a scrambling mass exodus into the holes. A few dared peep out at the intruders.

"Now you've seen how clever *they* are," Rand said with a narrow look at Stirling. "So, Kate, don't worry you will bother the whole village because you won't even see one of them while we shoot." He went over to stick the pieces of bark in several of the closest holes. "Stirling," he said as he walked back over, "since you declared the other day Kate was your woman, I suppose you'd like to give her the first lesson."

"You are the one who volunteered for this, Rand," he retorted, his voice on edge.

"Now look, you two, let's not argue," Kate interjected. "Stirling, maybe you can show me how to load the ball and powder, and Rand can teach me how to aim."

Stirling nodded and took his shiny, pristine-looking gun out of its spotless deerhide case.

"A beautiful gun," Rand observed. "Looks new and expensive."

"I borrowed it from General Clark's collection."

"You sure knew which one to pick," Rand said. "I've observed that most of his collection are the old smoothbore flintlocks—the upriver trade guns. He never lets his good hunting one out of his sight."

"Rand!" Kate protested, but she might as well not have spoken.

"One thing the Indians never seem to be able to learn is that if you pour in too much powder, you get an awful punch." Rand went on as Stirling poured a bit of powder down the barrel. "A few of them have learned to measure the right amount in a deer antler tip drilled out, but most still get blasted backward right off their horses. Then there are the honest ones who admit they don't know how to shoot at all but decorate it with brass tacks, put it in a fancy case, and tote the gun around just for show."

Kate fumed at Rand's needling of Stirling, but she soon had to admit she might be more adept at pouring the black powder and ramming the patch ball down the bore than he was. And then she realized Stirling had probably just learned to shoot since he arrived in St. Louis, and maybe that was why he seldom brought back specimens he set out for. He had been too embarrassed to tell her, of course—especially with Rand's obvious prowess with a gun. It would be just like Rand to know Stirling was a novice at this and be planning to show him up in front of her.

"This gun of mine is more like the upriver trade gun, isn't it, Rand?" she asked. When he nodded, she went on: "Then you go ahead and show me how to shoot it, since Stirling's obviously a more sophisticated weapon."

Rand's lifted eyebrows showed her he got her subtle challenge. He took over, explaining how to open the pan to pour in the other, finer powder from the second powder horn, how to close the frizzen, then sight the barrel, and pull the long trigger.

"And be prepared to flinch when you pull it," he said. "There's three little sounds as the hammer hits the frizzen up and the powder explodes to expel the ball. See?" He shot the farthest piece of bark neatly in two. "And there's a little kick from the stock against your shoulder, even if you have measured the powders right. Here, we're going to lose the light soon, so we'll let you load another day, and I'll just get mine ready for you to try a shot."

He deftly loaded again and put his gun in her hands. It felt warm where he had held it. He stood behind her, his hands over hers, his arms around her to help her sight the barrel.

"I see your game now, Major," Stirling cracked out, and stepped forward to pull Rand back. "Your intent is not only to humiliate me but, as you put it talking about your Sioux friends the other day, to paw my fiancée!"

"Stirling, we haven't actually—" Kate said before Rand interrupted.

Rand did not budge from nearly encircling Kate in his arms. But he turned his head toward Stirling and leveled a cold stare at him. "*Never* suggest that the Sioux are my friends, Mount. They are mortal enemies of the Mandans."

"Just like you want to be my enemy," Stirling insisted.

"The point is," Rand said, not loosing Kate when she tried to step away from him, "you may be able to keep a woman happy in the lap of city luxury, Mount, but there's no way you could protect one out here, you green, lily-livered—"

"Stop it, both of you!" she cried. She elbowed Rand back and pushed Stirling away with a raised hand to his chest. "This arguing is ridiculous, and though I don't have Gabriel's strength to separate brawlers, I just want you to stop it! I don't want to learn to shoot from either of you. Or maybe you'd like to have a duel at twenty paces as they do on Bloody Island just off the civilized shores of St. Louis! I don't care what you do, but I'm going back to the boat, and I certainly hope you will make your peace—or war—with each other and get it over before you come to my supper table this evening!"

Leaving them there glaring at each other—and at her—she picked up the otterskin case for her gun and stalked back into the trees toward the boat.

She stormed along at a good pace until her fury began to ease. She was angry with them, but with herself too. She had as good as decided she would accept Stirling's proposal when he made it formally, but she had nearly told him back there that he had no right to assume anything, to be possessive—as possessive as Rand's touch had been when he showed her how to take aim. And at first, even when she knew Rand was baiting Stirling, she had wanted to stand there close to him, in his embrace— even at Stirling's expense, she scolded herself. Curse her weakness and curse both of them!

She stopped and leaned against a slack-skinned red cedar. She saw fallen trunks here, so this was not the area the *Red Dawn*'s roosters had cleared out for firewood. She had obviously gone a bit too far to the north of where they had walked from the boat to the prairie. She began to retrace her steps as the sun settled lower and the forest darkened.

Her heartbeat quickened as she walked and recognized nothing, as she realized she might be lost. She wasn't even sure now where the prairie dog town was. But no, she could not be lost; the forest was not wide through here between the river and the open prairie. And the sinking sun was west, so if she just walked east—or did the river twist again near here, not really to the east? Which way was east?

She stood very still to listen. No doubt she would hear Rand and Stirling coming through the trees, still arguing. Or the steamboat's embarkment bell or even the dinner bell. She had not come far; it had to be this way.

But darkness soon swallowed the light, the trees. She went along slowly now, by feel, toward what she believed to be the eastern darkness that must surely be toward the river. Finally, when she emerged on the Missouri, it was a section she did not recognize. No steamboat, no lights, nothing. She leaned against a tree trunk and listened in the hush. Rippling water; a distant duck; absolutely nothing else. Even Blue Wing's Old Woman in the Moon was not in the sky to guide her.

She sat for a moment and mentally tried to retrace her steps from when she left Rand and Stirling at the prairie dog town. But she could not even fathom which way to walk on the river to find the boat. And there might be some of those soft, sandy spots that sucked one's feet right in along the banks. No, when you were lost, people always said, stay put and someone would find you. But she felt suddenly as frightened as a lost little girl, hungry, alone, afraid. This was wild animal and Sioux country, and Rand had jokingly implied they would like her light-colored scalp.

She held her gun close, but she had barely learned either to load or to shoot it. She resolved to learn to be a crack shot tomorrow when they found her. In this dark she could not load it anyway, but she would at first light so it would be ready in case someone unfriendly came along.

Besides, as soon as they realized she had not returned, they would send up a hue and cry for her, maybe steam up and down this stretch of river with lanterns lit to find her. Surely, surely, she would not really have to spend the night out here. She fought back panic, for Rand had said not to be afraid. She was suddenly very tired. She had worked hard today, then been emotionally exhausted by getting caught between Rand and Stirling. Now, from the chill or from the fear, her knees and hands shook.

She relieved herself in the bushes, then when she scratched her bare bottom and snagged her petticoat doing it, realized she was standing right next to the same sort of berry bush Blue Wing had been picking from. Although the briars rasped her hand, she gathered some by feel and gobbled them. A bit bitter, but as Mama used to say, "Hunger is the best pickle."

She sat, knees hunched up, in a little bark shelter she made for herself just back from the river and thought of Mama. Right now she felt like a child having a nightmare, wanted to call out in the black of night, "Mama, Mama, come help me!" But even as an adult dear Mama still suffered from her own nightmares. She blamed herself for losing little Leah; she still regretted she had not gone to nurse Father on his deathbed, even after all the cruel things he had done to them.

And her grandmother, for whom she had been named, had no doubt had her own mix of dreams and nightmares too. Moving time and again, never to put down roots, facing another departure from her beloved Ohio home to go west, being true to her wildfire minister husband through thick and thin, as Mama put it.

And Kate herself had stayed with Clive until he died, but would she have if she had known of his betrayals and deceits, which still haunted her? Marriage was an awesome, dangerous adventure you could get lost in. She must tread carefully with Stirling. Yet she loved him and valued him, didn't she?

Stirling, the mingled voices in her head went on, how

she wished he'd come along here like a rescuing knight
... how she wished Jamie were here to cuddle and comfort ... her guardian angel Gabriel, who had his own de-
mons from being deserted by his brothers, of being torn
the way his stepfather had been between fighting and
turning the other cheek ... poor, dead Captain Zeke, who
had lost his reputation, his career, and his wife in one fell
swoop of tragedy ... Rand—even Rand, the innocent
mother murderer, for he would have been the best of all
for protection out here. In her roiling dreams and plung-
ing nightmares, she was sure she heard Rand trying to
lure her from Stirling, calling to her.

She jerked so hard upright her gun slid off her lap and
her little bark fort toppled.

"Kate? Kate?"

"Rand? Here, by the river! Here!"

She had been so angry at him on the prairie, but now
she stood and hugged him when he emerged from the
depths of the forest. He clasped her to him, but she held
on too, talking into his chest, which smelled so wonder-
fully of leather, smoke, wind—and safety.

"Thank God, you found me. Where are the others?"

"Gabe and Stirling went the other, shorter way. I've
found when people wander off, they most often bear to
their right if they're right-handed. I don't know how you
did it, but you're a long way from the boat. I was just
about going to wait till light to start looking again, this
time along the river."

"Which way is the boat?" she asked, and stepped back,
amazed he had held her all that time.

"Behind you, but I don't want to fall in a ravine or
quicksand in the dark. Dawn will be here soon enough."

"They'll all be so worried."

"Just so you won't be worried—out here alone with me
all night."

"No. Why should I?"

"It won't do your reputation with Marbois or especially
your self-declared intended any good."

"I said I have not accepted Stirling's suit. I said I
would think about it."

"You hungry? I've got water and some bread."

"I was, but not now. Maybe some water. What time do you think it is out here?"

"Time to get some rest," he said, and handed her his parfleche water bottle. "You cold? You can wear my shirt," he said, and peeled it off his bare back. Rand half naked out here was not what she needed.

"I had made a little tent of cedar bark," she said, forcing herself to look away. "I know the Mandans are hardy, but you may keep your shirt. I'm fine, really. And I do thank you for finding me."

"I'm glad you didn't keep moving. You came far enough," he said, repeating himself. She realized he was as nervous as she now, trying to keep talk between them. He pulled his shirt back on and settled himself on the ground, making a rustling sound as he piled up leaves. "Here, a little bed for you, better than bark."

She sat, drank, handed him his parfleche bottle back, and wiped her mouth with the back of her hand. "I was afraid," she admitted.

"But you are something anyway, Kate Craig, Prairie Wind," he said. "I admire your gumption. Besides, I've been afraid lost in the forest too, though I was a boy and the hunting party found me before it got dark."

She nodded, wondering anew about his very different childhood, his very different life. He was close enough to her that she could see his face, though not his eyes in deep darkness. Still, she could feel them hot on her. No, she did not need to borrow his shirt to stay warm out here now. She felt so close to him, so open and vulnerable that she quickly grabbed for the only weapon she had ever really wielded well against him: an argument.

"I know one is not to look a gift horse in the mouth, but you were terrible to Stirling today."

"Does he need you to defend him? Yes, I think he does."

"What does that mean?"

"I mean, you're stronger than he is and that hardly makes a good combination for a marriage, unless you are totally taken by the idea of being your own master forever."

"I have found the hard way it is better than being ordered around!"

"Keep your voice down. We're probably alone out here, but this isn't the waterfront of St. Louis. No, I was thinking marriage should be a give-and-take, work-together kind of thing. I never have gone along with how the whites treat either their Indian wives or their white wives, but I can't say the tribes do things so well either. It's too easy for them to get into and out of wedlock."

"Judge and jury of both worlds, are you?" she asked. "What can a bachelor know of marriage?"

"Doctors don't have to be sick to diagnose a disease, do they?"

"What a wretched comparison!"

"Look, let's not argue," he implored. The palms of his hands shone white as he held them up as if to ward her off. "Let's try to get some sleep. And while you're at it, see if you can dream up a thing or two to say to the illustrious Stirling when he thanks me for bringing you back, then hates me even more for daring to spend the night with you out here."

"If he won't believe the truth, I can't help him."

"Damn good answer," he said, and rustled the leaves, nestling deeper into them as if the conversation were over.

Kate laid her rifle between them, wondering where he had put his to have it at the ready. She too rustled leaves as she got comfortable, flat on her back, then curled up on her side facing him. Strange, but she didn't feel the slightest bit afraid now, wild animals, Sioux Indians, or her endangered reputation notwithstanding. Her reputation: *That* was a laugh after all she'd been through in St. Louis, she thought. But when she'd told Stirling about that, he had accepted it very well. Her body felt heavy with exhaustion, but her mind raced.

Still, she fell asleep about the time Old Woman climbed into the sky to smile down on her. But she had to remember, she thought or dreamed, that Blue Wing had said Old Woman could be very dangerous. Why, there was a Mandan tale that Old Woman could be so fierce she kept a grizzly bear for a dog. A dog . . . a prairie dog . . .

peering out of its hole to spot danger ... and then fleeing into the dark depths for warmth and safety ... and love in her bed at Winterhaven ... her marriage bed with Clive.

She felt warm now, warm and secure, but her thigh kept pressing against a gun barrel and she was afraid it would go off. She came slowly, completely awake; silvery predawn dusted the forest. But she was not in her marriage bed with Clive. She was in Rand's warm buckskin-clad arms in the forest where she had somehow settled against him, or he her. No, she was the one who had rolled over her gun, which she had put between them. But when she tried to shift away, he did not budge.

"Rand. Rand ... I'm sorry I ... intruded. I was asleep ..."

She was horrified to realize he was already awake. His hands moved on her back; his arms tightened. "I'm sorry you did too, but I think it's too late for me. Maybe you can pull yourself out, but right now, I can't ..."

His chin moved; his mouth followed. His breath was hot, encompassing. His beard stubble scraped her cheek as he settled her closer to him. It felt so perfect, so right, even though it must be so wrong. But she lifted her mouth to meet his and pressed her entire body to the length of his legs and chest, which seemed to go on and on, devouring her as his mouth did. He moved to roll her under him, still cradling her body. A big knee intruded between hers, catching her petticoat and skirt there; his free hand raced over her hip and waist, then slid up to settle heavily on her breast, which rose and fell.

How could this be? She wanted Stirling in her life. And yet she wanted this dangerous, drowning power over this man more than anything in the universe.

Her hands grasped his shoulders, the nape of his neck, and fastened in his tousled hair, much longer than Clive's or Stirling's. But no, she did not want them to intrude, not in this perfect blending of bodies. She bit his earlobe and splayed her fingernails into the soft, stretched fabric over his hard back muscles.

She didn't mean to say the words, was horrified to hear them, but they came unbidden and raspy from her throat, which he now rained wet kisses on. "I need you, Rand. I need you!"

He lifted his head as if she'd spit on him.

"What is it?" she asked, not moving now. "You heard something?"

"Only my own good sense, damn it. Kate, this is my fault. You were just trying to get warm, and I let you come too close. And I do not need this . . . complication!"

He pulled away, sat up, and put his mussed head in his hands.

"I didn't mean anything by it. I can't believe I said it."

"Let's forget you did. It was the moment . . . my fault."

"Last time we blamed the place," she said, but she was grateful he had stopped; of course, she was. She could not believe she had gone to his arms and responded like a wanton when she should have pushed him away. It was just her gratitude at being rescued, that was all, and she told him so.

"Then we're friends," he said matter-of-factly, and smoothed his hair back with both hands. His voice actually shook.

"Yes, of course. That suits me," she declared, and stood to shake out and brush off her skirts.

She was suddenly amazed by everything in this moon-enchanted morning forest: that she had gotten lost, that he had found her, that they had come together after she had seen what he did to Stirling yesterday. That he had stopped and that she had actually thought she was glad. For, she admitted to herself, though she would never, never tell him, she had wanted him very badly, even on the leaf-littered forest floor by a river so wide and twisting it might as well be the abyss that stretched between them.

Chapter 11

The next week, when Kate entered the common room to set the table for dinner, Stirling was waiting for her. Since her night in the cedar forest he had evidently dedicated his life to making certain she and Rand were never alone again. If it meant rising at first light, staying up late, or learning to help in the pilothouse—from which Gabe had banished him yesterday after he nosed the prow into a half-sunken tree—whenever, wherever, Stirling was there. Including here and now.

"Stirling, you haven't been observing flora, fauna, or much else lately," she told him, and walked by him to get the utensils from the sideboard. "That is, except for observing me."

"You've been listening to MacLeod."

"No," she said, and stopped his intended embrace by holding the prongs of forks and points of knives outward, "I've been listening to myself. At first I felt flattered to have you in constant, avid attendance. But if you can't trust me even on board ship around Rand, you obvious don't credit a thing I said about our night in the forest together."

"That is not true. I do believe and trust you about that. It is just—just that being near you makes my day. And I will admit it," he said, speaking through gritted teeth, "I am so blasted jealous I could tear those snags out of the river with my bare hands!"

She leaned against the table. "At least you have enough honesty and humility to admit it. Most men wouldn't, I suppose."

"Kate, I am *not* most men."

"I realize that. But you've got to let me be myself *by* myself sometimes. Otherwise—"

"I understand," he said, holding up a hand to stay her next words. "If I didn't care so deeply for you . . . but I see now one of the reasons I adore you so is your strength and independence. I have always admired that in you, my dearest. And this won't happen again. I know you'll come to me if you need help to keep safe from anyone or anything—if it is something you cannot control on your own, I mean."

"Apology accepted, but as they say, the proof is in the pudding, Stirling. And speaking of which I need to get things ready for dinner."

"Then I shall get out of your way . . . for now."

"For now," she said, and smiled at him. Their eyes held before he turned and walked out on deck. Sometimes when they had their heartfelt talks, she thought nothing could be more wonderful. To have a man to love who listened, who could adapt, who was protective, possessive, yet trusting. And one, unlike Clive, who wanted to be near her at all costs, even humbling himself to admit his weaknesses. She sighed as she began to set the table.

"You like being shadowed?" Rand asked Kate that afternoon as he came up to take a turn with Gabe when she was leaving.

"Stirling, you mean? All that's over. And to answer your impertinent questions, yes and no."

Gabe grunted. "If it's yes and no with the man, you can't be thinking of marrying him back home."

"I *am* thinking about it. But the more we get into the wilds, the less time I have to agonize over it."

Gabe grunted again, his eyes on the river ahead. Rand looked at Kate. She stood sideways in the door of the pilothouse, taking advantage of the cool river breeze off the plains, for the sun could pour through the windows so hot here. She knew she should go down now to help Willy Nilly lay out supper, but she lingered.

"The ruins of an old Ree village," Rand said as he turned away and pointed. "That's the Arikara tribe, much fiercer than the Mandans, and you can see what the Sioux did to this place."

"The Sioux did that?" Kate asked, her voice rising to a squeak. Nothing stood but burned-out and tumbled foundations of round clay huts.

"You'll see Mandan villages upriver that met the same fate. Just remember that the Sioux even fight other Indians next time you want to go walking into a nest of them, white woman. They may admire strength and courage, but they want to test it, to prove they're stronger and more courageous any bloody way they can. It's one of my goals as agent to the Mandans to parlay for better relations with the Sioux. The Mandans will fight, but they're peacemakers at heart, as the Plains tribes go."

"I heard that," Gabe put in. "Bless their heathen hearts."

"But only in comparison to other tribes," Rand said. "Mandans will go out on raid, but they are generally defensive, not offensive, fighters. They even used to have walls around their towns. Their Ree and Hidatsa neighbors are aggressive warriors, and the Sioux—the Sioux are a scourge from hell, and don't either of you forget it. And there will be more Sioux at Fort Pierre."

"I remember," Gabe said. "Place was crawling with them last time I was there. I thought they were living better'n the white workers at the fort."

"The place is run by one of Chouteau's favorites, a Mr. Laidlaw," Rand explained. "He operates by keeping people in their place—as low a place as he can stomp them. He embezzles and shorts his workers so he has more to trade with the Sioux. And he hates what he calls white Indians."

"What's that?" Kate asked.

"What the rest of the world calls half-breeds, like me."

"He sounds like a dreadful man."

"About on a level with Chouteau and Marbois. I still say you're going to regret you let Marbois aboard, Kate. He'll show his true skunk colors at Fort Pierre, I bet, unless he's saving himself for Fort Clark."

"Rand, as subagent at Fort Clark," Kate said, "besides

trying to protect the Mandans from the Sioux and the smallpox, what else will you try to do?"

Rand took the wheel from Gabe to give him a rest on the captain's tall stool, but Rand seemed to watch her yet in the reflection of the glass as he looked upriver. "Encourage the tribe to keep a balance between growing corn and hunting buffalo—to keep their main livelihood independent from white trade. And when they trade, to be sure it's fair trade. I really admire how you're willing to help with that, and for the right reasons, Kate."

She felt deeply touched, as if he were holding her again. She nodded to encourage him to go on.

"In short," he continued, "I want the Mandans to be able to rely on *their* strengths, not those of the white traders or government. To keep their land intact, of course, so it isn't ripped from them through false treaties, though most Indians have no real concept of owning land. And to get the chiefs to realize that if they use white ideas— tools, weapons, religion—that's fine, but they must *not* be forced to do so. They have got to protect their heritage and themselves."

"I understand," Kate said. "If there's anything I can do to help . . ."

"I was thinking, if you make another trip upriver next year, you could bring the smallpox serum for inoculations to the tribe. Surely General Clark will have gotten it past President Jackson's tight purse strings by then."

"Yes, I could do that!" she vowed. She was so moved by what Rand had said and his trust in her that she forgot to look to see if Stirling was still waiting and watching for her.

They reached Fort Pierre on their fifty-second day out of St. Louis. When Kate toured the stockaded trading post with Stirling and Gabe, she saw that Rand and Gabe had told the truth about the way Mr. Laidlaw treated his white workers here. They looked as mangy, beaten, and hungry as stray dogs; they even snarled at one another, standing in lines for greasy bowls of meatless stew that turned her stomach to look at it. She had just seen how well Mr. Laidlaw and his few chosen compatriots dined when they had stopped by to "pay their respects" at his house within the compound. Marbois, as one of Chouteau's other fur-fort factors, had been at Laidlaw's lavishly laid table. And she felt terrible that many of their deck passengers had disembarked to work here through the end of the season.

"I can't believe Mr. Laidlaw thinks he will get more out of these men by treating them badly," Kate observed.

"Some overseers," Stirling said, "just like broken workhorses instead of spirited ones. A man like that ruined my father's spirit and his life years ago, and I swore it would never happen to me. I intend to be certain my superiors are willing to pay well for what I give them."

"But these poor souls," Kate said, taking his arm, "aren't as clever or strong as you. I wish we could do something to buck them up a bit—feed them too, though we have to save our trade goods for the Mandans. I can't believe that coffee, sugar, and flour were a dollar a pound at that dirty little store where they can supposedly buy extra goods!"

"Exactly what're you thinking?" Gabe asked as the three of them started back toward the steamboat.

"That, since tomorrow is Sunday, we could give them a little church service with some comforting words about holding up under duress. And though we don't have much food to share, we could give them a bit of something after—coffee and biscuits with some of that honey Rand and Pete found near the White River."

"And who's gonna preach?" Gabe asked, though he gave her that all-knowing, cross-eyed smile.

"Why, Gabriel, I think we both know you're a preacher at heart."

"I'm game if you are, but you'll have to break the news to Willy Nilly that we might have nigh on fifty guests for tea and crumpets."

Though Stirling looked glum, she and Gabe shared a laugh, which died as Marbois blocked their way up the gangplank with the tallest Indian Kate had ever seen. The Sioux brave was elaborately painted and bedecked in feathers, beads, and embroidered buckskin.

"This here's Big Buck, son of the Sioux war chief

White Raven," Marbois told Kate. "Says he'd like you to
trade with his people here, and he's got beaver, wolf, and
coyote fur."

"Please tell Big Buck I am very honored," she said.
"But our trade goods are promised to the Mandans up
north."

"*I said* this here's a real important Sioux brave,"
Marbois said. "Now lemme just give you an idea about
the Sioux by telling you about their fancy hairstyles, see.
A horizontal feather in their hair means the warrior
touched a dead enemy. Upright one means the enemy was
kilt with a fist. And the piece of wood in the hair means
he's kilt enemies by musket. Big Buck here's a real good
example 'cause he's got *all* that in his hair, now don't
he?"

Kate had already noted that lesson well, and she re-
called Rand's cautioning her not to challenge or cross the
Sioux. But she decided to keep her word about the Man-
dans. She wished that Rand had not gone hunting or that
Blue Wing would notice them and come down, but her
Mandan friend went out of her way to walk around the
Sioux.

"Wal, I'm waiting," Marbois said. "You're lucky he's
even dealing with a woman, but some Sioux from Fort
Lookout told him you ain't afeard. Don't want me to
translate a refusal now, do you, gal?"

"Mr. Marbois, I don't want to have to refuse him any
more than I want you to call me gal, but that's the way
it is." Her voice shook; she tried to steady it and her
knees. "Please tell him I have given my word, and it cannot be broken. And tell him to wait, for I have a gift for
him, for the great medicine he represents in his tribe. Stirling, if you would go aboard and bring down some tobacco in one of the pouches we were stuffing last night in
the common room, I would greatly appreciate it."

Marbois spoke to Big Buck in his language; the Sioux
frowned but stood still as stone, staring at Marbois, not
her, until Stirling hurried back with a leather pouch. Kate
was glad to see he had stuffed extra tobacco in it. Silently
Big Buck took the pouch from Stirling before Kate could
offer it and stalked away.

"Int'resting how brave but how foolish you can be, Mrs. Craig," Marbois observed.

"Interesting how you can apparently speak passable Sioux when your Mandan is so bad, so I keep wondering which tribe you are really serving," she replied.

"Hellfire, if'n I was you, Mrs. Craig, I'd be thinking of getting on Jacques Marbois's good side."

"I'm afraid I'm yet to see a good side to get on, Mr. Marbois," she snapped before she could pull the words back. She had no chance to reconsider or apologize as he swore under his breath and stalked away on Big Buck's heels.

The next morning they delayed their departure for a church service, to be followed by coffee and biscuits. More than forty white traders sat on the ground. Mr. Laidlaw himself, a short, burly man, appeared and stood under a nearby tree to watch.

"I believe we're under surveillance," Kate said, and Gabe nodded.

While Blue Wing and Willy Nilly worked on board to prepare to feed the crowd, Gabe gave a message about not being afraid to stand up for what was right—as long as it was done in a "peaceable" way. Gabe was large enough so that they gave him their attention at first before whispering and shifting about began.

But two louts in the front row seemed more rapt with each word. They elbowed each other and whispered. Kate noticed they were both about Gabe's size and shared his rusty hair color. Gabe seemed to be so intrigued by them he kept forgetting what he had just said.

"And now—just before we share some victuals—I'm gonna tell you a little story from the Good Book," Gabe went on. "A tale a real good mother—a foster mother to me—read me at night after she took me in when my own two brothers deserted me. See, there was this boy in the old times called Joseph, and his brothers sold him into slavery in Egypt. But later, when they were starving and had real hard times, and Joseph was working a real good job, they come before Joseph to ask for help. Now, Joseph, he could of just thrown them out or had them put in prison or 'bout anything he wanted, but he still loved—loved his brothers . . . even after all those years . . . and how cruel they been . . . to him— You two is Dan and Jeremy Smithfield from Cincinnati, right?" he suddenly demanded of the two tall redheaded men. "Right?"

The big men got up and stared at Gabe. Others behind them yelled, "Sit down and shut your mouths so we can get some grub!" Then, when Willy Nilly and Blue Wing came down the gangplank with plates of biscuits, the crowd made a mad rush at them. Kate ran to put herself in front of the plates to hand out honey-soaked biscuits, and Willy Nilly poured coffee into their bowls, shouting for silence and order.

While doling out the food, Kate kept trying to look around shoulders to see how Gabe was doing. She almost panicked when she did not see him or the two others—his brothers—and Mr. Laidlaw had disappeared too.

It hit her then what a mess she might have made of things with this idea. What if those two took advantage of or hurt Gabe as they had years ago? Wouldn't that be about like her father's coming back from the grave to haunt her again? Or what if they talked Gabe into staying here with them, to be a family?

But she got hold of her fears. Even if Gabe left her, she would find a way to see this through. Surely, somehow— sandbars, snags, and Sioux be damned—she would get the *Red Dawn* upriver to the Mandans.

Later, when everyone else was aboard but Gabe, and the time to cast off approached, Kate paced the boiler deck, hoping, praying he would return. This would put them another day behind, but if she had to steer, the trip would be terrible and interminable—perhaps impossible. Less than two hundred miles yet to go after the more than one thousand they had covered, but they were the worst miles, the wildest, with the most dangers both on and off the river.

Just in case Gabe did not return, she thought, they would wait until morning. That would give her time to inquire about him, find him, and talk to him, although she had no desire to come face-to-face with Marbois, Laidlaw, or Big

Buck again. But when, without her permission, Stirling dinged the embarkment bells from the pilothouse right on time, she saw Gabe emerge from the fort alone and stride straight for the steamer.

She waved wildly to him, and he acknowledged her with a nod. He came up the gangplank, up the stairs. "What's Mount doing in the pilothouse when I told him to stay out?" he muttered. He looked bleary-eyed, but his usually kind face was stern and hard.

"I'll get him right out. We—I was afraid, perhaps if those two were your brothers, you wouldn't come back."

"Why not? I got a job to do, and they're not family to me anymore. Even tried to deny who they was at first, though they recognized me sooner'n I did them. Guess I changed the most. But they want handouts, spect me to get them jobs here and steal stuff for them off the steamer. No, I told them, you're not my kin, though I'm willing to forgive. I figure a real family is those who take you in and trust you, not ones who take care a their own needs first. You're my family now, Kate—you, Jamie, Blue Wing, and the rest. This steamer's my home, and that's that."

"Gabriel, I'm so sorry you had to go through all that!"

"Blessing in disguise. Now I'll quit lying to myself they didn't mean to lose me on the dock in New Orleans when I couldn't fend for myself. I told them they let our mother down and wasn't worthy of her. And I showed them I turned out fine and got folks who believe in me and care about me, and all they got is that bastard Laidlaw and Chouteau sitting like kings above them all. Now get Mount out of the pilothouse 'cause we're pushing off for Mandan country!"

She hugged Gabe hard. Surprised, he froze, then squeezed her once and patted her shoulders hard when she let him go. "I don't know what I'd do without you, Gabriel!" she told him, swiping tears from her lashes.

"You, Kate Craig? Why, you'd have your other protectors like Mount or Rand Cloud just standing in line."

"Gabriel, not really. Stirling, of course, but not Rand."

"Better get the blinders off those pretty eyes. Truth is," he called back over his shoulder as he started up the steps, "you'd go on, even alone, and show the whole world how."

She stood amazed for a moment, for that was exactly what she had vowed to do, somehow, no matter what.

Ahpcha-Toha sat on the highest deck with her back against the pilothouse, where Dark Water steered and Gabe watched the river. She scanned the hills and hollows. She knew that in this area woodcutters sometimes had to leave cut wood and run when an armed band of Rees or Sioux attacked. Now, with fuel low, the crew was looking for a place to put in that had both wood and enough open terrain to defend while cutting.

When she began to see signs of home, Blue Wing was so excited she felt as if butterflies were trapped in her belly. She noted the familiar strips of burning coal in rocks along the buttes in this land which was rainy in the spring, but dry now in the summer and autumn. Buffalo berry bushes and Indian tobacco grew here—*kini-kenick*—to be mixed with the inner green bark of red willows. She saw more mud wallows and paths to the river made by antelope and Brother Buffalo.

Both on Big River and the side streams how she loved to see the humped huts of beaver, *warapa*. Though they seldom revealed themselves near the noise of this thunder canoe, she saw other signs of their presence: tree trunks gnawed through and wood chips scattered on the ground. *Warapa* flourished here, and only the most stupid of trappers tried to take them from this area. The Crow tribe sometimes hunted here. They believed that their departed ones came back as beavers, and they defended the little animals to the death. Blue Wing thought their beliefs were wrong, but she honored them, just as she did some of Prairie Wind's strange ideas.

At the mouth of the river the whites called the Cannonball, the steamer edged in under a line of flat hills. Blue Wing could tell that last spring, when the ice broke up, it roared through here two men tall, for bark was scraped off trees that high above the ground. As the roosters tied up the boat, everyone made ready to go ashore to help, including Pete and Dark Water, who would guard them with their guns.

The Cannonball River was full of rounded rocks which rolled down from the buttes to give the place its name. On its banks Blue Wing worked hard gathering driftwood, pulling it to the boat on a crude travois she had quickly made. Prairie Wind worked with her; they exchanged smiles to see Marbois helping gather woody brush. That man felt anything but trapping and trading was beneath his place. But Blue Wing's thoughts took flight and soared northward to the Heart River, the old home of the Mandans before they moved even farther north to the Knife River, where they lived now.

For near the Heart lay one of the two sacred Baby Hills of The People. If only it could be a wood stop like this, for Blue Wing must visit that place and take Prairie Wind with her! At that place Blue Wing would pray for a union with Swift Raven to produce a fine son. And Prairie Wind—she should pray for the return of her daughter, but would she want the father to be Stirling? Prairie Wind smiled at him with her mouth, but Blue Wing thought she smiled at Dark Water with her eyes.

The wind was cold this day, but Blue Wing soon felt warm in her work and dreams. She took out her skinning knife and cut some vines to hold the travois together better. It had rained here last night, for she stepped in a halfburied puddle on the bank and soaked both moccasins. *"Ahde!"* she muttered as she slogged about in their cold wetness.

"Hey, Blue Wing gal"—Marbois's shrill voice sliced through her thoughts—"drag that travois over here."

Blue Wing straightened and stared at him. Her knife in her hand, her feet wet, she did not take one step in his direction. She did not like or trust the man and did not wish to give him one word. Prairie Wind too stood and stared at Marbois.

Prairie Wind answered the man. "Bring your wood over here if you want to use this travois."

He stomped over with an armload of wood and threw it on the pile. "I think," he said to Prairie Wind, "we need food as bad as wood, since you been saving stuff for those Mandans you seem to be so enamored of, Indian lover." He squinted over in Rand's direction, where he stood on a rock with his gun ready. "So I'm gonna catch a few fish from the deck now. If you weren't so hellfire stubborn not to let me get off to trap at night when we tie up, I'd have us some good rabbit stew."

"The rules are no one gets off in hostile territory unless a group goes together, Mr. Marbois," Prairie Wind insisted. "Though I'm tempted to make an exception for you, since you'd evidently do well enough chatting with any marauding Sioux."

"Now I know where this Mandan gal learned her stubborn lip she gives out," he said, and turned to go.

At that moment the memories rushed at Blue Wing to drown her. Cold, wet, she had caught fish and had them with the wood on her travois beside that other river. That man—Scarface—he had dead rabbits for stew and came out on the snowbank to her. . . .

"You did try kill me!" Blue Wing screamed at Marbois.

He spun around. She saw panic on his face before it turned to anger. "What the hell you talking about, gal?"

"Along the river near St. Louis. Prairie Wind, this man tried to force me lie with him; he hit my head on ice and ran away when I fell in. He left me there—me and his rabbits when I cut his wrist."

"She's loony!" Marbois shouted. "She would have said something long before."

"Not if you hit her head, Mr. Marbois," Prairie Wind shouted back. "She had a huge bump and obviously some forgetfulness from what you did. You meant to defile her, then left her to drown! She nearly froze to death and could have caught pneumonia."

"I don't know what either of you's talking about! It wasn't me! Besides, Mandan gals give it out for free. No white man can *defile* them, as you put it so pretty! It's obvious she hates me. You do too. This is something you hatched up between you, that's sure. And you'd better learn that most Indians is liars!"

"And you were at Chouteau's house with him on the night before Christmas!" Blue Wing blurted.

"What's going on?" Dark Water demanded as he strode up with Stirling right behind him.

"Blue Wing just recalled," Prairie Wind said with her fists clenched at her sides, "that it was Marbois who tried to force her and then left her to drown last winter. She hit her head and didn't recall until now."

"MacLeod, the gal's demented! It's all a big, damn lie!"

"See if he carries knife scar on wrist," Blue Wing said. "Good cut, much blood. This wrist," she added, and thrust out her left arm.

"Marbois?" Dark Water said. "Just show us your wrist."

"The hell with all of you! I got scars all over my body, so it don't prove nothing!"

"At least now," Prairie Wind said, "you will get your wish to be given some food and be able to have time to trap ashore. I'm going to go aboard and get your things and some food for you when we pull away. I will not have an attempted rapist and murderer on my boat and I fully intend to protest your appointment to Monsieur Chouteau next time I see him in St. Louis. You have been grousing that the keelboats and mountain boats up and down through here this summer are better run, so I'm certain you will soon catch one of those and be much happier."

"You can't put me out here! MacLeod, your new boss, Major Blackwell, will have your head for allowing this! Is that the kind of start you want in your new post?"

"No, but I can't see Blackwell sanctioning the Mandan fur factor's trying to rape and murder Mandan women, at either Mitutanka and Ruptare or St. Louis."

"Hellfire, you idiot, it's a lying woman's word—two of them—against mine! And if this Mandan saw me on Christmas Eve at Chouteau's, I think she's a thief as well as a liar, as that's the night someone let his bison go, so what do you think about that?"

"Actually, Marbois, if it were up to me," Dark Water said, his voice low and threatening, "I'd simply chain you up in the hold and insist you be tried when we arrive at Fort Clark, preferably by the Mandans. But I'll let you

plead your own case to Blackwell—when you make it upriver. I really do not have the authority to overrule what
the ship's owner decides, as she employs the captain and
their word is law on the river."

"You smart-ass son of a Mandan bitch," Marbois muttered with a look so black at Dark Water that Blue Wing
shuddered. But when he called him that name, Dark Water exploded and put his fist right in Marbois's face.
Marbois fell back and hit the ground hard on the edge of
the river. Dark Water stood over him, legs spread, holding
his gun. Marbois did not speak again or rise to fight Dark
Water. He held his jaw, got up to sit on a boulder, and
glared.

But Blue Wing's heart was so grateful toward Prairie
Wind and Dark Water for honoring her words against
those of Marbois she did not care what the man did. She
felt tall and strong. And she decided then that somehow
she must help these two who helped her. She was sure
that was what Old Woman would want, she who loved
a-wa-sa-ta, the sacred water mirror. For even now, before
Prairie Wind went aboard the ship and as Dark Water
looked at her, their gazes met. Blue Wing saw they stared
into each other's eyes at the deep reflections they found
there.

Although it was late afternoon several days later when
Blue Wing led her to the Baby Hill, Kate saw the moon
was in the sky, as it had been the first day they met. Below them along the wide river the roosters gathered fuel.
Rand and Pete had gone hunting, but Stirling had accompanied the two women partway up, then, at their request,
sat down to wait. Below them Kate could see all that and
so much more.

The sky was a bright robin's-egg blue with clumps of
clouds which seemed to snag on the flat tableland called
Butte Caree to the west. To the east, in growing shadows
along the river, a dark, shifting herd of buffalo moved toward where Pete and Rand had gone. The great beasts
raised clouds of dust behind them as if to mirror those in
Old Woman's sky. Along the glinting ribbon of river below lay strips of forest, steep clay banks, and the *Red*

Dawn like the toy bank of Jamie's Gabe had carved for him. And on the hill where they stood, gold and blue wildflowers nodded as if to approve of the magnificent view.

"It's *sinashush* here, Blue Wing. I would love to paint it all."

"No time. Make prayers for children," the Mandan said, and sat cross-legged in the grass among the flowers. "Spirits of many unborn or babies died before they have names too, restless like blowing grass. Inside this hill it like a lodge of The People. An old man cares for little one's spirits there, waiting to be asked to come to life again. If one want a girl, bring cloth and a ball. A boy, bring small bow and arrow, see?" she said, and produced both. Awed, Kate sat beside her as she produced other treasures from her personal medicine pouch and laid them out in a half circle.

"You know," Kate told her friend, matching her quiet, reverent tone, "I don't really believe in fetishes for good luck, but I did pick up a lucky stone back at River of Sky."

"*Shish,*" Blue Wing told her. "Put it here."

Feeling sheepish and silly, Kate fished it from where it was tied in her handkerchief up her sleeve. She put it where Blue Wing pointed. "Good stone," her friend said. "Look, shape like half-moon."

"I didn't see that before, but I suppose. I didn't pick it up for that."

"Quiet!" Blue Wing insisted.

So Kate sat very still as the younger woman began a strange chant in Mandan. Kate caught only some of the words: *manuka* for "friend," *matka* for "heart," *chicka-dash* for "dream," and the repeated *hu-ta, hu-ta* for "come here, come here." But when Kate caught the words for Rand's Mandan name, Dark Water, she jolted as if from a trance.

"Blue Wing, why are you saying Dark Water's name?" she asked in her slow Mandan.

"He be best father for your daughter come back," Blue Wing whispered, and went back to chanting.

"No, he wouldn't! He has dark hair, not fair like Clive

or like Stirling, and his skin is much darker. Did Dark Water put you up to this? I noticed he did not say we shouldn't come up here."

"Quiet! Not disturb this place or prayers not heard."

"Just answer my question then."

"No, he not know of this."

"Thank God."

"And not mention your He Who Lives Above here in this place, for it sacred Mandan ground."

"I'm sorry, Blue Wing," she said, switching to English, "but I should not have come. I care deeply for you; my heart is good to you and your people and your ways. But this is not for me, not this calling of my daughter and certainly not to assume that—that Rand would be my child's father. My heart is not good to that, my friend and my sister. I'll wait down there with Stirling while you say your own prayers."

Kate snatched back her lucky rock, then realized she should not have kept it. She tossed it down the hill a ways and walked down to sit with Stirling, who was watching soaring hawks overhead with his telescope. When he let her use it, she scanned the sky, then trained it on the nearly full moon, *mihnang-ga*. It leaped at her big and bright, looking indeed like a woman's face watching all below.

Slowly Kate rotated the tube up the hill toward Blue Wing and readjusted the end to bring things in sharp. And there she watched Blue Wing get up and go down the hill, evidently to search for the rock she had thrown away. She was certain that was what she was doing. Evidently she found it, for she stooped to retrieve it, then went back and placed it with something else nearly on the spot where they had sat. Kate could not make out her expression from here, but she was certain the Mandan woman was smiling.

When she came down at last and they all walked toward the boat below, Kate asked her, "Did you find my rock?"

Blue Wing actually looked surprised for once; she covered her open mouth with her hand the way she used to do before she adapted more white ways. "How you know? Old Woman tell you?"

"Poppycock. I saw you through Stirling's looking glass," she whispered so he would not hear and think they both were crazy.

"I find and put with my Blue Wing feather. Good sacrifice to spirits at Baby Hill, near old spirit home of Mandan village here before Sioux and bad smallpox came."

"You mean The People have already had smallpox?"

"More than once, last time maybe fifty winters ago. Old grandmother, Buffalo Grass, have it and live, many marks on her face. Lost many people, babies too, so head north to live in new place, *shish, sinashush* place near Knife River. You see."

"Yes, I will see," Kate whispered.

Rand recognized the danger signs when they were but a few days out from Fort Clark. He had been watching for Sioux along the occasional narrow spots in the river with overhanging rocks or open prairie land for riding and shooting, but he had not anticipated this. One glance told him that Kate and Gabe had not seen what was chasing them from the southwest prairie. Gabe was steering and Kate was keeping old Captain Zeke's journal of landmarks up in the pilothouse, so they both were looking north upriver. Rand decided to watch for another moment to be sure it would hit them before he alarmed the others.

But all too soon he spotted wild ducks, their usually strict V formations broken, hurtling out of the sky overhead to flee destruction. Prairie hens and geese catapulted out, not making their usual noise, to save their strength. Small ground animals fled too, jumping or slithering into the river. And then, worse luck, the bigger animals like elk and deer—even two bears—appeared from the western prairie to cross the river. A herd of buffalo milled along the bank, then plunged into the water all around them. However much the big beasts feared the huffing, knocking steamship, they instinctively fled far worse. And the buffalo got everyone's attention.

"Prairie fire blowing in from the southwest!" Rand

yelled. "But I think those clouds are sand and dust, not smoke!"

He pointed to make them look at the distant sky instead of the swimming mass of buffalo around them. "Pete, don't waste time shooting them!" he yelled to his friend. "Get a pole and push them away from the paddle wheels. We've got to make the canyon, or the fire could get us!"

"But we're on water!" Kate yelled, leaning over the railing on the deck above. "The animals even know the river will stop it!"

"The flames could be as high as a building!" Rand shouted at her. "They'll leap the river! Get the crew to make more steam, and keep these animals away from the wheels!"

She did just that, yelling orders to Fynn and the roosters, while Gabe rang bells for more wood. Her decisive action both calmed Rand's panic and increased it. How much their relationship had changed on this voyage. Had she gotten weaker and he stronger, or was it the other way around? He wanted to hold it against her that she had become important to him when he should care for nothing but helping the Mandans. He wanted to blame her for the bad start he'd had with Marbois when he had promised General Clark he would get on with him and Blackwell. He wanted to hate her for making him desire her desperately because he did not need a woman, a willful white woman, in his life.

Kate could not believe destruction had descended on them so fast. From the moment Rand had pointed at the sky, she could tell they were in for it. To be so close, she thought, fighting down panic, yet so far from her goal . . . perhaps to lose it all in a roaring inferno, an act of nature, when she had been fearing the Sioux . . .

She ran everywhere, warning people, giving orders, but there was little time to prepare. The sand hit first. It swept and scoured the vessel, making it impossible for anyone to stay on deck. Some passengers packed themselves in the boiler deck compartments, some in the hold; the roosters, screamed at by Fynn Winston through the swirling onslaught, manned the machinery or scattered for cover.

Gabe, Kate, and Rand sealed themselves in the pilot-house, where giant fistfuls of sand scraped the glass. When it became impossible to see or steer, they killed the engine. Gabe edged the boat against the far bank so they could sit it out despite the wall of flame roaring closer.

The three of them huddled on the floor. Rand pressed his knee against her thigh; he held her hand until she had to pull it back to lift her skirt to her face. It helped to have him here; he felt solid and strong; Gabe's big back held the door closed. Still, sand seeped in everywhere to sift on their clothes and hair, to catch in their eyes, to make them cry. Kate flung her skirt completely over her head in an attempt to keep the sand from her eyes, nose, and mouth, but it got everywhere anyway. Finally she peered out in the dusky light through slitted, gritty eyelids.

"Sand's letting up," Gabe muttered. "Agh! Even got it in my teeth. Never seen the likes—never!" He pulled himself up and spit on the floor. "Blasted stuff scratched up the windows," he reported. Kate and Rand stood, shaking their head and bodies like dogs, trying to clean the corners of their eyes. "And look at that—scoured your new paint right off the ship, Kate!"

But there was no time to look at such dreadful wonders. Gabe rang bells to the boiler room for full steam again while Kate steered. The wind roared on. The prairie fire had leaped much closer now, orange and red and yellow, belching black smoke and racing toward the river.

"We have come so far," she told Rand and Gabe as she glared out the window. "And no storm of any kind—rain or sand or fire—is going to stop us now!"

"But if we don't make the buttes," Rand said, "and the boat catches fire, we'll have to jump in the river. Then just hope there's nothing else hostile between us and Mitutanka if we have to walk."

"And no snakes in the river," Kate added.

For the quarter hour they had left before the flames hit, the *Red Dawn* raced for the shelter of the rocks that would stop the building fire. They could hear it now, a crackling, roaring monster, clawing its way closer. They could smell it, feel it, sucking away the air and cool breeze. It loomed almost over them, a red-gold sun gone mad on earth.

On a treacherous stretch of river they pushed the little vessel to its limits. Kate prayed it would not explode. They had to grasshopper it over one shoal; with the ship shuddering and straining, they ran it right over two others. Along the west bank, flames devoured grass and brush, bushes, even the few trees. What paint on the vessel had escaped the scouring of the sandstorm now buckled and bubbled. But the buttes of the canyon were just ahead.

Stirling, Pete, and Rand hauled up buckets of water from the river and sloshed them down the decks, slipping on ribbons of sand there, hoping to keep cinders and sparks from catching. They dumped buckets on themselves to keep their hair and clothes from igniting.

And then Kate saw their salvation in the rocks looming through the smoke just ahead. She had to tell them, to urge them on, to assure them they would all be safe. She ran outside on the protected side of the pilothouse, dirty, wild-haired, sweating, soot-covered from her runs about the ship.

"The buttes! The buttes!" she screamed down at the men. Smoke seared her lungs with each breath, but she felt triumphant. From gritty, dry throats a cheer went up as they raced for the shaded shelter of the rocks.

She hugged Gabe, even though he still steered. Coughing, crying, laughing, she hurried down to the deck and into Stirling's arms, where he waited at the bottom of the ladder. She pulled away from him to embrace Blue Wing, then Pete, Fynn, Bill, and Willy Nilly, who ran up with a tray of mugs of beer everyone grabbed. No one stopped to toast their safety, for the wetness was too good on their parched throats. She'd thanked everyone but Rand, she thought. Where was Rand?

And then she saw him staring at her from across the deck, his eyes and teeth white in his smoke-smeared face. She put her mug back on the tray and walked toward him.

"Rand," she said. Her voice was raspy from smoke and

shouting. The crew was still noisy; she walked closer so he could hear, for this moment seemed theirs alone. "I cannot thank you enough for the good advice you gave, the help. For everything, Rand. We've as good as made it now, I just know it. Everything *has* to get better from here on out."

His big body tensed, his fists clenched, then unclenched at his sides as she approached. He nodded. Their eyes held, hot as flames that almost devoured them. And then she threw herself into his arms, and they whooped and spun each other around like cavorting children, while the world blurred by.

PART THREE

The Knife River

Old Woman in the Moon saw the swift, silver river knifing sharp through rocks and prairie. It separated buttes from buttes and tribes from tribes. She cursed the cruel river. And she cursed the way, within the tribe, people cut themselves off from other people.

Chapter 12

When the *Red Dawn* came around a broad bend of river, Blue Wing ran up to the pilothouse, where she never ventured, and pulled Kate outside to point northward. "Prairie Wind, there!" she cried, and pointed. "There! Mitutanka!"

At first Kate saw only a steep bluff above the west bank, then a wood-walled fort. But just beyond, on a broad tongue of land above the mirror of river, sat a cluster of bumps, like molehills, against the stark blue sky. Among those hills stood little blades of grass.

"Clay lodges of The People," Blue Wing said, her gray eyes shining. "Poles for prayers, scaffolds for food and honored dead. Home." Her friend ran down to join Rand on the prow of the hurricane deck as the steamer pushed toward its goal.

Emotions as varied as the view stunned Kate. A little stream pouring itself into the river before the fort, blue hills, and lush green prairie splashed with wildflowers made her yearn for River of Sky. Heavy-headed sunflowers edged corn patches worked by women, who were guarded by men along the river—Blue Wing's friends, perhaps her family, or her beloved Swift Raven. Kate wished she could help Blue Wing face her fears after this time away.

Children played and swam along the banks; how desperately Kate missed Jamie. Set back from the river, a pond, the size of the one owned by that cursed Chouteau in St. Louis, sparkled through a curve of forest. But here, so far away, St. Louis did not feel so much like home. How many times had Clive seen this peaceful, luring view and squinted to pick out his Mandan wife along the banks? And then, as they came closer, movement and noise exploded the restful scene.

"We been spotted at the fort too!" Gabe yelled as Kate stood outside the pilothouse. "They're running the Stars and Stripes up and down the flagstaff!"

Greeting guns boomed as they had at the other forts, but longer, louder. Then Kate realized, with the sandstorm and fire, she had lost track of the date. This was the Fourth of July; America's freedom was sixty years old on this National Independence Day. It made her feel even more bold about the future: a perfect day for her to see Mitutanka for the first time, for Blue Wing to come home, and for Rand to start his new career.

"Look at that crowd coming!" Gabe cried.

The rush became a brown blur of Mandans, salted with a few whites from the fort. The women wore deerskin dresses, but there was so much glistening gold-brown skin: men attired only in black-and-white-striped breechcloths, little girls in aprons, and hordes of boys naked as God made them. Though it seemed curious to Kate, she knew it would be this way. Blue Wing had told her; she had let Jamie run naked even in the snow that time. She must expect and accept some very different things, for *she* was the stranger in this strange land which Blue Wing and Rand dearly loved.

At first everyone, especially the men, looked alike to her. Most had bows and quivers strapped across their sturdy backs and held fans of white feathers. Some had brownish hair with white streaks like Blue Wing's, others had darker hair, but it all tumbled down to their knees. And each man's flowing mass was divided into three parts: the shortest lock hanging on the forehead tied with a bit of red ribbon; the two heavier hanks plaited. There, Kate noted, their physical likeness stopped. It was not the women but the Mandan men who stood out in the crowd.

Each brave's hair set him apart as if that were not just his style but his signature. Everyone had daubed his braided tresses with red, brown, and white clay in varied patterns. And each had bedecked it with a distinctive array of beads, shells, leather, copper wire, feathers, wood, or other ornaments. If their faces looked alike to her for now, she was certain she could tell them apart by their hair. How she would like to paint this scene and every Mandan here!

All around the people ran a shifting mass of dogs that were wolflike but not wolf-colored. They were white-and-black-spotted, and as Rand had warned her, they were outnumbered only by the big July mosquitoes along the riverbank. They all began to swat at them as the breeze died and the gangplank thudded on the shore. Yet it seemed to Kate the mosquitoes did not bother the Indians at all.

Nervous, smiling, she started down the plank with Blue Wing beside her; Rand and Stirling came behind. Mandans shouted greetings to Rand and Blue Wing. Kate could pick out some of the words, but the people talked so fast. She wondered which of these curious faces belonged to Blue Wing's family, but she did not have long to wonder.

The tribal women surged around her, touching her hair, patting her skin, feeling the blue calico of her dress, fingering her ribbon belt. One woman pulled up Kate's skirt and petticoat and peered beneath, evidently to see if she had feet and legs. Stirling pressed closer to protect her, but she was not afraid. She heard Rand laugh; he so seldom did that it thrilled her. Was it because she finally had her "belle of the ball" entrance he had teased her about at Fort Pierre? She wished she had brought the gifts for the tribal leaders and Blue Wing's family ashore, but there was time for that later.

Now, as the familiar smell of castoreum enveloped her, she summoned from the depths of her overflowing emotions a steady voice and said in loud Mandan, "I am happy and honored to be at Mitutanka. I am Kate Craig, called Prairie Wind, wife of River Walker, he who died. I am friend of Blue Wing and Dark Water. I come to trade fairly with The People."

Motion halted, and the babble hushed. Others repeated her words back into the crowd. Rand, who had been swallowed up somewhere, stepped forward with a slim, stately-looking brave with a commanding demeanor. He alone in this heat wore a buffalo robe, filled with picture paintings, thrown over one shoulder.

"Kate, this is Four Bears, one of the two main chiefs. He says, though two fire canoes of Chouteau have come and gone with furs and buffalo robes, The People will trade with the woman of River Walker, and—"

"Not much left to trade," a deep voice cut in, " 'less they get a bunch of buffalo hides on the summer hunt, but the first hundred been promised to Marbois."

Kate turned toward the commanding voice; some Indians shifted back a few steps. A white man with a carefully clipped auburn beard and sleek eyebrows stepped from the crowd. As immaculately attired as if he strode the streets of St. Louis, he carried a gold pocket watch on a chain. He doffed his fine beaver top hat to Kate with a flourish, then shook hands with Stirling and Rand.

"Some of the Sioux come in to trade for food last week said you was coming," he went on. "Got some cargo for me, I think. You see Marbois anywhere downriver?"

"Marbois and the cargo are a long story, Major Blackwell," Rand said, drawing Kate forward. "Mrs. Kate Craig, may I present to you Major Kellen Blackwell, General Clark's newly appointed Mandan agent I'll be serving under."

Kate exchanged polite greetings with the man. His face was so pale she wondered if he spent much time outside among these bronze people, but perhaps he always wore his hat. He continued to look down at his hands or his watch as he spoke, so it was hard to tell exactly whom he was addressing. But he was hardly shy. He seemed a bit brusque, but no doubt he needed to appear masterful before the tribe.

"Chief Four Bears," Kate said in her slow Mandan, aware they had been ignoring the Indians, "I am honored to be among The People. I would like to meet the family of Blue Wing."

The chief nodded; Rand spoke in quick Mandan to him, then told Kate, "Later, at their lodge." He indicated a group of Indians on the edge of the crowd, standing around Blue Wing and wailing, even as she was. "They've just heard officially, Kate, that her husband is dead, and custom decrees a show," he whispered to her, while Stirling leaned closer to hear.

Rand reached down and took Kate's hand, while Stirling held her other arm. Gently she disengaged her arm from Stirling, but she squeezed Rand's hand before she let go of it. She had noted that Major Blackwell did not understand even her halting Mandan; another white man had stepped forward to translate for Blackwell her words to Chief Four Bears. Perhaps, like her, Blackwell was just too new at this to have learned the challenging language yet. Despite Rand's earlier critical remarks about the whites here, she'd give Major Blackwell the benefit of the doubt. She wanted things to go well here for her and Rand.

"Time for this swarm to skedaddle," Major Blackwell announced, flipping open the face of his watch and closing it again. "And I don't mean these blasted mosquitoes," he added. If it was meant to be a joke, no one laughed. "All of you, party's over. Go on!" he shouted, and made shooing motions at the tribe.

None of the braves budged at Blackwell's bidding, though the children and dogs kept well back from him. Under his breath to no one in particular, he added, "You'd think July Fourth was their holiday, but 'less they're hunting or raiding, red men think every day's time off from work. Sad as that is, you'll see that's the way of it here, Mrs. Craig. Come on up to the fort now, ma'am, and I'll give all of you a good meal to welcome you."

"We'd appreciate that, Major," Kate told him, relieved that Rand's new boss was hospitable toward tired travelers. As for his comments about the Indians, it did seem the braves were at leisure, today at least. Still, there was a tone, an attitude to the man's comments that discomfited her. And she realized he had not yet met her curious gaze.

Rand said something to Blackwell Kate could not hear, while the crowd shifted and murmured. After parting rather formally from Chief Four Bears, Kate, Rand, and Stirling walked with the Mandan agent toward the fort for dinner, leaving Gabe and the crew to watch the boat.

Kate steeled herself to deal with Kellen Blackwell

about his lost barrels and the fort's fur factor. And she wanted to plead Blue Wing's case against Marbois. She hoped when the Mandan head agent heard all she had to say, her welcome would continue.

"But you've got to understand, ma'am," Major Blackwell told Kate over the lavish spread on his dinner table, "even if this Blue Wing was telling the truth, Mandan females give themselves to men so free Jacques wouldn't even know she wasn't willing when he approached her on the river near St. Louis that day."

"Whatever he thought of the Mandan moral code," Kate responded, "it gave him no excuse to beat her and leave her to drown in the icy water!"

"I understand your vexation, but see, ma'am, the Mandans don't have a moral code like ours."

Kate saw Rand clench his jaw and his fist, as he had from time to time throughout the meal. She could tell Blackwell deeply offended him, though he was obviously struggling to get along with his new boss by not taking him on publicly. However delicious the food and wine, their host's slanted views on the Indians were turning her stomach.

"You said the girl stabbed Jacques across the wrist," Blackwell continued. "Maybe he hit her head and fled to save his own skin because she cut him first. I'm telling you, ma'am—I'm sure you'll see it soon enough—a squaw with a knife, 'less she's skinning game or scraping a robe, can be big trouble."

"But Blue Wing is always purposeful with hers," Kate said, shoving down the memory of the young woman pulling her knife on Chouteau. "Surely we must judge members of the tribe as individuals."

"Look, ma'am, you only got here today, and I been living with the Mandans for more'n six weeks already."

"I realize that, sir. But I've been living with a Mandan woman for nine months and learned a lot about how they think and feel. And they *do* think and feel."

"Of course, they do. But living with one woman's not like dealing with a whole passel of them. Look, Mrs. Craig, as Major MacLeod will be the first to tell you, I'm the one with the final say-so on things here, and I say we let the Blue Wing versus Marbois problem pass. No use riling up bad Mandan-white feelings, now is there? Believe me, we've got bigger fish to fry here. I'm sure you understand that."

"I do understand that there are other problems, such as protection from the Sioux, and, of course, keeping a watch on fair trading," she said. "And arranging for the necessary smallpox inoculations to protect the tribe," she added, and caught Rand's avid expression.

Blackwell finally glared at Rand, who met his gaze steadily before the head agent looked away again. "Smallpox won't come this far north, ma'am," he went on, his voice constrained again. "My big regret is I was depending on those barrels of medicinal spirits to see us through diseases this winter. Indians wear so little, even in the cold, and I want to be able to dose them proper if they get the chills or ague."

He sounded concerned, Kate thought, yet his sincerity seemed counterfeit to her. But for once she followed Rand's lead and bit her tongue.

"Major Blackwell." Stirling spoke up, as he had now and then during dinner, evidently when he thought Kate needed more support than Rand dared give. "I would be happy to donate my four and a half barrels of brandy. General Clark will not mind if I don't take back preserved specimens when he hears it went for such a worthy cause."

"The offer of the barrels is much appreciated, Mr. Mount," Blackwell said with a hint of smile that lifted his auburn mustache. "And I wish you and Mrs. Craig the best, living in St. Louis. As for your trip up to Fort Union, you can go on the monthly mail boat. It's really good of General Clark to let you see all the places you'll be keeping the books for."

"The experience of a lifetime. The only thing I regret on the entire trip is having to leave Kate here for a while, but I know you will help keep an eye on her, Major Blackwell, and I will return before the *Red Dawn* heads for home."

At least, Kate thought, Stirling's sense of diplomacy

diffused the tense talk, but she had no intention of letting this man keep an eye on her. That would be worse than Stirling himself watchdogging her and Rand. And why did Major Blackwell think she and Stirling would be living *together* in St. Louis? She'd certainly have a word with Stirling in private before he left.

Suddenly she felt closed in at the fort when it was obvious that its inhabitants valued its tall walls and looming, guarded bastions. After weeks on the river, it seemed so crowded: the huddled store and warehouses, this combined Indian agency office and house, the men's quarters, picketed horses, even this cluttered table. It was still the Mandan village that lured her. But that, unfortunately, would have to wait until tomorrow.

"I do thank you for your fine hospitality, sir," she told Major Blackwell as he went back to clicking the etched face of his pocket watch open and closed. "And if you don't mind, I'll take you up on your kind offer to give my crew some white bread, though I know the Mandans eat a lot of corn bread."

"Just another friendly warning then, Mrs. Craig," he said, and the clicking stopped. "If you persist in this nonsensical notion to live with the Mandans, you'll be eating worse things than their precious corn balls. So I want you to know you are always welcome to dine at my table."

"Kate," Stirling said before she could respond, "Major Blackwell is right. I cannot allow you to live in the Mandan village while I am away."

"Stirling," she said as she rose and pushed back her chair before he could help her, "I believe we've already discussed things like this before. Whatever you may have told Major Blackwell in private, we are not betrothed and perhaps may never be. And even if we were, I do not appreciate being ordered about. I shall conduct myself within the laws of this place—and the customs of the Indians, which I plan to honor as I do the people themselves. And I am sure, Major Blackwell, as General Clark's and the government's representative here, you certainly understand and back that plan of behavior."

"Now that's quite a speech, ma'am," Blackwell said, staring down at his watch. "Too bad ladies can't run for office." He lifted his eyes to hers at last; they were a piercing dark brown. Still, she could not read whether he teased, scolded, or derided her. She could, however, read Stirling's angry gaze. She regretted rebuffing him publicly, but he had overstepped his bounds. Rand, though not a flicker of emotion crossed his stern face, winked at her. That made her feel that flags still flew and cannon boomed again to welcome her here. She excused herself and stepped outside into the slant of late-afternoon sunlight soon to be swallowed by the shadows of the walls.

Sturdy and strong, Swift Raven did not feel the effects of his fast until just before dawn the third day. He sat cross-legged with his medicine bundle and the sacred buffalo skull on the brow of a cliff overlooking the swift Knife River. He had come two days ago on a mission to seek the sun. Last night, after communing with it all day, he had met both victory and defeat.

He chanted his gratitude that his first request had been heard. For last night in the blaze of setting sun he had received *chickadash*, a prophetic dream. But that sacred dream had also broken his hopes. For the strong medicine of his family and the tribe, he must forgo the woman he wanted.

When the sun lifted his face above the eastern buttes, Swift Raven again lifted the horned skull of Brother Bull Buffalo over his head. Through its shaded eyeholes he stared at its golden glory. The vision returned to him, his *xopini* spirit of the raven soaring to meet Bright Star, daughter of Chief Four Bears, maternal granddaughter of the family of the turtle drum medicine bundle.

His union with her must bring him power. For Wolf Trap, his rival, had much medicine as a war leader. He would no doubt replace the head chief called Wolf Calf, his mother's brother, as the years took that man's strength away. So Swift Raven must get more influence to take the seat of Chief Four Bears, the honored tribal peacemaker, when he was no longer strong. To earn this honor, Swift Raven knew he must be chosen leader of the summer buffalo hunt and bring great bounty to the tribe. And he must marry a woman whose family had much more power in its medicine bundle than that of the buffalo robe artist Long Hatchet.

Then Swift Raven could blunt Wolf Trap's sharp lust for power through war and trade, for treacherous times stalked The People. The prices Chouteau would pay for furs went down, down with Marbois's tricky trading. Yet Wolf Trap wanted more trade from Chouteau; he smoked the pipe with Marbois and Blackwell, hoping for guns and other gifts.

But Swift Raven, like his friend Dark Water, saw things with other eyes. The path of The People must be preserved; the white man's ways must not become Mandan ways. As always, The People needed a balance of peace and power which the counselor could give the fierce fighter. *That* was the difference between Chief Four Bears and Chief Wolf Calf, however great were both men's exploits in battle. *That* was the difference between Swift Raven and Wolf Trap—that and their discord over the woman Blue Wing.

Swift Raven's arms shook from holding the skull aloft; his thoughts drifted to other times, when he first knew he loved Ahpcha-Toha in the days of his youth, when he was first friend to Runs Quickly, the half-breed, the other fastest boy in the tribe. Not once, but three summers, after Runs Quickly lived among the whites and only came to The People in warm weather, they both had beaten bold Wolf Trap in the corn harvest races.

Shame had burned a hole in the heart of Wolf Trap ever since. Wolf Trap, unlike wise men, had a ravenous hunger to be best at, to control everything, including Blue Wing, who had dared defy him.

Finally Swift Raven lowered the skull and sat again, his head up, his eyes closed. He concentrated on the stream of sunlight through his eyelids, the dull bloodred color there. Then he gazed down upon the slender, silver Knife River roaring its torrent of tears. He must return to Mitutanka and ask Four Bears for his daughter and the leadership of the hunt. He must do all this, no matter how the beautiful eyes of Blue Wing made such a river when she heard, no matter how his own heart took the knife of grief, again, again, every time he saw and could not touch her.

The next morning Kate found Blue Wing standing outside the door of the fort just staring at the river. She was relieved to see her friend had not hacked her hair again, nor did she wear crimson mourning paint. Perhaps that public wailing for Clive yesterday had been enough since he had been gone for nine months.

"You go to *Red Dawn* or come to Mitutanka?" Blue Wing asked when she saw her.

"I was hoping to find you and meet your family," Kate said, showing her the hemp sack full of gifts. "And have you seen Swift Raven yet? Blue Wing, what is it? He hasn't been hurt in a raid or something?"

"Swift Raven not here, gone three days to seek the sun—seek wisdom. My mother tell me this. To build his family medicine and chance to be a chief, he must take a wife again, and it must not be me."

"But if you have loved each other all these years, can't the two of you just decide——"

"No!" she interrupted, and started away from the fort. Kate hurried to catch up. Blue Wing's expression was bitter—eyes and mouth drawn down—when she turned to Kate, then looked away again. "No, it not like you choose Stirling or Dark Water."

"I have no intention of——"

"Not like for you because much medicine, future of the tribe important here. When Swift Raven returns, I will see his face and know he must go to her, this Bright Star, Corn Basket tell me."

"But if he went to seek wisdom, the answer might be to have a woman at his side who has loved him for years, a good, strong, clever woman."

"Prairie Wind, if you not trust Baby Hill, you not see our ways. And never trust love—only love! Duty, honor, what is right—*ahde,* all that so strong in tribe and must be best path to walk! At least I trying tell to myself that."

Kate stopped and pulled Blue Wing back to face her. "You're very brave, my friend, if you can put duty before love. Brave but perhaps foolish."

"But love sometimes make you to take man not right for you—like River Walker, you tell me."

"I don't know if I ever loved Clive. Perhaps it was just a desire to be cared for and admired. I don't want to choose a man that way ever again. And I cannot bear it when Stirling assumes I am already his and orders me about. I won't have it, so I guess I won't have him. Meanwhile, my feelings for Rand have changed so much lately . . . become so powerful . . . that it's frightening."

"Maybe you have real love this time for Dark Water," Blue Wing said. A hint of smile lifted the corners of her mouth and eyes. "You not worry all this now. You come to Mitutanka, like you already come to my life, welcome and honored."

Kate felt closer than ever to her friend as they walked the beaten path across the grassy stretch to the outthrust of land that held the village. Ruptare, the smaller Mandan settlement, about half the size of this one, lay two miles beyond. Because Mitutanka perched on a steep three-sided bluff above the Missouri, in case of attack it needed to be defended on only one side. As they crossed a ditch, guards with spears met them at a narrowed entrance set in a stockade fence that stretched from bluff to bluff.

"Black Mouth soldiers tell your name to village," Blue Wing said as a brave jumped up on the nearest domed clay roof just inside the gate and sang out, "Oh-karachtah Scha! Oh-karachtah Scha!" He also shouted some quick words she could not catch.

"What else did he say?" she asked Blue Wing.

"That Prairie Wind, wife of River Walker, he who died, come visit us. That you trade in his name but not today."

"I come to trade in my own name, but the rest is right," she said as they walked into the village. "No trading of goods today, only trading of greetings."

Kate was impressed by the cleanliness of Mitutanka, considering the tethered horses and packs of wandering dogs. No streets crisscrossed the area, for the dwellings were scattered in a hodgepodge around an open central court. Blue Wing told her there were sixty lodges of twenty to forty people, which Kate could tell consisted of three generations. Old grandmothers sat outside to watch toddling children or to rock babies laced in leather pouches dangling from poles. This was not so different from home.

"What's that dried thing hanging above the babies?" she asked Blue Wing, and pointed.

"Stick out finger bad luck here," Blue Wing scolded, and shoved Kate's hand down. "That thing dried birth cord, good luck."

Perhaps *everything* was not like home, Kate reminded herself again. Besides umbilical cords on display, she noted several ugly, stuffed figures hanging from the poles or scaffolds before the lodges.

In the central courtyard, beyond the rounded, cone-topped lodges, she glimpsed a six-foot cedar altar. It looked like a barrel, which Blue Wing said protected the sacred cedar post of First Man, who saved The People from the flood. Atop each lodge staring Mandans took the sun and air or worked amid an array of household goods like round leather boats, extra pots, drying buffalo hides, gourds, even weapons. Smoke and the smell of meat drifted from the vent holes in many roofs to mingle with the ever-present aroma of castoreum from so many bodies. It was that oil, Rand had told her last night, that kept mosquitoes off the Indians, and Kate could well smell why. But she was getting used to it; it suddenly seemed sweeter than the smoky smudge pots at the fort.

"Here, lodge of Long Hatchet and Corn Basket," Blue Wing said, and lifted a buffalo robe flap to lead Kate through a short wooden entryway into the dim depths. The interior was larger than she had guessed, built partly underground and about fifty feet in diameter. Sunlight splashed into the center through the vent hole. She had little time to look around the lodge itself as it was fairly full of people as well as dogs and several horses.

On a low scaffold near the door sat a wiry man, Blue Wing's father, Long Hatchet, wreathed in pipe smoke; Kate could identify him by the family resemblance. It appeared he had crude paintbrushes stuck in his hair. He raised a hand in greeting. Behind him in the center of the lodge sat a sturdy woman, who rose quickly to her feet, spilling her handwork off her lap. Still sitting was the oldest-looking woman Kate had ever seen. White hair framed a brown face seamed like a clay bank, from which two aged yet ageless dark eyes peered out. And when Kate came close in the slant of light, she saw she was marked with smallpox scars, just like the Omaha women.

"My honored father, my mother, and my grandmother, the wise one," Blue Wing said in Mandan, also reciting the lengthy list of names of each person. "These others," she went on as women so young they seemed to be children, some with babies at the breast, came forward from the shadows, "my cousins, their children, all called here aunts, little sisters, little brothers. Their husbands, uncles of the lodge, be here tonight. Come, sit. You welcome in the lodge of Long Hatchet."

Kate indeed felt welcome as she was immediately seated against a comfortable curved-stick backrest and fed before she could even give her gifts. She ate something called four mixture that seemed to be a combination of mush and vegetable stew. They also served a rich green potent-smelling soup of buffalo meat the others ate with relish, smacking their lips, while she barely managed to get it down because of the smell, if not the taste.

Using her deliberate Mandan, she spoke with the family and tried not to gawk at the surroundings. She understood now how Blue Wing could think even a fine house like Winterhaven with all its fancy purchased and manufactured trappings or General Clark's big place was barren. For here were gathered people and their many purposeful activities in one room: a place for the dogs and horses; slightly elevated, enclosed beds around the edge of the room, one of which they offered her for as long as she wished. Stewing food, fragrant hanging herbs, tools, utensils, Corn Basket's pottery, and Long Hatchet's painted robes all clustered here at the hearth and heart of the family.

Kate accepted their invitation to stay for as long as she wanted and told them she would bring her things before nightfall, after she bade farewell to a friend who was leaving for Fort Union. She gave them gifts they nodded and whispered over with great delight.

It was then she noticed that all the adults, especially

old Buffalo Grass, were missing parts of their fingers. She shuddered, telling herself that maiming themselves to show grief was just their way. When she finally stood, Buffalo Grass insisted the willow wood backrest she had leaned against was now hers. Kate noticed how the old woman rocked rhythmically back and forth against her own; she thought of her own grandmother, whom she had never met, sitting in her rocking chair on that porch in Ohio.

Kate's departure stretched out longer than her visit. More questions, good wishes, many thanks for taking in their Ahpcha-Toha, for nursing her through her illness, gratitude for fair trading, for a good heart toward The People. Next time she must bring her son, Much Questions; they hoped, they said, with a pointed glance at Blue Wing, Kate would be married soon again.

Even in this short time Kate felt she began to know them. Buffalo Grass, who had no doubt seen so much, appeared interested in each thing Kate said. She had a bright, young mind in that wizened body. Corn Basket seemed serious and stern but also concerned and kind; Long Hatchet solemn and proud; but not too proud to be considerate of a stranger.

The Mandan women did most of the talking. The younger ones deferred first to Buffalo Grass, then to Corn Basket if either of them spoke. And anytime Long Hatchet so much as muttered, the lodge fell silent. Only one little boy kept squirming and squealing even while Long Hatchet spoke. When his mother leaned down to hush him, he slapped her face with a resounding smack.

Kate held her breath, expecting swift punishment for the naked little boy, who made a face, even at Corn Basket, and ran outside with two dogs at his heels. As much as she loved Jamie, Kate would have spanked him soundly for such behavior before a guest.

"Bold heart in boy," Long Hatchet announced with a nod. "Make good brave someday. And someday," he said to Kate, "I see your good picture drawing too."

Thrilled that Long Hatchet seemed to encourage her art, she replied, "I want very much to make good drawings of The People. If that would be allowed."

"Good," he said, and from his hair, drew a wooden stick with stiff bristles bound on it and presented it to her. "But no drawing O-Kee-Pa if Blue Wing take you see it."

"O-Kee-Pa?" Kate repeated.

"Ceremonial dance," Blue Wing put in, "to call Brother Buffalo before the summer hunt. The People visited by a man once make very good drawings of it, but they angry. Too much medicine in dance to draw."

Kate knew Blue Wing must be referring to George Catlin, but Kate did not admit she had met and admired him. Perhaps she would tell Long Hatchet someday if he showed her how he did drawings on the buffalo robes. Now she thanked him for giving her a brush to paint; she felt that was his permission for her to pursue her art here. It touched her deeply, for there had been times when those in authority over her life had broken her brushes and her heart.

Just as Kate and Blue Wing were about to leave, in dashed a handsome young man with small mirrors in his hair—and one tied to his wrist in a wooden frame. Before he even greeted the rest of them, he squinted in his wrist mirror, straightened his two hair feathers, and gave his tresses a shake. All he had displayed there clanked and clattered. Then he nodded to them all and greeted Long Hatchet in a string of blurred Mandan.

"This Arrow Point, youngest brother," Blue Wing explained. "Fine brave. Other brother, Gray Eyes, he married to Red Flower and living with her family, out guarding women with the corn this day."

Kate tried not to smile as she spoke with Arrow Point. He was carefully painted and seemed to preen. An Indian dandy if ever there was one, yet a fine brave with feathers and paint which indicated exploits.

"And this year again he be part of the men's ceremony of O-Kee-Pa." Blue Wing continued her lengthy recital of Arrow Point's virtues, points of obvious pride in the family, who nodded at the telling of each deed. "And he has one of most decorated love exploit sticks of anyone in the village—see?"

Proudly the boy, who could not have yet been fifteen, drew from his hair and thrust out for Kate's inspection a white foot-long stick painted with black stripes. By now Kate was used to the way Indian men displayed their battle braveries with paint or other symbols, but she could not grasp what this was for.

"Love exploits?" she asked, repeating Blue Wing's own words.

"For each girl he lying with, he not married yet," she announced, and the entire family nodded while the handsome boy again glanced in his mirror and rearranged his tresses.

Kate had to admit it had been quite a day already as Blue Wing walked her out of the village and Kate headed alone down to the river to bid farewell to Stirling. He might be gone almost a month to visit Fort Union. She wondered if she would miss him. But no matter what she had tried to convince Blue Wing earlier about being reasonable about love, it was Rand she wanted to be with, not Stirling.

She saw Stirling watching Blackwell's man loading the fort's keelboat; she called to him and waved. He looked relieved to see her and hurried to meet her.

"I just wanted to say farewell," she told him as they strolled back toward the river, "so we didn't end on a sour note when you're heading off into danger."

"Kate," he said, and captured her hand, "I don't want you to talk about us ending. When I come back, we'll start over. As for dangers upriver, you must not worry. Everyone's armed on board, and one fellow told me the Sioux won't do anything to upset the whites or Mandans now because they would like to get in on the Mandan corn harvest next month."

"Oh, no. I never want to see that Big Buck again as long as I live."

"Come on then, Mount!" the keelboat captain called. "Though I can see with my own eyes you're a danged fool to be leavin'!"

Stirling turned and kissed her. She meant to keep it a mere peck, but when she tried to step back, his hand cupped her head to hold her to him.

The keelboat crew whooped and hollered. Stirling

seized her wrists and stared into her eyes and said, "I want your promise when I return. Your promise for forever. And I *will* let you be your own independent woman, Kate. We'll be happy, rich, *and independent* together, you'll see."

"I can't promise, Stirling. But don't worry about it and take care of yourself. I—I do love you as a friend."

Even at that crumb he grinned, triumphantly, she thought, and vaulted aboard the boat. She chided herself for not telling him definitely no, now and forever. But it would be unfair with everyone staring when he was leaving. As soon as he came back, she would make it clear.

Now she waved as the boat set out, being poled and sailed upriver. How silent it seemed with no pounding of the paddles, no fireboxes roaring or steam valve shrieking. She stood there a very long time.

"I know," Rand said behind her, "Stirling asked Major Blackwell to keep an eye on you, but I thought I'd at least escort you back to Mitutanka with your things. I hear you're going to live for a while with Blue Wing's family."

He looked very pleased with himself, standing there leaning his outstretched hands on the barrel of his gun with the stock propped between his splayed feet. She wondered how long he had been behind her and decided it must not have been long for him to have that grin. Was he just happy to be back here, or was he that happy to have Stirling gone for a while?

"Word travels fast in Mandan," she said, rather than rise to his bait about Stirling and Blackwell. They started to walk up toward the fort.

"Long Hatchet's my adopted tribal father," he reminded her. "If I didn't have to sleep in the fort, I'd live with them rather than my mother's people, though they would take me in. But as I'm only half Mandan and half white, I guess I can sometimes get away with obeying only half of everyone's rules."

"I don't think you want to obey *any* of Major Blackwell's."

"But I have to if I want to help mediate problems

here," he said with a frown that darkened his eyes. "So, what do you think of Mitutanka and The People so far?"

"I like them despite the surprises. Is it impolite to refuse certain foods?"

"Why?" he asked as a hint of a grin softened his expression. "Did they feed you their delicacy of rotted buffalo carcass soup?"

She blanched and stopped walking in the shadow of the fort. Thinking she might be ill any moment, she pressed her hands to her stomach. "Is that what it was, the green stuff? A delicacy? It smelled worse than that skunk Blue Wing brought in once!"

"As Blackwell told you, you take a risk eating with the Mandans. You noticed at his table you might as well have been dining in one of those fancy St. Louis hotels."

"I don't care," she declared. "I'd rather eat with the Mandans anytime!"

He smiled so broadly for once that his teeth gleamed white against his face. "If you ate that stuff," he admitted, "I admire your fortitude. They snag carcasses from the spring river and bury them till they are 'ripe and ready' to make that green soup. That will get you off to a bold, brave start with Blue Wing's family."

"Ugh! You should have warned me about it earlier! Never mind grinning at my stupidity, Dark Water! And if you're an adopted son of Long Hatchet, do you go around showing strange women your love exploit stick?"

The moment the words were out of her mouth, she regretted them. When she said it in English, it didn't come out quite the same, though surely the man must know what she meant. She hadn't intended a joke—or worse, something obscene. He went stone still, then burst out laughing. It too was the rarest of sights and sounds, but it annoyed her. He evidently saw that and held up his hands as if to ward off a physical attack that was tempting.

"Kate, I swear, anytime you want to see my love exploit stick, I'd be happy to show you."

She almost pretended she didn't have a notion what he meant, but it was far too late for any pretense between them. Whether or not he really had a love exploit stick, he was going to confound and needle her now.

"Rand Cloud—Major MacLeod—Dark Water, or whatever they call you around here, stop it! You know what I *meant* whatever I *said*!"

"Ah, damn," he muttered, and leaned back against the stockade near the fort gate to wipe tears from the corners of his eyes with one thumb and index finger. "Sorry. I just needed ... I wanted ..." He floundered. "It's just I feel so pent up here with Blackwell piously pronouncing judgment on the tribe, then scheming to make things worse. I didn't mean to cut loose at your expense."

His apology deflated her anger. "I'm sorry too. I didn't say it right."

"You said it exactly right. I had a love exploit stick one summer when I was here, Kate, when I was about seventeen. I was proud as a young rooster of it, what it meant. It's long gone, like a lot of things. Better go in to get your belongings, and we'll go over to Mitutanka. Just like the fort, they close the gate at sundown, and I need to get back over here. I think Blackwell's actually planning to build a still. I've got to find a way to stop him without getting in more trouble than I already am. I don't want him petitioning Clark for my dismissal."

"A still? Whatever for, if the Mandans don't want the whites' firewater? He's got Stirling's brandy now, unfortunately."

"He's hoping the tribe can be lured or coerced. One of the young leaders, Wolf Trap—the one married to Blue Wing's sister—is not so averse to drinking or other white ways. I'm afraid Blackwell and Marbois have as much a vested interest in getting him the chiefdom as I do getting someone else in a position of power."

"Are Chiefs Four Bears and Wolf Calf planning to retire?"

"No, but they will gradually have their duties assumed by younger men the tribe approves, while the new chiefs learn from the older ones. It's a darn sight more civilized than a knock-down-drag-out presidential election with one man immediately ousting the other."

As he spoke, he leaned one shoulder against the peeled

tree trunks of the stockade. She leaned her back against it, one boot sole on the wall, her face turned to him. The river breeze ruffled their hair and her skirts. She felt so close to him lately: trusted, trusting; at ease instead of on edge, as she used to feel. Yet jolts of tension crackled and surged between them, and she was certain he was aware of that too.

"Rand, may I ask you one more 'Mandan' question? Blue Wing said she'll take me to the O-Kee-Pa ceremonials, and her brother's going to be in the young men's part of it. What is all that? It would be all right to go, wouldn't it? It's safe, I mean. Are you going?"

"If you really want to understand the Mandans, you should go. But I would be prepared for surprises beyond anything else here, more than green soup, more than the way they mourn their dead or take more than one wife. It's safe for you physically, and yes, I'll be there, but just be prepared."

"They dress up like the buffalo, I take it? Lots of wild dancing?" she said, trying to probe what he meant.

"Yes, you'll see. And I'll bring you back to the lodge or the fort if you don't like it, all right?"

"All right," she said with a smile as she pushed a stray, blowing lock of hair from her eyes. "I'm grateful again."

His rugged features softened at that, but he said, "Kate, among Blue Wing's family, did you meet Loud Fox, her uncle?"

"No. Is he special?"

"Special to the tribe. He's a sort of holy man, a berdache. You know the word?"

"No. Like a medicine man?"

"No—berdaches are rare in number, but many Plains tribes have one or two. Loud Fox is the only one here now. They are men who dress like women, do women's work, even have ... physical relations with other men. But they are believed to have special powers of prophecy and can call the buffalo. You'll see him at the O-Kee-Pa, and I just wanted you to know. They don't regard it as outcast effeminacy, as the whites would."

"Strange, so strange. And wrong, I'd say. But here, where things are so different, it seems harder to judge.

Did you want to warn me that is what will be shocking at the O-Kee-Pa?"

"No, O-Kee-Pa has more to it than that revelation. Do you still want to go?"

"Yes. Rand, how much of their religion do you believe in?"

"I respect it all without believing much. My Scottish aunt Alice made me a Presbyterian, if not a very good one when it came to how strict and stern they can be. She had me a lot more years than my mother did, even though every summer, over Aunt Alice's protests, I used to set out to work my way up here on a keelboat. But I'd always come back to her . . . till now," he said, and stared, suddenly forlorn, past her shoulder.

"But still," he said, looking back at her, "sometimes I see certain powers at work among the tribe I can't explain. I don't know, maybe just because they believe in their ways so much it makes things happen."

"I was raised pretty strict Methodist, but I've felt the same way about it—like I'm not a good one," she admitted. "But each person still has to find his or her way to the Lord even if there's someone in the family who is strong for it, like my mother or your aunt. Strange, but I've felt closer to God—He Who Lives Above, as they put it here—out on the river, on the prairie, even in the forests than in the town. Sometimes I think I must have been a square peg in a round hole in so many ways, back in St. Louis. And I agree with you about feeling pent up in the fort and respecting, if not accepting, Mandan beliefs. I guess we're very alike, you and I. And I'm glad you'll be there at O-Kee-Pa because then I won't be a bit worried about it."

The lines of his face tightened; shutters seemed to drop over his luminous eyes. His voice came taut as he looked away. "We have very little in common, Kate. Not our pasts, not what we want for our futures. Go get your things. And hurry up because I've got a lot to do."

For once she didn't want to argue over his swift change of mood. She had glimpsed a dark, empty space inside him before he closed her out again. She knew a void of fear and self-blame from childhood could haunt an adult;

it had been her legacy from her father, as perhaps Rand's was, inadvertently, from his mother and later others who had shut the half-breed out. But she dared not risk telling him she understood, not yet.

Still, she almost reached out to touch his shoulder, gone stone-hard again as he stared out toward the river. Why, she wondered, did it always have to be this way between them? Each time she felt a bond, he yanked it back and cut it, blaming her, however subtly. He might have been an outcast at times, but he had also, obviously, been loved. She knew now how much she wanted to plumb the depths of this man The People called Dark Water.

"I'll hurry," she said. "I'm dying to start painting, and I've got a lot to do to prepare for trading tomorrow. I don't think your boss, Major Blackwell, despite all his city manners and shrewd concern, is going to let me use that fur and robe press, so I'll have to find some other way to pack them."

"You'll find another way," she heard him mutter. She did not say more, for she did not want him to know she had also heard his unspoken words of loneliness and longing, his silent plea to be loved.

Chapter 13

Although Ahpcha-Toha had long ago purchased the right to make her own earthen pots, today she helped her mother with hers. Outside the lodge, kneeling in the sun, the two women kneaded the mix of clay and sand, then formed the bowl sections of two-mouthed water pots by molding a lump around a stone. Intent, not speaking now, they cut the stone out and rejoined the form, finally pulling out the pouring lips and pressing their distinctive family pattern into the surface with a piece of coarsely woven cloth.

After the pots sun-dried during the four days of O-Kee-Pa, the craftswomen would smear them with corn boil scum and bake them in ash fires. They came out light but turned black with use. When she had set her first vessel in its willow bark ring and tied the thong for packing it on the hunt, Blue Wing recalled, how full her heart had been. Today, when she thought about Swift Raven, her head was full but her heart empty.

Corn Basket sat back on her heels and washed the clay from her hands. "Will you do as I asked now?" she said to her daughter. "Will you take one of the new-baked pots to Clam Necklace in her lodge? You gave few words to her last night and would not look at Wolf Trap. You, like Swift Raven, must learn to do what is best for family and The People."

"I went away once and wed another because it was best I not be here to see either Wolf Trap or Swift Raven."

"This time," Corn Basket said, and grasped her daughter's wrist with her wet hand, "you must stay but still not see Swift Raven. You must keep your eyes and thoughts away from him, but not from Wolf Trap. You belong to him in the way of The People."

Blue Wing did not move for one moment. She felt as if she were being pulled and molded, sliced in two, but not mended. She felt her hopes and heart harden. Surely her mother could not know what Wolf Trap was really like to ask this thing of her. Surely her family could not have known what he and Clam Necklace did to her.

"I will take the pot to Clam Necklace," she said, thinking that just yesterday she had told her friend Prairie Wind that a man could not always be chosen for love among The People. "But I cannot say what I will do about Wolf Trap. He will be chief someday with or without me. But I know it is not good that I, alone in the tribe, seem not to heed my family or The People's wishes. I will give the pot and good words to my sister, Clam Necklace."

Blue Wing washed her hands and headed with a baked pot across the village, around the edge of the courtyard, where the important medicine bundle families were preparing for the first day of O-Kee-Pa tomorrow. She must tell Prairie Wind more about it before she saw it, yet much of it was not to be told outside the tribe. Only a few whites The People trusted had ever seen it. Dark Water, of course, but his blood was half Mandan. River Walker, but he had married Mandan. Some trappers and that artist Prairie Wind admired.

She knew there were bloody, brazen parts of O-Kee-Pa that shocked the whites, but her Prairie Wind loved The People. Surely she would understand and accept. *Ahde,* if only she herself, Blue Wing, could accept The People's ways to bend her neck to Swift Raven's rival, the brutal, grasping Wolf Trap!

Blue Wing wove her way past the medicine lodge where the young male initiates for O-Kee-Pa would soon gather. Chief Four Bears, beloved of the tribe, had been chosen the Kani-Sachka, the overseer of the four days.

She spoke and nodded to several who called her name. She smiled to see boys playing on the domed roof of a lodge with their stick bows and arrows. It made her miss Much Questions; as ever, it made her long for a son of her own. Perhaps, even if his father must be Wolf Trap, it would be enough to have that son. She walked around the big lodge of Four Bears, set near the medicine lodge because he had married a woman of the powerful family of the turtle drum medicine bundle.

And there, as he walked away from that lodge, she came face-to-face with Swift Raven.

They both stopped and stared. She had heard he had returned; she had not seen him, not for twelve long moons. For her, all the noise, the motion stopped. They stood alone as the earth shifted under her bare feet.

"Ahpcha-Toha." He spoke first. "I heard that you were back."

"I too . . . heard you returned from seeking the sun on the Knife River."

He looked so handsome and strong to her. Yet she felt like a pot shattered on the rocks to see him so close and not run to his arms. "I hear you seek a new wife." She choked out the words.

"I have had a dream. I must do this. I have asked Four Bears for his youngest, Bright Star."

"And?"

"He has named me leader of the buffalo hunt and will decide about Bright Star when it is over."

She nodded. Then that was to be Swift Raven's great test. If the hunt was a success, he could have Bright Star and a bright future. If he "kicked the stone," as the tribe said—if men were lost or horses gored, if, even after the buffalo calling of O-Kee-Pa, Brother Buffalo did not offer himself—that would be the sad, shameful end of Swift Raven's quest for power.

"In the O-Kee-Pa ceremony I will become Night with your Old Woman in the Moon painted on my back," he said.

Though he moved not a step closer, his soft voice, his remembering how much Old Woman meant to her touched her deeply. The role of Night was not a main part in the dancing, not like one of the eight bull buffalo, but then Swift Raven was unwed right now and had no wife to offer for the walking with the buffalo. Oh, she thought, if only she were his wife, she would do that, do anything for him!

"I will be watching," she whispered.

"I think you are going to your sister's lodge. Will you go to live there now you have no husband?"

"I do not know."

"For the good of your family, the tribe, you must. That is what guides my steps, Blue Wing."

She felt furious that he asked this of her, to give herself to his rival, whom he did not respect any more than she did. But she realized he was telling her again that he sought a new wife and power for his family for the good of the tribe, not for his own happiness. Then he must still love her, Blue Wing! She spoke before she could pull the words back.

"Then on the night when some women walk with the buffalo, I will walk with Night and lie under the moon. For one last time before I go to the lodge of Wolf Trap and Clam Necklace as you have asked, I will be free to do as I wish."

She could see he took her meaning, her fervent request. His dark eyes widened; his nostrils flared. Joy flitted across his face before it plunged into shadow.

"You are the bravest woman I have ever known, Ahpcha-Toha!" He turned and walked back toward the busy courtyard.

The sounds and sights of the village seeped back into her. She stood clutching the pot to her breasts so hard they hurt. Four nights from now—would he come? They had not spoken of the place—their place—but surely he must know. One night to hold each other forever before she gave herself, as he did, for The People.

Now she knew she could sacrifice herself because the only man she would ever really love had asked this of her, not because of her family or the tribe. Never because of Clam Necklace's and Wolf Trap's wishes! For they had both betrayed her, even as some of Prairie Wind's family had hurt Prairie Wind.

Blue Wing's betrayal had happened the day after Clam Necklace heard her younger sister, Blue Wing, had refused to join her in her new lodge because she dared love another. Clam Necklace had lured Blue Wing to pick sacred sage on the prairie. There a grim Wolf Trap had been waiting like a snake in the grass. Clam Necklace held Blue Wing's arms and stopped her cries while Wolf Trap thrust himself between her thrashing legs where she had known only the tender touch of Swift Raven.

Punished, shamed for her willful disobeying of her family's wishes and tribal ways, fearing her parents and The People might even know of this retribution, she had told no one. But neither had she gone broken to the lodge of Wolf Trap. She had lifted her head and run away to where she found the protection of River Walker. But now, now that was long over, and she stood here alone, for Swift Raven had gone.

Such a sacrifice for him to send her to his enemy! It showed he put The People first. It proved he knew he would find great success and many buffalo on the hunt. And as much as she wanted to wait to see what happened there, she realized she must promise herself to Wolf Trap now to show Swift Raven she believed he would succeed and earn Bright Star's hand. And if Blue Wing did this thing in the way of The People, would it not placate the spirits and Brother Buffalo to give a good hunt?

The price was great. She would promise it now and, after the summer hunt, move to Wolf Trap's lodge as second wife. But over the years, living unloved, as Swift Raven became beloved of the tribe, just as her man, Chief Wolf Trap, was obeyed but feared, she would overflow with pride for Chief Swift Raven alone, just like a pot full to bursting with white river water!

That afternoon in the common room of the *Red Dawn,* Kate received the leaders of the tribe Rand had invited for her. Gabe stood behind her chair, Rand at the door in case she needed an interpreter. But her hands clasped on the table before her, she managed to speak for herself. However much she hesitated or floundered for a word, Rand said nothing. She was piqued he did not help her at first but soon realized the Indians were pleased she struggled to speak in their tongue.

Four Bears even smiled, though Wolf Calf looked forbidding, as did his nephew Wolf Trap. But it was Blue Wing's Swift Raven whom Kate's eyes kept coming back to. He spoke with authority, yet his voice was calm. Still, it was Wolf Calf doing most of the talking.

"Good prices, like with your man, River Walker. But not much robes and fur left after Chouteau's fire canoes leave. Summer beaver coats thin, no good," he said, gesturing with many of his words.

"But my friend Blue Wing tells me," Kate said quietly, "that there will be a good buffalo hunt under Swift Raven's leadership. I will trade for robes if they are not thin ones. The whites use robes for blankets, especially in their sleighs and carriages in winter," she added, using a few gestures herself.

Swift Raven and Four Bears nodded; the other two frowned. She was beginning to see clearly the dividing line of leadership here. "I understand," she went on, "that many robes of Brother Buffalo have been promised to Marbois when he returns. I understand about giving one's word. At Fort Pierre, when Big Buck of the Sioux wanted me to trade with his people, I said I had promised my goods for the Mandans."

Much muted muttering followed that revelation. Perhaps she should not have mentioned she had spoken with the Sioux. But soon there were admiring nods from Swift Raven and Four Bears.

"I tell you, woman," Wolf Trap warned, "never trust Big Buck and his father, White Raven. That name Raven bring bad medicine even wh—"

Whatever the rest of the insult he intended, Wolf Calf lifted his hand to halt both Wolf Trap's words and Swift Raven's quick reaction. And Four Bears put in, "There be good O-Kee-Pa, good hunt, we trade good with you and Marbois, Prairie Wind. You want we make our marks on paper like with Chouteau's factor?"

"No, for I trust the word of the great chiefs of The People," she said, and got to her feet next to Gabe, though she instantly regretted her diminutive height among them. She chided herself again for often forgetting she was so small, for even among these men, she had not felt so.

"And now I and the captain of my fire canoe give to you these gifts to pledge our trust," she told them.

Nodding, the men solemnly took the offered leather packets of tobacco and folded squares of bright blue calico from Kate. But they turned as wide-eyed as Jamie when Gabe handed them his carved wooden banks shaped like the *Red Dawn*. They shook them to hear their two pennies clink together inside; they squinted in the coin slot; they turned the wooden plug to get them out so they could plunk them back in again. Kate wondered if they believed that in possessing the replicas, they had some power over the steamer.

As he accepted his due, Wolf Trap's eyes glistened. Slowly he reached in his parfleche pouch and pulled out a leather thong strung with beads and clamshells. "From my wife, Clam Necklace," he said. "She have good heart to you bring her sister, Blue Wing, back to us, back to me, promised as my second wife after buffalo hunt."

Taken unaware by that revelation, Kate hesitated. She had seen Blue Wing not long ago; she had said nothing of this. Wolf Trap pushed the necklace into her hands and stepped back.

"She didn't . . . tell me . . . that news," Kate stammered in English, and then remembered to repeat it in Mandan as her eyes sought Rand's. He shrugged and shook his head to show he hadn't heard either. Kate saw Swift Raven's lithe body tense, his hand close hard around his leather pouch. But he said nothing else.

"Go now, prepare for tomorrow O-Kee-Pa." Four Bears' voice soothed the sharp silence. The men filed out, Rand included, Gabe following after, coins in banks still rattling. Kate heard their voices drift back, talking about smoking together, that women never smoked even if they had much medicine.

Kate dropped the heavy necklace, sat down hard at the table, and hid her face in her hands. No, curse it, she thought, women didn't do a lot of things they should be able to if they wanted. Indeed, they seemed not to have much medicine or anything else that mattered to men sometimes. Like choosing whom they would wed. Like standing up to bullies like that Wolf Trap and his grim uncle.

Worse, once again Kate could not understand or accept the ways of her Mandan "sister." Now Clam Necklace dared thank her for bringing Blue Wing home to her own destruction. Why did what seemed reasonable to her family and friends have to dictate whom a woman wed if she loved someone else? Kate hurled the necklace across the room, where it skidded into a dark corner and lay still.

The first day of O-Kee-Pa Kate found nothing upsetting but the fact that Blue Wing was determined to become Wolf Trap's second wife and would not discuss it. The People assembled to hear stories of the tribe's past, but all were told in an ancient dialect no one, especially Kate, could understand. Still, Blue Wing whispered to her about the creation of First Man by He Who Lives Above and of that man's salvation in a floating cedar boat during the flood.

Rand kept his promise to be nearby, for he lifted a hand to her as he sat on another roof across the way with boys and young men. She did not see anyone else from the fort, but then she could not imagine Major Blackwell wanting anything to do with this. Or perhaps he had not been invited.

The droning recitation was accompanied by the dull thud-thud of the sacred turtle drums. Kate saw no links to the buffalo hunt at all in the performance until Blue Wing told her that within each buffalo skin drum were balls of buffalo hair to represent the unborn buffalo yet in their mother's wombs.

"And I soon hope to have a child to make all well," Blue Wing whispered to her as they headed back to the lodge.

"If you do not love Wolf Trap, couldn't a child by him just make things worse?" Kate dared.

"Why you give bent words to me?" Blue Wing asked. "You once say your son was your life when River Walker hurt you and betrayed you and you not love him anymore!"

Kate bit her tongue and mourned Blue Wing's ever-bitter one. Her friend was on edge, desperate about something, deeply unhappy, yet wildly excited. Was it only exhilaration about the ceremonies that all The People seemed to feel? Kate could not bear to lose Blue Wing's friendship any more than she could bear to have her go to live with Wolf Trap and his haughty wife, for she had met Clam Necklace that morning. All Kate could think was that with a change of language, Clam Necklace would be right at home with some of the matrons of St. Louis, even to the pinched face and pouty mouth.

"I hope you wear your new necklace tomorrow," Clam Necklace had said to Kate, pointedly fingering her own. "Where is it? My gift to you means *we* friends."

"I left it on the fire canoe—for safekeeping, of course," Kate replied.

"I tell to you, wear it, for your safekeeping here. Gift from wife of future tribal leader, first wife of lodge of Wolf Trap," she had said, more to Blue Wing than Kate. Then, pulling her two young children behind her, she had swept on her way to a closer seat than their intended perch on the roof.

The second day of O-Kee-Pa eight buffalo bull dancers made their appearance. Their bodies painted black, they wore buffalo robes, fur side out, on their naked backs. Clothed only in that and dark breechcloths, they ran, leaped, danced, and roared in imitation of the beasts. Kate noticed that the bull dancers were older braves; two of them—the leaders of the herd, as Blue Wing put it—were garbed in headdresses made from the entire horned head of the animals.

The turtle drums pounded on, and Four Bears as Kani-Sachka leaned against the sacred cedar boat of First Man, moaning for communion with the buffalo herds out on the prairie. Soon a handsome, tall, elaborately attired woman joined him to add to Four Bears' piercing cries.

"My uncle Loud Fox," Blue Wing whispered, and looked as if she were awaiting more of Kate's questions. But forewarned by Rand, Kate just nodded. Perhaps she would not even have known the woman was really a man if Rand had not prepared her.

The third day the buffalo were joined by masked, fur-and feather-clad animals of all kinds that imitated the brother beasts of the Mandans. Coyotes howled and prowled, birds fished and preened, the beavers smacked their tails—Kate thought it was wonderful and ingenious. But most intriguing—to Blue Wing too, Kate could tell—was Swift Raven depicting Night. Nearly naked with only a feather girdle around his lean hips, he gleamed shiny ebony with white stars painted everywhere. On his back was the moon, and on his chest the sun.

Clam Necklace, who sat with them this day, had interrupted Blue Wing's narration so many times the girl sat sullen and silent on Kate's other side now. But when Swift Raven leaped on the scene, she elbowed Kate and whispered, "Old Woman in the Moon—a good painting, yes?"

"Yes, very good," Kate said, and elbowed her gently back.

"*I* really think," Clam Necklace said loudly enough for the whole cluster of women to hear, "it good that Swift Raven has bright stars all over his strong body, for he will soon lie every night with Bright Star." Corn Basket leveled a look at her elder daughter that she ignored. "I only hope Swift Raven leads a good hunt so he can have her soon. She cannot wait to be his, that is sure."

Kate turned to silence the woman, but Blue Wing seized her wrist. "Listen to the cries from the medicine lodge," she said. "The young men are walking with the buffalo."

Wails and occasional shrieks pierced even the beat of turtle drums. "Come," Blue Wing said to Kate, and they slid down from the roof.

"What's happening to the young men there?" Kate asked her. "That sounds awful, and Arrow Point's with them."

Blue Wing leaned back against the slanted side of the lodge as if she were in pain. "He will be many times prouder than he was of his mirrors or love exploits," she said. "To honor the buffalo, the older men pierce the young men's skin and muscles here and here," she explained, and hit her chest above her breasts. "They drag buffalo skulls around or are pulled by prayer poles until they faint from pain or blood loss."

Kate's mouth fell open. So that was what—one thing, at least—none of them, even Rand, had wanted to tell her. Self-torture. She thought she would be sick. And the Mandans dared call the Sioux bloody!

Blue Wing's eyes shot open. "I feel with them for the first time," she whispered. "For here I am torn too that Swift Raven will never be mine and I agreed. For the others, I agreed," she said, and ran toward her lodge.

But Kate saw that when Blue Wing met her father coming out the door, she stopped and stood erect, greeted him, and walked slowly in. Long Hatchet nodded to Kate as he walked past toward the dancing. Over his shoulder lay one of his most elaborately painted robes. She wondered if he was in the performance tonight, but even so, she could stomach no more of it. For the first time since she'd arrived, she heartily wished she were back in St. Louis. Still, she went in to see if she could comfort Blue Wing.

Although Kate had off and on decided she would not attend the last climactic night of O-Kee-Pa, the new intensity of the drums and chanting drew her. She stood amid a crowd of strangers, not wanting to climb one of the roofs, not wanting to sit with Clam Necklace or even Blue Wing. She did not see them anyway. But how grateful she was when Rand suddenly appeared.

"I thought you might not come," he said, standing close behind her.

"I had to," she told him as they watched the building action. To chants, pipes, drums, and even piercing screams from the crowd, the eight bull dancers got even wilder. Now they were joined by eight dancing women, including Clam Necklace; Red Flower, Blue Wing's sister-in-law; and two young matrons from Long Hatchet's lodge. The women too were scantily clad in aprons and collars of willow leaves. The buffalo approached the women and held out sacred bundles, which the women pressed to their bare breasts, sighing, swooning. Kate began to feel hot—embarrassed, ashamed, fascinated, even aroused—by it all. She dared not ask a question of Rand, but she felt his presence.

And then, amid shrill screams, in leaped a horrible-looking figure, painted black with huge white rings around his eyes. He wore a tail, a cap of coxcombs, and large fangs; like Swift Raven's depiction of Night, he had a sun on his chest and a moon on his back.

"That's not Swift Raven?" she asked Rand, who leaned over her shoulder to squint at the creature too.

"No, it's someone else as O-Kee-Hee-De. It's the closest thing they have to a devil."

"That's the stuffed figure hanging above the medicine lodge and chiefs' houses," she said.

"To ward evil away with his own terrible mirror image," he said. "That stick with the red ball on it is to represent an enemy's head."

He said no more in explanation as O-Kee-Hee-De ran amok, "terrifying" the women. And then Kate saw the element of his costume Rand had not described. For the black figure had produced from between his legs a huge carved wooden phallus the women fled from when he chased them. Then Four Bears as Kani-Sachka stepped forward, brandishing a medicine pipe—a tribal calumet, which Kate knew always stood for safety and peace in the tribe. At that O-Kee-Hee-De ran from the women but pretended to mount and rut each buffalo in turn. Shrieks and cries from the tribe intensified.

"Rites for the fertility of the buffalo—for all of nature," Rand said close in her ear, and put his hands on her shoulders. She jumped at his touch, then stood more steadily, still amazed by it all when she knew that she should refuse to look at more, should go off in a huff. But she was not offended. She knew now why the tribe seldom shared O-Kee-Pa with the whites; she certainly would not be telling her mother, Jamie, or Stirling about all this!

Now there was a mad melee as the women of the tribe beat O-Kee-Hee-De with sticks, even broke his phallus and drove him off.

"The defeat of evil," Rand said, and squeezed her shoulders.

"Or women taking their rightful place in the world," she said. He amazed her by a chuckle deep in his throat. He turned her away from the scene and steered her through the twisting path between the lodges, toward the gate of the village.

"Isn't there more?" she asked.

"Yes, but you're supposed to be fainting at that much."

"What else happens?"

"Now those eight women walk with the buffalo, but it is not voluntary torture, as when the young initiates walk with the buffalo to manhood. Kate"—he went on as they stopped in the cool, deeper shadows near the gate, still guarded by members of the Black Mouth Society of tribal soldiers—"the Mandan hunters believe if their wives lie with those older, veteran hunters dressed like the buffalo, that will appease the real buffalo. Then the herds will come nearer to the village and give their lives in the hunt."

"What? The husbands—like Wolf Trap, because Clam Necklace was there—want their wives to lie with those older men?"

He nodded. "One of the reasons the whites think the Indian women are loose is that they are willing to bed men to have their power and medicine . . . well, rub off. Then when the Indians bed them again, the power of the whites, the buffalo, or whatever transfers to them."

"I can't believe it."

"I'm not making this up."

"I didn't mean that. I just . . . I can't believe I'm here, seeing this, hearing this, accepting this. So their having several wives is nothing next to this," she said in wonderment.

"Small potatoes, as my aunt would say—if my father or I had ever told her this, and I assure you we did not."

"And yet you encouraged me to see it."

"You're hardly my aunt Alice. Kate, you're not like any woman I've ever known. I mean that as a compliment. Want to walk outside? When they're finished, it gets louder and longer. They shoot guns into the air, and the buffalo finally fall down as if dead to end the ceremony."

"After all that wild dancing . . . and breeding, I should
think they would fall down dead of exhaustion," she said,
then once again could not believe she had said that, and
to Rand. Nor could she believe she was willing to go off
into the dark alone with him. But something beat hot and
hard in her blood tonight. Rand took his rifle from a
brave who held it for him near the gate and pulled her out
into the blowing night.

"The mosquitoes will eat us," she said, trying to cling
to a last glimmer of protest.

"I won't let them get you. The wind will keep them
off, and they don't like where we're going."

"Where are we going?"

"To a little ravine along the stream where there's a
cave. Swift Raven and I used to hide there when we were
young. During the day bats are there, but they're all out
now."

She strode along at his side. She was going to a cave
where bats lived, alone with a moody man she had once
considered her enemy. Such strange things she had seen
this night had really happened. Back in the village, men
in buffalo hides were having sexual congress with women
who were not their wives to public approval and ap-
plause! It was a world gone mad, yet it lured her.

Beyond that she could not, did not want to, think. She
only wanted to feel how good it was to be alive out here,
holding Rand's hand under the grand star-lit heavens
arching over the prairie and the river. She only knew that
of all places on the planet, this was where and with whom
she wanted most to be this night.

Their eyes adjusted to the dark. And then the moon
rolled over the southeastern horizon, low and big like a
ripe peach, and slowly lifted to shrink and fade.

"Good evening, Old Woman in the Moon," Kate called
to the sky.

"Sh!" he said. "At least till we get by the fort."

The little stream made its own night sounds as Rand
led Kate down a path along its narrow banks. An owl
hoo-hooed, and the cottonwoods and willows muted
sounds of the distant revels. The moon was much smaller

now when they could glimpse it through the rustling trees.

Rand's feet were swift and sure, but hers were not. She stumbled once and skidded, but he pulled her up—right into his hard arms. He kissed her once, powerfully, then more softly, as if tasting her.

"Want to go back?" he whispered.

"Can I trust you?"

She saw his grin flash white before he sobered. "You can trust me to let nothing else touch you."

"Then I don't want to go back," she said recklessly, and meant every word.

He guided her on again, more slowly, then pulled her off the path. Her blood rushed through her veins; her ears buzzed with it. The mouth of a cave yawned to swallow them as they shuffled in.

"There's a second entrance out the other side of a ravine," he said, speaking in a normal voice now. "Once Long Hatchet came here looking for Swift Raven and me when we had spilled his paint on a new robe he was doing, and we were out the back and to Mitutanka before he found us."

"You have happy memories of the Mandans," she said.

"Both kinds. I came back to help The People because of the good and bad in my past and the good and bad in their future."

"I don't suppose you brought a candle?" she asked as he led her back into the cave, feeling his way along the wall. "Are you sure the bats are out and there is nothing else?"

"Not much farther. Here."

He sat and tugged her down beside him on a buffalo robe. So he had planned this—this tryst. She must be careful it did not turn out to be seduction, a little voice in her head warned, but she shoved it away. Tumbled thoughts of what must be happening back at the village threatened her composure again. She should not have come, but she was glad she had. She would just talk to him, that was it. Be warm and kind but not dare to—

He turned away to put his gun down. She could see his form against the slightly grayer distant mouth of the cave.

He reached for her, lifted her into his lap. She held tightly to his arm to keep from tipping back too far in his embrace, but his other arm, like an iron band, came behind to support her shoulders. He leaned so close she breathed into his nostrils. Then they were lost in each other's touch.

It was always the same with this man. Her emotions churned and rampaged, leaving her as breathless as before when she matched his demanding kisses. His free hand roamed her throat, her shoulders, squeezed her breasts, moved to cup her bottom and lift her closer. She fought, not to escape him but to be even closer. His big calloused hand clasped her ankle, then her knee. His skin felt wonderful on her bare thigh above her stocking. She moaned deep in her throat and pulled him closer as they rolled over once and lay side by side on the buffalo rug. It was then, when Rand straddled her, keeping his weight off her by both arms beside her head that they heard the strange sound.

They froze, breathing hard. Rand covered her mouth gently with one hand, but she knew not to speak or cry out. A wild animal, a Sioux scout? Sioux had been spotted across the river. Rand was breathing hard but silently through his open mouth. His chest and belly moved against her, still pressing her down. Leaning his weight on one arm, he groped for his gun. And then they both heard the voices in Mandan and froze again.

"My Ahpcha-Toha, if anyone learns the leader of the hunt slipped out the last night of O-Kee-Pa, I will be cursed."

"It was the only way, our only night, maybe forever."

"And I would curse myself forever if I could not hold you, could not touch you like this."

"Swift Raven, this one time of all the nights of our lives, before we must part, make me your woman!"

Rand slumped heavier over Kate at the sounds that came from toward the front of the cave. They both knew, Kate thought, they should make their presence known. But would this be Swift Raven's and Blue Wing's last time together? Those two were wrong to come here, but so were she and Rand. For with their very different lives, they were as doomed, Kate thought, as those other lovers.

"Now or not till later," Rand breathed in her ear, and rolled off her. She wasn't certain what he meant at first, but he silently lifted his gun, then pulled her to her feet and steadied her. Slowly he led her farther into the cave. They left the robe where it lay and stepped carefully, so carefully. When cobwebs draped across the face, Kate closed her eyes and held more tightly to his hand. At last, after an eternity within, she breathed cool, fresh night air.

"If we had given ourselves away, it would have ended everything for them," he said, his voice normal now as they emerged in a ravine and climbed out of it. "And they don't have tomorrow, not together. As for us," he added as his arm came out to a tree trunk to stop her progress, "the drums and the dance went to our heads."

Kate nodded, but she still tingled everywhere he had touched her, and her pulse pounded like those turtle drums. Her spirits sang and soared just for being with him.

He turned her to him and held her close. They both were covered with cobwebs and dirty from their back door exit. But she wrapped her arms around his waist and pressed her cheek to his chest to hear the dull thud of his heart.

"I don't know where all that . . . between us . . . could have led," Rand said at last, and cleared his throat, pressed against her forehead. "In a few weeks you're heading south, and I'm dedicating whatever it takes here to do this job for as long as I can. No more future in that than what Swift Raven and Blue Wing face."

"I know."

"But first," he said as he set her back to look into her face, "do you want to go on the hunt?"

"The summer buffalo hunt?"

"I talked Blackwell into sending me. Nearly the whole tribe goes. Besides, you should be along to pick out the best robes for the trading. On the summer hunt the big beasts can be mangy."

"I'd love to!"

"The women will probably put you to work. I'll pick you out a horse from the stock at the fort. You don't need one of those feisty Indian ponies. Actually, Kate, Blackwell's letting me go because shortly after we return, after the corn harvest when the Sioux come in to trade, I'm going to arrange with them to visit their autumn camps to parlay for peace with the Mandans—on behalf of the tribe and the U.S. government. Usually, as soon as the corn runs out and the game gets scarce in the autumn, they'll start to raid here."

"It sounds like the Mandans almost have to buy peace from them with their corn. But won't your going out be dangerous? I wouldn't want to trust the likes of Big Buck."

"It's his father, White Raven, whom I will ultimately have to convince. It has to be done, and I'm in the best position. I told you it was important to me, so important, in fact, that if that damned Marbois makes it back here, I'm going to try to mend fences with him and convince him to go with me to translate."

"I wouldn't trust him any more than Big Buck," she said, "but I'm sure you know what you're doing."

"Sometimes I wonder," he said, and shook his head, "but the stakes are high enough to risk it. And we'll have some time on the hunt together first."

"Then I will really enjoy it!" She knew, once again, like seeing O-Kee-Pa, like walking in a pitch-dark cave, she wanted whatever came with him. She felt somehow better and bolder out here among the Mandans than she ever had.

"The buffalo hunt with the whole tribe will certainly be something to tell Jamie about," she said as they walked back toward the fort and village. "And someday, when I'm old and gray, my grandchildren."

"When you're old and gray, tell them about this too," he said. He dropped his gun, grabbed her hands, and leaning back to swing her around in a wild circle as if moonstruck, they danced.

It was more special than their celebration on the boat after they escaped the firestorm because they were alone out here. She laughed and laughed, giddy with joy and the heady sense of freedom. When she got dizzy, he pulled her close. She held to him, matching kiss for kiss in the vastness of the dark, blowing prairie.

Chapter 14

In the lodge of Chief Four Bears, Rand sat just behind the smoking circle of the tribal leaders. The People would depart for the hunt this morning, and he knew these ceremonies were as important to them as the packing. He watched with pride as Swift Raven, leader of the summer hunt, burned the sacred sage. Then he lifted his pipe to He Who Lives Above, to the four cardinal points, and to Brother Buffalo out on the prairie.

To seal their unity for this great communal endeavor, the men inhaled the smoke at the same time. But each held his pipe in his characteristic way, which was as much a part of his personality as his hair or exploit robe. Over the years Rand himself had learned to bring his pipe to his mouth swiftly to signify the first name he was given in the tribe, Runs Quickly. Though he had long since been renamed Dark Water, he yet honored the name his mother's family had given him. Swift Raven lifted his with a swooping motion of a raven in flight. Wolf Calf held his importantly with both hands; Wolf Trap's fingers spread to cover his pipe stem as if it were caught in a snare; Four Bears lifted his to his mouth slowly four times, even as he now offered a prayer for success for The People.

But as hard as Rand tried to keep his mind on Four Bears' incantation, his thoughts kept drifting, thick like this smoke, back to Kate.

He had tried not to want her; he had tried to convince himself it was best that Stirling marry her and keep her in St. Louis. Once the two of them began their partnership, they could send Gabe upriver to trade fairly and deliver the smallpox vaccine Rand was trying to get through

General Clark. Rand did not want Kate endangered or himself enticed by her coming back upriver. For when he was near her, he was sorely tempted, and that was a threat to both of them. It was bad enough to have to worry about protecting The People; having her about to protect—and desire—would keep him from his duties and the solitary life he had chosen for himself.

He had also tried not to admire her, but he did for many reasons. That first day here how boldly she had stood up to Blackwell about the Mandans' being individuals with feelings and thoughts. Though President Jackson would probably not heed a woman's words, Rand half wished *she* had been sent to take on the government in Washington. While many looked down on half-breeds, even when he had treated her rudely or roughly, she was strong but kind to him. And though Kate, like all women, seemed motivated by emotions, she displayed loyalty to principles and boldness to act—two traits he most admired in some men.

Still, despite Kate's claims that the two of them had much in common, Rand saw and stressed their differences. He did not want her to come closer, yet he wanted her with all his—all his desire, damn her. How he wished she could be his, really his! But he was so afraid that he would in turn become hers. And then wouldn't he lose something of himself in having to tear down the walls of control and seclusion that protected him from his fears? He could never face losing a woman he loved again—any more than he could face losing The People.

When the men dispersed and walked outside, Rand saw the packing was in full swing, both in the village and on the brow of the hill where the line of march formed. Only the elderly would remain behind, watched, like the ripening corn and the village dogs, by a few guards.

As he walked past lodges and then out toward the fort, he saw women down on the lowland patches, mounding soil around each cornstalk to keep it moist and strong in the summer winds while they were away. On the plain between the village and the fort, braves had tethered their two horses, one for the ride, one for the chase. Women harnessed travois to packhorses to drag the tepees and

household goods. Children ran everywhere, either helping
or hindering. The Black Mouth soldiers, under Swift Raven's command for the duration, hurried here and there,
overseeing and organizing. And then Rand saw Kate.

Amid the beige- and brown-clad Mandan women, she
stood out in her cornflower blue dress. She was helping
Blue Wing and Corn Basket pack their travois. Striding
closer, he saw she was tying down her easel and roll of
canvas among the bowls and water pots.

"I found a good mare for you. She's with my horse in
the fort, but I'll bring her right out," he told her as she
looked up. Did her eyes, blue as her dress, light to see
him or was it just the slant of sun or azure sky behind
her?

"I'm grateful. Everyone is so generous. Corn Basket
has a robe for me to sleep on, and Long Hatchet gave me
this painted parfleche to carry my brushes and paint in.
See," she said, and held it out for his perusal. "It's the
story of my arrival in Mitutanka and the first coming to
their lodge nine days ago. I'm going to learn to read Long
Hatchet's symbols. I guess this will have to do for now
until you get that exploit robe you promised me," she
went on, her tone teasing now. That lilt in her voice and
lift of her lips made his toes curl in his boots.

"I promised you?"

"When my rocking chair helped save you from the
river, remember?"

"Yes. I won't forget," he said, but forced himself to
look away from her. Swift Raven rode by, calling out orders, which were instantly obeyed. Rand thought he had
the good nature of Four Bears. People cooperated because
they liked him and wanted to help, not because they were
intimidated, as with Wolf Calf and Wolf Trap, who sat
glowering on their horses at the head of the line, apparently impatient for an overlong departure.

"Swift Raven is a kind but firm leader and in his element today," Kate said as if she could read his thoughts.

"I just pray this hunt has no catastrophes. Too much
hangs on what happens." He made the mistake of looking
at her again. She nodded and pressed her full lips together, but he felt she read him then, the way Captain

Zeke and Gabe had taught her to read the river or she would learn to read Mandan picture writing. He feared she saw his need for her. It made him feel naked, and he did not like it. Without another word he turned toward the fort.

Before he could reach it, he saw Marbois, on a painted Sioux pony, ride through the entrance. Almost immediately Marbois and Blackwell strode out toward the activities.

"Marbois, you're back," Rand said. "I see you met some friendly Sioux on the way."

Marbois ignored the jab. "Here just in time to see *this* tribe honors its buffalo robe deal with me," he muttered, and went right past Rand, who spun around to follow. "They ain't clearing outa here till I got Wolf Calf's word on them one hundred hides."

"They're aware of their bargain with you," Rand said, walking along with him and Blackwell. "They're hoping for a big hunt to have some for Mrs. Craig too."

"That right? The major here says she's been sitting real cozy with them. You still guard-dogging her?" Marbois asked, his voice bitter and accusing, but he did not break stride.

"Just plain dogging her's more like it," Blackwell muttered.

Marbois walked right up to Wolf Calf and Four Bears. "I'm sure you're gonna fetch me back the best robes—least one hundred of them, Wolf Calf!"

"I gave to you my words, and we smoked," Wolf Calf said.

"You," Four Bears said to Marbois as Swift Raven rode up, "and all white traders, you get your due from Mandan people." Rand noted the usually hospitable chief spoke with barely concealed menace; Marbois evidently caught the undertone too and only nodded.

"The time is right," Swift Raven announced, "for tossing the feather to begin the hunt. Time to go to Brother Buffalo and pray he comes to meet us. Marbois, we bring back to you robes and painting by the white woman of our great hunt," he said, and rode away, followed by the two chiefs.

Marbois rounded on Blackwell. "Hellfire, Major, you didn't tell me that white gal's going too!"

"She told me she's going to use some of the profit from her robes to buy smallpox serum for the tribe," Blackwell explained with a shrug, fiddling with his watch chain. "Told me it would be better for the Indians than those barrels of spirits you was supposed to get me here, Jacques, and then you didn't even show up till now! Besides, it's hard to stop a lady that has such high principles and friends in high places, right, Major MacLeod?"

"As for friends in high places," Rand responded, "you ought to know, Major. I'll see you both when I get back."

When Rand saw everyone mounting and that Blackwell and Marbois were not going to bother Kate, he loped back to the fort. He mounted his chestnut stallion and grabbed the reins of Kate's saddled horse and his packhorse.

Once again Kate had stunned him with her high-mindedness and bold plan of action. He had not known she had decided to spend some of her trade money for smallpox serum. Why had she told that damned Blackwell and not shared it with him? But he had to admit he had avoided her some days, trying hard to keep his eyes and thoughts and hands off her. No, he could not be angry with her for any aspect of this. If it was true, he was awed and deeply touched and must find the courage to tell her so.

For if General Clark failed to get the money, Rand had been planning to use his entire savings, which he had left with Aunt Alice. Now, without being asked, even when Kate needed every dollar to rebuild her own life, she shared his dream to protect the tribe. A chill swept him, prickling the hairs on the nape of his neck, racing up his backbone. Perhaps they did have some deep-seated things in common, goals to share, a life to build on here.

Outside the fort he urged his horse to a canter straight toward Kate. She was waving farewell to Gabe, who waved back from the top deck of the steamer down the hill.

"Here's the mare, name of Polly," he told her as he reined in. "Sorry there's no sidesaddle."

"I haven't ridden sidesaddle since I met Blue Wing," Kate said as she hiked up her skirt and mounted before he could get down to help her. "I see our friend Marbois is back."

"Came in on a Sioux pony. Kate, Blackwell said you were thinking of putting some of your profits toward smallpox vaccine."

"Yes, all I can afford. I'll need some trade goods for another trip next summer, and I might start to build a small cabin at River of Sky too. But as for the pox, I know from personal experience how important it is."

She looked away at the tossing of the feather and the long line ahead beginning to move and went on. "A doctor friend in St. Louis warned me about protecting Jamie. And though I haven't told another soul, my mother—she just recently told me I had a baby sister who died from it when the Omahas were ravaged. It's just plain wrong for our government to miss the Mandans, who are so good to whites, when some of the other tribes they've vaccinated aren't. I haven't lived here long, but I honor and care for The People. And," she added, looking directly at him now, "I know how much it means to you."

Whatever else he could have said caught in his throat. He nodded and reached out to cover her hands on her reins, then pulled back. As Blue Wing rode up, he urged his horse to the head of the line with the other scouts.

Marbois and Blackwell moved a bit downwind when the hundreds of horses and travois kicked up a cloud of dust. "Seems to me things been going to hell in a handbasket since I been gone," Marbois told his friend as they watched the exodus toward the western plains. "It don't maybe matter what old man Clark thinks, but Chouteau ain't gonna be too pleased."

"Don't start with me, Jacques. We decided we're in this together, so it won't do any good to bicker. That's all we need to have getting back to the headman who likes everything to go real smoothlike. I'm not going to say another thing about you getting yourself tossed off that steamship, or trying to rape that Mandan whore in St. Louis, not even about failing to deliver my booze. Besides, we're going to have to put our heads together on getting rid of MacLeod one way or t'other. Might as well have Swift Raven or Four Bears as subagent as that Mandan half-breed son of a bitch."

Marbois spit into the grass. "The white gal's a real fly in the ointment too."

"Not for long. She'll be heading back, and the headman has a plan to clear the decks of her. Come on in for some whiskey," Blackwell said, consulting his watch, "and I'll tell you about it. No, she's just a woman. It's the man the tribe calls Dark Water we've got to take care of—real good, lasting care. So I don't want you arguing with him because I'm going to have you go among the Sioux with him, supposedly to parlay for peace. Get him out from under foot, and maybe you can make yourself some sweet deals on the side since you can talk their tongue. After that who knows? Accidents can happen even to half a savage out here on the wild frontier," he declared, drawing out his last words. He snapped his watch face closed with a flourish.

Marbois managed a laugh. "I'd like to find some way to get rid of Four Bears and Swift Raven while we're at it," he admitted with a shake of his head as they walked toward the fort. "Too bad the pox they're all steamed up about can't come calling real soon—and carry off only certain tribal leaders, if you get my meaning. That would leave us dealing with Wolf Calf or, better yet, Wolf Trap, and then we'd be in clover. Say, that whiskey you mentioned—you gone ahead with building that still so Wolf Trap could get more of the braves to drinking?"

"Not after MacLeod smelled it out and protested. Don't want to give him any excuse to tattle to Clark, or Chouteau'll have my head. The still's going to have to wait till after we rid ourselves of several problems, cleverly, carefully. Meanwhile, it's going to be pretty fine without the place crawling with those red rascals! Let their so-called Brother Buffalo deal with them for a while."

Marbois's laugh rang out even as they went within the wooden, waiting arms of Fort Clark.

* * *

Kate had seen that the Indians, like the whites, greatly divided labor by the sexes, with women doing most of the daily manual work. But out on the hunt democracy reigned. Perhaps, she thought, it was because on these vast grasslands under the huge reach of sky, it would be impossible not to know that freedom was possible for all.

When buffalo chips or wild turnip roots could be gathered, Swift Raven halted the march, and all scavenged and dug for them. The women might unload the packhorses, but the men would help erect the tepees. Everyone labored to set up camp, to butcher the meat, and share it equally, whoever had his arrow in the beast.

And Kate was continually amazed at the many equally allotted uses of the bodies of Brother Buffalo, not even counting the huge array of cuts of meat. Sinews could become bowstrings or sewing thread; braves shaped the shoulder blades to hoes or scraping tools or knives, though they favored now the steel ones they traded for; hide became buffalo boats owned jointly; hooves turned to hatchets or dress decorations; grease and hides had a hundred uses; the skulls served in funeral and other ceremonies for both sexes. The march and the hunt were a revelation to her of how well men and women could work together, sharing labor and materials for the common good.

After the third day, one on which the tribe had made a "surround" and killed about thirty buffalo, Kate entered the tepee of Long Hatchet and Corn Basket to fetch her painting supplies. She had already filled herself to bursting with roasted ribs, turnips, and corn balls. It all tasted wonderful to her, especially after a day of riding and hard work. Now she wanted to paint for a while before the sun sank.

She had to stoop to enter the tepee. She admired these portable houses: The hides were scraped so thin that like parchment, they let light filter through, making Long Hatchet's paintings of earlier hunts on the outer walls seem to shimmer and move when the wind blew. The flap at the top gave both air and more light; inside, things were carefully stowed. As night approached, a small wheel-shaped

fire in the very center of the floor gave warmth and a gold-
en glow.

Old Buffalo Grass, who had told Kate she used to love
the summer hunts and took her name from one on which
she had spotted a large herd from her hiding place in the
grass on a hill, had taught Kate proper tepee etiquette before they left the village. Once inside, Kate turned left,
for the men turned right. She walked carefully behind
those seated, and they leaned politely forward to allow it.
After life in a Mandan lodge, living in this slanted tent
took some doing, though most of The People slept out
under the stars within the shelter of the encircled tepees
and ropes strung behind them to corral the horses.

But Kate's careful training went for naught when her
roll of canvas sprawled open nearly to the fire. Long
Hatchet, who wanted no interference while smoking after
supper, rescued it. He frowned and shook his head but did
not scold or hesitate to help. For one moment Kate recalled her own father; he would have raged that she was
going off to paint and had disturbed him. Mama never
would have dared to calm him merely with a narrow-eyed
look as Corn Basket did Long Hatchet. And all this while
Blue Wing sat against the back, slanted wall, watching
but not moving.

With Corn Basket's help, Kate settled just outside the
rope boundary of the camp behind the tepee. She set up
her easel, cut and fitted her canvas to the square wooden
frame, and nailed it on with her little hammer. She mixed
her paints quickly on one of Long Hatchet's buffalo
shoulder blade palettes.

The sky was alive with many different shapes and
kinds of clouds. She wasn't sure what first to paint of all
that she had seen on the hunt so far. Her mind was filled
with images of The People and their places. The whole
tribe was a great canvas to her: their personalities, their
daily lives, both mundane and colorful.

She began to plan a scene of women scraping hides and
smoking meat on scaffolds, while men dug turnip roots
beyond. But, she thought, she must not just show the
good times. Especially if, like her hero, George Catlin,
she displayed these paintings later in St. Louis, she must

also emphasize the trials the Mandans faced: unfair prices for furs; winter hunger; attacks by Sioux; smallpox, which once ravaged the tribe, forcing The People to move from their old villages on the Heart River nearer to the Knife. And now they had to live under the watchful eye of government agents and Chouteau's traders. She had heard the stories; she had not seen some of these griefs with her eyes, but she saw them in her heart.

She jumped and smeared the grass when Blue Wing spoke so close behind. "Oh, you startled me!" Kate scolded. "You know I still can't hear footsteps like you do!"

"Not thinking of that."

"You're not still worried the hunt is not going well enough? Seventy buffalo in three days is good, isn't it?"

"I afraid Wolf Trap try to do something bad, make Swift Raven kick the stone as leader. Then Wolf Trap have me, have all the power too."

"But Swift Raven has been vigilant."

"Tell to me that word."

"Vigilant, watchful. He's everywhere, doing a good job."

"Yes," she said. A little smile hovered on her pinched lips. "But since it not rutting season yet, the herds small and scattered. And you saw some thin hides. Prairie Wind, Swift Raven not can give you many good hides if not more found."

"I know. I may have to go back with much less than I hoped. But whatever happens, I will have so much more than I ever hoped for, Blue Wing. A new sister in you, a second family, just like you said Jamie and I gave you."

"But I losing you, taking back Clam Necklace. Losing Swift Raven, taking Wolf Trap. And already you become the daughter in the lodge of Long Hatchet and Corn Basket," she said, and turned away, to duck under the rope and disappear back into the tepee.

Kate stood stock-still. How could she comfort her friend if she was now to be included in the blame? But she understood how Blue Wing felt, how it seemed as if everything were closing in on her and going wrong. For Kate had felt like that herself when she'd lost Clive and everything she'd once held dear except Jamie. But she could hardly go in now before them all to try to buck up Blue Wing, not in that small public tepee.

With a huge sigh Kate began to paint out the smear she'd made across the stretch of thick grama grass Brother Buffalo loved. She created clouds hovering on the horizon that perhaps threatened rain, just like the real ones glowering from the sky. Surely rain would make the hunt harder tomorrow. She balanced sunlight struggling with the gray cloud masses, her mind lost, floating in her work and dreams.

What of Stirling? He had a golden, sunny personality to match his looks, not a dark, stormy one. What was best for her was to wed Stirling, but that no longer felt possible or right. And if she really loved him, would she not have said yes the first time he asked, not put it off? Gabe had said if it was "yes and no about the man," he was wrong for her. Yet their goals and plans meshed seamlessly. Stirling promised love, a life, a future—all the things she was risking here each time she took a walk with Rand or smiled his way or longed for him to come to her. But he must be struggling with himself too, for he had not approached her since the first evening they strolled about the camp.

Rand. She longed to see Rand every day and watched for him when he wasn't out with the scouts. As she rode, as she packed or unpacked, as she listened to the drums or horse or buffalo hoofbeats, she heard the thud of his heart when he'd held her against him in the cave. She knew she could not blame the drums of O-Kee-Pa or the moon or anything that night but that she wanted to let him love her. She wanted him whatever it cost her. But for how long would she have him? Until she went downriver? As long as it took him to spend his passion in her?

Dangerous passion. A rampaging river of emotion had flowed between her and Rand from the beginning. Anger turning to arousal, then attraction. That had to be all it was at first, but now—at least for her—it was so much more. Still, she must shed this deepening desire for him the way the lumbering beasts of the plains had shed their thick winter coats and now grew new ones to protect themselves.

Rand had been smarter than she; he had been right about holding to his commitment. How had she so taken leave of her senses—common sense, he called it—to dream of a future with him? If they married among the Mandans, would it be legal at home? Would it be a common law, if not a commonsense, marriage? How surprised Jamie would be to have Rand for a father. Would they eventually have to live here year-round? Would Rand come to St. Louis or at least to River of Sky? She never wanted to be separated from the man she loved—thought she loved—ever again. Yet all this agonizing was fantasy, as much fantasy as her own painting here. . .

She heard a distant rumble, not this chaos of her thoughts. She scanned the darkening sea of grass for a distant blur of the herd, but it was thunder. Veins of lightning bled from clotted clouds. She scrambled to gather her things. She was deeply touched when both Blue Wing and Corn Basket ran out to help her.

At dawn on the fifth day, after two nights and one day of rain, the skies cleared. The tribe broke rain camp and went on again, heading west below the southern border of the Knife River. A stiff wind refreshed them, but dew was dense; they moved slower because of slick grass and hidden sinkholes. But this pace gave Kate time to study the stark scene.

She saw rills slashing toward the Knife River, carving the rocky landscape into amazing shapes. Just as she often did with clouds, she picked out imaginary forms: the silhouette of the *Red Dawn,* a Mandan lodge, her long-lost rocking chair, the shape of "her rock" at River of Sky, Rand's profile. Now and then, between or below the bluffs, the Knife glinted sharp silver in the sun. Old Woman in the Moon would never approve of the Knife River, Kate mused, for she would never see her reflection in its wild rush.

The People passed through land mostly inhabited by the Hidatsas, a friendly tribe. Fortunately the more hostile Assiniboins, a branch of the Sioux, lived across the Knife and traded at Fort Union. Still, the buffalo scouts kept a good watch for Teton Sioux, who might be passing through. Kate marveled again that certain tribes bore each other enmity, some for reasons lost in the past, but, then, was that not the way of white civilization too? As she watched Blue Wing on the horse just ahead, she prayed that nothing would ever sever their friendship.

Now white sagebrush mingled with reddish blazing star and blue asters, reminding her of the American flag, flapping in the breeze on this prairie. They followed a buffalo road, trampled three or four feet deep to watering spots or wallows. But so far today neither they nor their scouts riding farther out had found grazing herds.

During the rattle of the rain on the tepee roof last night, Rand had eaten with Long Hatchet. He had said he was worried the buffalo had moved much farther on during the tribe's delay in the unusual summer storm. Wolf Trap had even been murmuring, Rand said, that it was a bad sign from the heavens for the hunt: Why had not the rain blessed the corn back at Mitutanka and left the hunt alone? No one had spoken at that. Long Hatchet had frowned, and Blue Wing had tears in her eyes. Everyone knew Wolf Trap would love to see Swift Raven discredited and ruined.

So far, as even Rand had admitted, it was not a hunt to bring bounty to the tribe and glory to Swift Raven. And in the broad valley that now lay below them, Kate realized there would be no place to trap strays by a surround. Any chase after a rain was dangerous. Still, the entire tribe had seen Swift Raven offer his morning prayers for a fruitful day; they saw his broad shoulders did not slump, his head lifted as they set out. And because the leader of the hunt had faith, The People—most of them—clung to that too.

When Swift Raven ordered a rest stop near a stream just after midday, Kate and Blue Wing overheard him say, "No biting bugs here, good sign."

"Thank heaven," Kate whispered to Blue Wing. "A holiday from mosquitoes was the only good thing in all that rain. Is it because of the wind they are not here now, or are we farther from water?"

Without taking her eyes from Swift Raven, Blue Wing said in an awed voice, "It may mean much Brother Buffalo near. Biting bugs leave little people if big beasts near."

A scout returned to camp and rode straight for Swift Raven. The leader went out with him and returned to announce from the back of his horse, "Brother Buffalo has heard our prayer! Over there, in the broad valley, the land is black with buffalo. The camp stays here, and those who can chase come now, come now. If the wind shifts, they will scent us and move on!"

The men scrambled for their mounts, the buffalo ponies with the distinctive cropped ears; they could be guided by the pressure of the riders' thighs. Each brave thrust his legs through the rope girdle around the horse's belly to keep from bouncing off when he used both hands to shoot; each made certain he dragged the long rope a thrown rider could grab to snag his horse and remount, he hoped, before he was trampled or met the wrath of his would-be victim. The braves adjusted their quivers stuffed with their uniquely cut arrows. Wolf Trap with his wolf pelt bouncing behind him and Swift Raven on the leader's white horse led others trailing behind them over the rim of the hill.

With the other women, Kate walked up on the grassy bluff and peered down into the broad valley. They all knew the perils of the chase after a rain: Grass slicked over gopher or prairie dog holes. The odds of a big kill were good in such a massive herd; the odds of being crushed or trampled were good too. And whatever happened would hang on Swift Raven's judgment, as did his future in the tribe.

The wind was in the women's faces, so the huge black sea of beasts below could not scent them. Kate went back for Gabe's telescope, which she had brought along, and hurried to focus it and stare down at the scene. Below them braves on their ponies began to run the herd.

Kate soon saw Rand was with them. Though he had gone out to scout, he had not returned to camp. She picked him out, as she did the others, by the color of his horse, the chestnut in the ribbon of riders.

The herd began to bolt. A rumble filled the women's ears. Despite the recent rain, a cloud of dust soon shimmered in the sun above a thousand curly ebony heads and humps and backs. Hooves flung clods of sod. The riders closed, pressed. Men drew their bows and fitted arrows; Rand raised his rifle.

The women could see more clearly as the herd thundered this way. "One down," Blue Wing said, squinting to count buffalo dropped to make the following herd divide to get past them. "Two, three, many."

But Kate soon saw that buffalo were not the only thing down. A man—she was sure it was Wolf Trap with that white wolf pelt across his pale horse's flank—had put his arrow, then another in a great, running beast not too far into the herd. But it turned on him; his pony arched, then spilled him off. He disappeared into the blur of hides and hoofs.

"Wolf Trap's horse is down," Kate reported.

Behind her Clam Necklace wailed so loud Kate jumped. Blue Wing grabbed Kate's arm and held tight. "A man on a light horse," Kate said, "has gone back for him."

"Swift Raven," Blue Wing cried. "He risks his life for Wolf Trap!"

The herd thudded by endlessly, charging down the valley, leaving dotted heaps of themselves behind. The women squinted into the dust, trying to count men. Buffalo bellows and human shrieks drifted to them even above Clam Necklace's wails. Kate saw Wolf Trap's horse lying among the dead animals. If there was a man trodden there, they could not tell from here. She could pick out Swift Raven's white horse, but it bore no man on its back. All the others saw that too. If the leader of the hunt had been lost, the people would be cursed for years.

The women mounted their horses and headed down the same winding path to the valley to help with both butchering and healing. Blue Wing rode ahead of Clam Necklace, who was chanting, more quietly now. The other women ignored her, for this was bad luck, to mourn what was not yet known.

And then, on his chestnut mount, Rand rode at them. His horse still foamed from the chase; gunpowder clinging to Rand's sweat had blackened his face; his buckskins were dirty and bloody. He held a slumped, bleeding brave before him. Kate and Blue Wing gasped, expecting it to be Swift Raven. But Wolf Trap lay limply in his arms.

"Battered with broken ribs," Rand called out to them in Mandan. "But the leader of the hunt, Swift Raven, using their horses for a shield, saved Wolf Trap's life to make this a great hunt day with much meat and many hides!"

The women chanted in joy; Kate even sang along with the three-note tune. Blue Wing looked both stunned and proud. Clam Necklace quieted at last and reached out from her horse to touch her husband's shoulder. Wolf Trap weakly hit her hand away.

But for everyone else, especially Swift Raven, Kate thought, it had been a victorious day.

It was nightfall before the tribe finished the hard work of skinning and butchering and returned to camp. Tomorrow hides would be scraped and meat smoked before the return journey. But even if they went home today, the hunt—and Swift Raven—would be a success. Tonight they stacked their uncured hides, filled their bellies with food, and celebrated with games, eating, dancing, and more eating.

Kate saw Blue Wing rejoice outwardly with the others but grieve silently. Soon after they returned to Mitutanka, she would move to Wolf Trap's lodge. His medicine had been greatly weakened today. The first animal he shot had bested him and killed his horse. This would have reflected badly too on Swift Raven's control of the hunt had he not saved his rival, who everyone knew had subtly disparaged him. Even Clam Necklace had disgraced herself.

But Kate knew Blue Wing was hardly grieving for all that. She had seen that across the camp, Swift Raven had received Four Bears' permission to be alone in the tepee with his daughter, Bright Star. Kate sighed and bit her lip as Blue Wing went into the tepee of Long Hatchet and did not appear again.

Kate sat cross-legged outside, sated with food, wanting to be with Blue Wing but not wanting to go inside. Besides, when she tried to reach out to her lately, Blue Wing had insisted she did not want to talk. Now how Kate wished she could see Rand across the way with the other scouts. She knew she would grieve if she saw him go off with someone else, yes, even if Stirling Mount were sitting here beside her this very moment.

And then a new thought hit her. It was as stunning as her realization of independence when she sat alone that day at River of Sky. Blue Wing's mother, her society, and the man she really loved all said she must marry Wolf Trap because he was the proper, suitable husband for her. Blue Wing was doing what was supposedly *right,* yet it was so *wrong.*

Was that not her own predicament exactly? Kate's mother, her society, Stirling himself all counseled her to marry and assumed she would marry the man who seemed proper and suitable. But she realized now that Stirling would be so wrong for her. Wrong, because she loved and wanted Rand. She wanted to share his dreams, his life, and that was that.

She stood and paced, then stopped when she heard snarls and growls from just beyond the line of light behind the great circle of tepees. She hurried to the center of the camp to tell Long Hatchet. He cocked his head and listened through the noise.

"Wolves, Brother Coyote smell our feast," he said. "But they not dare come in, not with us all together here with light and songs."

Although the animals still made her nervous—she could sometimes glimpse the feral gleam of their eyes in reflected firelight—she believed Long Hatchet. But she did not go back to her seat. For there, across the way near the tent of his mother's people of the white sage medicine bundle, she saw Rand.

Her stomach careened to her feet as if she had jumped off a cliff and hurtled downward. She might, she thought, be trembling from the wolves or from her new decision she wanted Rand, but her heart and mind felt strong as she walked directly toward him.

She passed Arrow Point, combing his locks and laughingly adorning them with the ribs of buffalo; Loud Fox danced off by himself in a sort of trance, looking every bit like a handsome woman; boys shot a storm of arrows outward by torchlight to see who could keep the most aloft. She saw all these things, but she saw only Rand.

He looked at her and smiled. "I was coming over to see you," he said. "I've been taking a bath way up the stream. I was a mess."

"But the wolves are out there."

"I went with a group of loud, armed fellow hunters. Kate, you know my mother's oldest sister, Scatter Corn." The two exchanged greetings; then the woman ducked inside her tepee to bring out a bundle she gave to Rand. Scatter Corn looked Kate over with a most proprietary eye. "I have something for you in a bit," he explained to Kate, "if you want it."

They said farewell to Scatter Corn and strolled across the camp to sit on a grassy spot between two tepees. Kate was aching to see what he held, but she didn't intend to tease for it.

"Want to sit and watch from here?" he asked.

"Yes, fine."

She could have laughed aloud from the pure thrill of his presence, but she tried to calm herself. He had indeed been bathing. His thick, unruly hair was slicked to his head, and his buckskins had evidently been washed so they clung tightly to his hard body and squeaked a bit when he moved. Suddenly she was not sure what to say, what to do to convince him of her new, powerful knowledge they were right for each other.

"It's hard to tell with the firelight, but the stars are bright," he said, and swept his arm expansively above them.

Especially when she shaded her eyes and squinted, she could pick out a handful of diamonds flung across black velvet sky. For once she was glad there was no moon; sometimes she was certain Old Woman bewitched her.

"To see the stars really well," she observed, "we'd have to wade through those wolves out there."

She was surprised to see him grin, though he looked as nervous as she felt through their small talk. Little butterflies of anticipation beat their wings in the bottom of her belly. "One of the prices," he said, "we pay for paradise."

He was obviously in a soaring mood because of Swift Raven's success today. But he did not know yet that she planned on victory too. If only she could conquer him to make him see things her way! The old housebound, citybound, fear-bound Katherine Warfield Craig never would have dared, but Prairie Wind did. She had come so far, so very far to this special place and moment: The People rejoicing together, success on the hunt, the beauty of the night, despite lurking dangers beyond the boundaries—and this man.

"You've gotten used to it all," he said, leaning back on his hands.

"The ways of The People? Yes."

"Just remember, there are things you still don't know about them, like a dark side of the moon."

"I don't want to talk or think about dark sides tonight."

"All right. Here's something for you, if you will accept it." He extended a garment toward her, letting it fall open from his hand.

She took it and shook it out, then clasped it to her, stretching her legs straight out to see if it was a shirt or dress. Its fringed hoof-decked hem would fall just below her knees. Soft, cropped animal fur was sewn into the seams to decorate it further. It would fit her perfectly, and she would take that for a sign if she were superstitious.

"Oh, Rand, the softest smoked deerskin dress!"

"Elkskin. But if you wear it, it means you will lie with me, so you'd better think twice about it."

She clutched it harder to her. "You haven't given it to others? It isn't something like a love exploit stick?"

"No, it was my mother's. It has a rain cloud sewn on the back with porcupine quills. See—Rain Cloud, my mother's name. So if you wear it, people will know I gave it to you. And what it means."

"They will think we are lovers?"

He cleared his throat. "Yes, you could say it like that. Then there goes your reputation among the whites."

"And among the Mandans?"

"They will nod and smile and ask if you will be staying the winter."

"But, Rand, you know I can't—can't stay the winter, not this winter anyway. And not because of what others will say, but because of my own beliefs and desires. I can't lie with a man and then just leave him—even one I realize I love—unless he means to marry me."

"Better give it back then."

"No!" she said. "I like it, and I said I love you. I suppose that threatens your—your memories or your medicine to be dedicated only to the tribe. So will you fuss and fume?"

"Threatens me? Fuss and fume?" he said, his voice gruff. "Is that the way you see it?"

"I must admit I'm weary of it too."

"Kate, damn it, I—"

"Let's talk common sense, as you put it," she said, and seized his thick wrist. "Obviously I can't marry Stirling when I'm in love with you. Now will that revelation make you turn temporarily mean and hightail it?"

He reached for her and pulled her to him, sprawling them both on the ground, whoever might walk by and stare. "Stirling, curse him," he said, "illustrious saint that he is, will still take you—but, no doubt, *not* if you're wearing that dress and the village thinks you're my woman!"

"I never took you for a coward. Offer me the dress, then warn me not to take it. Is Swift Raven noble to urge Blue Wing to wed a man she does not love? You're no better. You want to possess me from time to time but just temporarily. In the long run you would let Stirling have me so you don't have to take on the burden of a wife. You don't have the backbone for promising me at least tomorr—"

"Stop goading me! Besides, I'd kill Stirling Mount with my bare hands before I'd let you marry him! But what the hell has gotten into you?"

"You have—you and this—this heart of the frontier.

The Mandans, the freedom out here, my own courage—I don't know. I vowed to myself at River of Sky I would make my own decisions, do things for myself, my own way. And I am."

"But you said 'marry,' woman! You can't mean to marry me and live out here!"

"I—I don't know. Surely we could work something out."

"I won't leave here, Kate. I am completely dedicated to these people . . . completely . . . until you . . ."

He kissed her hard, then gently, then hard again. He leaned into her, but she held to him just as fervently. He slid his mouth down her throat to the valley between her breasts. He pressed a bent knee between her legs, though her skirts snagged it there. She arched her back and neck for him before sanity seeped back in.

"Rand," she gasped, "I want you. But it cannot be just this once, not just for the summer, and certainly not here. Let me up. I know The People do things differently here, but—Rand!"

He lifted his head, his face in stark shadow. "I know. But there is no one in your family I can ask for you. I can't buy you with horses. There is no real betrothal—"

"The betrothal would be that you ask me—we ask each other—and accept. We choose to love, to be together, to wed . . ."

"Yes! Kate, I adore you, but—"

"But it will not just be the passion of this moment. We *decide* we can do it somehow; we *dedicate* ourselves, and we *do* it!"

"Yes, yes!" he exclaimed. "Kate, I've been hesitant, maybe afraid to say it, but I've admired, cared deeply for you—"

"Loved me, Rand? Can you say you love me?"

"Yes. Kate Craig, Prairie Wind of the Mandans, will you marry me?"

"Yes! Yes, curse those wolves out there so we can't be alone."

"We will be and soon. I can come to your bed in Long Hatchet's lodge the first night we're back at Mitutanka."

"This heirloom gown is dearer to me than any betrothal

ring could be," she said, reaching for the dress where it was caught between them. "It—it wasn't your mother's wedding gown, was it?"

"No, it's her name dress—you know, after she had her *xopini* dream that made her a woman. But it can be your Mandan marriage dress."

"Yes. Buffalo Grass told me I could take corn porridge to you at the lodge of Scatter Corn and, if you ate it, we'd be wed. She knew what I should do long before I dared to know. And Gabe as ship's captain could preach us a good church ceremony."

"And then both halves of the half-breed would really be married," he said. A new tone darkened his voice, but he was smiling. He had said yes, she exulted. He had!

Later, as they kissed, whispering, Katc prayed that it could always be this way for them, together in love, promised and dedicated. It was nearly dawn when she looked up into the sky again. She startled to see there a sliver of moon had risen and tilted overhead to look like not Old Woman but the blessing of her broadest smile.

Chapter 15

The morning after the tribe returned to Mitutanka, Rand and Kate prepared to be married by Captain Gabe aboard the *Red Dawn*. Nearly twenty people, mostly Mandans, crowded into the common room, which Kate had decorated with swags and bowls of prairie flowers. Out on deck they had set up a table with the three-layered blackberry corn cake Willy Nilly had managed to put together on such short notice.

Although Kate was determined to wear her precious Indian dress for the Mandan ceremony that would bind her to Rand in the eyes of the tribe, today she wore her best gown, a burgundy moiré with double-puffed sleeves, a low-cut neckline, and a bodice bow. She had even dug out suede gloves and, instead of boots or moccasins, wore her black slippers laced over her last pair of white stockings. She carried a bouquet of pink prairie roses, which she also pinned in her loosed hair with her tortoiseshell combs.

It would, she thought, have been a perfect day if Jamie and Mama could have been there. And Blue Wing had not yet appeared, though she had told Kate she would come. Later, she thought, she would feel guilty for being so elated and in love when Blue Wing was so unhappy, but now she could not contain her joy.

"Gabriel," Kate said as they waited in the small kitchen before the service, "have you got the vows I wrote out?"

"Right here, Kate. 'Love, honor,' and all the rest."

"I can't tell you how much it means to me to have you do this for us—and to give me away. We've been good friends through both thick and thin." Her eyes misted, and her voice snagged.

"Now you just stop talking like it's some funeral we're holding, like our friendship's all in the past." Gabe scolded her and patted her arm. He was dressed in his best coat and the only clean shirt she had seen him in for months. He too looked teary-eyed. "We're still gonna be friends whatever happens, Kate!"

"That we are," she said, and reached up on tiptoe to kiss his bearded cheek. "Well, we can't wait for Blue Wing all day. I do understand, since Swift Raven is moving into Four Bears' lodge as Bright Star's husband today. Why would Blue Wing want to sit through any sort of wedding? Let's go, my guardian angel!"

"And make this a real gimcracker of a day!" he whispered as she took his arm.

He smiled proudly as he escorted her in to join Rand, waiting with the guests. Rand too wore his best—she assumed his only—broadcloth coat, waistcoat, and trousers. His white shirt made his face look very dark; he had his usually unruly hair combed. But he looked very edgy. His hand was even cold when his skin was usually so warm to the touch.

"Dearly beloved, we are gathered here in the sight of God to join this man and this woman in holy wedlock." Gabe intoned the words Kate had set down for him. Her wedding and Mama's second one were the only two she could recall, but the words were burned in her mind. "If there is anyone who knows a reason why these two may not be joined, let him speak now or forever hold his peace."

A flurry, a scuffling sounded in the back of the room. Gabe looked up past them; Kate and Rand both turned to see Blue Wing hurry in, edge past Scatter Corn, and stand in the back corner behind her parents. Was Blue Wing forever going to come late to weddings and wakes? Kate wondered. She saw now that both Marbois and Blackwell—with his little translator—had dared come, but perhaps Rand had thought he must invite them.

"Go ahead, Gabe," Rand said. Kate could have hugged him for that. He did want to wed her. Any fears she had that he would change his mind or regretted this were foolish ones.

"Do you, Katherine Craig, known here as Prairie Wind, promise to love this man, Randal MacLeod, known as Dark Water, for better or for worse, for richer or poorer, in sickness and in health as long as you both shall live and . . . till death you do part?" Gabe added as he flipped his piece of paper over.

Blue Wing's Mandan translation of the vows, which Kate had asked her to do, echoed in the small room after each sentence Gabe spoke.

"I do!" Kate declared.

She held Rand's hand tighter as he gave his vows. It was all really happening, she thought, this glorious day of dedication. He would be a good father to Jamie. She smiled as she recalled how he had taught the boy to swim, something Jamie's own father had never done. How Jamie followed him about the boat; how Rand used to refer to him as "son" from the beginning as if he were prophetic. In her journey up the wide Missouri she had found a new father for Jamie, a new people to love, and a man to cherish forever who could bridge both her worlds.

The Mandans looked on wide-eyed as Gabe waxed eloquent on the topic of how Jesus attended the wedding at Cana and changed water into wine, and Blue Wing stumbled through translations.

"Much medicine, that man, but where Cana?" Kate heard Long Hatchet ask loudly in Mandan. She and Rand had to smile. After all, Kate thought, Long Hatchet was used to speaking and being heeded whenever he wished.

Gabe plunged on, explaining that a strong belief in God could change people the same way the water at Cana was changed to better wine. It could make them learn to love peace and turn away from warfare.

"But drink no good, warfare very good!" Long Hatchet bellowed after Blue Wing's translation. Various assenting grunts followed with much shuffling of moccasined feet. Marbois snickered and Blackwell laughed outright when Blackwell's little translator explained.

Gabe took the hint, pronounced them man and wife, gave a quick benediction, and ordered, "Rand, kiss your bride."

As Kate and Rand kissed, whoops and hollers sounded not from the congregation but from the riverbank to make the common room empty out but for them and Gabe.

"Where are they going? What's all that noise?" she asked.

"I'd better go see!" Rand said, and ran out on deck too.

"Wait for me!" she cried as she ran to the rail to stand beside him. Below them, Wolf Trap, despite his injuries from the hunt, was doing most of the whooping and waving a decorated spear in the air. "What is it, Rand? I can't tell what he means."

"Two of The People were just found killed by Sioux to the west where they went berry picking," he explained. "He wants braves to form a party for revenge."

"If that don't beat all!" Gabe cried as he stood behind them. "Don't do a whit of good to preach peace and love 'round here! They'd rather have a revenge party than a wedding party!"

Kate was glad she had taken Rand's advice to give small gifts with the invitations to the service, for there was no time to give them now. She stepped over the pile of the presents her guests had brought them; she gazed forlornly at the wedding cake. "At least we can celebrate with the crew," she told Rand.

"What? Yes, as soon as I get back. Kate, if they send out a big raiding party, any attempt to parlay for peace later will be hopeless. I've got to go make certain only a few go out, as the attacking band was probably just a few hotheaded renegades."

"You're not leaving too! And why would the Sioux dare attack now if they want to trade for the corn that's almost ripe? It doesn't make any sense!"

"You don't understand how they think. Kate, sweetheart, I'll be right back. No one said this was going to be easy for us. I will be right back."

He kissed her hard and dared leave her standing there. But yes, he was right. She should not have expected things to be perfect for them. Only why did problems have to start now? "Love, honor, and obey . . . till death us do part," but at least they shouldn't have to part on their wedding day! And then Blue Wing came to stand at her side.

"Blue Wing, I'm so glad you're here with me."

"Again the man does go and we here."

"He said he'd be right back. Did you know either of the two that were killed?"

"Two women from Ruptare."

"Oh, I didn't realize they weren't even from here." She shuddered to think the Sioux had no qualms even about killing women just picking berries. "But a party from Mitutanka will go after the killers of Ruptare people too?"

"That the way."

Kate sighed. Unfortunately Rand was right that she still did not understand how Indians thought, even the ones she lived among. But she would stand by them—Rand's and Blue Wing's people—and now her people too.

"Bloodthirsty as mosquitoes, aren't they, ma'am?" Kellen Blackwell said as he stepped from the shadows.

Kate was surprised to see him still here. At least she didn't see that wretch Marbois anywhere, but then Blue Wing would not be standing here.

"It's their definition of honor—mutual protection and their future survival," Kate told him, surprised she defended them when she did not think their actions were right.

"Speaking of honor," he said, drawling out his words as he consulted his watch, "a certain Mr. Mount's going to be devastated to find his fiancée's married another. A cruel kind of dishonoring a man, of torture really. Despite your civilized outer trappings, you'd make a real good little savage warrior."

"I made it very clear to Stirling, and to you that first day, that he and I were not betrothed, sir."

"You made lots of things pretty clear that day, Mrs. Craig—Mrs. MacLeod. So let me be real clear about something. I hear you did a lot of painting on the hunt but not only of the hunt. I hear some of it makes my agency and the fur factor here look real bad. Those so-called artworks better be for your own eyes only. See, like General Clark and Mr. Marbois's boss, Monsieur Cadet

Chouteau, I expect the wives of underlings to be well be-haved. Or it could cost Major MacLeod his job as sub-agent."

"Whatever I do, Major Blackwell, it will be to help the Mandans—and with my husband's approval."

"Approval? Permission, don't you mean? If a man can't rule his own roost, I can't trust him with the Man-dans, and 'specially not the Sioux. Good day, Mrs. Dark Water MacLeod."

Kate felt like hurling epithets and herself after the man as he slowly descended the gangplank and walked back to the fort. He had insulted and threatened her, yet in a sly, subtle way. Perhaps she had underestimated him as a real threat to Rand and her, let alone to the Mandans.

"Blue Wing, you're not leaving too?" she asked as her friend turned away.

"You not need me now Blackwell go. The man you love come back soon. Tonight he share your bed in the lodge of Long Hatchet."

"I know you are determined to go to Wolf Trap at the time of the corn ceremony. But what if I asked you to go south with me again and then return in the spring? Could it delay things and help—"

"No help for me now. Only if you bend the thoughts of Corn Basket, Long Hatchet, even Buffalo Grass. Prairie Wind, do not look so sad for me. This day you be happy. You have man you love. Tonight maybe Dark Water make child for you, and your Sally come straight back from white man Baby Hill."

As Blue Wing walked away, Kate didn't even have the strength to argue about the Baby Hill. Standing alone at the rail, she watched her last wedding guest depart. For one moment she felt she had been jilted at the altar, but that was crazy. Rand would be back soon; they had a whole honeymoon, a whole life together. And Blue Wing's blessing was indeed a good one: Be happy ... have the man you love ... make a child.

She stood on the hurricane deck of the *Red Dawn*, waiting for Rand while a raiding party of four men gal-loped out of the gate of Mitutanka and headed west. Finally, when she saw him coming back down the hill with Scatter Corn, she ran to him with outstretched arms.

The day Rand and Kate were married in the month of Wild Ripe Plums, August 15, 1836, the day the Mandan raiding party chased the Sioux, was also the first day some of the corn turned ripe. Kate could hear the messengers of the Black Mouth Society running through the village, shouting the news that in four days the Corn Dance would be given.

In the lodge of Long Hatchet she stood, nervously fingering the fur fringe on her elkskin dress, waiting for Rand's arrival in late afternoon. Because Major Blackwell had insisted Rand sleep in the fort the nights when the raiding party was out, these hours before the sun set and the gates were locked were to be their wedding night. Though it was not the Mandan way, Corn Basket had made everyone vacate the lodge of Long Hatchet; it seemed empty and vast to Kate without the bustle of the family. And Blue Wing's face still haunted her, for she had paused at the door and looked back at her to say, "Now we no longer sisters through one husband."

"But always sisters in friendship," Kate had called to her.

Blue Wing said no more, and the buffaloskin flap closed behind her.

Now Kate paced. Why was Rand late? Surely Blackwell had not given him something to do at the last minute! It was bad enough he was keeping him in the fort at night!

Despite her trying to keep calm, her mind raced back to her first night with Clive. He had been gentle but so eager to possess her; she had not really known what he expected of her but to kiss him back and hold to him. But that was another life ago; she had great expectations of this night and this life now. Even if she could go back and erase all the pain it had taken to get here, she would not trade who and where she was for anything.

And she wished she were better at trading! He was tough but fair, Clive had always said. Unfortunately, she thought, she was too fair and not tough enough, especially here at Mitutanka. Marbois still claimed he had first rights on the best hides from the hunt, since some of the buffalo had not fully grown in their cold weather coats. She'd probably have to take Marbois on, or she'd go back with mangy, scruffy hides to sell.

But though she'd done it before, she hated tangling with Marbois. He always made her feel sullied, as if a skunk had sprayed her even if she'd chased it off. And she certainly did not want Rand to endanger his tenuous position here by coming to her aid. But she wouldn't mind one bit, curse it, if he'd come to her bed right now! If he didn't get here soon, perhaps she might just be a bit late tomorrow when she took that symbolic corn porridge to Scatter Corn's lodge for him!

But suddenly there he was, lifting the door flap, striding in out of breath. She ran to him. "I was afraid Blackwell or someone delayed you!"

"Let them try. This night—time together, I mean—has been long months, maybe years in coming."

He lifted and carried her through the slant of sun toward the beds along the back wall. "Which one?" he asked.

"That one. See the steamboat Long Hatchet painted on it?"

"I don't want to look at anything but you," he said, and put her down. "Your Mandan dress is lovely, but I think we could do without it now."

"Your things too," she said, tugging at his fringed shirt.

He stripped it over his head in one quick motion, then helped her undress. She felt so eager she wanted to dive into the bed. All during their small reception today—just they, Scatter Corn, and the crew—the two of them had watched each other and longed for this. In the cedar forest the night she was lost, in the cave, in her dreams, she had come to this point so many times only to turn back. But now all of him—he was really hers.

And there was so much more of Rand than she had ever envisioned: stretches of skin, dark, curly hair, everything. She stood straight while he looked and touched his fill. It all seemed so very right. And soon she was exploring him until it was his knees which buckled first to topple them into the soft box of the bed.

No linen-laid, quilt-clad, curtained bed in the city could compare with the privacy and pleasure of a Mandan bed. It was a long, two-person-wide box over springy willow sticks and a bouncy, stretched buffalo hide. It was padded with pelts and herb-filled pillows, and tanned hides enclosed it on all sides but one, which faced the outer lodge wall. And now Rand lit up the dimness of the bed and filled its depths with his big body, holding her, pressing her down.

They came together in a blur of sweet fierceness, a heady brew of emotions she had never known before him. She felt vulnerable but powerful, shy but bold. She was herself yet some new, transported being. She wrapped her arms, her legs, her life around him. Surely they had always been like this, raging with the need to be closer, even closer. Locked together, for now, for tomorrow, for always, they sealed their love.

Kate was not sure how or why, but her marriage to Rand and her "lessons" in picture drawing from Long Hatchet freed her painting abilities as never before. When Rand was busy and she was not trading or packing the hold of the *Red Dawn,* she painted here and there in the village: people, scenes real and recollected. And despite Blackwell's veiled threats, she did a painting of the soldiers at Fort Leavenworth letting illegal barrels pass through; she did one of Marbois demanding the Mandan chiefs give him his due; she sketched Blackwell standing aloof from the Indians who went to see him at the fort, trailing their dogs, which he took a good kick at, as she had seen him do at the Mandan children.

And she drew many of the tribal women. She did a very detailed one of her new "aunt," Scatter Corn, for Corn Basket told her Scatter Corn looked like Rand's mother and she wanted to surprise him with a painting later. How kind Scatter Corn had been to her the day she took the corn porridge to Rand to make the Mandan marriage official. She drew Buffalo Grass, even Clam Necklace, who grabbed the sketch of her from Kate the

moment it was done and went off with it, gloating, showing everyone she passed.

Kate felt happier than she had ever been, however
much she still missed Jamie. Despite some questionable
Mandan meals, she bloomed with health. But she dreaded
the idea that Rand would head out once they heard from
the raiding party, and she would go back to St. Louis. All
that—and Stirling, who had not yet returned from Fort
Union—seemed so distant, so undesired.

The one thing that continually grieved Kate through the
blur of her joy was Blue Wing. Her going to Wolf Trap
had been delayed by his leading three other braves on the
retaliatory raid, however sore he still was from the hunt.
After all, if he led a successful raid in his weakened condition, some of his disgrace would be blotted out in the
minds of The People. Sometimes, though neither of them
said it, Kate was sure she had the same harsh but hopeful
thought as Blue Wing: that perhaps Wolf Trap would not
return at all.

The day before the Corn Dance, heading for her father's lodge, Ahpcha-Toha went the long way around the
edge of the village so she would not have to pass by the
lodge of Chief Four Bears. For Swift Raven lived there
now with his new wife, and she could not bear to see
them coming or going. But when she went to the lodge of
Wolf Trap, they would be neighbors and see each other
often. *Ahde,* what did it matter? she tried to tell herself.
She saw her beloved Swift Raven anytime she so much as
closed her eyes anyway, waking or sleeping.

She hesitated before entering her father's lodge,
strengthening herself to keep from telling her parents how
Clam Necklace and Wolf Trap had betrayed her long ago,
telling herself she must not ask them not to send her to
Wolf Trap when he returned. For she had given to them
words of promise which could not be broken.

As she stood outside the open door flap on this warm
day, she heard Long Hatchet inside explaining to Prairie
Wing more signs for the *mih-sha,* the traditional painted
buffalo robe. Each *mih-sha* was cut in short, decorative

strips on the bottom, he told Kate, and fringed on the sides, but there all similarities ended. Each robe told the tale of a brave's—or a brave woman's—exploits. Her friend's answering voice was so light and bright that it stung Blue Wing by comparison with how dark and heavy she felt.

"So those marks stand for 'how many days,' and the *X* means 'I will trade.' " Prairie Wind repeated all he told her like an eager child. "And this sign means 'husband,' so this could mean 'I will trade my husband.' "

Blue Wing froze as Corn Basket and even the old one's laughter drifted out to her. "You know," Kate went on in her deliberate Mandan, for she still had trouble with many deep-throat sounds, "I realize the Mandans can change husbands if they want, so why must Blue Wing go to Wolf Trap if she could just walk away from him later?"

Blue Wing jerked even more alert. Her fingernails bit into her palms as she stood there, not daring to enter. She had not really believed Prairie Wind would try to bend her family's thoughts.

"Not good thinking," Long Hatchet said. "Not the way of The People. Clam Necklace go to man with much medicine. Next daughter go too. Big medicine bundle in Wolf Trap family. Blue Wing go."

"You know, Blue Wing has told me about the sacred geese of Old Woman in the Moon—her messengers that teach the tribe."

"Yes," Long Hatchet said. "This sign of the goose I make now."

"Blue Wing told me how the geese would die to protect their children, and that is a good lesson. But," Kate said, her voice rising, "since geese mate for life, how can The People put a mate aside and why should Blue Wing go to a man she cannot love in the first place?"

"You say too much." Buffalo Grass's voice came, subdued but stern.

"I am sorry to offend my dear sister's family," Prairie Wind said. "But since I admit and all of us know that the white man makes many mistakes in his ways, could not just some of the Mandan ways be wrong too?"

"You here learn paint, not think," Long Hatchet insisted, and from the ensuing silence Blue Wing could tell Prairie Wind dared no more. How she loved and admired her for this attempt, yet how she resented that she sat among them already taking her place, in her Mandan dress, being listened to by all of them, however much they did not heed her. Unlike Prairie Wind, their own daughter of this lodge dared not even argue.

But as Blue Wing straightened her shoulders and prepared to go in, she heard the telltale shrieks of the Black Mouth messengers from the roofs: "The warriors return! Victory! Scalps! Scalps!"

Blue Wing scrambled up on the roof, as did others in the village. Corn Basket and Prairie Wind ran out and climbed up too, surprised to see Blue Wing already there. Long Hatchet and Buffalo Grass came out to see the proud procession.

Blue Wing squinted to count the returning Mandans. Yes, four men, Wolf Trap at their head. He had returned, so she must go to him the day of the Corn Dance as promised. Now she joined in the women's shrieks of victory, but her cries were of inner dismay and devastation.

"What are they saying?" Prairie Wind shouted at her over the din.

"Calling all to Scalp Dance!" Blue Wing explained.

"They took scalps and are going to dance over them?" she demanded, grabbing her wrist. "Will the men at the fort allow that?"

"Not can stop The People's ways, not your man either!" Blue Wing retorted. "Even your new mother and grandmother will dance," she said, and pointed at both women as they slid down to the ground to shriek and jump and turn.

Now Wolf Trap rode straight toward them. His eyes lit to see Blue Wing. He thrust at them one of his two poles, with a dangling long-haired black scalp, then handed both poles to his mother-in-law and the old one, who increased their cavorting and cries.

"It's—it's awful, and I defended it to Blackwell," Blue Wing heard Prairie Wind say. Blue Wing pulled her wrist back so hard her friend almost rolled off the roof before she caught herself. "Rand told me there were some things

I didn't understand," she said, "but . . . Corn Basket and Buffalo Grass—it makes me sick."

"Go live with your man at the fort then," Blue Wing cried. Once again the bad heart words to Prairie Wind burned her tongue, but she said them. "And look at you— Sioux scalps on your dress!"

"What?" she said. She looked with eyes as big as clamshells at her Mandan dress instead of at the crowd of shrieking dancers, waving scalps on poles while the painted Wolf Trap sat triumphant on his horse.

"There and there!" Blue Wing exulted, pointing at the seams of the dress, though she detested herself for wanting to hurt Prairie Wind. "More scalp hair of the Sioux!"

Prairie Wind ran her hand down the side seam with its black hair sewn there, then pulled back as if it burned her. She slid off the roof and ran out of the village, going way around to avoid the dancers.

Blue Wing felt hollow as she watched her go. She wanted to run with her, to hold to her friend. Wolf Trap and The People claimed victory today, but Blue Wing felt defeat that she had wounded her friend and danced on her pain.

Kate met Rand loping toward the village while she ran away from it. "I hear the raiding party's back," he called to her. "What's happened?"

"They're all safe, and everyone's going wild over the scalps! Rand, is this scalp hair on this dress? I thought it was fur or buffalo or something! It's terrible!"

"How many scalps did they take?" he asked as he turned her and propelled her along with him toward the village.

"Four, I guess. Rand! *Is* this scalp hair?"

"Traditional. My grandfather's trophies, I imagine. If they only took four for two dead, things won't spin out of control so we can't trade corn with them and still talk peace."

"Peace? These people don't want peace!"

Despite his hurry, he swung Kate around to face him, holding her upper arms in a firm grip. "Kate, I told you that—"

"I know, that they had a dark side. You do too."

"I never pretended anything else. But I believe you were willing to take me on, to vow we'd solve whatever differences or problems came our way. Did you mean that?"

"Yes."

"Mandan manhood and leadership are based on raids, I hope in place of major warfare. Besides the family medicine bundle, warfare and prowess on the hunt mean everything. Those make their reputations, their wealth and power instead of owning a lot of land or goods ... or people."

"I know. But I didn't know scalp hair was on my dress!"

"We can talk about it later. Blackwell sent me here to keep control of things so they don't send another party out. Why don't you just go on back to the fort and wait for me if you can't stomach how they're acting now?" He started off again.

She stood there, watching him walk away, thinking of all she'd seen, all she'd learned at Mitutanka. As she had tried to tell Blue Wing's family today, some things here were wrong, and this—this rejoicing at murder and scalping for revenge was the worst she had seen so far. It was harder to abide than love exploit sticks, dead bodies on scaffolds until the bones fell down, self-torture in O-Kee-Pa, polygamy, berdaches, divorce, and Baby Hills!

Yet for the love she bore them all, especially Rand, she told herself, if she kept trying, maybe some of these things could change. She could give a long list of cruelties and crimes and sins in the so-called civilized world too.

She wanted to run after Rand, though she did not budge. She had to go back to The People and take the bad with the good. Only she could not bear to go in to see them that way, not the models of Mandan womanhood, Corn Basket and Buffalo Grass too! And she was starting to think she and Blue Wing could never patch up what they had once shared.

And then she glanced down toward the tethered *Red Dawn*. She could talk to Gabe for a while, help him, Pete, and Fynn pack the goods they had traded for already. Anything to keep busy while this was going on. Then she saw not only her steamship but, just passing it and tying up beyond it, Fort Clark's big keelboat on which Stirling had gone to Fort Union weeks ago. Resigned to tell him his bad news before someone else did, she strode resolutely down to the river.

Stirling stood on the prow, wildly waving his hat. Hating what was coming, she waved back. He vaulted off the deck while the crew cheered. As he ran up toward her, arms outstretched, she held up her hands to stop him.

"My love!" he cried, coming to a halt just in front of her. "What is it? You're not ill?"

She could not keep him from hugging her, but she gently pushed him back and stepped away. "I'm afraid I have a sad surprise for you, Stirling. I am very sorry, but I cannot marry you."

"Thank God, that's all," he said with a broad grin, flipping his hat around in one hand. "I will change your mind in a trice, my love. I swear, you looked as if someone had died. You know we are fated for each other, my beautiful Kate." He hooked her arm in his and pulled her up toward the fort.

"No," she said, and tugged free. "I'm not joking. You don't understand. I—I'm sorry, but I married Rand. I mean, I'm not sorry I did, but that I let you down, and—"

"You what?" he shouted. His usually placid demeanor crumbled; his complexion, as rosy as it was, stained sunset red. "Now you *are* joking. I thought it was just—just animal attraction between—"

"*Animal!* Stirling, Rand and I want to share our lives. Don't you dare degrade—"

"Are you demented to marry that loner, that renegade half-breed? A woman like you living in a place like this? And he is a fish out of water in civilization. You certainly led me a pretty dance, led me on!"

"No, I only responded to your lead—your fervent friendship and clever courtship. You'd think after I was swept off my feet by grand promises once before—and I don't mean by Rand—I would not have let it happen again between you and me."

"Then he seduced you, trapped you. The moment I left here, or that night you were so conveniently lost in the woods, he—"

"That's not true. Everything was mutual, despite the fact we didn't even like each other at first."

"By damn, I will have his head!"

"Will you? I suppose you'll call him out on a point of honor over this? Pistols at forty paces like the old days on Bloody Island off St. Louis? Talk about uncivilized. Or challenge him to a rifle duel with your prowess? I said I am sorry to have hurt you, and—and Rand is too, but I won't have you blaming him for something that was shared."

"Then *you* are the traitor. A liar too! Don't worry about anything but taking care of yourself, you said when I left. You said you loved me!"

"Stirling, I said I loved you as a friend. I loved that you seemed too good to be true because of all the things you offered me, and as with Clive before, that was wrong of me."

He snorted indignantly, leaning against a tree, slapping his hat back and forth against his thighs. She could tell he wanted to say more, probably give her a good cursing. When he just pressed his lips together, she thought—she hoped—the initial shock and rage had begun to drain from him.

"So, Mrs. Kate Craig, you have made a country marriage out here in the pagan wilds, even after you said you would not accept that your first husband did just that."

"I said that I didn't accept it at first and that he never told me. And I am not married to someone else as he was. Besides, when I got to know Blue Wing—"

"Oh, how noble of you, always noble about the savages. Well, if you like the red man's ways and can accept what your first husband did, then I can be your city husband, Rand your country Mandan one, and everything will be fine and dandy. Then you can be *both* the city and the country wife. And everyone far and wide from

Blackwell to Clark to Chouteau and your own mother will know you are demented!"

"Stop it, Stirling! I know I've hurt you!"

"By damn, woman, you have hurt yourself, and you don't even see it. And yes, you have let me down, made things exceedingly ... difficult." He cleared his throat and looked away toward the river. "I suppose you do not want me going back on the *Red Dawn*."

"If you can stand it, and Rand doesn't mind, it's fine. General Clark did buy you a return ticket."

"What a hellish ride it has been. I cannot believe you married him over me, that's all."

"I said I won't listen to disparaging words about Rand. And I do not have to defend him. Stirling, with all you have to offer, the ladies in St. Louis will fall at your feet."

He snorted again. "I had everything so planned out I cannot believe it, so perfectly planned." He shook his head, looking for a moment as if he'd caught himself in some admission. He shoved away from the tree and faced her squarely.

"I cannot wish you the best, Kate Craig MacLeod. And yes, I want to head home on the steamship, the sooner the better. I've seen quite enough of frontier life. I have kept my bargain—with Clark, I mean. And the sooner I am out of it all, the better!"

She had never seen him look so hard and bitter as he walked away, but then it wasn't every day a man of Stirling's qualities and virtues met disappointment and defeat, she thought. As he trudged toward the fort, she ran back toward Mitutanka, more eager than ever now to be reunited with Rand and, yes, the Mandans. Over the coming years, visiting or even living here, she might try to change some of their ways. But even if she detested a few of their actions and beliefs, she could never detest The People themselves.

Although Ahpcha-Toha had not wanted to talk to Prairie Wind for days, and when she did, she tried to hurt her, today she wanted to talk and talk to her. It was the day The People first ate some of the ripe corn and sacrificed some of it to Old Woman in the Moon, known in planting and harvesttime as Corn Mother. It was also the day Blue Wing would depart from living under the hand of Buffalo Grass and Corn Basket and come under the hand of Clam Necklace. It was the day she would leave the lodge of Long Hatchet and go to the lodge—and bed—of Wolf Trap.

She took Prairie Wind with her down to the stream near the cave where she had met Swift Raven the night of O-Kee-Pa. She would have liked to peer inside the cool, dim cave to remember, but she dared not with Prairie Wind here. Blue Wing spoke on and on to her friend, explaining about the ceremony they had been watching, telling her all about how the old women dancers must be members of the Goose Society, to which Buffalo Grass belonged. She told her why the corn ears they danced with were on a stick, pointing at the sky to honor Old Woman. Why a few grains would be given to each family to be mixed with seed corn for the next spring planting. How the Old Woman's sacred geese would see this and fly into the sky to tell Old Woman that The People honored her so she would send good grain next year. How Prairie Wind should paint the ceremony, especially Buffalo Grass as she danced.

On, she talked, just so she didn't have to think about going to Wolf Trap and Clam Necklace. She told how she would try to be another mother to the two children of the lodge, a boy and a girl, how she, and Prairie Wind too, would have children of their own. Finally, when she had prepared on the face of a flat rock a base of clay and filled it with water to make the sacred mirror, *a-wa-sa-ta,* she peered down into it and fell silent at last.

The woman staring up at her looked beautifully arrayed. Her hair and skin shone with castoreum, her beads were bright—but her eyes were dull. If she turned her head just right, the mirror caught the top of Prairie Wind's golden head and, beyond, the treetops above the entrance to the cave.

Just recently Blue Wing had seen she had not conceived a child that night with Swift Raven, however fervently she had wished it. Now she sat back on her heels and stared into the blue eyes of her friend sitting in the speckled shade. This was like a sheltered cave of leaves she and Prairie Wind could hide in forever.

"I am glad you brought me here today," Prairie Wind told her. "Just to be with you."

Blue Wing could not trust her voice. She shrugged, something she had learned from the whites.

"It is a beautiful place here"—Prairie Wind went on in the sudden silence—"like so much of the Mandan land. I know you will not forget that there are many beautiful things in life, Blue Wing, even if your heart is not good as you go to his lodge."

"Yes. A new life. Always women must make the best of a new, different life."

"That's exactly right." Prairie Wind reached out her hand, which Blue Wing clasped. "When we can help each other, we must. And even if we are far apart, we will think good thoughts and hope for fine things in life for each other. And whatever happens with our men or between our men, we *will* be friends, Blue Wing."

"Yes," she said, and stood before she dropped tears to make *a-wa-sa-ta* ruffle like the river. She smacked her hand in it to splash the water out. "I go now alone. You not come farther than the village walls."

"All right. I was going to let you say farewell to everyone in private. But I would like to walk all the way to the village with you."

Unspeaking now, shoulder to shoulder, they walked the beaten path to Mitutanka. Again in her thoughts, Blue Wing walked with this white woman sister by the beaver pond where they had first spoken on that other prairie. She recalled they went together, Much Questions too, down the snow-slick hill to the warehouse on the muddy Mississippi where they made their winter home. Tracing the boundaries of the land at River of Sky with Prairie Wind, Blue Wing saw again that lovely day. They stood on the Baby Hill, though they argued there. Again they walked the deck of the *Red Dawn* steaming up Big River and rode the buffalo hunt path side by side. But for now they must walk no more together.

"You turn back now," Blue Wing said, and dared not look at her friend. "I go on."

Ahpcha-Toha, Blue Wing, second daughter of Long Hatchet and Corn Basket, went to her family's lodge and bade them all good-bye. Her things, pots and all, would be sent later, for Clam Necklace was a maker of jewelry, not pots. Although Blue Wing could tell her parents were proud of her, even relieved and joyous, she still wanted to cling to the support pole of the lodge and cry to stay.

Corn Basket handed her the dish of porridge made from fresh new corn. Buffalo Grass, still tired after the dancing, did not rise, but she lifted her hand as if to give a blessing. Long Hatchet nodded his approval, then looked back down at the robe he had been working on. With a quick glance Blue Wing could tell it was a woman's robe, and then she knew. The steamboat was on it again, and a chair with rockers, and the sign for Dark Water: The robe was for the new daughter of the lodge.

Eyes straight ahead, Ahpcha-Toha walked to the lodge of Wolf Trap, feeling it was just that: Its entryway with the flap lifted loomed like a wolf's den or a trap. Grateful she had seen no one from the next-door lodge of Four Bears, she shoved the flap wider and went in.

She fought to calm herself when she saw the scene. This was no wolf's den, no trap. Clam Necklace sat in the center of the lodge with her two young children playing at her feet. Two of Wolf Trap's unwed sisters stood to greet her; the man himself sat with his pipe on a scaffold just before the second bed, his eyes gleaming through the curls of smoke. That bed would, she knew, be hers as Wolf Trap's second wife. Head high, she walked straight to him and offered him the porridge, which he ate quickly, greedily.

After all had formally exchanged names and greetings, Clam Necklace said, "This day long overdue."

Wolf Trap grunted. "I will get back lost days, lost nights."

Clam Necklace looked down at the beads she was stringing in her lap. Since she was not watching, Blue Wing smiled at the children, a girl of four winters, a boy of two. Clam Necklace had always tried to keep these two from her, though that was not The People's way any more

than the younger sister's refusing to go into marriage with
her elder sister, especially to a man of so much medicine.

Blue Wing fought to beat down her still-festering resentment that Clam Necklace had helped Wolf Trap attack her that day on the prairie. She knew she must forget
and forgive to go on, but bile from it still tasted bitter in
her mouth. This future chief of The People was as low as
that defiling Marbois the tribe detested. But she was married to Wolf Trap now; they were a family. All else—all
others once loved—must be put away like girlhood
games.

The hours before dark became a blur for her. They ate;
Wolf Trap smoked and sipped water; the children darted
about with the dogs. And then her new husband lifted his
hand and firmly took her wrist.

"Now I make you my woman, only mine," he whispered.

His narrow eyes slid over her; she smelled something
sharp on his breath that was not tobacco. She recognized
it then: liquor, which Gabe drank once a day, which
Marbois had on his breath, which Prairie Wind said had
made her father beat her and her mother. Without another
word or glance at Clam Necklace, Wolf Trap pulled her
to her feet, and she followed him back into the dim
depths of the lodge.

Blue Wing wished he had given her a moment alone
first to prepare, but what did it matter now? She took off
her moccasins and climbed into the dark space. She tried
to close out thoughts of other such places of privacy and
pleasure nearby: Clam Necklace's bed, Bright Star's in
the next lodge, that of Dark Water and Prairie Wind, who
loved so wildly that they squeaked their bed upon its
stretched hide and willow sticks.

As Wolf Trap climbed heavily in beside her and closed
the flap, she shut her eyes, willing herself to accept. Then
his hands roamed her, tugging up her dress, separating
her legs, moving his mouth with that harsh scent across
each stretch of skin he bared.

"The first time you fought me like a cornered dog," he
whispered. His breath burned her breast. "You have
fought me ever since, but no more. Turn your defiant face

away. On your knees for me, my fighting dog bitch still in heat for that cursed Swift Raven. I will leash you every night and him later."

He twisted her wrist behind her back to make her comply. She gasped aloud once at the insult, at the indignity and pain. But she would make no more sound. She would not give to him one more word in this bed than she would have given that other drunken animal Scarface Marbois. She bit her lower lip in her teeth until she tasted blood.

How she had hoped for something to build on here, something to help her forget. But even as Wolf Trap took her cruelly, the real Blue Wing eluded him. For there, there behind her eyelids screwed tight shut even in this dark cave, she saw her beloved Swift Raven. And in the shaded shelter of her thoughts she still gripped the hand of her strong friend and her real sister, Prairie Wind.

Chapter 16

At Blackwell's dining table in the fort he and Marbois stuffed themselves with the succulent ears of freshly picked corn Clam Necklace boiled for them at the hearth, then carried to the table. It smeared their mouths, caught in their teeth and Marbois's beard. They washed it down with gulps of whiskey and talked as they chewed. The only other guest, Stirling Mount, ate too, but slowly and silently.

"Good, eh, Mount?" Blackwell demanded. "Only red man food I'd about kill for."

"It is delicious," Stirling said, but he pushed back from the table and wiped his mouth and hands with his handkerchief.

"Losing his gal's done put him off his food," Marbois muttered.

"Leave him alone. He's got more'n that to worry about. But look, man"—Blackwell addressed Stirling now—"she's stupid to marry MacLeod, and who needs a stupid woman underfoot, at least in St. Louis with the company you'll be keeping?"

Stirling shoved his chair back from the table. "I cannot appreciate your logic or your humor. I should like to see you go back to St. Louis if you failed so miserably." He rose, walked out, and slammed the door.

"Failed in a big, big way," Marbois said, and frowned toward Clam Necklace. He heaved another cob on the growing pile of them in the corner of the room. "You sure this gal don't know English?"

"Naw," Blackwell responded. "The only ears she got for us is these." He grinned at his own pun and waved his corn. "But the new Mrs. MacLeod's friend Blue Wing is living at Wolf Trap's now. She's been taught some English by that meddling white woman, and I suppose Blue Wing could slip this one an English word or two. But it's having a new bride that made Wolf Trap kind enough to loan out wife number one more lately. To partake"—he became more eloquent and loud, waving his half-ravaged cob—"of my great white medicine to increase his own the next time he beds her." Blackwell shook his head as he laughed at himself. "Guess that's the second thing about the Mandans I like: their belief in sharing women."

"Say," Marbois asked, going back to whispering, "you think . . . when Wolf Trap gets a bit weary of his new gal, he'd share her too? I swear I got a score to settle with the whore, and I'd be willing to rub off on her a lot of my medicine about trading and working for Chouteau and all."

They snickered and clinked pewter mugs. Blackwell snatched at Clam Necklace's skirt, and Marbois smacked her rear as she came over with four fresh ears.

"Well, now," Blackwell said, his voice still low, "soon as the white woman leaves and before you head west with the half-breed, maybe we can arrange something like that. Wolf Trap knows the whole leadership of this tribe's at stake, and we can help him get it."

"Speaking of which," Blackwell said, leaning farther forward and picking his teeth with his knife from time to time, "Mount told me some trader up at Fort Union says the smallpox been out among the Kaws and Pawnees, in and out of the southern plains. Can get kicked off just by infection from sick folks' blankets and such if the victims ain't been inoculated, and I don't think any of the Mandans been. Now, if we could only get a few blankets like that to give Four Bears and his lackey Swift Raven— maybe Wolf Calf too. You know, get them off alone to keep it offa the others Wolf Trap could then control for us. Chouteau'd be so proud of both of us he'd probably let us marry into his clan like he done with others, and we'd be set for life."

"Set 'cept for dealing with MacLeod—both MacLeods," Marbois muttered.

"When Chouteau gets my letter going back on the *Red Dawn,* I don't think we'll see her coming back up here to trade. Or if she does get past your friend Big Buck next time and we can get those blankets, we can just put the blame on her. Heard her say she'd be bringing blankets next time to trade for buffalo hides. As for MacLeod among the Sioux, you just never know what can happen," he added, and stabbed his next ear of corn with his knife.

Marbois stopped chewing long enough to grin. "I'm sending a note to Chouteau myself—in French," he said, still whispering. "I'm suggesting neither of them—the MacLeods—oughta ever come back. Meanwhile, we got our first and second line of plans all laid, I'd say. Now, you're real sure this red gal don't know what we're saying?"

"Most of them's too stupid to learn English if they had to, especially the squaws," he said, and hiccuped. "Now just go on over there and latch the door so we don't get disturbed, and I'll show you the language she does get good and clear." He flung the skewered corn off his knife as Marbois hasted to obey. "Now that we're partners in all this, I don't mind sharing. Just make sure you give her a little present after you're done with her, 'cause she and Wolf Trap really like what the white man's got to give."

They laughed again as Blackwell cleared the table with a swipe of his arm and grabbed for Clam Necklace amid the mess they'd made.

Stirling walked the rampart walls of the fort, scuffing his feet, kicking the logs now and then. He had really cared for Kate, had wanted her from the first time he saw her. Granted, he'd been warned she was independent and sassy, but he had not believed she'd choose MacLeod and a life out here over him and St. Louis. He should have paid more attention to how she blossomed on the river, how she loved that place of hers, River of Sky, and the prairie here, despite the hardships. He should have believed the danger signs he saw. Success through Kate had been his just for the plucking, and she'd turned out rotten.

Muttering under his breath, he went down the ladder and into his cubbyhole of a room to pace two steps out, two back. Damn, but he couldn't wait to get back to civilization, a decent bed, oil lanterns, carriages, the rest of it. He only hoped his mentor would still be willing to sponsor him, to trust him working in the superintendent's office. He jumped and hit his head on the low-beam ceiling when someone rapped on the door.

"What is it?"

"It's Jenkins," Blackwell's Mandan translator called to him. "The major, he sent you a little present, knowing you was feeling low."

Stirling opened the door to reveal Jenkins grinning sheepishly ... and a nubile, scantily clad Mandan girl. "Who is she?" he demanded.

"Your gift, man. One of Wolf Trap's sisters."

"I don't want her. Take her away."

"Well, now, she and Wolf Trap might get real insulted."

"I don't care. Tell Blackwell I am insulted that he thinks I can forget, get over my loss like this. Tell him, I'm sorry, but no." He couldn't help himself, but he slammed the door.

Kate might be able to forget and forgo all they had once had together by bedding someone else, but he could not. For whatever reasons he had wanted her, he had loved her too. But no more, if he could help it, no more! She had ruined everything! And now he would have to be near her on the way home.

He sat on the edge of his bed without lighting a candle and stared into the darkness. And cursed Kate, above all else, for ruining his prosperous future.

Through the first week of September Kate still lingered at Mitutanka when she knew she should be on her way. She missed Jamie terribly and had told him she would see him before the leaves changed. This far north an early frost had wilted the flowers and silvered the grass. Still, the leaves clung to their summer green as she clung to Rand, who would be leaving soon too.

A band of Teton Sioux, led by Big Buck, had come in to trade for corn and camped for several days. Kate could not believe that these two tribes, members of which had recently killed each other, could get along at all. Renegade Sioux had murdered Mandan berry pickers; Mandan raiders had done their duty; the Sioux would perhaps retaliate for that later. But for now both sides accepted a temporary truce, evidently traditional. As Rand had said before, she realized, she did not understand the way the Indians thought. But she did avoid Big Buck and his camp.

Rand, with Marbois as his translator—a man she warned Rand not to trust—had tried to get the Sioux and Mandans to parlay for a permanent peace. When Big Buck said his father, the war chief, White Raven, was the only one who could promise that, Rand made plans to visit their autumn camp out on the plains. He and Marbois would head out with Big Buck's party when they went in a few days.

When Kate heard that, she finally accepted that her days with Rand were numbered. She feared his dealing with the Sioux; she dreaded leaving him. But she must go to Jamie and St. Louis so that she could return as soon as the spring ice melted on the river.

Today the sun was warm, but the brisk air hinted at colder days to come. Rand got away from the fort for the afternoon, and the two of them borrowed Corn Basket's bullboat. Laughing at their shared balancing act, they carried it to the lake back of the woods where the Mitutanka Mandans had the smaller, warmer winter village they would move to in the early snows.

They launched the circular boat made from buffalo skins stretched airtight over willow hoops. The craft was rough river-worthy and could carry great loads. But Kate had to laugh because every time Rand moved it with the oar pole, the boat revolved halfway around in its progress.

"Don't laugh, or you can do this!" he said, grinning himself.

"It's just I've never been in a fur-lined boat before. Oh, look, some sort of water lily. Take us over there so I can pick a few for Buffalo Grass."

"I think they've all adopted you—the old woman especially," he said as he slowly moved the rotating boat toward the small gold blooms perched on their green pads.

"I'm deeply touched by their hospitality. But I don't think it's endearing me to poor Blue Wing lately. Rand, I don't care if I'm not welcome at Wolf Trap's lodge. I'm going there to see her before I leave. And if Blue Wing gives the word, I'll take her south with me."

"You can't," he said. "That is, I don't think she'll go, and nothing would turn Long Hatchet's lodge against you faster. Their prestige has been greatly restored by her doing her duty."

"Doing her duty," Kate muttered as she reached for a lily. Its stem was slippery and seemed to go down forever without snapping off. "And I've got to do mine by setting out south and soon. But I can't bear to go until after you do."

Rand sat beside her in the boat and propped the long oar across the rim. "One thing I need to tell you today, Kate, is that the Sioux will be setting out tomorrow, and I'm go—"

"Tomorrow! Not tomorrow!"

He nodded. "We knew this time would come. Separation this year of necessity, but somehow never again."

"Yes," she said, abandoning her struggle with the lily stem. She threw her wet arms tight around him. "We're not going to have a marriage apart, not after I get things set for trading and bring that smallpox vaccine up here."

But even all that faded as they kissed. Floating like a big lily pad on the little lake, the boat finally bumped against the bank. They both startled from their embrace; Rand peered up over the edge. He helped her out, grabbed his rifle, and dragged the boat up on the bank.

"The last official day of our honeymoon," he said. "Our first but not our last Indian summer together. Come on. Let's really make time fly."

He held out his hand to her, and they walked into the trees. He led her into what the whites at the fort called Point of Woods. The trees here would keep their green cloaks before another frost or two would paint them red and gold, but Kate knew neither of them would be here to see that.

He took her into the sheltered winter village with its smaller lodges set more deeply in the soil. They stopped before the closest one. Rand used his gun barrel to pull out the twisted thorns and briars blocking the entrance.

"Scatter Corn's family's winter lodge," he said. "They

won't mind. If I come to the winter village, I'll stay here or with Long Hatchet."

He led her down into the dim shell, where light spilled in only from the door. It reminded her of the cave near the stream the night they had gone there to love but had been interrupted by Swift Raven and Blue Wing. Today nothing would stop them, but again Kate felt the clinging sadness of her friend, even though she rejoiced in her own life and love.

The interior looked so empty compared with the big village lodges, but when The People came, they brought what they needed. Still, looped over a vine hanging from the ceiling, Rand found a buffalo hide and flung it on the floor. He pulled her to him.

They explored each other with eager hands, eyes, and lips as if they had never loved before. Shedding their skin garments to make soft puddles at their feet, they sank to the robe on their knees. They touched and tantalized, awestruck anew. He tumbled her over, then under him. Her arms entwined around his neck; her knees and thighs clasped his narrow hips to seek a mutual possession. They linked their bodies and their lives, moving in a rhythm so fierce they moved the robe across the floor out of the sun into the chill shade. Yet they felt nothing but the heat between them. Finally, breathless, sweating, they collapsed but still held tight.

"I keep thinking," he said later, his voice rough, "we shouldn't make a baby until you get back. We've been breeding like minks."

Though exhausted, she took a limp-fisted swipe at his chin. "What a terrible comparison. You mean we should have been celibate until I came back next spring? Now that's a good one, even for someone as self-disciplined as you."

"Not self-disciplined around you. You've changed me so much."

"For the best, I hope."

"You've given me more to care about, but more to worry about than The People."

"Rand, I'll be all right. And you've got to realize you

alone are not responsible for saving The People. You blame yourself too much and always have."

He frowned and turned her in his arms, so she faced away from him but was cuddled back against him as if she were sitting in his lap. "For my mother's loss, you mean," he said, his voice almost a whisper. "Damn it, that *was* my fault."

"You were a little boy who happened to find his father's gun," she said, and twisted back around in his arms to face him. "And please don't worry you will lose me the way you lost her. I don't mean, with a gun, but just don't think you will lose me at all! Everything will be good for us, I know it. We'll have our cabin inside the fort you're going to have built, and Long Hatchet said we can still have our bed at the lodge. Once in a while we can visit your aunt in St. Louis, where I'll have the business going to support things we do here, and on our way back and forth we can stay at River of Sky. I'll build us a cabin there or something even better."

"No big houses," he said. "Not like that Winterhaven of yours."

"Winterhaven was Clive's even though he never really owned it. It was his dream of grandeur and success, of being someone important and rich. It was never my house, but more like—like a cage. A very pretty cage I was hiding in—hiding from myself, from life really. No, I would not want a mansion at River of Sky, but something that fits the land there. . . ."

Already she had packed away in her things sketches of the interior of Mandan lodges, diagrams of their support and crossbeams, their dimensions, but she had not told Rand. And she had not told him she was doing a portrait of Scatter Corn for him because she looked like his mother. It was her dream to have that painting hanging in a Mandan-style lodge at River of Sky when he saw the place next time. And it was her dream that Rand would be able to gaze on that with a peaceful heart, not with the grief of self-blame.

"Rand, you know what George Catlin, that artist at General Clark's, told me the first night you and I met?"

"That you could be a great painter."

"Sort of. But he said something more important. He told me never to let anyone make me forgo my dreams. I've clung to that since, even when what I thought I wanted in life changed and deepened. Now I want us to be a family, Jamie too."

"I will try to be a good father to him—the best!" he declared, and hugged her hard. "There's so much I want to show and teach him. And, Kate, you know what has always signified my dream for me—to help the Mandans? Something I heard years ago. It stuck with me, just like your Catlin quotation did with you."

"Tell me," she said, stroking his shoulder and upper arm.

"My mother," he began, and cleared his throat, "used to tell me a story her family owned, a myth about the Children of the Sun. Once those children were given thunder and lightning as weapons with which to kill monsters that were afflicting their mother's people. And they did it—protected her and her people. That's all I remembered of the story over the years until Scatter Corn told it to me again the other day. But that part about the children killing the enemies of their mother's people always stuck with me and grew in my mind as I got older. . . ."

She took his chin in her small hand and turned him to look at her instead of the ceiling. "And your weapons of thunder and lightning are your position as subagent and the love you bear The People when others only want to use them."

"Yes," he whispered, and his dark eyes filled with tears. "Yes!"

"I share your dream now to help and protect the Mandans. But, Rand, even if you somehow lost your position, we could still stay here as traders. We could build up a St. Louis business and defy Chouteau if we had to. We can try to make the whites understand that The People are real people too! Nothing can stop us if we hold to our dreams and to each other!"

His hands cradled her face; he tipped her head back. His eyes blazed, and a smile trembled on his lips. "You are a wonder," he whispered. "And yes, I will do everything to work with the way things are, even to trust Clark and President Jackson for the vaccine. But if worse comes to worst with the government, you and I will find some way! Kate, I have been so determined but so down-trodden, so alone in this. But no longer, with you."

He clung to her so hard she almost could not breathe. She stroked the back of his head and molded her soft flesh to his angles and planes. Surely their love would keep them safe and united, however far the miles between them stretched, she thought. She pressed her cheek to his slightly stubbled one, then kissed him strongly. And though that afternoon they loved again, and swam in the lake, and visited Scatter Corn, and strolled the village, Kate knew that their moment of fervent farewell—but also their deepest binding—had already happened. For in the winter lodge by the lake they had sealed themselves and their dreams forever.

That evening at the fort, before Rand went to spend the last night with Kate at Long Hatchet's lodge, he sought out Stirling Mount. He had expected Mount to accost him earlier, but Clark's man had obviously been avoiding him and seething in private. Or perhaps the man just did not have the backbone for any sort of real confrontation, no matter what the stakes. Rand would have let things slide, except for Kate's sake on the trip back downriver. So when he looked up and saw Stirling along the top of the wall near the south battlement, he went up the ladder to him.

Stirling turned and saw him coming. He'd been resting his chin on his arms atop the stockade logs, but he seemed to stand at attention now.

"You are a fool to be taking time out from your honeymoon, MacLeod," he said. "But then you were a selfish fool to marry her. If you cared for her, you would let her go back to St. Louis and stay there."

"Is that the way you'd care for the woman you love: let her live apart from you forever?" Rand replied before he could take the calmer tack he'd meant to.

"You know this is no place for her and the boy!"

"I didn't come to discuss where my wife and stepson will live, Mount. I came to ask you man to man if you will be a friend to her on the way back, though not too damned close a friend."

Stirling stood even stiffer. "You have ruined all my dreams and dare to ask that?"

"For her sake, yes. If you can't swear it to me, I'll send you back on the last keelboat no matter what General Clark says."

"What? I'm going back on the *Red Dawn*! And your jealousy had better not affect that!"

"What's affecting that, Mount, is my deep concern that Kate get back safely to St. Louis with no one picking away at her decisions or dedication, though she's probably mentally stronger than both of us put together. So do I have your word, because if not—"

"Yes, you have it. As for the two of us, we will settle things someday, some way between us!"

Stirling stood his ground as Rand stepped closer. "That would suit me just fine, Mount, as long as it's just you and me and no one else involved. And I'm giving you an extra pouch of powder and ball to practice shooting on the way south. In case something happens where the crew needs an extra shot, you and that fancy rifle the general loaned you had better be ready. And maybe when we have that little meeting to settle things someday, you'll want to be a better shot."

He started away, then turned back to the man. He had meant not to threaten him but to impress upon him that he held him partly responsible for Kate's well-being. "And give my best to General Clark," Rand added. "Kate will be reporting to him, just like you will, you know."

Stirling assumed his earlier nonchalant position, leaning against the logs, but he hardly looked at ease. "Actually, MacLeod, I hope I never see you or this godforsaken land again."

"That would suit me fine. I'm glad you didn't convince her to marry you, Mount, for lots of reasons. For one, she loves this land, the people too. But they'll still be just numbers and amounts to you, even though General Clark sent you to learn to appreciate them because he cares for them too."

The two men stared at each other in the dimming light.

Rand could tell Mount wanted to fling some other insult or challenge at him but stifled it. Rand glanced out toward the village beckoning to him. He went down the steps without another word or glance at the handsome, suave city man Kate might have—perhaps should have—chosen over the rugged, rough half-breed she said she loved.

The next morning Kate and Rand rose from their bed in the lodge of Long Hatchet at first dawn. Kate already grieved to see Rand looking rushed and preoccupied. Neither of them had slept well even when they had finally tried to get some rest; their thoughts, first whispered, then unspoken, disturbed their sleep.

Now Rand quickly ate the stew and corn balls Corn Basket gave him. He smoked a last pipe with Long Hatchet while Kate helped Corn Basket prepare more food and straighten the robes strewn in the beds, but not for Buffalo Grass, who still slept.

Kate's stomach twisted tighter as she tried to watch Rand's every move, tried to memorize his face, his voice. For one moment she could not believe that the big dark man etched by dim firelight across the lodge was hers—and that they were really parting. But she would not let herself think of that. Nothing bad would happen; it could not, not when they had found each other and made a marriage. She was angry with herself that she had agreed she would not go to the Sioux camp to say a final farewell. She would be willing to face Big Buck just so they could have a few more moments!

When Rand came over to her, he was carrying a buffalo robe. "Come outside with me," he said. "I have something for you."

In the light of pink dawn he flapped the robe open. With all of Long Hatchet's tutoring, she could read the Mandan picture writing signs quite well. In the tribal artist's distinctive hand, the *mih-sha* told the story of Kate's befriending Blue Wing, of being named Prairie Wind, of nursing Blue Wing through the winter, of bringing her upriver. And there was Rand finding her lost in the forest, teaching her to swim and shoot, and Rand saved from the river by her rocking chair. And on this row, for the pic-

tures and signs were read up one line, then turned to be
read down the next, Kate came to the lodge of Long
Hatchet with her presents. Here she painted on the hunt.
Then she and Rand were wed, man and wife, once on the
steamboat and once here in the village.

"You see, I didn't forget," Rand said.

"It's wonderful. And at least it doesn't show us parting." Tears now blurred her view of it all. "What a beautiful exploit robe. I will thank him for it—and you too, of
course, if we just had time. . . ."

"He's left space for our children and our future here,
see?"

"Oh, Rand, it's lovely, it's all been so lovely," she said,
and hugged him hard with the thick robe pressed between
them.

Without another word he held her. He rocked her
slightly as the village came to life around them.

"I've got to go, Kate, and soon you do too."

"Yes," she said, and stood back from him, though it
was one of the hardest things she'd ever done. "Just a final day of trading, I think. It is a rather sparse haul with
Chouteau's previous demands on them for furs, but it will
be enough to profit what we want to do—you and I."

"Don't forget to give Aunt Alice my letter. She'll be
thrilled to know you, to have you and Jamie stay with her
this winter. Give her my love!"

She nodded. "Yours and mine—I will."

He ducked inside for his pack, gun, water bottle, and
parfleche with buffalo and berry pemmican. "Kate," he
said as he came back out, "I will see you next spring. Be
here, or you'll make me come looking for you!" He tried
to sound gruff, but his voice broke.

"I'll be here!" Holding the heavy robe to her, she managed to smile at him through her tears.

He nodded, then shouldered his pack to free one hand.
She thought he would hug her again, but he reached
around and patted her bottom. He turned and hurried
away; she watched him until he disappeared into the red,
rising sun.

She just stood there, dazed, staring after him as the village got noisier and busier. Dogs barked; naked, laughing

little boys ran to the cliffside to see which could launch his little stream of urine farthest over the side; women went on their tasks of fetching and tending. Many bade her good morning, and she answered them back. But she felt hollow inside. Finally she heard the tent flap behind her, and old Buffalo Grass tottered out.

"Pretty painting on robe," she said. "Come inside. I want show you my husband's robe, many coups, many scalps."

Kate stood for one moment, staring at her. Just a few days ago she had run away from Buffalo Grass's horrid pride in scalps. But the old woman was trying to comfort her, to keep her busy, to share with her the love and loss of her own man. Kate felt the emotional ties knotting tighter despite the things she disliked here.

"Thank you, old Grandmother," she said. "You know I do not like taking scalps, but I realize your man must have been brave to have a woman like you." Swiping at her tears, she went into the lodge of Long Hatchet to praise his painting and be comforted.

Later that morning Kate took gifts for Wolf Trap and Clam Necklace and went to see Blue Wing. She was relieved to find her friend sitting alone before their lodge in the sun, making pots. Blue Wing looked up at her familiar footfalls, but she did not smile.

Without a word Kate could see why. She looked exhausted, thinner, haunted. How could she have so changed in the few days—was it a week?—since she had gone to her new home? Her full mouth was pinched and drawn; dark circles rimmed her once-bright eyes. Kate's heart twisted even more when her friend's face lit to see her.

"Good morning, Prairie Wind," Blue Wing said when Kate just stared. "Sit down. I was so afraid you would leave when your man did."

"Tomorrow," Kate said, still not budging. "We leave tomorrow. And," she added, whispering now, "whatever Rand or your family think, I want you to come with me. Blue Wing, you could stay at River of Sky. I'm going to build a cabin and maybe a lodge there too. You could live there and—"

"I am here, home," she said. "Will you not sit?"

Kate sat, holding the gifts in her lap, watching Blue Wing's swift, sure hands on the clay. "One thing," Blue Wing said, not looking at her now, "I ask you again. You stop at Baby Hill, be sure the gifts I left still there? Not for yourself, you not believe in medicine there, but for your old *manuka,* Ahpcha-Toha, you ask for a child come to me?"

"Yes. Yes, if you want. And—"

Clam Necklace emerged from the lodge with a clatter of shells held in her lifted skirt. "Ah, my friend I give necklace to comes see me!" she declared, though it was obvious whom Kate had come to see.

Kate rose to her feet with the smooth motion she had learned from Blue Wing. "Here are gifts for you and Wolf Trap," Kate told the woman. "I am leaving tomorrow and wanted to ask my friend Blue Wing to come to see the *Red Dawn* depart."

"Much of The People see every fire canoe come and go," Clam Necklace assured her. "But Blue Wing stay here, work. It make her too sad see you go."

"Blue Wing, please come down to the ship so Gabriel, Pete, Willy Nilly, and all of us can say good-bye," Kate said.

Blue Wing shrugged. "I very busy with these pots, Prairie Wind. But if I not there, you know my thoughts: Always they are with you."

Wolf Trap appeared from somewhere in the village and looked pleased at his gift. Kate stood awkwardly with the three of them, wanting to grab Blue Wing's wrist and pull her away from these—these vultures! It turned her stomach to think of the cruel things they must be saying or doing to her here. She would insist Corn Basket and Long Hatchet at least visit the lodge despite their ideas about not coming too soon. She felt guilty for her own blissful marriage.

And then she thought of what she could say to Blue Wing in farewell, in case she did not see her tomorrow, something to let her hold to hope, deserted as she was by Swift Raven, who lived in this next lodge, and by her parents and their foolish Mandan ways.

"Every time I look up at Old Woman in the Moon, I will recall our happy days together—and our happy days to come," Kate said. "I will be back next spring, Blue Wing, and then we will renew and build on our days together . . . our many good times. . . ."

Clam Necklace was babbling something about trading Kate for some necklaces; Wolf Trap just glared. But Kate excused herself and hurried back to the lodge of Long Hatchet.

"Blue Wing's very unhappy," she told them the moment she entered. "It's wrong that she go to a man and his wife who do not care for her but to keep face. I would take her with me if she would just come. I should never have brought her back!"

Buffalo Grass shook her head; Corn Basket frowned. It was Long Hatchet who spoke. "You have much yet learn of proper paths, Prairie Wind. You can walk with us only when you see this is true. I think many ways much bad of the whites, but I not say so to you."

She stood in the door of the now-familiar lodge, feeling torn in half. Every time she felt Mandan, felt she understood, she found she did not, could not understand. Had Rand felt like this, pulled between both worlds, a half-breed half loving and half hating?

"I'd best spend this last night down at the boat." She choked out the words. "I've so much to do before we leave. . . ."

"We bring your things later," Long Hatchet said with a sage nod, as if giving his permission.

She turned and went.

Kate deeply regretted that she had left Blue Wing, Long Hatchet's lodge, and the village that way, but she did have much to do on the boat. They finished packing the hides by hand as best they could since Blackwell wanted an exorbitant amount for use of his fur press, which was standing idle in the fort. If she'd had a lot more furs and robes, she would not have been able to fit them in the hold anyway without their being properly pressed and crated. But she resented the fact that

Blackwell knew this and intentionally kept the press out of her reach.

Kate felt vindicated that she and Rand had decided last night she should publicly display her paintings in St. Louis, however subtly Blackwell had threatened her about Rand's position here. When Kate reported what she'd seen to General Clark, surely he would safeguard Rand's assignment for him. If not, the two of them would remain near the village as rival traders. They were through having to bear Blackwell's insults and his control of Rand, though Rand wanted to keep his place long enough to parlay for peace with the Sioux. Besides, the national government did not seem to heed pleas for change to better the Indians anyway. Kate and Rand thought they could perhaps lend even more encouragement and support as private allies to the Mandans.

In the cabin on board that Rand had used, Kate stowed the few pieces she had of Indian pottery, wrapped in furs or packed with quilled moccasins between. At least there had been many Indian-crafted items to trade for; since Chouteau put so little commercial value in them, his traders had not wiped them out. She intended to sell these distinctive and beautiful things when she showed her paintings.

Surely that would be a good way to create interest in this far north tribe and generate money to put toward the vaccine too. Kate had no idea how much it would cost, but she knew she needed to get enough for nearly sixteen hundred souls if everyone in Mitutanka and Ruptare was to be protected. As far as she knew, Blue Wing was the only Mandan inoculated, though Rand thought the few old ones with the pockmarked faces, like Buffalo Grass, might be immune from having survived the onslaught of the disease years before.

Kate went up on deck to count a few more furs, bartered for deck passage fees from the trappers and *engagés* who would be riding back with this last steamer before the snows. Most of the men were Rand's friends; some had come up with them for a short trading and trapping season, but the return passengers were far fewer than had come upriver. Their blacksmith, Bill Blake, had taken a

Mandan wife, but she was staying here until he returned
next spring. Now most of these men were spending a last
night ashore. Stirling was still in the fort, passing his
time, no doubt, at Blackwell's bounteous table since Rand
had deprived him of his friend Marbois. She shuddered to
think of Rand off in the wilds with that amoral wretch—
and Big Buck.

Again Kate could hardly sleep on her hard, lonely
bunk, though the river rocked her gently. If Long Hatchet
and Corn Basket did not bring her things down this last
morning, as they had said, she must run up to say good-
bye. Though she had her Mandan dress on board, her exploit robe was still up there, and she would not leave
without it. But most of all, she would not leave until she
smoothed things over with them, her Mandan family.

At first light Gabe rang the *Red Dawn*'s bells for all
departing to come aboard and ordered the roosters to fire
up the boilers. Kate knew he was anxious to leave and
thought they had stayed overlong, but he had been too
good a friend to say so.

"Gabriel!" she called up to him. "I'll be right back, but
I have to run up to the village for a few good-byes."

"Don't think you have to," he called down from his
loftier position in the pilothouse. "Looks like the good-
byes is coming to you."

Kate gasped as she saw the procession that wended its
way down from Mitutanka. It reminded her of that morning when the buffalo hunt assembled, but there were no
horses. Swift Raven and Chief Four Bears came first with
Long Hatchet just behind and then other men, including
two of the Black Mouth Society town criers she recognized, calling for her to delay her departure. Scatter Corn
and her family, Corn Basket and hers came among the
women. Kate saw Arrow Point, his hair mirrors glittering
in the first sunlight, and the handsome berdache Loud
Fox, balancing Buffalo Grass between them. Most of the
Indians carried something. Kate estimated that about half
of Mitutanka was here—the half that had ties to Four
Bears and Swift Raven. Not one of the allies of Wolf Calf
or Wolf Trap was to be seen.

Kate went down the gangplank to greet them just as Stirling and Blackwell came from the fort and stopped to stare. But it was the brown, eager faces of The People she saw: her people. Still, she scanned the crowd for the family of Wolf Trap and saw no one.

"Woman trader, once wife of River Walker, him who died, now wife of Dark Water," Chief Four Bears addressed her in Mandan. The crowd hushed. "You trade fair with The People, you live with The People, talk with their words. Prairie Wind good friend. You give gifts; now we give you gifts. But *not* trading gifts," he went on, glaring directly at Major Blackwell while the crowd murmured. "Not counting like trade with Marbois or numbered like gifts from Great White Father in Washington!" he concluded, and spit on the ground in contempt.

Kate almost cheered at Four Bears' bold speech. She saw his intent to make a protest to General Clark about being treated unfairly by Chouteau and the government. She would write it all down to tell the general, for Blue Wing had said he greatly admired Four Bears. Had Marbois been here and understood Mandan, Kate thought, he would have burst a blood vessel; Blackwell, despite the language barrier, got the message and stood there sputtering as if seized by an apoplectic fit.

For this time his little translator did not scurry to his side. He seemed almost naked without his other prop, Marbois, whom she'd seen shout and swear at the tribe in Sioux. In this crisis Blackwell could neither understand what was being said nor berate the big crowd.

"What did he say?" Blackwell called to Kate. "Four Bears, what did you say? I want to have a word-for-word explanation!"

"Even big chiefs not talk your words too good much," Four Bears said in English much poorer than Kate had heard from him before.

Four Bears turned his back on the man and nodded to Kate. She smiled broadly back as if he'd made the grandest joke at Blackwell's expense. Kate too turned her back on Blackwell, even as Stirling hurried on board and hissed, "If you understood all that gibberish, tell the man for heaven's sake! You've sat at his table."

"And feel guilty for even that," she retorted, apparently sending Stirling straight to his cabin.

In comparison with the pile of wedding gifts she and Rand had received, this bounty from the tribe was a mountain, she thought, as crew members carted the items bestowed on her to the deck. She saw good winter buffalo robes from beds; wolf, coyote, even beaver pelts from backrests; cured buffalo and elkhides fresh off the stretching frames of the village. A few blankets, beautifully made baskets, wooden bowls, strings of feathers, a few baskets of corn. These were more than gifts, she thought; with winter coming, they were sacrifices. She wished she could refuse to take them, but it would be a deep insult to these people in their public protest. Their gifts were the battle flags of victory over Marbois, Blackwell, and Chouteau, at least this day.

"Even my Mandan words"—Kate shouted to be heard from the deck of the ship—"cannot tell how much I thank The People. Next spring, when I return to live among you, I will bring you gifts to say my thanks. And I hope while I am gone, The People will be good friends to my husband, Dark Water, and my friend Blue Wing, the new wife of Wolf Trap."

Her eyes met Swift Raven's. He stood on the bank with his hand on his young wife's shoulder. His expression did not change but for the flaring of his nostrils. And then, as if her name had summoned her, Blue Wing hurried down the hill with bulging blankets tied to both ends of a shoulder pole. She was flushed and out of breath as Kate ran to meet her amid the crowd.

"I was afraid you wouldn't come, Blue Wing!"

"Clam Necklace did say no."

"But you came anyway!"

Though Blue Wing shook her head, she told her, "Pots for you take back—sell or use in your lodge at River of Sky. Someday, with my children, I visit you there." When the crowd murmured, Blue Wing glanced up to see Clam Necklace and Wolf Trap come running. "Quick, take now, go," she cried. "And another little bow and arrow inside for you leave at Baby Hill!"

Kate took the heavy load of pots and passed it on to

Willy Nilly, who was helping carry goods aboard. She saw her exploit robe and other possessions pass from Corn Basket to Pete.

Kate hugged Blue wing, then set her back. "My dear *manuka, ptanka,* always!" she said, then repeated, "My dear friend, sister, always!"

They clasped hands, then let go just as Clam Necklace and Wolf Trap pushed through the crowd. "You not going away, dear sister!" Clam Necklace cried, and clung to Blue Wing.

"No," Kate told Clam Necklace. "She chooses to stay with you for the good of her family and The People. And all will be watching to see that you treat Blue Wing as a good sister." Kate's gaze collided with Wolf Trap's brutal stare. His jaw was set; his eyes narrowed. With a final nod to Blue Wing, Kate turned away.

From the hurricane deck of the southbound ship, Kate MacLeod saw Mitutanka shrink to that same silhouette of mole hills and blades of grass she had seen the day she came. As she waved and watched The People grow smaller, they grew larger in her thoughts. Of the rich gifts Kate took away with her, she valued her marvelous memories of the Mandans more than even the fine things they had given her today.

The familiar vibrating of the vessel stirred her to recall the blood racing through her veins that night on the buffalo hunt, in the lodge of the winter village, in the cave— anywhere and anytime Rand had looked at her or touched her. The straining engines shuddered the decks as she had been shaken to see Blue Wing so distraught yet so determined. The steam valve shrieked as she had wanted to when Blackwell and Marbois so abused The People. The chug, chug melded with memories of the thudding of O-Kee-Pa drums, the pulse of the tribe beating in the heart of the frontier where she had plunged beyond the frontiers of her own heart.

Finally the *Red Dawn*'s bells jolted her back to reality. Rand and Blue Wing were not here. She was on the river again. And she had much to do.

PART FOUR

River of Sky

Old Woman remembered how well she loved The People when she saw her face in River of Sky. But the dark dangers of Big River swallowed its green calm and churned it to writhing white. In the rushing roar and crash even Old Woman was afraid.

Chapter 17

Once the *Red Dawn* departed Mandan land, Kate felt in a terrible rush and, as a result, was tired all the time. She wanted to hurry back to Jamie, then St. Louis. She must accomplish her goals and make time fly so she could return to Rand and The People. Though they were heading downstream, they had many frustrating delays as another sandbar, snag, or repair delayed them. The river ran low too, for it had not rained since the buffalo hunt. At least, the southbound ship moved about four times faster than a northbound one. Even without steam, when afloat, they could make good progress heading home.

And yet Kate seldom felt they were heading *home* now. She wrestled with the same dilemma which had haunted her after she had lost Clive and Winterhaven: Where was home? She felt no longer lured by St. Louis, except for the tasks she must accomplish there. Her only kin awaited at Bellevue, but she intended to see Mama and Tom, take Jamie, and push on. Mostly now home meant Mitutanka and River of Sky, the place where she would most like to have a house and hearth of her own with Rand and Jamie at her side.

When they approached Blue Wing's Baby Hill near the Heart River, Kate did not want to stop, especially because it was raining at last to swell the river. But she had promised her friend. Over her crew's concern—and a sullen Stirling's protest—she had Gabe put the boat in. She wrapped herself in an extra piece of canvas tarp for a rain cape and, taking her rifle and Blue Wing's little offering of a bow and arrow, trudged up the hill.

Because they were in Sioux country, Bill Blake, Pete Marburn, and even Willy Nilly escorted her with their guns loaded too. But Kate feared this place not as much for the Sioux as because it called to her, and she did not want it to.

The climb made her hot and even more exhausted, despite the cool wind and rain in her face. The wash of fresh water felt so good that drenched with perspiration anyway, she just carried her cape and enjoyed the bath. Pete went up all the way with her; he had admitted he had promised his friend Rand he would help "keep her safe."

But returning to the Baby Hill somehow did not seem safe to her. She did not believe the way the Mandans did, however deeply she cared for them. She had told Blue Wing time and again that "her thoughts were bad toward the Baby Hill." So in a hurry now to get it over, she went to the spot she was certain Blue Wing had left her offerings before.

She was not surprised to find nothing remained; the winds would have taken things long ago. And yet was that the little rock she had brought from River of Sky, which Blue Wing had retrieved and left here? Kate bent over to pick up the odd-shaped stone, which Blue Wing had insisted looked like a half-moon. Almost dizzy from the height, Kate knelt and placed Blue Wing's new bow and arrow on the slant of wet hillside.

She squinted into the gentle, blowing rain to gaze below. The sight was a smear of grays now, but the view was still majestic. And when the wind blew amid the patter of the drops, she could almost imagine strange sounds: little scurrying feet; moaning, muted cries; whines or whispers. No doubt that was how this place got its reputation among the superstitious Mandans. She only hoped Blue Wing could have the child she desperately desired. And Kate prayed that somehow her friend could find peace and happiness in her marriage, but the thought of Blue Wing in Wolf Trap's arms churned Kate's stomach. Blue Wing should be with her beloved Swift Raven now, just as Kate should be with Rand.

Kate fingered the little rock, closed her eyes, and tipped her face skyward. When the next thought came to her, her eyes shot wide open.

Her exhaustion, this light-headed feeling, and—and she

had just missed her monthly, which had always been so regular. She heard Rand's words falling on her with the rain: "I keep thinking we shouldn't make a baby until you get back. We've been breeding like minks."

She had laughed then, though she'd been slightly annoyed at the way he'd put it. But now the thought both awed and terrified her. Could it be? She dropped the rock in her lap to count on her fingers, just the way Blue Wing always did: they were married August 15, and September 9 was their last night together. And she'd been gone not even a week. So little time!

But she'd had this—this tipsy feeling only after she had set out on the river. She had thought it was grief at parting, just being back on the swaying current again, a sort of seasickness and exhaustion, naturally. Yet this was exactly the way she'd felt two other times, carrying Sally and Jamie.

She forced herself to sit still in the steadier pour of rain, ticking off on her fingers October, November, December . . . "June!" she cried. "A June baby! But that's when I'll be heading back—in the eighth and ninth months!"

Frightened and furious, she got to her feet. If she were indeed pregnant, she would not stay in St. Louis until she had this child and it was big enough to travel. If she did, she'd never get back upriver at all next year, and she had promised. Promised Rand, The People, herself! She would just have to go upstream as big as a barn and have the child at Mitutanka. She was going to take that smallpox vaccine and new trade goods and herself and Jamie to Mitutanka, no matter what next spring! Instead of being the last steamer to leave, they would be the first, that was all, she assured herself. The ice would just have to melt early.

But it might be a problem if she were "showing," as they said, when she went among the citizens of St. Louis this winter and spring to tell about the plight of the Mandans, to display her art and ask for whatever aid she could get for vaccine. She would do it anyway, no matter what people thought about women who should be staying home, unseen and unheard, when they were "in a family way."

And then, as she stood to go downhill, the joy hit her. She felt ashamed for feeling anything but rapture at the possibility of carrying Rand's baby, their love child, a true blending of his Mandan and white blood in her. She hugged herself, though she was trembling now. Listening to the sounds here, she stood remembering Blue Wind's prayers on this very spot that Prairie Wind have Dark Water's child, that her lost Sally return to her.

She gripped herself more tightly as a shudder shook her. This was a fearsome place but somehow a fine one too, this Baby Hill.

Even as far south as Bellevue the trees had begun to turn their paint box reds and yellows. Kate stood beside Gabriel in the pilothouse, staring out the front window, watching each turn in the river for the landmarks that would lead them to her family.

"I told Jamie we'd be back before the trees colored up, Gabriel," she admitted with a sigh. "I've let him down."

Gabe, who had seemed so solemn lately, even though he reveled in being on the river again, shook his red head. "You couldn't help it, Kate," he told her. "He'll always love you anyway, whatever you do."

And then there it was, Bellevue, on its wooded bluff, its chimneys trailing fingers of smoke into the sky this brisk late mid-October morning. Gabe clanged the bells; the firemen cut steam. Kate rushed to the main deck and across the gangplank the minute the roosters plopped it down. People appeared from cabins and warehouses; shading her eyes in the steep slant of sun, Kate scanned the scene for her family. She saw her mother at last, waving by their cabin, her sleeves rolled up, her arms floury white to the elbows. But where were Tom and Jamie?

In Mandan Kate greeted the usual cluster of curious Omaha women and their children as she went up the twisting path. Perhaps they understood, for they called out words and streamed after her. Near her mother stood the same two smallpox-scarred women she remembered from before. It served as another reminder that she must not stay long, that she had things to do. But where was Jamie?

"Mama!" she cried, and hugged her. "Where's my boy?"

"I thought he'd gone down with Tom to the smithy, but don't know where they are," she said, returning Kate's hearty embrace. "Mercy me, I'm just so blessed to see you in one piece again. And you're looking fine, Katie, filled out a bit too, though those freckles are worse than ever."

"Mama, I've so much to tell you—"

And then Kate heard a shriek and saw Jamie tearing down from the fields above. He had a willow fishing pole over his shoulder that bobbed as he ran. Tom came trotting along behind.

"Mama! Mama!"

She knelt and hugged him hard when he thudded into her. He had sprouted in just these few months; his baby-soft limbs had gone leaner and longer. She didn't mean to, but she cried as they went into the Barton cabin.

"And I know how to shoe a horse, 'cause I saw Grandpa Tom do it lots of times, and I can work a little bellows, and I'm going to be a blacksmith, if I'm not an Indian when I grow up. . . ." Jamie chattered on so she could hardly get a word in.

"So you'd like to live with the Indians for a while?" Kate ventured.

"Sure! Which ones? I guess we got Otoes and Omahas here."

"With the Mandans," Kate answered, seizing her chance. Mama turned to face her from kneading bread dough to bake in the Dutch oven on the hearth.

"You're going back again to trade?" Mama asked, then turned back to thump at the bread. "Thought after this one trip you intended to send others, build the business from St. Louis—with Stirling."

"Mama, Tom, Jamie," Kate said, staring down into her son's bright blue eyes, "I'm married but not to Stirling. I married the man I love and a new way of life. Jamie, you have a new father: Rand Cloud, Major MacLeod."

"He taught me how to swim," Jamie said, drowning her mother's gasp. "Can he teach me how to shoot?"

"Yes, and how to be a man, lots of good things, just like your Grandpa Tom's been doing," Kate said with a smile at her stepfather. At least he was on her side, for he smiled back and winked. "We'll be spending the winter in St. Louis," she went on in a rush, "but come next spring—"

"Such a shock," Mama said, and sank onto the settle by the hearth. Her eyes dropped to Kate's middle, and that really riled Kate. That *was* the other news she was aching to share, but she didn't now. The implication that she might have married Rand because she had to was all too clear. Mama had no right to think that. Not her own mother!

"You can't mean to go upriver to live, Katie," her mother said, her voice calm but strained.

"Mama, you went upriver to live with your husband, and here you are, hale and happy."

"But not so far upriver, so far into a different life. Jamie, dearie, why don't you and Grandpa Tom go on back to the smithy, where I thought you'd gone anyway?" Miriam Barton coaxed, and Tom took the hint if Jamie did not.

"Naw, Grandmama, we went fishing, but nothing was biting."

"I'll bet something's going to bite now," Kate dared to say with a wary look at her mother, then added, "but you go ahead, and we'll call you for dinner soon."

"Katie," her mother said when they were alone, "of course, you're all grown and surely must know your heart, but I thought we decided Mr. Mount was the man for you."

"No, Mama, you decided, and I listened. I just didn't know then, and I cannot live my life by what others think, however much I care for or admire those others. I have married the man I love, *not* the circumstances I used to think I would love to be in. Besides, I really feel right living with the Mandans most of the time. Please be happy for me, Mama."

"And you propose to raise a family up there in—in

Mandan and Sioux country," her mother said as she clanged the lid over the bread. "Mercy, Katie, that's way beyond frontier up there!"

"In some ways—yes, I know. But the way the government agents and Chouteau's factor at the fort treat them they need less of white civilization, not more. I love it there, and the people are very hospitable. Mama, just like the whites, the Mandans do some things wrong and immoral, but that's true of all people."

"What about other children?"

"What about them?" Kate asked, pressing her hands to her stomach beneath the table where she sat. "There's a walled fort and a walled village. If the Sioux raid, it won't be right there. Jamie and any other children Rand and I have will be quite safe as long as they don't go wandering off on the plains. Besides, Rand is parlaying for permanent peace with the Sioux."

"That's all fine and good, but I'm referring to your children's futures. Since your husband's a half-breed and looks more Indian, everyone will judge the children that way too."

"Mama, I've learned the hard way I can't live my life by how others will judge me or mine. I have followed my heart, just as you did to take Tom on. I married the first time because I was swept away by the trappings of a man's dreams. This time I married the man himself with both eyes wide open—for my own dreams as well as his."

"I see," Mama managed to say, though she still looked stunned. "And I mustn't judge others, for that's God's business. It's just Stirling seemed . . . perfect. But you're right, it's the man himself that really matters, not his prospects. Just so he doesn't drink, this man of yours, just so he doesn't have something from his past that will make him act amiss—you know, Katie, a dark streak in that silent, stoic nature of his that will turn him violent. In his own way I'm sure he will provide for you. I recollect you said he worked for both Chouteau and Clark in St. Louis. Maybe he can do so there again."

"He needs to help his people where they live, Mama, and I'm going to be with him."

"I won't even mention the fact you vowed no more separations in a marriage ever again."

"Thank you for *not* mentioning it," Kate said. "It's only a necessity this year, and never after."

Mama jumped up to turn the kettle in the ashes. "You know, Katie, I do recall he went right out and shot us some venison for dinner instead of just standing about to be introduced like Mr. Mount when you were here. Besides, here's your chance to go preach the Gospel among the heathen, just the way your grandfather wanted to do his whole life."

"If I preach to them, it will be by example as well as words, Mama. Like I said, they've got some major things all wrong, but so do people I've known in St. Louis who already get preaching."

"Yes, well, let's just get this dinner on the table, and you can go fetch Tom and Jamie and a few of the crew, even poor Mr. Mount if you want. Go on then."

Kate stood in the doorway, looking at her mother's back, stiff and imposing, even bent over the hearth. She wanted to run to her, to hug her and tell her about the new baby, to explain again how much she loved and believed in Rand and the Mandans. But some strange new glimmer of pride, of independence or strength, even a sense of separation held her back. She hurried out to fetch the men.

Over dinner—which Stirling fortunately refused to attend—they toasted Kate's new husband and Jamie's new father with beer flavored with honey. Kate had Gabe bring up the painted wedding portrait she had made of Mama and Tom from a sketch and, for a second gift, a drawing of her and Rand. Gabe had carved lovely wooden frames for both. Mama cried over the presents, dabbing at her brimming eyes with her apron. But Kate feared she was really crying for her lost hopes for a daughter she evidently feared had made a terrible mistake. And so even though Mama had shared about her baby with Kate, Kate could not bring herself to tell her about this child she carried. She felt proud of Rand, now defiantly so, no matter what Mama really felt. So far no one else knew that she was pregnant.

While the men went down to the steamer and she and Mama were washing dishes, the ever-present Omaha women with their little ones peeked in the door and hung in the single window. Kate saw they were gawking at the newly hung artwork. She smiled at them and did not let Mama shoo them off. In their string of questions Kate finally discerned what they must be asking.

"Yes, my man. My husband there!" she declared proudly in both Mandan and English, pointing to Rand in the framed sketch.

"Pretty!" one Omaha woman pronounced, and Kate laughed, however close she felt to crying. A tendency to cry, even when laughing, was another thing a pregnancy always did to her, she thought. Carrying a child seemed to push her emotions right to the edge of a cliff it was so easy to fall off.

"Mandan?" the same woman demanded, holding her little girl so her legs draped over the windowsill.

"Yes," Kate said. "A pretty Mandan!" The Omaha women tittered behind their raised hands.

Mama had nothing to add. Kate realized that if her own mother, who loved her dearly, reacted this way to her marriage, she must steel herself to face those who didn't care a bit for her in the city. But she'd show them all that they were wrong, that Rand was the perfect man for her, that this child she carried was as good as any. She would convince them that they must allow the Indians to remain strong and independent so they did not have to be outsiders merely looking in the window on the bounty of this country that was rightfully theirs too.

Kate also knew, as her own words to the Omaha women echoed in her head, whether her child was a boy or a girl, what she would name him or her: Mandan. Mandan MacLeod.

Kate was surprised to find what a relief it was to be on her way again the next morning. She did not shed a tear, though Jamie did. He kept shouting from the rail of the

Red Dawn, "I'll be back, Grandmama and Grandpa Tom! But I have to take care of Mama now!"

The Bartons stood on the riverbank, arm in arm, whispering, waving. Kate waved back to them and to the wildly gesturing Omaha women.

"So what did she think of your rather hasty marriage?" Stirling asked from behind her. Kate was surprised he stood so close; he had been avoiding her, however small the ship was, even taking his meals at off hours.

"She admitted," Kate told him, "I was right to marry the man himself and not his prospects."

"You have as good as ruined mine," he blurted.

She spun to face him. "I don't see how. General Clark's job and support awaits you. It was in no way contingent on me."

"I only mean my personal prospects for happiness," he said, and went up the steps to the cabin deck.

"Why don't Mr. Mount like St. Louis anymore, Mama?" Jamie asked.

" 'Why *doesn't* Mr. Mount,' Jamie. And he does. He can't wait to get back there. He told me so before," she explained.

But then, as they picked up steam and current, Kate's mind snagged again on her son's question. Stirling had said he wanted to get back, yet he seemed to be dreading it. It reminded her of other apparent paradoxes in him: that he wanted to draw but had no talent for it; that he carried an expensive gun but couldn't shoot it. At Fort Leavenworth he had been relieved to keep his barrels of rum for specimens, then hardly gathered any. And he had been only too pleased to hand over those barrels to Kellen Blackwell, though she had thought at the time he was doing it to protect her from Blackwell's anger.

"Mama, you said I could go up in the pilothouse with you and Gabe. Come on!" Jamie cried, windmilling his arm.

Thrusting aside her foolish thoughts, Kate went.

Kate's heart was full the next week when they left River of Sky. She had chosen the site for the Mandan lodge and staked it out in the grass on the broad brow of the hill. She had laid a line of rocks where she would like the foundations of the storehouse, which could later become a trading post. Now she stared dreamily into the clear trail of the Sky River as it spilled, yet unsullied by the Missouri's dark flow, miles south of the site.

She felt lulled by that ribbon of green as if she were floating in bright, clear memories of her days at Mitutanka, her days with Rand and Blue Wing there unsullied by what others thought or would soon think of her decisions. Again she took out Rand's words to polish and replace among her treasured memories: "Separation this year of necessity, but somehow never again." But when the big river below won the struggle to swallow up her smaller river in its dark currents, she turned to go back to her tasks.

She jolted when a gunshot crackled nearby. Though they were well out of Sioux territory, she ducked. Then she realized the shot had come from the prow of the boat. A dead gray goose hurtled from the sky and splashed in the river off the aft side.

She strode forward and saw Stirling with his rifle. "Got that one with my first shot!" he exulted, and raised the barrel again.

"Stop it, unless you intend one or two for the table," she said. "You didn't even try to snare that one. Besides, those are geese."

"So?" he said, and sighted again at the low-flying Vs of the geese migrating overhead. "They are a lot easier to hit than smaller ducks, and it is your illustrious husband who gave me the shot and powder and suggested I practice." He pulled the trigger and hit another one; a flapping flight ended as it spiraled, then fell.

"Use a tree or something on the bank if it's just practice. I'm sure Rand meant for you to practice *before* we left Sioux country."

"I thought the sound might summon them, and we did not need that."

"And the sound of the steamboat itself would not summon them? Why didn't you practice this summer? I did. Look, Stirling, I don't want to argue, but you're a bit late to learn now, especially since you say you're never coming back upriver. The next few days all you'll have to shoot at is settlers. And Rand never shoots anything but for necessary meat."

Again it annoyed her that Stirling seemed to act contrary to logic. In case of attack up north, they could have used another rifleman, but here and in his soft city life, he'd not need this gun—but, of course, to shoot game out at General Clark's. Yes, no doubt, that was what he was practicing for, to please his new boss, not to protect her ship.

"Here, hold this while I try to snag that goose if you're so particular," he said, and thrust the still-warm rifle in her hands. She followed him while he ran to the stern to unhook a sounding pole, then leaned out to snag the second goose.

"I've changed my mind," she said. "I can't allow you to shoot at those geese even for food, not from my boat. They mate for life and will die protecting their young. They're sacred to Old Woman in the Moon, who is sacred to Blue Wing, so—"

"Listen to yourself, for heaven's sake! You've turned into an ignorant barbarian!" he said accusingly, and let the goose go in the current. "I, for one, cannot see respecting the unholy ways of savages, their trickery and deceit, their loose morals, though I can see how some of that might appeal to you."

"You pious prig. Try listening to yourself! You've turned into a Marbois or Blackwell, a Cadet Chouteau! And I'd rather think like a Mandan than one of them any day. Here, take your gun and get out of my sight."

But as she held it out to him, her eyes caught the carved, entwined initials in the bottom of the gun butt. She had not noticed them before, but the slant of sun etched them sharply now: C C.

"Why is this gun marked with a *C C* when you said it was General Clark's?" she asked, and pointed out the letters. "It should be *W C* for William Clark."

He squinted at it; his eyes widened as they met hers. "I didn't even see them before. They are so close together it is obviously *G C* for General Clark. How should I know everything even if you do?" he muttered, seized the gun, and stalked off.

Leaning on the railing, she felt Gabe's eyes on her from the pilothouse. She could sense her guardian angel was watching over her and would have shouted or come down if she needed him. But she could handle Stirling Mount. Still, the thing was, she was certain those initials of the gun's owner were *C C*. It had certainly not been Clive Craig's gun. She knew of only one other possibility for the owner of that rifle—and perhaps the owner of the present owner too. And somehow, first chance she got, she was going to look into her suspicions. As Rand had said, Cadet Chouteau had a very long arm.

The last Sunday of October they sighted the silhouette of St. Louis and steamed in before Sam's warehouse just as the setting sun began to stain the city crimson. Though Kate had come to think of the *Red Dawn* as security on the Missouri, it seemed tiny among these already tethered behemoths along the Mississippi. Word that they had made it back spread quickly. People stared, and Sam came running. Greetings and news flew between them.

"Can't wait to hear all about the trip," Sam told her and Gabe. "Many a time, I tell y'all, I wished I'd gone along!"

"Sam, Gabe's going to keep Jamie on board for a little while, but do you have a horse I can borrow?" Kate asked. "I know it's crazy to run off like this, but it's important."

"It's getting dark. Where you goin' in such an all-fired hurry? But sure, sure, I'll go saddle one and get the boys to start unloadin'. I can't believe you're back. I mean, I knew y'all'd make it, but to be gone so far so long. . . ."

Yes, Kate thought as she surveyed the familiar scene of wharf and city above, she had gone so far so long. St. Louis seemed almost alien to her now, too cluttered, too busy, part of another life. But she must not let herself think it was forbidding. She had much to do, beginning with following Stirling Mount, who had disembarked without one word.

She watched him walk along the wharf with his gun

and portmanteau and turn up Oak Street. That was the
general direction of the road out to Clark's Marais Castor,
but he certainly could not intend to walk the entire way,
not this late in the day. At least not as many people
crowded the streets on this chill Sabbath evening so she
could spot him if only Sam would hurry with that horse!

Once mounted, Kate rode quickly not to lose him; there
had been talk of gaslights before she left, but none had
been installed yet, and the hanging oil lanterns cast wan
light. When she saw him turn down Main Street, she
slowed the horse. Stirling might not be going to Clark's,
but he was not going to Chouteau's place out at the edge
of the prairie either. Nor was there a livery stable down
here where he could get a horse. He must be heading for
either the Union or the Missouri Hotel. She would find
out which one, just so she knew, but her surveillance
plans were ruined now. She could hardly hang about a
lobby waiting for him to visit or receive a call from
Chouteau. Her theory was probably just based on her distrust of both men anyway.

But she sucked in a quick breath as she saw Stirling
stop at the intersection of Main and Market streets, directly across from Cadet Chouteau's father's house. On
Sunday perhaps Chouteau had come into town to visit the
old man here. Realizing she was too close if Stirling
glanced her way, she dismounted and walked the horse.
But he did not look back. Even after six months in the
wilds he had not learned to be aware of his surroundings
or cover his tracks, the greenhorn! Had observing Rand,
the trappers, or Indians taught him nothing? But he was
wily, she thought, if he was in with Chouteau, for she and
Rand had not suspected all this time.

As she stood down the street and watched him go to
the front door of the lantern-lit old French-style mansion,
several things Stirling had said taunted her. How he
dreamed of being wealthy and would do whatever he
must to make that dream come true. How she had ruined
his great prospects to have a job with a very influential
man.

She had thought then, of course, he had meant General

Clark, who had hired him and bought his steamboat
ticket. But could he have meant Chouteau, who might
have set him up and sent him to Clark? The general had
told her Stirling came highly recommended, and she had
assumed he meant by people he had met in the East. But
could he have been recommended to him by Chouteau?
And here she'd thought Stirling's avid attentions were
caused by his caring for her. Perhaps his passion for her
was intended to get her out of the trade, to tie her through
trickery in marriage to Chouteau's alliances.

It was so like Chouteau to snare those he wanted to
control in his web one way or the other. She had defied
him when he tried to take her into his household last winter. So he had sought to govern her through a man he no
doubt "owned," a man he hoped would be her lord and
master, Stirling Mount—a man who courted her and proposed marriage for his own rapacious purposes.

She sagged against the side of the horse, feeling weak
and ill. Once again she had not read a man any better than
she had her father or Clive. Because she wanted to be
loved, needed, and admired, she had not seen the real
Stirling. At first he seemed such a sunny contrast with
Rand's dark moods. If all this were true, how she had
played the fool. But what if she had not read Rand well
either? She shoved that fear down; of course, she knew
her beloved husband!

And no doubt, General Clark had been taken in too, for
surely he could not be a party to this, however much he
and Chouteau fancied they were friends. She had seen
that the general sincerely cared about the Indians, while
Chouteau cared only about using them.

She pulled her horse after her toward the mansion, then
decided to go around in back, through the gardens. Any
covert approach to the house would have been impossible
in broad daylight, but in the gathering gloom she would
risk it. She had to find out if she could see Stirling actually talking to Chouteau inside.

She tied her mount to a grape arbor far behind the
property and moved down an arch of bare-leafed vines.
Only muted light emanated from the two-story house, for
most draperies were drawn. Amazing, she thought, that

Stirling had known to come here, exactly where Cadet Chouteau might be—unless Stirling had come to report in to the old man, Pierre. But she knew that Cadet had been the power in the family business for years.

She moved carefully along the back of the house, listening, squinting through cracks in draperies. And then, yes, in a room lined with books there was Cadet, pacing and gesturing. She could not see Stirling, not hear the words, but she stayed fixed by Chouteau's anger. And then she saw Stirling's rifle on the round polished table in the middle of the room, and she knew for sure. Worse, a hand smacked a pile of letters down on the table, and Chouteau snatched them up.

So, she thought, Stirling had been Chouteau's messenger, his eyes and ears up north, as well as Clark's. Was he tattling that Rand had made waves at Fort Clark? That she had traded for fair prices? That Chief Four Bears and the tribe had not only traded with her but bestowed gifts to defy Chouteau's might? How she would love to get her hands on those letters. And on Stirling's throat!

Instead she pressed both hands over her mouth. What she had reasoned out hit her now with stunning force. She stood shaking, furious, wanting to pound on the window, wanting them to know that she recognized their treachery. But knowledge was power against them if she did not tip her hand. She must warn General Clark especially if Stirling turned up to work for him. Chouteau's grasp was everywhere, but if it was the last thing she ever did, she—she, Rand, and the Mandans—would defeat him!

Now Stirling rose and walked before her narrow line of vision. Chouteau reached out to grasp his shoulder, to shake it once. Then he clapped Stirling on the back as if to encourage him, as if he had another chance to make good.

"To do evil," Kate muttered, and turned away. The grape arbor was deep and dark now as she fled through it toward her horse.

Kate and Jamie stayed aboard the *Red Dawn* one more night, so they could look more presentable to visit Rand's aunt, Alice Forbes, in the morning. Kate carried a note

from Rand asking that the woman take them into the
boardinghouse she ran for her landlord, but Kate knew
there might not be room available or that the woman
might be unwilling. She did not want to get her hopes too
high, so she was fully prepared to rent some small room
somewhere else if need be. But oh, how desperately she
hoped Aunt Alice took them in, so she could feel a bit
closer to Rand this winter.

Kate borrowed Sam's horse again since the house was
way across town on Cedar Street. Despite her wanting to
feel rested today, Kate's seething about Stirling's deceit
and her own stupidity had kept her awake most of the
night. She jolted from her still-agonized thoughts as
Jamie spoke, sitting before her on the horse as they trotted along.

"Since you're married to Major MacLeod now, does
that mean this lady's our aunt too?"

"That will really be up to her," she said calmly, but she
was feeling as nervous as she was tired.

The yard on Cedar Street had many trees and neatly
brick-lined flower beds. An old man was painting the
porch pillars of the two-story house. Kate dismounted,
helped Jamie down, and tied the horse to the hitching
post. When she inquired after Mrs. Forbes, the painter replied without breaking his stroke, "Round back. Beating
rugs. Most women's satisfied just with spring cleaning.
Not Alice Forbes. Most women would wed a man been
helping them nigh on twenty years. Not Alice Forbes."

More anxious than ever now, Kate led Jamie around
the side of the house. With a wire beater a tall, spare
woman was taking swooping whacks at a flowered maroon carpet hanging over a clothesline. The crisp wind
yanked puffs of dust away. She wore a long apron over a
dark green dress, a head scarf, and a handkerchief tied
about her mouth and nose.

"Mrs. Forbes? Excuse me, Mrs. Forbes!"

The woman stopped and turned. Her hair was salt and
pepper and pulled severely back from a high forehead and
sleek brown brows. She tugged her face scarf down to ex-
pose a pinched, plain face. Kate could see little resem-

blance to Rand, except perhaps in her lean limbs and height.

"Didna hear you. Speak up now. Come about the room, have you?" she asked before Kate could say anything else. "I'm the housekeeper, but I can let the extra room. A bonny one, right up there, gets the morning sun. Your name, lass?"

The woman spoke with a lilt to her language Kate had never heard before, but then Rand said she was Scottish. Kate fumbled with the letter from Rand in her drawstring purse and extended it to her.

"I'm Kate, and this is Jamie," she said, not wanting to shock her but wanting to tell her so much, to mean so much to this stern-looking stranger. "Kate *MacLeod*. You see, I was a widow, and your nephew—Rand—Randal— went upriver on my steamboat last spring, and we fell in love and got married there at Mitutanka. . . ."

Alice Forbes's icy blue eyes widened. The firm mouth set hard, then dropped open. But she threw her rug beater up into the air and whooped, "Rand married? Good glory, can it be? Come in, come in, and this fine-looking lad too! Oh, dearie, you canna ken how long I've wished for a family again. You say you've been upriver to Mitutanka? Here you are and done it all!" she added with tears in her blue eyes as she took Kate's trembling hands in her strong ones.

But Kate could not act even that restrained: She hugged Rand's "city aunt" while Jamie grinned and asked if he could call her Aunt Alice. Kate felt, at least, at last, this well-tended little piece of St. Louis could temporarily be home.

Kate and Jamie spent the rest of the day with the woman they were to call Aunt Alice. She hung on Kate's every word about Rand and Mitutanka, wanting to "ken" all about their adventures there. She plied Jamie with buttermilk and gingerbread and stories of Rand as a boy, a rather rebellious boy. She explained her deep sorrow when she got word her brother, Gordon, was dead and every time Rand left her to go upriver after that.

"But he always came back, though this time he told me

it would be a long spell," she said with a sigh, before she perked up again. "But now that he's sent me you—a new family—it will all be easier to bear, at least till you head back next spring."

"Perhaps someday you can visit us there," Kate suggested.

"How I'd love to, but I promised myself when I got off that boat in New York from Glasgow nigh on thirty-two years ago, I'd never get on the water again and never have. Lost my husband during a storm at sea, and Rand says there's bad blows on the rivers too."

"Yes," Kate admitted. "Yes, there are, but you just have to want something so much you get bold enough to go."

The next morning, after Kate and Jamie had moved their meager possessions in, Aunt Alice insisted she leave Jamie for the day and see to her errands. Jamie was playing with Rand's old miniature metal War of Independence soldiers, with appropriate sounds of the booms and blasts of battle. Kate could tell Aunt Alice reveled in having a boy to tend to again. She recalled how Rand had said his aunt had never remarried, however much she had wanted children of her own. She thought of Blue Wing again, hoping she was happy, hoping she might have a child, and then she hurried on her way.

She paid a condolence call on Captain Zeke Pickens's family to explain his death, give them his possessions, and praise him for all he had done for her. Next, she stopped by the cemetery to visit Clive's and Sally's graves. How she wished Blue Wing were here to keep her company again, but now she had Aunt Alice.

Then she remembered something Rand and Gabe had told her at different times: Even if she had no one, she would go on. Yes, she thought determinedly as she turned Sam's horse toward the prairie, that was truer now than ever before. She chose her path in life now because *she* thought it was right, not because of what her father or husband, her mother or other folks thought or said.

As she headed toward Marais Castor, she only hoped that she could warn General Clark about Stirling and

Chouteau. She had letters for the old man, one from Rand and one of her own, in case he was not able to have an interview today. She had written down, as best she could recall it, Four Bears' speech of protest on the riverbank. How she hoped the general would have good news for her that the government was ready to support immunizing the tribe—something Rand had asked for since last year.

Last year, she thought as she urged the horse to go faster, she had first begun to understand Blue Wing at Marais Castor. Four years ago she had met Rand and George Catlin there. Now, like her painter hero, she had a collection of her work she wanted to share with St. Louis. Besides her output from Mitutanka, she had painted and drawn many nights aboard ship heading back when they were tied up and the decks were somewhat steady. Perhaps the general could put her in contact with someone for a public showing, one which could help raise interest and support for the smallpox vaccine. Today, more than ever, so many hopes rode with her as she reined in at Marais Castor.

Amos, General Clark's elderly majordomo, met her at the door, announced her, then, thank heaven, showed her directly into the general's study. Clutching her letters, she faced William Clark, who rose, smiling, from behind his desk to greet her. But hovering just behind him, pen and papers in hand, stood Stirling Mount.

Chapter 18

Dear girl, so good to see you safe and sound!" General
Clark said, and shook her hand. His grip was cold
and trembled. Despite his imposing height, he looked
frail. "Stirling tells me congratulations are in order," he
added.

"Yes, for my marriage as well as a successful trading
trip." She tried to glance at Stirling, but the general's
shoulder blocked him. She would like to rebuke the
wretch, but she dared not now.

"So sad to leave a new husband there. But of course,
he has his duty. How is Major MacLeod?"

"Good, sir, but he could be better if you could help him
with several problems. I have an important letter here for
you from him and one from me—both for your eyes
only," she added quietly.

"Fine, fine. Won't you sit?" he said as he took the letters. He indicated the settee across the room. Grateful to
get away from Stirling, she followed. "I wonder, General,
if we might not have a private conversation," she inquired.

"You see, I've made Stirling my private secretary as
well as accountant," the old man said as they sat side by
side. At least, she thought, Stirling stayed put across the
room, bending over the general's desk, apparently shuffling papers. "Stirling Mount is a godsend," General
Clark went on, loudly enough for Stirling to hear now.
"I'm so fortunate he came back now, as I've been very
overworked. Demands, demands. Now, let me look at
you. I believe the fresh air and adventure put bloom in
your cheeks. And how is Major MacLeod?"

Kate's eyes widened. He had just asked that, but then

he must mean to get more details. "He is very concerned about the things you have discussed before," she said, her voice still low. "Fair trading, good relations at the agency, the threats of the Sioux, and the fact the Mandans have never been immunized against smallpox as so many other plains tribes were. He hopes—"

"Smallpox, a deadly curse. You know, I had a friend who was living with the Omahas when it swept through and took some of them, even after they'd been vaccinated by our doctors. Evidently they missed protecting some of the women and children. Anyhow a few of the poor females got so desperately ill they took pox infection from the few who were recovering—right from their healing blisters—and put it in cuts in their bodies. A false, amateur inoculation as it were. Evidently some survived that way."

"Really? I've seen scarred Omaha women at Bellevue. But the point is the government missed *all* the Mandans, who have been their strong allies, and I need to take vaccine back with me, enough for the entire tribe, women and children too."

"The Mandans always have been our friends, Meriwether's and mine," the general said as his gaze grew distant and drifted past her shoulder. "Sacajawea lived among them too. . . ." He went on, rambling off into memories. Sometimes in his convoluted recounting of the Lewis and Clark Expedition he called Kate "my dear," sometimes "Mrs. Craig," but never "Mrs. MacLeod." Yet twice again he injected, "How is Major MacLeod? His father went west with us, you know."

Sitting there looking at and listening to him, Kate became more alarmed she could not get through to him. Obviously he could no longer function in his position. For the Mandans and Rand this was a worse catastrophe than if he had died and been replaced. It did not take a leap of logic to realize who controlled the orders and allotments that crossed the general's desk now. Yet while she was here, she must try to communicate.

She asked General Clark for help with money for the vaccine from Washington, but he talked of his first meeting with Andrew Jackson. She asked if he could recommend some place in town to display her art of Mandan life. Each time she asked a question, he smiled and patted her hand and digressed. Her stomach knotted tighter and tighter. Should she try to retrieve her and Rand's letters lying in his lap?

"General"—she interrupted at last—"may I please have a word in private with you about Cadet Chouteau?"

"He's well, isn't he? Stirling told me he was and was coming to dinner, today, I believe. Isn't that right, Stirling?"

"It is indeed, General," Stirling answered to show he was in on all they said.

"Besides," Clark said, plucking at his own shirtsleeve, "I promised my dear wife not to have interviews alone with fetching young women. But about your drawings, if you'd like to hang one or two about here, she would not mind a bit."

At that Kate admitted defeat with him. The general's wife had been dead for years. "Thank you, sir, but I don't think so. I need some place in town to display my work, for unless there is an event here, I don't think people would ride out."

"Why ever not? You came out clear from Winterhaven with Captain Craig, didn't you? And Stirling vows he'll be here to help— Oh, Stirling here is some new correspondence that just arrived to be dealt with—"

Kate watched horrified as he extended her letters to Stirling, who crossed the room in several quick strides.

She rose and snatched the letters before Stirling could. "You know, General," she explained, "I just realized these letters I brought you need to be revised a bit, in light of all you've just told me. I will redo them and return them to you soon."

"Very well," he said, and slapped his knees before he stood. "You did remarry, and it was Major MacLeod, wasn't it? How is he doing?"

"I imagine Stirling told you many other things," she said, glaring at the traitor. He did not even bother to pretend concern anymore, until the general glanced his way, when he wiped his smug smile from his countenance.

"Then, my dear, again you have been a pioneer, just

like going up the river," General Clark pronounced in a booming voice, as if he were addressing a crowd. "The first white woman perhaps to make a country marriage when it's always been the man who marries Indian."

"My husband is proud to be both Indian and white, General Clark," she managed to say, though she felt more angry than beaten now. "And that is why"—she raised her voice too—"he wants the white government, which you represent, to safeguard the Mandans from small-pox—and safeguard them from the plague of Chouteau and those who work for him, some secretly! Even Chouteau should see the use of vaccinating the Mandans so they can continue to be bilked of furs and buffalo robes—and eventually their land!"

She wished she could pull those last accusations back, but they had just exploded from her. Now Stirling and Chouteau would know she was on to them. She did not say good-bye. The poor old man would not remember it; she feared it would not be a farewell to Stirling anyway. And if Chouteau was coming out here for dinner, she had no intention of meeting him—not yet.

She rushed from the house and mounted her horse before the hovering Amos could even offer the refreshments on his tray. She had to move quickly, and she knew only one other who might help her. She urged her horse to a run down the long lane lined by now barren fruit trees.

Kate's horse was lathered and foaming when she reined in before Dr. Beaumont's house on Chestnut Street. His plumply pretty brunette wife answered the door. "Why, Mrs. Craig, you're back! We've been so concerned about your voyage. Is anything wrong? You look rather harried. Are you quite well? Come in, come in, and I'll fetch the doctor."

Kate was grateful for that rather demanding greeting, despite the fact Mrs. Beaumont had not gotten her name right either. But it wasn't for reasons of senility or cruelty or hatred; the Beaumonts just hadn't heard she'd married Rand. She must remember that there were friends in this city as well as enemies.

"Mrs. Craig, welcome back!" the doctor said as he hurried into the parlor, wiping his hands. "I can't wait to hear all about the voyage."

"Dr. Beaumont, you have always been good and fair with me. If you're willing, I need your help. Are you General Clark's doctor by any chance?"

"No. He's used Army doctors for years. He's not ailing—more than his creeping forgetfulness, I mean?" he asked as he escorted her into his office just off the family kitchen.

"More like rampant forgetfulness. And I recall you said you never tended Monsieur Cadet Chouteau and did not wish to."

"The man's a despot running loose in this democracy of ours! Mrs. Beaumont," he called back over his shoulder, "since I'm between patients now, could we possibly have some tea? And won't you come join us?"

Kate sat across his desk, but she felt closer to him than she had to General Clark with no desk between them. Imagine, a man who saw Chouteau the same way she and Rand did!

"Tell me where all these questions are leading then," he said.

"Doctor, you were so adamant about immunizing my son from the smallpox and were good enough to vaccinate Blue Wing too. Now the sixteen hundred some Mandans need the same. The government missed them somehow, and money to help is not forthcoming. I will try to get the funds privately, but I need your help to order enough by the spring to take upriver—"

"Whoa, now," he said, sitting forward in his worn leather chair. "For sixteen hundred people? That cowpox vaccine is twenty-five cents per person, but most of that amount would have to be shipped in from New Orleans or points east. That will raise the price considerably, especially with the rivers icing closed soon. And that four hundred or so dollars doesn't include a doctor, you know, though I suppose a layman could be taught the necessary skills of application. I'll be happy to help as much as I can, but I'm afraid I couldn't leave my practice here to go upriver. . . ."

Despite his caveats, she was overjoyed. Surely Dr.

Beaumont could teach her and Gabe to give the vaccine! Only four hundred dollars, plus shipping costs! Rand had left nearly a hundred dollars with Aunt Alice, and Kate's profits would clear several hundred, even with restocking her goods and buying that exorbitant but necessary insurance for the *Red Dawn*. It was the best news she'd had in weeks, that and the fact she'd finally found an ally here not controlled by Cadet Chouteau.

Besides, as she had tried to imply to Stirling at General Clark's, it behooved Chouteau to have the Mandans immunized. And she planned to weaken Chouteau here by displaying her art, which clearly showed his cheating hold on the tribe. She'd heard of the power of the pen; this would be a test of the power of the paintbrush.

"Dr. Beaumont, I cannot thank you enough!" she told him as Mrs. Beaumont carried in a tea tray. "You've made my day, and I would venture to say you've made the Mandans' entire future!"

They touched teacups to seal their bargain. Then Kate realized what other surprise she had for them, something she had told the ecstatic Aunt Alice but not even her own mother. Her cup clanked a bit loudly as she replaced it in its saucer.

"I must tell you, both of you, that I need a doctor for another reason too. I married Randal MacLeod, the subagent for the Mandans, this summer. And I am carrying a child I think will be born in June."

"Oh, my!" Mrs. Beaumont managed to say, though Kate did not want to consider which revelation she reacted to.

"But you said you're going back upriver," the doctor said.

"I'm sure it will all work out, as Mandans deliver their infants without a doctor's help and bring them up there too, of course."

"Of course, they do," he said quickly. "But I was just thinking of your going all that way when you are nearly ready to deliver."

"I can do it, Doctor."

"You know, Mrs. MacLeod, I believe you can. You're even hardier than that Mandan friend of yours, though I thought she was going to leave us when she fell in the frozen river last year. But come hell or high water—pardon that old saw, ladies—I believe you will come through, just as you say."

Rand tried to tell himself that he had come through—that he had both a major and a minor victory in his grasp—but he still felt melancholy and lonely. At least for the next few days he was getting out of the oppressive atmosphere of the fort, away from being cooped up near the sly Blackwell and brazen Marbois, and that alone was a short-term victory. And his trip among the Sioux last autumn had arranged a Sioux treaty visit here next summer—he hoped a major triumph for the future safety of Mandans. But he thought, squinting against the glare of sun on snow as he walked along on his snowshoes toward the winter village, sometimes he thought he'd forfeit all that to be with Kate right now.

He shook his fur-capped head at that admission. Despite his dedication to the tribe and his duty, he thought about her all the time. He worried for her, even prayed for her, and missed her desperately. But surely, as strong and determined as she was, her getting help from General Clark and her standing up to Chouteau would result in her swift return next spring. In his travels on the *Red Dawn* he had come to see the boat was sturdy and riverworthy, even if it looked fragile. And the same could be said for Kate MacLeod.

He stopped on a hill above the edge of the little lake where he and Kate had gone out in the bullboat last autumn. He tugged the leash on the lead dog of three pulling his goods on a small sled so they would wait for him. Down on the snow-swept banks, lightly garbed Mandan boys were setting horsehair snares to catch snow buntings for winter pets, just the way he and Swift Raven had years ago. They did not see him, and he trudged on, half mesmerized by the scrunch, scrunch of his snowshoes and his thoughts.

When it got this cold—let's see, this was December 20 in what The People called the Month of Freezing Rivers—he stopped dressing like the tribe. Each brave went about in little more than additional leggings with a buffalo *mih-sha* thrown over his usual breechcloth. But Rand wore wool instead of elkskin now and blanket legging wraps over his trousers that didn't shrink when dried by the fire. For extra foot warmth, he stuffed moss and dried leaves between his stockings and his boots, while the Mandans wore just moccasins. Yes, more than ever, in cold winter months, Rand knew white blood pulsed through his veins along with the Mandan. And right now his father's part of him was longing for a cabin with a hearth—and Kate. Shaking his head again, he plunged among the bare tree trunks at Point of Woods.

When Rand entered the winter village to shouted greetings, he pictured Kate yet again, for he had brought her here to bed her. But that poignant memory was soon tugged away by the noise and motion in the village. On a cleared-off space of snow, men played their favorite large-group gambling game, *Tchung-Kee,* in which they often wagered great wealth on one throw of the hoop. Though they evidently played in teams today, each man in turn tried to get his rolled little leather circle to fall over particular tabs on a long spear. He saw Blue Wing's brothers, Arrow Point and Gray Eyes, even the usually aloof berdache Loud Fox shouting out their bets, but it was obvious Wolf Trap led their team. On the other side stood Swift Raven and Four Bears and their male relatives, shouting challenges and insults.

For one moment Rand was tempted to go over, to put himself between the sides. It reminded him of the rift in the tribe that needed dealing with, as had the rift between the tribes, but he knew better than to get into the middle of the boisterous game.

But he stood and watched a moment, wishing instead it were the time of year the tribe played their other game with hoops, when the river ice broke up and even the women raced across big pieces of rampaging ice to toss them, for then Kate would come back soon.

"Dark Water, enter! I see you will be with us awhile." The woman's warm voice came so close behind him that he jumped at his own yearning. He turned to see his aunt, Scatter Corn, standing in the doorway of her winter lodge. "Come in, come in here, and I will unhitch the dogs and unpack your things," she said.

"I'll help you."

"No," she said, but smiled. "When you are in the village, you are one of us. So let women do that work. Go in now and rest."

He ducked inside. Though sweating from his exertions, he loved the closeness and warmth in here. With snow banked around the outer walls, hide curtains hung inside, and the fire, it was a warm winter haven. But standing here only made him remember Kate in his arms, her warm, open body welcoming his thrusts. . . .

Sounds from the gambling game outside were more muted now, like memories. He sat down and stared into the fire. He only hoped and prayed that his and Kate's big gamble to be apart this winter was a wager they would win.

On December 20, as she would be doing each day before Christmas, Kate greeted guests at the big, open double doors of Sam's warehouse. Stomping snow off their feet as if they were entering a grand house, the cold and the curious came in from their festivities on the winter river ice or, as word spread, took time out from their holiday shopping uptown for the opening of Kate's display.

Because she had not been able to locate any other space for her paintings and Indian art—it was once again obvious to her that "someone powerful" in town pulled people's strings for their excuses and refusals—she had decided to use the front of Sam's building. Besides, most of the goods stored here, including her Mitutanka cargo, had been sold and shipped to empty this part of the vast place. Unfortunately the fur warehouse still stank a bit despite the wide open doors and the tart aroma of heating cider. But when Gabe and a few others passed out handbills offering a hot drink and a free art exhibition of Indians, people paraded in.

How Kate wished she had the *Red Dawn* itself here to put on display down on the wharf, for it was a real work of art in its own way. But now in a southern bayou, it was sitting out the ice and its eventual rampaging breakup.

Gabe would be going after it in March, when this cold weather broke.

Today Kate kept her cloak pulled tightly around her for another reason besides the bite of wind. Even in her third month she showed more than she had with her two earlier pregnancies. It was either that she was older or that the father of this child was different. A little smile lifted her lips at the thought of her moody man, who had learned to trust her, and at the memory of his hands and mouth so hot on her. Even in the river breeze she felt herself flush at the mere thought of him.

Though she felt wearier than usual and her ankles were swollen, she circulated among the small crowd, answering questions, explaining the art for sale was to obtain money for the vaccine. Having Gabe and Pete about answering questions helped too. Jamie had been shadowing Gabe but was now up in Sam's room, playing with Rand's toy soldiers. The "lad," as Aunt Alice always called him, now declared he wanted to be a soldier as well as an Indian when he grew up.

"Why you calling these sewn moccasins art?" one man asked her. "Your paintings, sure. But shoes—even fancy ones made in civilization—are hardly art."

"If you'll look closely at the beautiful designs and pictures done in quills and grasses and beads on them and the fine stitching, you'll see it's not unlike a painting or drawing," she said. "And that buffalo robe on the wall over there tells a story too, as a book or drawing does." The man just shook his head, but he did drop a coin in the barrel.

She was grateful for any contributions; it had turned out that shipping in so much medicine had doubled the price Dr. Beaumont had first quoted. Aunt Alice had given some money, the Beaumonts some; she had visited everyone from Mayor Derby to her old friends Samantha Lautrec and Lilian de la Forest for donations. But she was still short almost two hundred dollars, which were evidently going to have to be raised this way.

And so her precious paintings were all for sale today, though she didn't want to let them go. She had trouble convincing several buyers who wanted to cart them off right now why they must stay until the end of the exhibit on Christmas Day.

"Jethro, look how crude those pots are," Kate overheard a woman say. "Not even symmetrical, are they?"

Kate sighed and almost swooped in to defend them, but Aunt Alice was making straight for her, with that determined, no-nonsense expression Kate had come to think of as her "Scottish" look.

"Change places with me and just serve cider for a wee spell, lass. You've been on your feet long enough, I'd say."

"I'll take a little rest later, Aunt Alice. I'm just so thrilled to see people coming. And the works getting the most comments are these I put in front," she said proudly, indicating the series of drawings and paintings that showed the trials the tribe faced.

Hanging from a set of upended crates near the entrance, Buffalo Grass's wise but smallpox-pitted countenance stared down on the visitors from one frame. In the next, a Mandan brave—she had used Swift Raven's stoic face—traded a whole pile of pelts for one mere harness Marbois offered from a Chouteau steamer along the bank. Then, inside the dark walls of Fort Clark Kellen Blackwell kicked at both Indian dogs and Indian children. In the hold of a steamboat Fort Leavenworth soldiers shrugged to let pass a barrel of booze marked "Fr. Chouteau's Fur Factor to Gov't. Agent Blackwell." Traders hauled boxes marked "Gov't. Annuities for Mandans" into Fort Clark past angry Indians. And Mandans with tight mouths stared at devastated, empty beaver lodges on the Heart River while in the last painting men stood in the lobby of the Union Hotel here in town, exchanging money and smugly tipping their elegant beaver hats to each other.

Later Kate turned from thanking a French couple for a fifty-cent donation and bumped into Cadet Chouteau with Stirling right behind him.

"Oh!" she gasped, then composed herself. Both men wore beaver hats they pointedly did not tip or remove in her presence. "Stirling," she managed to say, "I see you are now on the leash of your master. Why stand behind

General Clark's chair so apparently obedient when you are actually leading the poor man about by the nose?"

"Madame MacLeod," Chouteau said, and dared bow over her hand, which she snatched back. "Always so angry, eh? Such passion becomes you. Don't you agree, Monsieur Mount?"

"Yes, because it always gets her in trouble," he muttered.

"Now, madame, before you lash us with your tongue or summon one of your louts, let me tell you I have brought quite a few louts of my own if you choose to make a foolish protest. And I assure you I am here to good purpose, to help your grand and noble cause, eh?" Chouteau said mockingly, and drew a leather pouch from the depths of his velvet-collared greatcoat. "Word is, you see, that you are two hundred dollars short of paying for the smallpox vaccine when it arrives."

"How did you—" she said, then stopped. "Yes," she admitted, staring at the purse as if it were a fanged snake. How desperately she wanted that money, but not from Chouteau. In accepting it, she would be allowing him to control things again, the Mandans, her. Folks could even say that she, like Clive, was on the take from him. The need was great, the cause just, yet she just glared at him.

"Will you be so stubborn and stupid to throw it in my face?" he asked tauntingly, and tossed the pouch once to jingle it and flaunt its weight. "Actually it is not a donation, but the purchase price for these paintings closest to the door here," he said, and swept his hand in their direction.

"Those are the only ones not for sale. At least not to someone who will not display them prominently and who ignores their message. I imagine you would just collect them as you have so many other things for a pretty price, including Stirling Mount."

"Really, madame"—Chouteau ignored her attacks on Stirling—"you should just draw flowers and birds, not political propaganda! So with this money I will have your promise that you will go back to Mitutanka and just breed half-breeds. Stay there and do no more of this ah, incendiary, art."

She wanted to scream and hit him. Her fingernails bit painful half-moons in her palms as Stirling dared snigger. But she knew she must play his game, ignore the taunts to be able to fight back with careful logic, not raw emotion.

"You know," she told him, her voice loud but calm, "sometimes before certain ceremonies, the Mandans make a medicine mirror—*a-wa-sa-ta* they call it. They gaze in it to try to see their real motives—to learn about themselves, even to ally themselves with Old Woman in the Moon, a nature god who likes to see her face in river water. And those paintings, just like a mirror," she declared, raising her voice even more, "show the reality of the way you Chouteaus run and ruin the precious places and people upriver! And I hope to heaven you will change before it's too late for the Mandans, as it has been for other tribes!"

He'd looked flabbergasted at first but was furious now. "Ah, a female philosopher, an art critic! She's a critic now, Monsieur Mount."

"She always was," Stirling said. "Let us just get this over."

"Ah, of course. Madame—"

"I would like to add your filthy money to what we have"—she interrupted him—"but I'm trying to decide if it would be worth the adulation you will expect as a result."

"If my money is too dirty for you, toss it on the pile with your work, for it is a pittance to me!"

As he finally doffed his hat to her, the crowd in the warehouse seemed to explode. Men rushed forward to remove the paintings near the front and ran outside with them. Others with Chouteau—including Stirling, no less, who had a pistol!—drew guns and held them on Gabe and Pete and other visitors, though Aunt Alice shoved through to Kate's side. Just before Chouteau turned away, he emptied the sack of clanking coins at her feet and, in replacing his top hat, evidently gave a second sign. Outside in the street the paintings of her protest were dumped in a pile and ignited with a torch.

"No!" she shouted, but slipped in the puddle of coins

and went down to her knees, before Aunt Alice grabbed her.

"Lass, dinna take them on! You have the money."

"No!" she repeated, and got up. She pulled away from Aunt Alice and ran forward, before several of the guns, including Stirling's, pivoted her way. She stared Stirling down; his wrist wilted. Striding past him, she halted in the big double doors as the wooden frames Pete had built and Gabe had carved and the linseed oil thinner and paints and canvas caught and flared.

People out on the ice looked and pointed at the bonfire; those on the street stopped to stare. Gabe's face reflected the conflagration, but it was also livid with rage; his ham hock fists clenched, then unclenched at his sides. Chouteau ought to be eternally grateful, Kate thought, that Gabe was pledged to peace, or the big man might have torn him limb from limb, even with a gun still poked in his ribs.

"Get back, woman!" Chouteau muttered at her, then raised his voice so the crowd both in the warehouse and on the street could hear. "She sold me the lot of them," he said, pointing to Kate and then the burning paintings, "so I ought to do what I will with them! Wretched art, frilly and feminine! Her work stinks as bad as this warehouse!"

Several dared laugh at that. Glaring at her, still gesturing grandly as if he were making a public speech for office, Chouteau plunged on. "Women, especially married ones breeding half-savage whelps, ought to stay home— and home for this woman is upriver!"

Stunned he knew of her pregnancy, Kate gasped. When he had mentioned her breeding before, she did not know he meant he knew. But she thought triumphantly, if he thought the crowd would cheer him, he was wrong. Apparently surprised to be gaped at and not cheered, he lowered his voice at last.

"Paint any more of this threatening trash while you are in town, woman, and I will burn the next ones *with* this warehouse and your ramshackle boat. Come on, Mount."

"Wait!" she shouted. The two of them turned back to her. "Monsieur Chouteau, you may own spies, slaves like this man"—she pointed at Stirling—"but you do not own me or my trading company. And you most certainly do not own the proud, free Mandans, however much you cheat them, however this price you've paid may save some lives!"

Chouteau stepped closer. "Best worry about saving your own skin!" he hissed at her as Gabe hurried up. Her mouth dropped open at that whispered threat, but he strode away. Only Stirling dared stay. She was surprised to see his face looked anguished, for she'd thought he reveled in all this.

"Kate, I—even though he told me to watch you going upriver, to court you, I swear to you: I cared, I came to love y—"

"Liar! How can I believe anything you say ever again?"

His countenance crumpled. He bit his lower lip and plunged away into the crowd.

Kate walked once around the ashes of her work, then strode back into the warehouse. She no longer tried to conceal the beginning swelling of her body. However that bastard Chouteau had known about the child she carried did not matter now. She must protect that innocent life and herself to deliver the vaccine, for all that meant a safe future for those she loved.

"I would have put a hole through that fork-tongued son of a snake polecat, but I didn't know I needed a gun here!" Pete said while everyone trailed behind her as she went back into the warehouse.

"I didn't guess you were ... with child," Gabe whispered as if awestruck. He hung his head until Sam slapped him on the back.

"You all did the right thing," Kate told them. "I would never forgive myself if anything happened to any of you on my account. He took me by surprise, but he's not going to get me down. At least now I think he's done his worst, for he'll look a fool if the vaccine or any of us are harmed. And we got what we wanted: enough money to protect the entire tribe!"

She gazed at the yet wary faces of her friends: Aunt Alice, Gabe, Sam, Pete, even Dr. Beaumont and his wife, who had come in too late to see Chouteau's display of destruction. Jamie ran down from upstairs and hugged her. Kate leaned down to embrace him.

"Kate, I hope you're thinking you'll at least lay low till spring," Gabe said.

"She's thinking," Aunt Alice declared, "that you are all invited to my house for Christmas dinner. And that she's going to take it slow and easy till this baby arrives."

"If," Pete put in, "you call heading back upriver to Mandan country come spring taking it slow and easy. Ding-danged, but Rand's gonna be happy about that baby!"

"Kate, maybe it's not the time to ask," Sam said, "but I been thinkin' about hirin' on with y'all for the next trip. I got a friend can watch this place. With what all I heard about the frontier from Pete and Gabe, even Jamie, I'm rarin' to try it once. Seems it's a more dangerous place 'round here lately anyway."

"And you?" Kate asked Aunt Alice, turning to the old woman.

"Me? I told you, you willna catch me on a ship again. And neither are you going, lass, not till you've had that bairn here with the doctor and me to help you!"

"I'm going, Aunt Alice, as soon as the ice breaks up if I have to swim."

"Good glory, but you're too stubborn for your own good!"

"Maybe so. But I suppose folks once said the same to you, Alice Forbes, when you left Scotland for the New World with the man you loved, shaky ships and storms at sea notwithstanding."

The old woman's eyes misted; she sniffed and nodded. "You're my family now, right along with Rand," she said while the men drifted out in the street to poke at the charred, smoking rubble. "You and Jamie and that bairn you're carrying. So . . . well, just maybe I might have to go with you."

They hugged with Jamie hanging on between them. Despite the ruination of the day and the destruction of her work, Kate felt strangely, deeply blessed. Like this baby growing within her, she now had both a white and an In-

dian family and more than one home. For now let
Chouteau think he had defeated her. In a new way he had
set her free, just as her friendship with Blue Wing, as her
land at River of Sky or the wide, open prairie had. Just as
loving Rand had.

While the men swept up the street, she went back into
the warehouse and sat on the floor with Jamie, gathering
and counting coins. She kept thinking with each dollar
that four more Mandans would now be safe to trade with
MacLeod and Company, independent dealers, so that,
with the help of The People, they could run Chouteau
right out of business, at least on Mandan land.

"We're in business," Marbois gloated, and took a big
swig of Stirling Mount's rum, which they were using for
Christmas punch. "Soon as this weather breaks, I'll head
south to Fort Pierre to get that chest with them infected
blankets! Then I'll catch the earliest keelboat or steamer
heading back."

"Just be sure you get on a steamboat where you won't
get tossed off," Blackwell warned, and refilled both their
mugs. He prided himself in always dressing well despite
the dirt out here on the prairie, and he had worn his best
suit and shirt today. But what a miserable holiday season.
He regretted that Marbois and Indians were about the best
he had for company.

"Next time I see that MacLeod gal again," Marbois
muttered, "I'll get even, the bitch! As for them blankets,
all we gotta do is make sure we get Four Bears, Swift
Raven, and any of their kind off alone a ways with us—
maybe to plan for that summer Sioux peace parlay, eh?"

"And then be sure once they get hit with it, they don't
go wandering back to the tribe," Blackwell put in. "I hear
pox spreads like prairie fire. I don't want this getting out
of hand, Jacques. I only want those red allies of
MacLeod's gotten rid of, so Wolf Trap can really start to
take over—and we can control him. No more of your
sloppy work."

"I told you, nothing ain't gonna go wrong."

"Then that means getting MacLeod off the premises
again for a while," Blackwell said with a sigh. "You

know, if I send him off on some wild-goose chase and his wife's not back yet when we deal with Swift Raven and Four Bears, we can hardly pin the pox on the MacLeods."

"I know, but we can't wait. Not every plan's perfect. But guess what I'm gonna do to really celebrate the day—not today or New Year's but whatever early spring day the ice breaks up so I can head south?"

"I have the feeling you're going to tell me," Blackwell said as he clicked his watch lid up and down.

"I'm finally gonna ask Wolf Trap for the loan of Blue Wing in my bed! He's been real possessive of her, but the more I think about her and her tight friendship with MacLeod's gal, the more I itch to do some taming of her."

"I told you, take a temporary Mandan wife."

"Naw, can't stomach none of them squaws that long. But a few nights' loan of Wolf Trap's latest bride will do me just fine and settle a coupla old scores. Just can't wait till spring. Chouteau's gonna really owe us after we pull this one off. Just can't wait till spring!"

Chapter 19

Even from the winter village Ahpcha-Toha could hear the excited squeals and shouts of the tribe. Through the woods, down on the banks of Big River, The People played and rejoiced at the breaking of the ice, the messenger of spring. She had even started out to join them, hoping to take part in the women's game of spinning the hoop across the ice, hoping to catch a glimpse of Swift Raven as the men hurled a lance through their flying hoops. But Clam Necklace called her back: Wolf Trap had returned to their lodge and wished to speak with her.

"What does our husband want?" Blue Wing asked as she passed her sister.

"Must I always know everything?" Clam Necklace retorted, and, with her leather hoop around her neck, ran toward the river, holding her children's hands.

Frowning, Blue Wing stared after them, then turned to trudge to their lodge at the far end of the village. At least her sister had responded. Sometimes she did not answer at all when Blue Wing asked her where something was to be kept in the winter lodge or when she requested to tend the children. Clam Necklace let Wolf Trap's female relatives watch them, but because she knew the children were dear to Blue Wing, she seldom let her play with or teach them. Still, though it was a victory she did not savor, Blue Wing had won something over her sister.

For these last months Wolf Trap spent many more nights in her bed than in that of Clam Necklace. Perhaps it was because he knew his new wife did not love him, and he thought commanding her body would capture her mind. Perhaps it was because even in their most private moments, she never gave him warmth, and he thought his strength—his medicine—would wear her down. Or perhaps in overpowering and punishing her, he thought he could hurt her for loving Swift Raven, hurt Swift Raven through her. She did not know or care. She only knew that as dreadful as her nights were with Wolf Trap, sober or drunk, the fact he chose to be with her was her only triumph over Clam Necklace.

She lifted the layers of furs aside and ducked to enter the lodge. Wolf Trap sat, not smoking, not drinking, just waiting for her.

"You wish to speak to me, husband?"

"Sit. I have a special honor for you—for me too."

"Have I not honored you enough by living here?"

"Why will you dare to talk back in the day but never talk at all at night?"

She said nothing, though she almost blurted out that he was a sneaking creature of the night, which was sacred to Old Woman in the Moon. Instead she sat and concentrated on the now-muted cries of The People. She had seen Swift Raven and his Bright Star run out of their winter lodge with hoops and rope. She longed to escape too, to exult in the departure of the ice, which meant Prairie Wind's return to Dark Water and to her.

"Chouteau's fur trader Marbois a man of much medicine," Wolf Trap said to yank back her straying thoughts.

"Marbois? What of him?"

"I told him you honored to walk with him this night in his bed at the fort. He is heading south to Fort Pierre soon now that the ice has broken. Why do you look at me that way? It is an honor, more white medicine for me."

She jumped to her feet. "Not Marbois! He tried to force me! He tried to kill me, hitting my head on river ice near St. Louis! He left me to drown!"

"What? You bend words! That white woman put snakes in your head. She told you say this. She and Dark Water have a bad heart toward Marbois!"

"That is not why," she said, backing away from him as he rose. "I will not walk with Marbois. That is not a good way of The People."

"Blind woman! Always you take another path, dare to

judge me and The People! If your words are straight, why did you not tell me before?"

"Why should I tell my first defiler about one who only tried to defile me later? Would there be comfort or justice there? I will not bed with a white who hates and cheats The People, who tries to harness you and Wolf Calf! Clam Necklace is wrong to do so; perhaps those who walk with the buffalo are wrong too! Women must wed a man they can love and respect . . . and not be given to others—"

He roared in fury and grabbed at her. She ducked, eluded him. She scrambled for the door. Before she realized he was not pursuing her, she was across the village clearing. To chase and scold a woman was weakness; to beat one's wife where others would see, disgrace. But Wolf Trap no doubt already planned what he would do to her this night in her bed—before he forced her to spread her legs for stinking Scarface tomorrow.

She stopped running on the far side of the woods. Out of breath, glancing back one more time, she leaned against a tree. She watched The People, most of them naked, leaping from floe to floe with their hoops. Some of the men roped Brother Buffalo, dead and drowned, floating by. The animals would be buried along the banks until warm weather, when they would make fine soup. She slid her shoulders down the tree, huddled on the ground, and sighed.

Before she would lie with Marbois, she would kill herself. But she hated to go against the ways of The People, however much she thought sometimes those ways were wrong. Wolf Trap had said true that Prairie Wind had changed her thinking on some things. Two wives for one husband seemed as wrong and unfair as the fact she bore no children. Sisters should not have to go to the lodge of the same man. Maybe even raiding and scalp taking were bad because they just turned the eternal wheel of revenge between the tribes. But all that hard thinking aside, she knew one thing for sure: She would not—could not—return to the lodge of Wolf Trap, however much it grieved her family and The People.

She stood now to see better as the men dragged another

dead buffalo up on the bank below her. Swift Raven stood among those men, his sleek brown body shiny in the sun. Next to him Brother Buffalo looked still and limp, so peaceful amid the noise and revelry.

And then she thought of it. If she lost herself on the ice, decided to slip in, not to swim, it would be peaceful for her too. No more Wolf Trap, Clam Necklace, no Marbois, no hurting her family. They would honor and mourn her, never knowing she had turned away from their ways again, for after all, she had but been lost through the ice on a day so wild Old Woman could never see her face in the river.

She started to run. She kicked off her moccasins but left on her dress. White woman's modesty—another thing, perhaps, her dear Prairie Wind had taught her.

She leaped and slipped across the careening white-blue blocks with the others. She had no hoop, but one went by, and she winged it skyward, then chased it. Her spirit soared, free of Wolf Trap, amid her beloved people. Would Prairie Wind and Much Questions come to the scaffold where her bones lay wrapped until they dropped to the earth? Would Prairie Wind mourn for her as deeply as The People did—if they found her body? For like Brother Buffalo, she could be swept miles away, miles down, clear to the shores of the Baby Hill or River of Sky or even St. Louis to tell Prairie Wind to come—come soon.

She saw now she was nearly in the middle of the wide river. A group of naked braves—young, unmarried ones, Arrow Point too—raced by her, screeching. Then she saw Bright Star ahead. She too had chased the hoop Blue Wing had thrown and now bent to retrieve it from the water. The slim body of the girl, the skin Swift Raven had caressed gleamed golden. How much Blue Wing wished to trade places with her, to snatch that hoop and hurry back to her husband, Swift Raven, laughing, loving. In the tumult of the tribe Blue Wing stood and stared one moment. And saw Bright Star simply slip and disappear.

Blue Wing started, then jumped and slid closer to where Bright Star had gone in. No head bobbed in the frothing rush of water; the heavy chunks here closed and crunched. Not thinking her loss was possible—for would she not just come up farther on?—she still turned and shouted to the braves, "Bright Star fell! I cannot see her!"

They stopped and stared, then raced downriver, leaping, looking. Others on the bank saw how far they went. They too ran closer, riding the ice, running along the bank. Swift Raven tore out toward Blue Wing, who tried to stay near the spot Bright Star had gone under.

"Bright Star?" he asked.

"I saw her from a little ways. She slipped!"

He turned away. Some now searched the riverbanks, shouting when they saw something black bobbing in the river like a dark head. But always it was another buffalo or the tip of a tree. Swift Raven ran up and down the banks; Bright Star's father, Four Bears, joined the search, though he seemed to lumber along behind Swift Raven.

Now, Blue Wing told herself, now was the time. No one would see her go, as easily missing as Bright Star. But something held her back, not a chance with Swift Raven but the fact she had thought of Bright Star's death—perhaps wished for it—just before she disappeared. She had not meant that this should really be. And this was so much like what happened to her last year when Marbois left her to drown—frenzy first, disbelief, then numbing cold, the sad sense of loss. Had Bright Star thought last of Swift Raven as the river sucked her down and swept her away? That was what Blue Wing had thought of last year: being saved by Swift Raven, even as she nearly drowned.

They found Bright Star's body downstream, caught in driftwood, forever silent and still. Blue Wing yet walked the river ice, not going back to shore, trying to decide what to do, not wanting to see Swift Raven's face. But at last she did, for he himself came out to her on the ice. She trembled from the cold and shock.

"I am grateful you gave the alarm," Swift Raven said. "Several saw you run to her and try to help. Come back to shore now."

"Yes, but I . . . lost . . . no help . . ."

"Come to shore now. Come," he said, coaxing her. She took his hand and let him lead her to the bank.

He turned to her again, speaking very low. "She was a good wife to me, but she was never you." He loosed her hand. She watched him climb the snowy riverbank, head bent, while the wails of mourning began.

It was then Blue Wing decided to go back to her family's lodge and tell them what Clam Necklace and Wolf Trap had done to her years ago. If they took her in, she would stay with them until Prairie Wind returned, then go south next autumn with the *Red Dawn* to live at River of Sky, just the way her friend had said she could. If Long Hatchet and Corn Basket would not take her back, she would go to live in the cave down by the stream until the steamboat came. She was leaving Wolf Trap, no matter what, and it had taken that poor woman's dying in her place to make her go.

On April 10, as soon as the heavy ice from up north swept through the Mississippi, the *Red Dawn* pulled away from the wharf at St. Louis. The Beaumonts waved, and the doctor called to Kate, "Remember now, judge the dosage by how heavy and tall each person is. And to babies, including your new one, just a dab."

"Yes, Doctor! Thank you again for all your help!"

"And sometime," he shouted back, walking along the wharf now to be heard, "Mrs. Beaumont and I will go too—at least for a visit to your River of Sky and . . ." The chug of engines and rumble of the boilers drowned his last words.

Kate saw Sam standing at the stern, gawking as his big warehouse shrank with the rest of the city. On the first curve she watched hills and budding trees swallow the wharves, the silhouette of buildings, even the lofty spire of the cathedral. Now dwindled the roofs of the neighborhood where Winterhaven stood, next the area where Aunt Alice had left her home of many years in the hands of Lawrence Lockwood, the old man who had worked with her and apparently loved her for years. Kate had loved St. Louis for years but blessedly never felt wedded to it either.

Startled from her reverie, she looked around to be sure Jamie was with Pete. She glanced up to the pilothouse at

Gabe steering, lecturing their new redheaded first mate, Martin Reilly. Then Kate hurried up from the main deck to be sure Aunt Alice was all right. Though she had boarded stoically, she stayed in her cabin and refused to step out on deck.

Kate moved carefully on the stairs she used to race up and down, for she was already big for her seven months. If her mother didn't believe this baby was not conceived before her marriage, that was just too bad. She knocked on Aunt Alice's cabin, the one which had been Rand's last time.

"Come in." Aunt Alice sat on her bed, glaring at the opposite wall.

"Outside, it's not like being at sea at all," Kate said, holding the door open.

"I thought you hadna been to sea."

"No, but you can always see land on both sides here. And believe me, it will get shallow lots of places before we arrive."

"Good glory, if it weren't for the lad and that bairn you're carrying, I'd never have let you talk me into this."

"Rand will be so pleased." Kate tried again when Aunt Alice didn't budge or look at her.

"I do want to meet that country aunt of his, Scatter Corn, I tell you that!" the woman declared, but her voice lacked conviction.

"Aunt Alice, whatever your motives—this baby, Jamie, Rand, and all the Mandans aside—*I* am so glad you came!"

At that the woman squinted up at her and almost smiled. "Better go check that barrel of medicine, like you been doing for weeks," she said in her best scolding voice, and made a shooing motion with her hand. "I swear, but the landlord would have kicked me out forever instead of just a year if he'd known we had a barrel chock-full of live pox in your room this last month. Off with you now, and I'll be out for a tour later. The lad promised to escort me."

Kate went directly down in the hold to check again on the special wooden cradle Pete had built to keep the small glass jars of serum safe in a sawdust-packed barrel. It sat at the most inward section of the hold so a limb or rock banging the hull could not harm it. Barrels of beer for the crew surrounded it, but could not bump it. And if, by chance, the worst happened and the precious barrel somehow fell in the river, it would float dry, nestled inside its oilskin sack inside the staves. Kate put her hand on the barrel, encouraged by the solid, rough feel of the wood, by the clearly printed words "FRAGILE: GLASS AND MEDICINE," as she rehearsed in her mind how she and Gabe had learned to administer "the matter."

"The matter" was always how Dr. Beaumont referred to the cowpox serum itself, which would be carefully measured and smeared across scratch marks on a person's arm, then covered with a tied piece of cloth until a tiny rash was raised. The lesser disease and localized sore skin protected one from the deadly disease with its rampant pustules and permanent pockmarking—if one survived. One of Dr. Beaumont's medical books called the procedure, which an Englishman named Edward Jenner had discovered late in the last century, "elective infection with active cowpox virus matter." But Kate always thought of the task now ahead as "the great Mandan matter."

She went back up on deck and stood, hands on the rail one moment more, remembering the last time the *Red Dawn* had set out upriver. They'd had just as few deck passengers aboard then because they'd left late instead of early like this time. Rand had been sitting on the prow, and she'd thought she detested him; Stirling was dancing attendance on her already, and she'd thought he was wonderful; Jamie had seemed so much smaller and younger; Captain Zeke was at the helm and Gabe too nervous even to touch the wheel; Blue Wing wandered the ship. And Katherine Warfield Craig—she'd had no husband to love or baby growing inside her then. How times had changed, for she was not leaving home this time but heading for it.

At Fort Pierre in the third week of May Jacques Marbois patted his strap-bound box of blankets to be sure it was real again. His plan was working well, though he'd had to wait too long for this to be brought in by some trappers returning from the plains.

Still, since he spoke Sioux, he was more at home here than with the Mandans, but the Sioux had already had fur agents when Chouteau assigned him. Maybe once he and Blackwell got control of the Mandans, Chouteau would let him serve anywhere he wanted, and maybe he'd just pick here. Or maybe he'd like the life Cadet Chouteau himself lived at his mansion on the edge of the prairie where he'd mingled with the Chouteaus a year ago last Christmas. Sure, maybe that would be the life for him when he got good and rich off animal furs and Indian hides. He guffawed aloud at that.

But for now, he thought, victuals on Laidlaw's table here was as good as on Blackwell's. Spring was on the land, and that was mighty fine. But it was time to head back north, so he'd had some Sioux on the lookout for any steamboat coming through he could board. He needed to hightail it back to Fort Clark before heavy trading began and Blackwell's temper snapped.

He stretched and walked out in the sun from his tiny room in the shadow of the stockade. The fort traders and workers looked like winter'd almost done them in, the skinny, mangy dogs. He'd heard some of them had even eaten rats to get through. But his attention quickened when a Sioux brave he knew from Big Buck's band motioned to him from the guarded door of the stockade. Marbois hurried out to speak with him.

"Spot me a keelboat or fire canoe down south?" he asked the brave, named Beaver Rock.

"Small fire canoe, moving fast. On flag," he said in Sioux, making gestures for words he did not know, "painted a yellow sun, red rays. Two white women riding its back."

"The *Red Dawn*!" Marbois exulted, and couldn't help dancing a little jig. "I got a score to settle with her! Can't believe she's the first boat up this year instead of last! Hellfire, I won't get a ride from her, but I'll get a darn sight more! Justice!"

"You burn *Red Dawn* with hellfire?" Beaver Rock asked.

Marbois snorted a laugh. "Naw, 'cause that would rob Big Buck of some plans up north a ways where he's awaiting. No, I'm just gonna pay a little social call on that gal for all she cost me. Just for a little drink, a course. Tit for tat. Eye for an eye, that cross-eyed son of a bitch who pilots her boat would say with all his fancy preaching! This is Jacques Marbois's lucky day! Beaver Rock, can you ride me down near Big Bend, where they might tie up for the night? Just you, don't want no bunch of whooping, scalping braves, not yet, not till she knows we're even."

Beaver Rock nodded and started away, but Marbois ran back one more time to check his box of blankets and shove it under a pile of furs he'd paid the Sioux plenty for to keep their fickle loyalty.

As he grabbed his rifle and shot and headed out the door, he smiled and muttered, "What a damn pretty spring day!"

Enjoying the beautiful spring day, Kate sat on the hurricane deck in her new rocking chair—a belated wedding gift from Gabe and Pete. A fine carpenter, Pete had built it from violet- and white-tinged cedarwood, and dear Gabe had carved the *Red Dawn* and the river on its headrest. Yet she did not let the chair lull her any more than the rhythmic motion of the boat. She kept her eyes on the passing shoreline with her loaded rifle at her feet.

She tried to calm herself with happy thoughts of their brief stop at River of Sky and Bellevue. She had left two builders on her land with her instructions for the Mandan lodge and small storehouse. Covered with a stout piece of canvas, she had left her painting of Scatter Corn to be hung in the lodge where the sun would light it. Just being there one day before they hurried on had restored her strength.

At Bellevue she had explained everything calmly to her mother: how her sense of independence had grown with her love for Rand; his concern that she not conceive a child until they were reunited. After that Mama did not look askance at her blooming belly again. Perhaps she did the same finger counting to realize the child was not due too soon. The only disagreement she and Mama had this time was when Mama insisted she stay there until the child was born. Aunt Alice sided with her mother, but Kate had pushed on without a moment's worry—until now.

They had just passed the Dry River, the official Sioux boundary. The landmarks were familiar: the ruins of that old fort and the Ree village destroyed by Sioux that Rand had pointed out before. Next came Big Bend, the huge, shallow turn in the river that was twenty-five miles around but only one and a half miles across on foot. Eight miles south of that, the dark humps of the so-called Medicine Hills seemed to press in on her. She shifted her bulk in her chair and continued to squint at the shadowed passing banks despite the headache perched between her brows.

Shoreline scenery changed here too. Brambles tangled themselves around bushes and stunted trees, but long, open sections stretched between ravines. From their rocky dens, wolves and foxes shrieked piercing howls heard even over the noise of the steamer. Blue Wing had liked to see black smoke blowing from coal layers burning in the rocks here, but it reminded Kate too much of the threat of fires.

She picked up her gun and put it across her knees, for her thighs almost disappeared when she sat like this. She saw nothing human, nothing amiss. Still, when they stopped that night after the slow steam around Big Bend, she put two roosters on guard instead of one.

She slept fitfully despite her exhaustion. Every little noise aboard seemed magnified over Jamie's shallow, regular breathing across the tiny cabin. Her head and back hurt. But at last she lost herself in slumber and wakened late, groggy to hear the engines churn to life. She could hear Jamie's voice up on deck. Horrified she'd slept so late, she threw on her clothes and tied her wild hair back with a ribbon. She flushed with embarrassment to see Aunt Alice had taken over her chores to serve the men breakfast; a place for her alone lay on the big, empty table now.

"Sorry I overslept," she told Aunt Alice. "What did Willy Nilly concoct this morning?"

But he rushed in before Aunt Alice could answer. "All them barrels of beer is gone from the hold. Gone like they been searched and seized by those soldiers at Leavenworth who passed them through!"

"That . . . cannot be!" Kate cried, and jumped up from the table. "Someone's playing a trick. I want to see those two men who were on guard last night. Fynn," she shouted out the door when she saw him near the prow, "what two were on watch last night?"

"Two the boys say they ain't seen, ma'am. I mean, they can't be missing, and I was just going to search the boat."

"Tell Gabe we're staying put. If they've gone ashore, we'll have to find them, and if they've done something with those barrels, I'll have their hides. . . ."

A horrid thought sapped her strength; she staggered back against the stairs. She hurried down to the hold—and screamed. Not only the barrels of beer but the barrel of serum were gone. Gone! Just gone.

She clutched her throat, dashing through the half-lighted hold, looking for it. No, just boxes, crates, sacks. She panted, panicked as Aunt Alice came down the steps. "If those lads went off to get themselves drunk—" the old woman said, then stared too.

Kate hurried back up, her heart thudding like her feet on the wooden deck. It could not just be gone. Not after everything. Not when it was the answer to safety, to salvation. Not just gone.

"Fynn," she ordered, "get the gangplank back down. Gabe," she shouted up to the pilothouse, "kill the engines and come down! Two crew are missing—and the serum!"

Some searched the ship, but Kate and four others went ashore. They found a few moccasin footprints on the muddy bank and a few booted ones, though someone had tried to brush a branch across them. And just downstream a bit, tied to trees, they found the two missing men gagged and trussed like pigs.

"The barrels—beer and the serum. Did they take them?" Kate demanded, fighting to keep calm as she pulled a wad of leaves from one man's mouth.

"Indians, least one was!" he said in a raspy voice. "One white. Don't know how many others, maybe lots. Saw them in the distance when I come to after they slugged me, Jack too. Think they took our guns."

"The barrels? Did they take the barrels?"

"I guess," the other man said between big breaths when Pete freed him. "They broke least some of them down yonder . . . on some rocks . . . dumped the beer in the river . . . if that don't beat all."

Kate's legs shook uncontrollably, but she went with the four armed men downriver. They found a place about twenty yards beyond where rifle butts or rocks had been used to smash the barrels; they saw a few splintered staves caught in brush that had evidently not floated off down the black river in the middle of the night. And sawdust—sawdust everywhere, damp and dirty now on river mud. Worse, the precious oilskin sack in shreds. Kate stooped, despite her bulk, to retrieve one broken bottle that had once held the costly, precious cowpox matter. Broken her plans and hopes, she thought. Rand's dream. Safety for the Mandans. Broken.

"Marbois," she whispered. "Somehow it was Marbois."

"Here?" Pete asked. "But why?"

"I guess because Rand and I broke up his barrels of booze. And because he's a demented bastard! I only hope, whoever it was, they drank from these bottles, thinking it was some fine, fancy liquor!"

She leaned against a rock, horrified at what she'd said. Tears burned her eyes, but she refused to cry. She felt sick, sick to her stomach and her very soul. Rand had trusted her to do this, and she thought she had been so careful, so clever! She should have kept the barrel in her cabin, however much it thumped around, despite the danger of storm with limbs crashing in windows. The barrel had been clearly marked, but in the dark— Anyway, could Marbois and an Indian even read? She had been so proud when the Leavenworth soldiers passed it all through.

Now disaster and destruction. She would kill Marbois, kill him, if she could prove he'd done this. Now they would only have to hope that despite the smallpox out on the plains, the Mandans, sheltered in their villages, would be passed by again this year.

Although her parents took her back and privately told Wolf Trap and Clam Necklace they were not welcome in the lodge of Long Hatchet, as the weather warmed, Ahpcha-Toha spent more time in the cave by the river. Once she had left Wolf Trap's lodge and told her parents the truth, she felt no fear—not of being alone here where wild animals or Sioux had sometimes marauded; not of Marbois when he returned from Fort Pierre. Not even of Wolf Trap, for he would suffer public humiliation if he so much as looked as if he missed or wanted a wife who had left him. A warrior's revenge was saved for slights and shame by other men and tribes; a wayward wife was beneath contempt.

She *had* shamed him, but as long as no other man claimed her, Wolf Trap could do nothing but hold his head up and suffer the loss of his medicine among the tribe. She knew it would make him even more desperate to get more white man's medicine from Blackwell and Marbois, but she could not help the man's weaknesses.

Yet on this sweet spring day she heard a rustle in last year's leaves outside her cave and lifted her knife in case it was an unwanted visitor. She shuffled silently to the mouth of the cave to see.

Swift Raven stood just outside in the slant of sun, with a fine winter buffalo robe in his arms and not one but two horses tethered down on the stream. His hair hacked for Bright Star's death had grown out to chin length; his face was not painted red in mourning today. When Blue Wing, uncertain for one moment he was not a longed-for vision, stood still and stared at him, he spoke.

"I had to see if you are well."

"Better than in years."

"Blue Wing, strong and free and unafraid."

"Yes, now. And you, Swift Raven?"

"In need of your help. Twice I have chosen the wrong woman. He Who Lives Above took them because I did not read the signs right. The signs of my own heart and head," he said, hitting his chest, his forehead, "no matter what tribal law seemed to say. How can I choose the straight path for The People if I cannot choose the right woman? How can I be brave enough to stand against Wolf Calf and Wolf Trap if I am not brave enough to claim her?"

He held out the fine robe to her, an offering, a promise.

She nodded. Extending her hand to him, she gently pulled him into the cave.

Now let Wolf Trap do his worst, she thought as she heated porridge on the fire for this man. She must feed him well before they fled, so that the declaration was formal and official. On the way to live among the Hidatsas for a while, they would tell someone to inform the tribe that Blue Wing, second wife of Wolf Trap, had left him for another man, the widower Swift Raven. When they returned, they would face shame, but in having each other, Blue Wing and Swift Raven would fly to the heavens above it. Together they would earn back Swift Raven's place among the tribe. And even if she never bore this man a child, she knew she would learn to be content.

She smiled, deep inside, as Swift Raven set aside his partly eaten meal to pull her into his embrace. By nightfall they had fled.

Kate almost lost heart after they lost the serum. Part of her purpose had been taken from her; the Mandans had once again been robbed of something that should rightfully be theirs. And she had not even had a chance to fight back.

After the initial shock wore off, she felt roiling anger: at Marbois and his Sioux friends, at Blackwell, Chouteau, even Rand, who should have been with her. Those two guards who had been surprised at their posts knew to walk around her on deck. Even Jamie seemed to tiptoe past her sometimes. Gabe, who had not forgiven himself for not breaking Chouteau's neck back at the warehouse, felt his ship had been violated. More than once he talked about having Pete teach him how to shoot, and Kate argued him out of it. Aunt Alice annoyed her by trying to coddle her. Everyone was tense, on edge.

But several hundred miles later Kate had to smile as

they steamed by the Heart River and Baby Hill. Her heart had been deeply touched by this land and its people, and Mandan MacLeod—her and Rand's child—would be here soon to treasure and protect the way she had not been able to safeguard the smallpox serum. Surely things would look so much better when this child was born— and when she and Rand thought of some way to go down-river next autumn to get more medicine.

Just beyond the big bluff called Butte Caree, the wide Missouri narrowed and ran between chains of prairie hills in long, naked ridges like fortress walls. Steep clay banks with deep seams and crevasses crowded long open spaces.

Kate was rocking with her rifle on her lap when Gabe began to clang the bell. She looked where he pointed at a line of figures on the hill above—mounted men, Indi-ans! And not Mandan.

"Sioux!" Gabe bellowed out the side of the pilothouse. "More up ahead, riding! Cover, take cover!"

Kate first thought of Jamie. Aunt Alice had been read-ing him a story in the cabin. Safe for now, if they stayed there. She repeated Gabe's warning down to clear the decks, to summon those with guns. Already her cries were matched by shrieks as both groups of Indians charged along the eastern side of the ship on the next stretch of open bank. Hoofbeats blended with the thunder of the engines; screams merged with escaping steam. Kate made it into the pilothouse to join Gabe and First Mate Martin. And from there she saw who led the attack.

"Big Buck, that tall one there," she said, and pointed him out to the men. "Is mine the only rifle up here?"

"No—mine too," Martin said, and grabbed it from the corner while Gabe rang for more speed and hung over the wheel.

"Kate," Gabe ordered, "sit down on the floor. You can load for Marty if it comes to that."

It quickly came to that. A few braves had guns, but most shot arrows. Some glanced off, some studded the wood. Two of the attackers went down under gunfire from the crew below; a horse and rider rolled into the river, just missing the paddles churning water and mud. It was shallow here, and the banks rose so high on the starboard side that the Indians rode even now with the hurricane deck, screaming, shooting a shower of arrows.

Kate, as heavy and as frightened as she was, moved in a blur. She filled a gun with powder, patch, and ball and rammed them down. Martin shot, handed the hot gun back to her, again, again, while Gabe steered and pushed the ship for all it could take. Then Martin seemed to fly out the door and jump the railing down.

"Marty!" she screamed. "Hit!"

She reached out to take the second gun back from where he had dropped it. Gabe grabbed her, yanked her back in by her skirt, though the wheel spun madly.

"Get back, stay down, I said," he roared, and slammed the door.

"I'm going to shoot!" she insisted.

But in that moment two braves had climbed the ladder to their deck. Big Buck loomed huge and dark just outside the glass, a painted, frenzied nightmare with hatchet and knife raised. Suddenly Kate remembered an early warning of Rand's: Don't be afraid or you will make mistakes. Still, she was afraid—afraid and furious. And she'd already made mistakes. But Big Buck ... the whole damned Sioux tribe ... their friend Marbois—they could not have her boat, her crew, her friends, her family, and her baby!

She thrust the loaded rifle barrel out the door and fired. The man beside Big Buck fell back and tumbled away. But before she could close the door, the tall Sioux lunged, pulling the door and her outward. Kate let go and leaped back in with Big Buck behind her. Gabe released the wheel and jumped at the Sioux. With a roar of rage to drown Big Buck's battle cry, Gabe pounded the big man, just his height, into the pilothouse glass, again and again, his hands around the Sioux's corded neck, trying to strangle him.

Kate scrambled for the unloaded rifle, but they were standing on the pouch of balls. She edged around, trying to stay out of their bouncing, banging struggle, to get clear of Gabe and reach Big Buck. When she saw her chance, she swung the gun butt against the Sioux's skull

with all her might. She closed her eyes, felt it hit, heard
the thud. She broke the forward window, but Big Buck
crumpled to a huge pile across the door of the pilothouse.

Exhausted by his efforts, Gabe fell forward on top of
the Indian. The shooting and shrieking stopped outside as
the tinkling of glass subsided. The ship, as if wounded,
nosed into the bank and just kept churning as if to climb
clear out of the water.

Kate tried to help Gabe up, then rolled him over. "No,
oh, dear God, no!" Big Buck lay still, slack-mouthed and
glassy-eyed, but just above Gabe's belt bloomed crimson
blood with a silver knife at its center. Pete thudded up to
the deck; she did not look but knew his voice.

"The rest rode off for now. First mate's dead on the
deck below," he gasped. "Kate, not Gabe!" He dragged
the dead Indian out on deck and fell to his knees on
Gabe's other side.

Kate knelt to cradle Gabe in her arms. Yes, he
breathed. He would be all right! Only then did she speak.
"He could have had that knife in him the whole time they
fought, Pete. All he ever wanted was peace for folks.
He's strong, we'll patch him up."

Gabe opened his eyes, dear eyes, she thought, however
they seemed to look beyond her now. "Kate, take the
wheel," he wheezed. "Keep it going."

"You saved me, Gabriel. Pete, take the wheel and try to
turn the boat out. They may come back." He obeyed,
clambering over them, grasping and turning the wheel
he'd never touched before.

"Jamie, Aunt Alice?" she asked Pete, but she still did
not take her eyes off Gabe.

"Barricaded in your cabin. I wanted to get to you, but
we were picking them off down there."

"I had Gabriel taking care of me," she said, and saw
Gabe's eyes flicker that he had heard her. Kate wanted to
pull the knife from him, but it seemed so deep.

"We come a long way . . . together, Kate," Gabe whispered. She had to bend so close over him to hear that
once-strong voice.

"You've been my best man friend ever, Gabriel, but

don't talk, so you can get better." But she knew then—
knew he did too—that he would not.

"Hope Mary Taylor . . . won't be disappointed . . . in
me now. She'd have to see . . . sometimes it takes fighting
to have love . . ."

Gabe's voice faded; his words gurgled, then stopped.
"Don't let him talk," Pete said.

"He won't again," she whispered. She reached out a
trembling hand to close those eyes which still seemed to
look two different places. "How—how many others hurt
down below?" she asked as she laid Gabe down and got
slowly to her feet.

"Fynn's got two arrows in him, but he'll live. A coupla
roosters and your friend Sam are slightly wounded. Kate,
this thing's steering mighty hard."

Glass crunched under her feet as she stepped over to
take the wheel from him. "Get that big Sioux off my
boat, Pete. Drag him out and throw him off! A few hundred miles, a few days to Mitutanka, that's all we have.
And lay Gabe out real nice in a crate, and we'll bury him
there on the prairie. We're not stopping for anything but
fuel. We'll run all night with the light of Old Woman in
the Moon. And tell the roosters to yank those arrows out
of the wood. I don't want the Mandans or my husband
heading out to take on the Sioux when they see us!"

Pete just gaped at that tirade of orders, at her bending
so bulkily over the wheel. "But even with Marty and
Gabe gone, you can't mean to steer," he said in protest.

"Go on, Pete. I can read the river. And ask Aunt Alice
and Willy Nilly, please, to tend the wounded."

The moment she was alone, she sucked in silent sobs.
She dare not look down at her beloved bloodied friend,
for then she would know he was gone for good. Was this
ship cursed that it lost its captains? And now here she
was next in line for it with this child coming soon, too
soon.

But she would make it. She could not stop, would not
stop. It was a race against the Sioux, but against her own
body too. For in the shock and grief and loss she could
tell the baby had shifted lower. Perhaps sensing her mother's fear, the child—was it a daughter, a new Sally, this

Mandan MacLeod?—would soon fight to be free. But until then Kate was going to stand here and steer this ship out of danger, back home.

"Gabriel, you were right to say I would have to go on alone sometimes." She began to talk to him as she squinted upriver through the jaggedly broken front window. "I'm going on without you, without anyone to help me steer. But maybe I'll pretend you're still here with me, urging me on, saying what a gimcracker of a day. . . ."

Another sob racked her, but she stifled it. She bit her lip and held hard to the wheel as a pain crunched low in her belly, then receded. As the crew came to tend to Gabe and drag off Big Buck, she stared straight ahead, shaking, but steering strongly around that next bend in the river.

Chapter 20

Eventually Kate let Pete stand behind her, helping her turn the wheel, holding her up if she swayed or wobbled, but she refused to rest. She tried to keep the pain inside, especially when Aunt Alice made one of her frequent trips up to the pilothouse to check on her. If the stubborn woman had known Kate was actually in labor and her water had broken during her last quick trip to the toilet, she would have had the men drag her away to bear this child belowdecks.

But now the only water they had yet to break was river water cresting against the banks below Fort Clark and the stockaded village. Even as her pain increased, her relief at that welcome sight was so great that she felt she had already labored, already survived the suffering.

Again the Indians spilled down to the river in a rich brown stream to greet them. Kate stood between Aunt Alice and Pete in the door of the pilothouse where Gabe had died to save her. She leaned both hands on the railing, squinting into the sun, searching for Rand, for Blue Wing. What if Rand had not come back from the Sioux? What if Wolf Trap had done something dreadful to Blue Wing?

But there was Rand, tearing down from the fort, waving, shouting. Pete yelled back and waved, for Kate's strength was gone. Rand raced up the gangplank, disappeared to climb the stairs. Somewhere belowdecks Jamie squealed and cheered, then charged after Rand. Even as he hurried to her, Kate saw the shock on his face at her appearance, his amazement to see Aunt Alice.

"Kate! Sweetheart!" he cried, and held her to him. "Damn the Sioux!"

"How did you know?" she asked, her mouth pressed to

his throat. He hugged his aunt, one-armed, not letting Kate go, then reached down to tousle Jamie's hair.

"Arrow holes everywhere," he said. Tears shimmered in his eyes as he looked her over. "And will you ask me how I know you're pregnant?"

"Pregnant and too bullheaded," Aunt Alice said, "to deliver this bairn before she got us here. Get her to wherever we have to go to bring it into the world, lad."

Kate managed the narrow stairs herself before Rand lifted her in his arms. She gritted her teeth as the next wave of agony wrenched her. Still, she had to know some things, to tell him others before this birth really began.

"Rand, they killed Gabe and our new first mate. Will you see to burying them here?"

"Not Gabe! Yes, yes, of course."

"And promise me you won't let anyone—you too—go out after the Sioux. Gabe fought Big Buck to save me. But I bashed in his head to finish him."

He almost stumbled; he clutched her closer. "He was the war chief's son, Kate. Someone will have to go to White Raven to head off a full-fledged war."

"He's the one who attacked us—ah!" She held to him, fighting the additional pain of being jostled by his climb up the hill, his jogging pace into the village.

Kate tried to smile at Aunt Alice over Rand's shoulder, but she had to close her eyes and press her lips tight to keep from crying out. How she admired the old woman anew, for she hurried behind, her thin arms full of linens, looking askance at the alien world she entered without hesitation. Kate knew Rand was taking them to Corn Basket; how she wished Blue Wing would come home for this—if she didn't hold it against her that she would bear a child.

"How's Blue Wing?" she managed to ask as he stooped to carry her into the lodge of Long Hatchet.

"She ran away with Swift Raven after Bright Star died. It may have cost him his other dreams, but I can understand."

"Rand, lost dreams . . . someone boarded the boat at night, broke all the bottles of serum, threw it in the river.

We paid eight hundred dollars for it, learned how to use it, and it's gone. . . ."

He stood, holding her to him, his eyes wide, his mouth slack. For one moment he ignored Corn Basket's orders, Aunt Alice's pleas. "G-Gone? Who—" he stammered.

"An Indian and a white man. Near Fort Pierre. And since—"

"Marbois! And in getting even with us, he ruins—"

"Put her down and go away." Buffalo Grass interrupted. "Take others with you but not this white-haired mother. Only old women bring a child. You know the way."

He knelt to lay her down on a smooth robe Corn Basket had spread on the floor before the fire. "Rand," Kate whispered, "whatever has happened or happens now, I love you."

"Always—I too . . ." he said before Buffalo Grass pushed him away.

Corn Basket threw a handful of fragrant, sacred white sage on the low fire before she shooed the others out. Long Hatchet shuffled away with pipe in hand, nodding in approval. Rand came back to grasp Kate's hand hard, then hugged Aunt Alice again before he followed, still looking stunned.

Kate had not known "the way" that only old women brought the child. She wanted Corn Basket here too, calm and capable; she wanted Rand, Blue Wing. She wanted this child to be born right now! But she submitted to their hands, cool on her burning body.

Aunt Alice and Buffalo Grass had no way of communicating but signs and pointing. Kate tried to translate for them before she was swept away. Everything began to flow past her like the river. Laboring to get the *Red Dawn* here, to fight the Sioux and Chouteau, to get the money, the medicine, get back safely to Rand and The People. And now she was here, but nothing felt safe. It made her want to scream, just scream. And so she did, once, again, yanking the leather straps tied to the beams. Then the river flowed through her, from her, and the guardian angel Gabriel had said the river was like life.

"A wee lass! A daughter, Kate!" Aunt Alice's voice

came from far away with the sound of wailing. Wailing for Gabe's loss, wailing for the loss of the serum, Sally's death, Blue Wing's mourning Clive that long-ago day at Winterhaven . . .

Buffalo Grass grasped Kate's chin and washed her face in cold water. Kate's eyes flew open; her thoughts settled.

"Girl child, not named for ten days, be sure she live," the old woman declared.

"She *will* live," Kate said. "And her name was decided long ago. Mandan MacLeod!" She held out her arms for the crying child.

After she nursed her new daughter, Buffalo Grass put a wide woven belt around Kate's middle—over Aunt Alice's protests. The two women argued with signs and gestures when Buffalo Grass told Kate she must walk down and bathe in Big River. Aunt Alice also objected when Buffalo Grass smeared bear fat on the baby; Buffalo Grass was just as appalled when Aunt Alice diapered the child in white linen and wrapped her in a little blanket when Buffalo Grass wanted her in cattail down in the leather bag suspended from the ceiling beam. And when Buffalo Grass tried to hang the birth cord from the hoop over the leather bag . . .

"Both of you," Kate said sternly in English and in Mandan, "stop arguing. Give her back to me, and send someone for Rand! Since this child is a blend of the white and Mandan worlds, Rand and *I* will decide what to do to honor both people. I am too tired to go wash in the river, but I would like a bath here. And I am grateful the skilled hands of my dear grandmother, Buffalo Grass, and my aunt Alice brought this child safely into the world."

"The Mandan world!" Buffalo Grass said, and folded her arms across her sunken breasts, glaring at Aunt Alice.

"But for her dark hair, she looks Scottish," Aunt Alice insisted, crossing her arms too. "Not a bit of Mandan in her face, not with those blue eyes."

"In the beginning," Kate said, "Mandan babies have blue eyes. And if this child has the stubborn strength of both of you, she can conquer this whole world!"

* * *

Rand felt awed. He knew his lower lip trembled and tears glazed his eyes as he held the baby, who clasped his finger in her tiny fist. Later he brought Jamie to see his new half sister.

"Now no matter what happens," Kate whispered to Rand, "we have all this."

He nodded, but when the three of them were alone again, he forced himself to broach the subject he was dreading. "Kate, you know I have to head off any retaliation from the Sioux, for everyone's sake." He cleared his throat and stared only at the child. The tragic news about the serum and the Sioux muted his joy at their reunion and this birth, and he must not let her know.

"No," Kate insisted. "Let Blackwell go this time. Wait until Marbois comes back and let him go talk to them. If they harm him, he deserves it."

"I'm going to kill him when I see him." He let the words slip out before he could control himself. He forced himself to unclench his fists.

"Don't talk that way, Rand, not now! And we can't be apart ever again. You promised!"

"I can't help it. I didn't foresee you and your crew would kill Big Buck. You don't know how they think."

"I'm tired of being told that. I'm just plain tired. Don't go now at least," she pleaded, looking so beautiful, however drawn and pale. She stretched out her arm to him, and he took her hand in both of his. "Wait until Mandan's at least old enough to have her name recognized and be treated as a person around here . . . ten days. See, I understand how they think!" she insisted.

"Kate, promise me you'll get some sleep. Pete told me how you got here after Gabe was killed, how you kept them all going."

"I *won't* sleep if you won't be here when I wake up!"

It scared him how shrill she sounded. The baby stirred and began to fuss, but he plunged on, hardening his heart.

"You'll have to, for the child's sake, if not your own," he said as he got to his feet, then squatted to stroke the baby's silken cheek with the back of one bent finger. His lovely little child—his daughter, Mandan—hushed at his touch to break his hard heart, but he must go. "Kate, I don't want to leave, but I've got to. And if that damned Marbois waltzes back in here, steer clear of him till I get back!"

He hated himself for being harsh, even cruel. But, he assured himself, he was actually being careful and kind. He did not tell her he had to face the Sioux before White Raven heard that the woman who had helped kill Big Buck was among the Mandans. The Sioux would not hesitate to take bloodthirsty revenge against a white woman and her children for Big Buck's life, let alone the tribe. They'd evidently attacked her ship because she refused to trade with them last year—and maybe because Marbois urged them on. But he did not want to burden her with all that.

"It's bad enough," he said, fighting to keep the bitterness from his voice, "that the serum was lost and we can't hold off smallpox if it slips in this summer. The Sioux range so far to other tribes they could even bring it in. It's out among the Pawnees, I hear. Not that any of that's your fault, but you're going to have to sacrifice me for a while. I won't have the Sioux charging in here when The People need to be tending their corn and hunting. I've worked too hard to set up a summer parlay to let it all go."

"And I've worked too hard," she said, her voice quiet now, "for this child—and just to get back here—to let you go! But I do understand the way they think about revenge too, Rand. Because," she said, glaring at him now, "if the Sioux do anything to harm you, I will find them and fight them!"

He clasped her face gently in his hands. At least she understood his need! She would be brave again! "My own warrior, my war chief," he whispered.

He kissed her quickly but hard. He did not let himself touch the baby again or look back. Leaving Kate to be guarded, even here in the village, by Pete and Long Hatchet's sons, he strode outside the village walls. On the brow of hill above the river, he mounted. Alone, so there was no appearance of a raiding party, and pulling a horse laden with gifts, he rode out to find White Raven's camp.

* * *

Five days after Rand left, Marbois came back to the fort on Chouteau's steamer, but Kate had not seen him yet. She refused to even worry about the trading competition, though the *Platte Warrior* dwarfed the *Red Dawn* on the bank below the village. For today her beloved Blue Wing had returned with Swift Raven to face the tribe. Leaving Jamie and Mandan with Aunt Alice and Buffalo Grass, Kate hurried to see what would happen at the lodge of Wolf Trap.

The People streamed that way too, eager to see the show of shame between the two young rivals in the tribe. For as was tradition, the Black Mouth soldiers had taken Blue Wing to her former husband's lodge the moment she entered the village with her new one. Wolf Trap's rights did not include punishing Blue Wing directly, but he had every right to humiliate her and Swift Raven to save face.

Kate almost ran to her friend when she saw her after these months away, but Scatter Corn pulled her back into the crowd. Pete, her shadow, and Blue Wing's brothers, Arrow Point and Gray Eyes, appeared at her sides as they did whenever she ventured out.

Blue Wing sat straight on Wolf Trap's new pony before the lodge. He had decked her in a fine fringed deerskin gown Clam Necklace had no doubt dressed and sewn; a huge clamshell necklace and a precious one of bear claws dangled from her neck. Her hair had been oiled and carefully braided. This ritual showed Wolf Trap gave her gladly as a gift to his rival, a gift Swift Raven would owe him for all his life. It was supposed to shame both runaways. Yet Kate smiled and the tribe stared and murmured, for Ahpcha-Toha had never looked more proud and radiant, daring and defiant.

Blue Wing did not see Kate, for across the sea of heads she stared only at Swift Raven, who sat mounted. He too looked brave and bold, not solemn or submissive. Kate thrilled for her friend. This is the way her reunion with Rand should have been and would be next time. Sioux and smallpox, childbirth aside, they would have their day of triumph too, soaring above any trials.

When Wolf Trap spoke, the crowd hushed. "At last Wolf Trap give Swift Raven not only cast-off wife but big gift. Marbois bring back two blankets from Fort Pierre, try to keep secret, keep hid much white medicine. But I take for good of The People. Now, give one to Swift Raven; he forever in debt to me for it and for his bad-heart woman. Wolf Trap give other blanket to true wife, Clam Necklace."

Heads turned to see Clam Necklace standing proudly with a bright red blanket wrapped around her shoulder—a Mexican blanket Kate had heard it called in St. Louis. With a flourish Wolf Trap flapped open an identical one and flung it over the horse's neck and Blue Wing's legs.

"Wolf Trap have much medicine of own, so he give this gift to man of fallen face," he boasted, and stood beaming as several nearest Blue Wing reached out to pat or stroke the blanket. Scatter Corn reached out to feel its finely woven texture. Others went over to admire the one Clam Necklace wore. Kate had brought many wool blankets as gifts for the tribe, especially since they'd given her so many fine buffalo robes and furs. But those were dull-hued; she could see why they loved these bright ones.

Just then Jacques Marbois appeared, out of breath, a man who never set foot in the village, especially alone. Kate would have lunged at him, but Pete held her arm.

"Wolf Trap, you took them?" Marbois shouted, and yanked the blanket back from Blue Wing. She let him have it; she kicked him back away from her. But when Marbois strode toward Clam Necklace, she ducked inside the lodge to save hers. Marbois spun back.

"You stupid, thieving fool!" he yelled at Wolf Trap. "You don't know what you done!"

"Shall I translate your fine words for The People, Marbois?" Kate shouted, and shoved forward in the crowd despite her coterie of companions. "But why berate him for that theft when you stole The People's smallpox serum from the *Red Dawn*?"

"What? I didn't—" he said before Chief Four Bears stepped forward.

"Leave things here for once," he commanded in English, glaring at Marbois. "You plan make us pay more like for government gifts? Go, or some bad thing could happen here."

"It's on your head, all of you stupid savages!" Marbois shouted, and flung the blanket straight at Swift Raven before he melted into the crowd.

Blue Wing slid off the horse and ran to Kate. "I did hear you have a new daughter, just like I said!" she cried.

"I hear you have a new husband, just like I said!" Kate retorted, and they held each other tightly. "Finally—as soon as Rand gets back—now that folks know Marbois for what he is, times will be better for us all." Kate smiled at Swift Raven as he came over with Marbois's beautiful bloodred blanket over his shoulder.

The Sioux raids that summer of 1837 began about the same time the smallpox struck, to bottle up The People in their two villages. Clam Necklace and her children were the first to break out with the rash, pain, and fever that signified the onset of the disease. Because Blue Wing was the only Mandan immunized against it—and despite everything, because of her continued duty to her family and the tribe—she tended her kin in Wolf Trap's lodge but told him he must stay away. It was, no doubt, the only reason she was permitted back in the lodge and the only reason she would go.

"So sad, Clam Necklace," Blue Wing told Kate later. "My sister out of her head with fever before she let me care for those children. And then it much too late— maybe for the whole tribe."

"Don't say that. We have to save as many as we can, even if it spreads."

The dead those first twelve days—for that appeared to be the course of the plague in one body—included those living in Wolf Trap's lodge, except him, and five in the lodge of Scatter Corn, where Kate worked day and night to tend them. At Blue Wing's suggestion, she had sent Jamie and Mandan with Aunt Alice and Willy Nilly to live in the cave near the stream, thinking stray Sioux would be more likely to raid the boat or winter village. The *Platte Warrior* had fled downstream immediately, but there was no one to pilot the *Red Dawn* but Kate.

In her most frenzied, exhausting moments, she was haunted by her mother's voice as they knelt together by her baby sister's grave above Bellevue. The Omaha women had spread smallpox to little Leah; she had died, and Mama mourned. Kate would not—could not—lose another daughter to disease, as she had her Sally. Yet though she feared for her newborn daughter, the only one among family and crew who had not been immunized, she was not going to desert The People, especially when it was partly her fault they did not have their serum.

As for laying blame at her door, the amoral bastards at the fort dared to accuse her. Blackwell put out the word it was the trade blankets Kate had brought that started the plague. But Chief Four Bears and many others knew whose blankets were at fault. They went looking for Marbois, but he had fled. Even that did not end the official fingerpointing at Kate.

Somehow Blackwell convinced the Mandan shaman, Old Bear, who went about desperately trying to stem the curse with his chants and dances and medicine bundle, that Kate had sapped the strength of many Mandans by painting their faces—that old belief she had first heard the night she met Rand at General Clark's.

"Blackwell tell shaman Old Bear," Long Hatchet reported to Kate, "that your paintings of Mandans burn, so that why The People burn now with fever and die."

"That lying coward! I'm sure he heard from those traders on Chouteau's boat that their lord and master burned my work!"

"The chiefs kill Blackwell if they get him now, but gates lock shut and many guns on walls," Long Hatchet explained. He looked out toward the prairie, his weathered face creased with new worry. "And Sioux wait out there like spiders if we try send those untouched by curse away. We must pray harder to He Who Lives Above, make sacrifices to sun and moon. But do not worry The People blame you, Prairie Wind. We know the wife of River Walker and Dark Water help fight this bad white man disease."

In a fit of rage Kate burned the crimson blankets, though she later wished she'd just buried them for evi-

dence against Marbois. But like Four Bears, like the
chiefs, she stood helpless in the relentless onslaught of
the contagion. As she had heard and feared, the Indians
had less natural resistance to it than the whites. Scatter
Corn's family died, one more each day, but Rand's
"country aunt" lingered, as if she had to oversee the departure of those she loved. Kate nursed her for a week,
watching the proud, once-lovely face ravaged by tiny
spots, then red pustules, then scabs that marked the stages
of the infection.

"If bad-heart Sioux not harm our Dark Water," Scatter
Corn whispered to Kate, "tell him blame gun his father
did leave, not himself. Tell your daughter all about us so
The People may live on."

"Yes, I will. And Scatter Corn, honored Aunt, I promise you that your wise, dear face will gaze down from the
wall of our home at River of Sky."

"That good—River of Sky," she repeated as twin tears
tracked from her closed eyes. "The People say one who
dies go down water trail to spirit village high in heaven—
river of sky."

She opened her eyes to stare upward, but her spirit was
no longer there. Kate bent over her, mourning all that was
lost.

Strangely Wolf Trap and Swift Raven showed the rash
on the same day, but at first neither of them slowed, as if
they dared defy the disease. Swift Raven had been overseeing the watch for Sioux, but they lurked just beyond
the hills and only raided, a threat to keep everyone closed
in here to face another kind of massacre. Kate pictured
Marbois out there among the Sioux, even directing their
occasional slaughter of Mandan hunters, scouts, or refu-
gees from the plague. Blue Wing turned her frenzied attentions to nursing her husband when the fever finally
prostrated him.

Now Kate and Blue Wing were often at the lodge of
Long Hatchet, for besides Swift Raven, Kate's worst
nightmare of all the horrors she'd seen had happened:
Corn Basket, Long Hatchet, and their kin were stricken
too. Corn Basket's mind wandered in her delirium. Just

like General Clark, she rambled on about the old days, about how kindly the tribe had received the Lewis and Clark party. It was long into one endless night, bent over Corn Basket to wipe her brow, while Buffalo Grass tended Long Hatchet and Blue Wing leaned over Swift Raven, when Kate seized on a desperate idea.

"I just recollected something General Clark told me!" she whispered to Blue Wing.

"Just like with Corn Basket, what help are memories now?"

Blue Wing's face looked gray with grief; Kate knew she feared most of all to lose the man she had waited for so long. She reached over to grasp her shoulder.

"Listen to me. He said some Omaha women once were so desperate to cure smallpox among their people that they took matter from the pustules of others and rubbed it in scratches on their skin. You see, they did exactly what a vaccination does, only uncontrolled. And it saved them. Why didn't I think of that before? Swift Raven and your father are not too bad yet. Blue Wing, we have to try! I'm going out and find a man about their size who is ill and get some homemade serum!"

"You out of your head too," Blue Wing said, grabbing at Kate's skirt to stop her as she rose. "The People not let you take disease and put it in them, not when they hear it come from others already ill! Smallpox vaccine brought in from city—white man's medicine—that maybe different. And what if you harm those untouched so far?"

"Who will remain untouched but you and Buffalo Grass? Everyone is falling ill, and the Sioux have trapped us here."

"Yes," Swift Raven spoke, and weakly grasped Blue Wing's wrist. "Yes, I will try this thing. The sun-god and your Old Woman in the Moon turn away from us, wife. And if I get strong, Prairie Wind, I will ride out and find my friend Dark Water and fight the Sioux!"

Kate was startled to see day breaking as she made her way through the cluttered Mandan streets. Once clean and orderly, the village seemed now the stews of hell with hungry dogs, deserted lodges, strewn possessions, and the fetid stench of decay. Bodies often swelled and turned black just before death. The first victims had been properly wrapped and placed on scaffolds outside the village walls. But now The People dumped their many dead in ravines or food caches because the survivors were terrified and ill. Some Mandans, convinced their gods had deserted them, unable to face the obliteration of all they knew and believed, even hanged themselves or jumped off the cliff. Demented souls sometimes ran shrieking through the streets to make everyone think the Sioux were upon them.

Kate stopped before the lodge of Chief Four Bears and called out his name. She clasped her scraper and bowl close to her breasts, wishing she could hold and nurse Mandan yet—nurse her with her mother's milk, a healthy child after all this other nursing of the sick. She longed to hug Jamie and hold Rand to her, as she had so briefly before he set out. But she must not think of Rand's fate now or she too would rush demented, shrieking, through this town of death. She called out again and knocked on a doorpost.

The chief came to motion her in. "Do not tell of other deaths," he said, "for my own all gone now to join Bright Star." Kate looked around the lodge. Empty when just yesterday there were four struggling for life here. In the light of the low fire she saw he was decked in full battle regalia. Now he threw his painted buffalo robe over one shoulder.

"I am so . . . very sorry and bent with grief," she managed to say in Mandan, "although words cannot say how I feel."

"Words can say much," he countered in English, "like your good painting say much. Today in heart of the village I want you write down my words in English, take to General Clark and that dog Chouteau. Tell many whites in St. Louis and Washington, even the Great White Father, he who is also lower than dog."

"I—yes, all right. Chief Four Bears, I came here thinking your sons were still alive and I could make a cure from their—their wounds. I think I know how, if you will let me use others."

He sighed. "All good medicine gone from The People." His voice rustled like dry leaves. Then, without another word, he walked outside.

She followed to see him mount a pony with a fine saddle. He began to ride up and down the twisting streets of Mitutanka bellowing in Mandan, "Braves, to arms! Watchmen, announce the raid! Glorious deeds await in battle! We must fight the Sioux! We must fight our enemies, even unto death!"

Kate ran back to the lodge of Long Hatchet and found her drawing pad and a charcoal pencil. With no one following him, no one pressing forward to hang on his every word, still shouting, Chief Four Bears reined in at the very center of the silent town. Kate stood alone in dawn's pale light to scribble down the words he said: "I have never wronged a white man but have protected them. The People never saw a white man hungry but they gave him food, drink, and a buffalo skin. But I do say now the whites are black-hearted dogs. People, think of all you hold dear who are dead. This is the last you will hear me!"

He charged his horse past her, out of the village. Kate heard later that he had gone only as far as the scaffolds of the dead where he dismounted, sat down, and starved himself to death.

That very day she concocted a diluted serum from the live smallpox fluid and rubbed it in scratches she made on the arms of Long Hatchet and Swift Raven. Though their faces still developed the crusty scabs that would turn to pockmarks, they lived! She tried it on the few others who would allow it, for the madman shaman haunted her steps, claiming she could not be trusted. At last, after most of the tribe had cast their once-precious bundles in the fire or died clutching them to their breasts, the shaman's voice fell eternally silent too.

But Kate found meager victory in saving a few Mandans when, by her own reckoning, seven-eighths of the inhabitants of Mitutanka were dead, and word came from Ruptare that only fourteen there remained alive. Yet she felt hopeful as well as fearful when Swift Raven rode out alone to search for Rand. She marveled at how stoically Blue Wing bade farewell to her husband, now chief of the tribe because the other leaders were all gone. But perhaps, since Kate's makeshift immunization had saved him, Blue Wing thought he would lead a charmed life out among the deadly Sioux.

Kate's guards had now shrunk to the ever-faithful Pete. Quiet Gray Eyes, laughing Arrow Point with his mirrored hair, even the handsome berdache Loud Fox were no more. Finally she felt the holocaust had abated enough that she dared to wash thoroughly in the river and go to visit her family. Yet she stood across the stream and called to them over it while Pete stood behind her with a loaded gun and Willy Nilly came out with his gun in his arms.

"No, don't let Jamie come over here, Aunt Alice! I think he'd be fine, but he might carry something back to Mandan. Oh, she's looking wonderful, even without her mother's milk."

"I dinna ever see a sturdier lass," Aunt Alice called to her, and held up the squirming child. "But I must warn you, Kate MacLeod, the wee bairn thinks I'm her mother now."

"And couldn't have had a better one. But we'll share her ... when Rand—when he comes back. Swift Raven's gone out to find him. But he'll be so devastated. . . ."

For the first time in the blur of days and weeks, Kate feared for Rand's mind and soul as well as his life. He had suffered so and blamed himself when his mother died. He had dedicated himself to protecting The People. Perhaps he would now blame Kate for failing to bring the serum. "You're going to have to sacrifice me for a while," he had said to her the day he left. But she could not bear it if he were gone for good.

"I'll be back soon again!" she called to her little family. "I love you, Jamie! Be a good boy, and do what Willy Nilly and Aunt Alice say. And soon we'll all be back togeth—"

She could not help it, but she turned away without another word and ran with Pete right behind, jogging so his bullets bounced rhythmically in his leather pouch. She had not really cried all this time, and this nightmare was not over yet, not until Rand came back and said he loved her and they would go on together. But she had seen so much death, learned not to hope someone would make it.

They skirted way around the fort and went back to the *Red Dawn,* which seemed poised for escape. For one moment she was tempted to send Pete back for her family and set out to River of Sky, where surely everything was calm and peaceful and safe. But everyone here among the Mandans was her family now too. She slowed her strides and squared her shoulders as she went aboard. She lifted her chin and blinked back tears again, refusing to give in to overwhelming fear and grief.

"If we had some good cannon aboard, I'd blow that damned government fort to perdition, where it belongs," she told Pete. "And then I just might burn the village too, so those bloody Sioux can't come in here and take it undefended as if the Mandans were nothing! And the remnants of the tribe—I'd take them to River of Sky to live."

"I know," he said, his voice a mere whisper. "So few left."

"We're left, and Blue Wing and Swift Raven," she declared. "General Clark once talked about sending Blue Wing to Washington. And if it's the last thing I do, our so-called white civilization's going to hear about this travesty of justice to the Mandans—the trading, the graft, the pox, all of it—if *I* have to take Four Bears' speech to the President and the newspapers myself!"

But inside her cabin, despite that bravado, at last she cried.

Swift Raven found his friend Dark Water when he had almost given up. The new chief had been clear to the camp of White Raven only to be turned away because they were afraid of the "Mandan sick." But he had learned that Rand had parlayed with White Raven to talk him out of total war—for half the Mandan corn crop this autumn, a crop now untended and unharvested. Heading back, Swift Raven was almost home when he heard gunfire on the buttes above the Knife River and saw someone pinned down by Sioux arrows and gunfire: Rand! Swift Raven hid his horse and, finding no good spot to attack the enemy from the rear, managed to crawl around the precipice to join his friend.

"A splinter band of Sioux, one White Raven doesn't control," Rand explained breathlessly. He felt overjoyed to see his friend, even though they were still desperately outnumbered. It touched him deeply that Swift Raven had risked his life to join him. His food was almost gone, though he had been rationing bullets.

They exchanged quick, whispered information as the sun rose bright in their eyes. Yes, the smallpox had been bad, but this situation was too, Swift Raven insisted, so they could speak of the other later. Rand briefly explained how he'd met some Hidatsas on the way home, who told him pox was among the Mandans. He'd raced back, and his horse had broken a leg in a prairie dog hole. He'd gone over a hundred miles on foot until this band, evidently harassing the Mandans, spotted him and nearly ran him down before he made it into a crevice in the rocks.

Swift Raven knew this area even better then Rand did, so he went first as they wormed their way from one crevice to the other in the morning shadows, carefully climbing higher, higher over the rampaging river, hoping to escape or at least get a good vantage point above their foe. But the stark sun reminded Rand of the other foe, for it etched the pockmarks on Swift Raven's face deep and dark.

"You had it too yet live, my friend!" Rand whispered. "Then what I feared is not so bad? Do many others live too?"

"Few," Swift Raven admitted. "Your Prairie Wind did save me and Long Hatchet. But we will not speak of death now, only of getting back to Mitutanka."

And then, as they shifted on their bellies in the shortening shadows, they caught a good glimpse of the enemy—and saw that Jacques Marbois was with them.

"Ayee," Swift Raven whispered. "That one least of all deserves to live, for he brought the pox with his red blankets."

"What?" Rand asked. "You mean Marbois deliberately

brought in the disease? That son of a bitch took the serum!"

As the sun climbed higher behind the Sioux, Rand saw only red. Red sky . . . red blankets . . . the blood of The People . . . the blood on his mother's chest when he pulled the trigger that day. Too long he had kept the fury leashed, for his father, for Aunt Alice, Chouteau, and Clark, then Kate. Kate, how he longed to hold her, to protect her from Marbois!

Before he even knew he would move, Rand went to a half crouch to be sure the bastard could not duck out of his sight. "Marbois, you demon," he shouted, "go to hell where you belong!"

He heard Swift Raven gasp at his daring. The Sioux screeched; Marbois leaped to his feet and lifted his gun. Rand fired, blowing him back away where he tumbled off the cliff and spun down to sprawl silently and grotesquely on the rocks below.

Rand reloaded while Swift Raven shot arrows. The daring of the surprise was still good; the Mandan fitted and shot four arrows before the Sioux returned one. Two Sioux went down; the dozen or so others scattered. Rand got another one.

"This way—more cover," Swift Raven said, and scrambled down the rock.

Rand slid after him, still trying to reload. They lost sight of the enemy then as they went around a ledge to change their position. The river roared below them. Suddenly two braves loomed on the shelf above. Swift Raven thumped an arrow into the first one. But the second sent a blur of arrow right at Rand. He tried to cling to the rock; he knew it would hit him low. He felt it thud into his back. The pain was intense and then nothing. But he tottered. He grabbed for Swift Raven, the rock. He grabbed for Kate, to keep her safe.

The last thing he saw was rising rocks and rushing river.

Kate sat stone-still on the deck of the *Red Dawn* while Swift Raven explained it all to her: how Rand had met success again with the Sioux, heard of the smallpox, rushed back, been trapped, killed Marbois. And how he had been struck by an arrow and fallen into the river, how he had been dead before he even hit the water. But Swift Raven had jumped in after him and been carried to safety from the Sioux. How he had searched for Rand's body but had not found it. And Rand had told him, Swift Raven went on, how much he loved her and wanted her to take the children to live in peace at River of Sky.

Still Kate sat, holding Mandan in her arms, with Jamie pressed against her knee and Aunt Alice's trembling hands on her shoulders. Finally, when Swift Raven did not budge even when Blue Wing went to him, Kate said, "Chief Swift Raven, thank you for trying to help, as I tried to help here, but it was impossible. The Mandans meant so much to my husband; perhaps he would not choose to live with their loss anyway." She thought Swift Raven looked almost sheepish when she said that, and she realized she had somehow embarrassed him. "Thank you," she said again.

But imagine, a little voice in her head prated, thanking someone for telling her she had lost her husband, that man who was never really her husband at all, not for more than a few wonderful weeks here last year. But all that was gone now, gone like most of the Mandans, like Gabe, like her dreams. She must begin all over again—as when she lost Clive—but she was so different now, perhaps stronger, however weak and wasted she felt. She had her daughter too, and memories. Why must they rub her heart so raw right now that she could not face them, could not face the kind, concerned expressions of those around her? Clasping Mandan in her arms, she stood.

"I will be back next year to trade with The People, Chief Swift Raven," she said. "Now I—I must go south to River of Sky, then perhaps on to St. Louis to be sure everyone knows the truth about—about these tragedies."

This was not real, she thought. All that Swift Raven had said about Rand's death was not real. He was going to come riding in here soon or run down from the fort and cross the gangplank to the ship. He was going to take her in his arms and help her rear these children. She handed the baby to Aunt Alice just in time because for the first time in her life she fainted.

It was nearly two weeks later when Kate was well enough to set out on the river. She had seen enough of her cabin ceiling these days to last a lifetime. She held hands with Blue Wing, trying to say good-bye for now, making plans to fight Chouteau and the government. The Mandans might be mostly gone, but the wrongs which had done them in were not.

At the last moment Long Hatchet came aboard with a buffalo robe in his arms. "The *mih-sha* of your husband, newly painted, tell whole story," the old artist whispered, and touched her hand. "You know how read it now, good as you know how paint."

Kate almost smiled at that, for Chief Four Bears too had said her work was good. These men from a supposedly hostile, savage world had valued her work as the men in the white world never had. She suddenly realized one way to make these mass deaths have some meaning was to paint The People again from memory. Yes, she would do Corn Basket making pots, Scatter Corn scraping a fine robe, Arrow Point shaking his mirrors in the sun and admiring his love exploit stick. . . .

She sniffed hard and waved farewell as the few Mandans disembarked. How many there had been to greet her here; how they had thronged last time she departed to give her gifts. But even now she took with her their gifts of acceptance, wisdom, and love. And she must admit, she took with her resentment, even hatred for Kellen Blackwell, who had told Pete he was worried that with so many hunters "gone," the fort would not clear its overhead operating costs this year. If it were only in her power, she would be certain he met the same fate Marbois had!

With Pete acting as first mate, though he had everything to learn, Kate rang the bell and cast off. She did not let herself look back again, only ahead toward River of Sky. They made good time those first few hours, riding with the current, but she felt haunted by the river she had once loved. Now, at each rack of driftwood, each shadowy thicket among the autumn reds and golds, she kept imagining she would find Rand along the banks, as she had once before. He'd be hurt perhaps, limping, but waiting for her, flagging her down to tell her he'd escaped the Sioux. Her legs went weak, and she began to tremble.

"Pete, get me that stool, will you?"

"Sure. Guess you put that new painted robe on it, though."

"Let me see it, and you just take the wheel a moment. We're right out in the middle of the channel."

She perched on the stool with the robe over her knees and fingered it almost reverently. It told the whole story, Long Hatchet had said. Steadying herself to see how he had done Rand's death, she glanced down at the bottom of the last row of picture drawings, where the paint was fresh and bright. And gasped.

"What's the matter?" Pete asked without taking his eyes off the river.

"This story Long Hatchet's painted . . . Oh, Pete, it can't be!"

She threw the robe back on the stool and reached around him to nose the boat into the bank. "What in tarnation are you doing?" he demanded. "It's not time for a wood stop a-tall, let alone—"

"We're heading back!" she cried. "Back to the winter village at Point of Woods! If this is true, I won't let him do this! Oh, dear God in heaven, it *has* to be true!"

"What?"

"Just tell everyone we have to go back!" Stunned by disbelief, shaking with hope, she rang for more steam and turned the *Red Dawn* back out to fight the current.

Chapter 21

Rand lay, his lifeless legs covered with one of Kate's trading blankets, on the floor of his mother's family's winter lodge. Beside him, stuck on the slanted wall, the sketch of him Kate had done years ago at General Clark's stared down at him and he at it like some awful black-and-white mirror of his soul. The drawing looked crumpled and still—just like him.

With his arms he hiked himself more upright against the willow backrest. He felt no physical pain; from his hipbones down he felt absolutely nothing, could move nothing. But emotional agony wrenched his heart, for deceiving Kate and asking Swift Raven to lie to her. His friend and Buffalo Grass cared for his needs now, solemnly, stoically, like giving the last rites to the dead.

Rand was sure that besides these two and Long Hatchet, no one knew he was alive. He wasn't really; today he'd died a little more when he'd heard the distant ding of the *Red Dawn*'s departing bells, the fading chug of its engine. Kate had to be set free, even if it meant the loss of the only woman he had ever loved, the only child he would ever have, his once-foolish hopes for harmony between the Mandan and white worlds. He had sobbed aloud then. Now, several hours later, he sat dry-eyed and ready.

As soon as Kate had left, Buffalo Grass had been asked to chatter to the sentry at the gate of the fort to let Blackwell know that he was alive, hiding paralyzed in the winter village, and that he was alone each afternoon. He had told Swift Raven he could explain it all to Blue Wing later but for now to keep her away. Soon, surely, his last two tasks on this earth would be done.

Buffalo Grass shuffled in. The devastation to the tribe had bowed but not broken her. He thought she too might never smile again.

"Old Grandmother, does Blackwell know?" he asked.

"The man ran tell him, but I say your thoughts crooked. Facing Blackwell alone, good. But not bent words to Prairie Wind. She strong enough for both of you over the years."

"There are no years left for me now—not this way. I can't control my body functions, let alone my legs. I've got nothing now of what it takes to protect and keep a woman."

She snorted. "In all harsh winters I learn much. Men can command a woman's body, not her heart. You throw away one like Prairie Wind," she muttered as she went out, "maybe you already dead."

"Soon enough," he whispered to the empty, echoing lodge.

He sat waiting, not for revenge but for justice, as he had planned these last weeks since Swift Raven had pulled him from the river. It was not long before the accused came into Rand's court, holding a pistol in his hand with a second gun stuck in his belt, next to that gold watch he always flaunted. And he had dressed well for his own funeral; even in the wilds Blackwell had always looked and acted the dandy.

"So it's true," Blackwell said, pointing the pistol at him. "The half-breed's now half a man, too."

"I want to know if you and Marbois schemed to start the pox here," Rand demanded.

"Only to wipe out a chosen few of the stubborn bastards, and it just got out of hand. It's the red men themselves spread it! I'm just hoping Chouteau reassigns me, as this bunch is gone. And since I hear you killed Marbois, I don't feel a bit bad to—"

Blackwell lifted his pistol, stiff-armed. For once the man looked directly in Rand's eyes. But before he could shoot, Rand fired the pistol he held under the blanket. It blew the blanket from him and Blackwell back into the wall. He hit, slumped, shuddered, and did not move again.

"Your crime was the rape and murder of the Mandans," Rand pronounced. "And mine—failure to stop it all . . ." As Swift Raven ran into the room, Rand lifted the pistol barrel toward himself.

"No!" The Mandan lunged, sprawled across him, to roll him over and knock the gun away. They lay panting, shaking, almost in an awkward embrace.

Finally Swift Raven rolled off and spoke. "I tell bent words for you, but I will not let you go. If I am chief, even of the few, I cannot do it alone! Always The People have two leaders!"

His eyes pinched shut, Rand shook his head. Swift Raven pulled him back to a sitting position and knelt beside him. "I can't be a chief here," Rand said. "And you know, if I want to leave like that"—he pointed as they looked at Blackwell—"I will. Anyhow, when Chouteau hears I killed both his lackeys here, he'll try to get me."

Swift Raven took Rand's gun and looked about to be sure there was not another. "Not when Prairie Wind tell everyone the truth," he insisted. "She be better than a gun to that dog's head."

Swift Raven went across the lodge and rolled Blackwell over with his foot. Grabbing him by his ankles, he dragged him out the door. His pocket watch fell from him and lay sprawled behind him in the trail of his blood.

When Buffalo Grass came in and swabbed at the stains and retrieved the watch, Rand asked her, "Do you want that?"

"No!" she said, and brought it to him, holding it by its chain as if it would bite. "That bad-heart man think it have white medicine in it, but it only have death."

Rand took it from her, held it by its chain, and smashed it to pieces, again, again, against the wall post. There, he thought, as it turned to a mass of springs and wheels and crumpled metal, time has stopped for Blackwell, just as it has for me.

Kate nosed the prow of the boat into the bank at Point of Woods and told Pete to keep it there. "I'm taking several roosters with me to bring him back if all is as I think," she added. She'd tried to explain what she'd read on the robe to Pete.

She ran down the plank and led four armed men through the woods at such a pace they were soon panting. The winter village, silent, deserted, loomed through bright autumn trees. She saw Buffalo Grass sitting in the sun before the lodge of Scatter Corn and ran straight for her.

"Is he here? Is he really alive, old Grandmother?"

Buffalo Grass's face webbed into a grin. "Good you here," she said. "He killed Blackwell, wants kill himself. You take him, help him."

Kate told the men to wait and yanked the flap aside. She darted in, then stopped as Rand gasped and heaved himself to a sitting position. "How could you?" she cried. It was not what she meant to say, but she felt as angry as elated. While her eyes adjusted slowly to the dimness, she walked to him in this lodge, where he had brought her this time last year to love, to make their child. Now he'd as good as sent her away. "Don't you know I love you," she demanded, "no matter what?"

Looking stunned, he held up both palms as if to ward her off. "Kate, it's for the best—for you. I can't walk, can't function as a husband or a man!"

"It doesn't matter."

"Of course, it matters! It matters to a man who was once called Runs Quickly among The People. A man who has a wife and children to protect but can't walk, ride, can't—"

"Fine job you're doing of protecting us if we're at River of Sky and you're here! We'll get a doctor; we'll all be together!"

"Kate, you're strong and clever. You can build a life again, but you don't need a third child to tend. Find someone else. I'll be gone soon enough, and we were only married here. Don't look at me that way! I've ruined everything in life I've touched, everything I wanted to protect and love!"

Desperate, she seized on the only weapon she had ever wielded well against him: argument, something that should have been buried between them long ago.

"It's just you want to be free of us, isn't it? Live here with your memories where you can blame yourself, live in the past? And you told me you believed in lifelong marriages, unlike the Mandans. You told me we'd always be together after last year. If you won't be a husband to me and a father to the children, I suppose I can use you for a secretary the way General Clark does Stirling now, because I intend to let everyone know about how Chouteau operates through men like Blackwell and Marbois!"

"I killed them both—Blackwell here, just a while ago."

"Am I supposed to faint or cheer?" Tears streaked her face, but she refused to gasp or sob. She yearned to hold him, to find comfort in his arms, but she saw she must fight for his strength and not submit to his weakness.

She went to the door flap and summoned her men. They came in, glancing around nervously. "Be careful about it, but Major MacLeod needs to be carried to the boat. His legs aren't working well now, but he'll get better. And he's a bit delirious from all he's been through, so ignore his ravings. Let's go! Just wrap that blanket around his legs, that's it."

"Who told you I was here?" Rand demanded, seeing he was trapped, not bothering to struggle.

"Let's just say I read it somewhere," she said, and snatched her old sketch of him off the wall. The fact that he had it gave her a shred of hope he still loved her, wanted her.

"I thought you'd left!" he said.

"So you could tell yourself I was deserting you instead of the other way around?"

They were partway across the clearing when Swift Raven ran toward them with Blue Wing. Kate could tell Blue Wing was shocked to see Rand. Despite how Blue Wing questioned and scolded her husband, Kate saw Swift Raven was smiling. As he bent to lift and carry Buffalo Grass on his back, the new Mandan chief's scarred face beamed to see Kate and Rand reunited. If only Rand too could be glad she'd come back for him!

The crew of the *Red Dawn* gave three loud hurrahs, and Aunt Alice cried and jumped up and down. Jamie looked as if he were doing a scalp dance, cavorting and screeching in his boyish joy. Pete and Sam bellowed their welcomes.

When everyone quieted, Kate called out to the four Mandans, "We will return next spring and hope Rand will be walking by then!" She waved to dear Long Hatchet too as he walked from the woods and gave a whoop. "You see," she shouted to them all, "Dark Water is the best gift The People ever gave me."

She made sure Rand was settled in the bed which had been Jamie's in her cabin. He was fuming now, not speaking at all, though everyone else—but their wailing daughter—was ecstatic. Kate trembled at her forced bravado, still wanting so to hold him. And that gave her another idea. She went next door and took Mandan from Aunt Alice. She marched back into the cabin, past Jamie gawking in the door.

"Since I'll be up in the pilothouse," Kate said, "and Aunt Alice is going to help Willy Nilly prepare supper, please make yourself useful by holding your daughter for a while."

Rand took the child but seized Kate's wrist in a bruising grip that bent her close to him. "I'm in diapers too, damn it. Will you also change me?"

She bit her lower lip. She must not fear this dark, furious stranger. Mandan cried loudly, so Kate raised her voice. "I think Pete and Sam will help you if you ask them with a civil tongue. And yes, I hope to change you, change your bad heart, Rand, convince you how much I need and love you. But until then I'll have to tend to things myself, won't I? Now let me go."

"I want you to let *me* go!"

"No! I've been betrayed by men before who loved their bottle more, or riches, or another woman. But not by one who loved self-blame more. I've climbed out of my past, however hard that's been, and you can too."

"Not without my legs, my manhood," he whispered, glaring at her.

"Mandan's crying for both of us," Kate said. "Please make the crying stop." She pulled away from him and ran past Jamie and Aunt Alice, past the others to the pilothouse where she could think. All that afternoon, even when Sam and Pete said they'd help, she held the wheel, trying to get a grip on her circling thoughts and fears. And making plans, plans that dug deep into her troubles the way the paddle wheels churned water.

When they pulled into River of Sky on a blazing blue and gold day in early October, Rand was sitting in Kate's rocking chair with his gun across his knees, where she'd had him carried each day, at first over his protests and then at his command. Still, he was not the old Rand; he was broken and needed to be mended spiritually and physically, and she did not know how. She could only hope that when he saw what she had done here to welcome him home, his heart would soften. In their moments together she had tried both gentleness and fierceness to no avail.

"What the hell, a Mandan lodge?" he said now, as Pete and Sam carried him up the hill, still sitting in the rocker. To her chagrin she saw his jaw set hard, his eyes narrow.

"Obviously, Rand, when I had it built, I did not know the tribe would be mostly gone when we came here. I only wanted to honor The People and show you we can live in both worlds."

"The Mandan world is gone. It hurts too much to see it now."

Still, she threw open the door and uncovered the vent hole to light the room. And there, just as she had intended, against a central support beam, hung the portrait of Scatter Corn.

Rand gave a strangled gasp as the men carried him in and put him down. Kate motioned everyone else out and closed the door—one concession to the white world here. Dust motes twirled in the shaft of sunlight striking the boxed Mandan beds with their buffalo robes—and the proud face of Scatter Corn.

"I painted her at first," Kate explained, gripping her hands together, "because I heard she looked so much like your mother, who loved you dearly. I wanted you to have a remembrance of her. But then when Scatter Corn died too—"

"I can't believe this. You are trying to help me feel better and you paint *this* to stare down at us?"

"I thought you'd—".

"You thought wrong. About this, about many things. They're all dead, Kate, dead, and I had a lot to do with killing them—especially my mother!"

"Would you stop it! Scatter Corn's dying words to me were 'Tell Rand to blame the gun his father left in the lodge, not himself. Tell your daughter all about us so The People may live on'—"

"Live on? Damn it, woman, just like my legs, all that's *gone*! The fatal forces of evil have won again, Kate. Your happy world where everything gets better—gets painted over with love and hope and pretty memories—is a sham, just like this painting!"

He threw his rifle and hit the bottom of the frame Gabe had lovingly carved. The whole thing shuddered, then hit the floor and toppled facedown.

"Welcome home, Rand," Kate said. "I'd tell you to go to hell, but I think you've already built a hell for yourself, right here where I see our chance at heaven."

He seized her wrist, but she yanked it back. "Tell Pete," he said slowly, emphasizing each word, "I need a drink of whiskey."

"Tell him yourself since you know that nothing frightens me more than that." She went outside and ran up the hill, with Jamie chasing her. Collapsed on her rock, she watched the boy tear up to her, running as Rand never would again. She hugged him when he thudded into her; for once he did not wriggle from her embrace but stood silently, no questions, no chatter.

Kate still reeled from Rand's bitter cruelty, the pain he so wanted to share. But share it she would. Gabe's voice that day of her marriage taunted her: " 'In sickness and in health . . . till death us do part.' " Perhaps Rand's anger would help drain his agony from him. No matter what, she would be at his side.

She remembered how her mother had regretted that she had not gone to nurse her father when he fell and was paralyzed, even after all the terrible things he had done to them. And she recalled her mother's warning that Rand might have a violent streak hidden in his stoic, silent nature. Would he turn to drink or brutality now, the very things he had feared for The People, the things she had hated her father for, those causes for pain and never a cure?

She knew Rand needed healing desperately. She had a good notion to put him back on board and go on to St. Louis to seek Dr. Beaumont's help. But Rand needed more than just to walk. He needed to believe that unjust, dreadful things which had happened to people he loved were not his fault. She would send a request to St. Louis, asking that the doctor come here next spring.

All that aside, she knew she loved this man the Mandans had called Dark Water however much in his own way he now betrayed her. Surely this was a man she could read. She could understand his pain, his blame, his fears. And she was somehow going to soothe those and turn them to bright hope again.

She kissed the top of Jamie's tousled head. "Let's get busy, my boy. We've lots to do to make this place our home."

That winter was both the best and the worst of Kate's life. The best because Rand and Mandan were alive when she could have lost both of them. Although Sam and the roosters had gone back to St. Louis, Willy Nilly, who adored Aunt Alice, and Pete had stayed on to help and keep them company. The two men lived in the sturdy storehouse she'd had built. And even though Rand seemed to detest the lodge and threatened once to go live with the men, Kate loved their Mandan wood, sod, and clay house. It was the best winter too because she found great purpose in painting The People from her memories of happier times.

But it was the worst winter because although Rand would not argue with her in the intimacy of the lodge with the children and Aunt Alice there, silence stretched endlessly between them. And the worst because he seemed to want to betray her in another way her father and Clive, even Chouteau had before.

"Those portraits are only making their loss more painful," Rand muttered, to halt her brush in mid-stroke. "I don't want you to do any more, like that one of Scatter Corn you put back up."

"So you will at least say her name? Rand, I'm sorry you don't like what I'm doing, but what else should I expect from you? And you *won't* tell me I cannot paint. I'm good, and I enjoy it. It helps me get through these terrible times. And I have not forgotten that the night we met, George Catlin told me never to let anyone make me forgo my dreams!"

"It's all been a dream turned nightmare, Kate, all we once hoped for."

"It's a nightmare we could turn to a dream come true, if you but had the courage," she insisted, and went right on painting Chief Four Bears, sitting on his horse, giving his final address on his last day in the heart of the dying village.

Rand frustrated every effort she made to include him in life around him. He refused to go out on the simple sled Pete had made to take him hunting. Even Jamie's questions could not pry much of a response from him. Eventually the boy too, though he still watched Rand eagerly for signs of interest, walked around him. Pete's camaraderie, Kate's concern, Aunt Alice's scolding or coddling could not lift him from the deep pit of his melancholy.

Sometimes Kate wondered if he hadn't fallen back into those dark years after he shot his mother when he did not speak, refusing to recall the tragedy of her loss. Now that he had lost The People and his pride, perhaps this was even worse. She searched and prayed for something to pull him from his despair. At least he did not take to drinking, as she had feared. But she felt that like the *Red Dawn* rolled up on logs and chained to trees on the ice- and mud-clogged bank of River of Sky, she and Rand were mired and frozen and fettered all that long, long winter.

When the weather broke, Kate worked outside while Aunt Alice tended Mandan and the house. Alone or with Pete and Willy Nilly, Kate did the things she had once planned she and Rand would do together: plant corn, squash, and beans; plan a trading trip upriver; build up a trade with the Ioways, Omahas, and Osages who drifted through. But their visitors reminded Rand of the lost Mandans. Even when he found he could twitch a toe and Kate rejoiced, it only made him realize all that was gone. In the sweet spring, even at her beloved River of Sky, Kate too began to despair.

And then, on the first steamer up the spring river, Dr. Beaumont arrived and gave her hope again. "You've both got to realize," he counseled after he examined Rand, "that spinal injuries are notoriously slow to heal, but some *do* heal. Kate, what you've told me about your father's broken neck is different from this. This may not even be a broken back. That twitch in your toe is one good sign, Rand. Though your back wound has healed over, I think it would be advisable for me to make an incision to see if splinters from the arrowhead are still in there. And you've got to begin to exercise whatever muscle strength you do have, even if it pains you. Walk on crutches, swim."

"Swim?" Kate said. "What a wonderful idea. River of Sky is calm and deep enough!"

"It takes legs as well as arms to swim" was Rand's reply, but he agreed to the operation. And so, with Kate's blessing, Rand downed nearly two bottles of "medicinal rum" to deaden the pain, bit a leather strap, and let Pete and Willy Nilly hold him down while Dr. Beaumont cut him open and picked out deep-set splinters of the Sioux arrow. Kate swabbed blood, remembering the night that Blue Wing and she had stitched him up and he had not made a sound.

But after Dr. Beaumont returned to St. Louis, even when the scar healed over again, no changes occurred but an occasional tingling in his calves and thighs. And because Kate was watching when he toppled and fell on the crutches Pete had made him, he refused to use them. Again he plunged into black brooding.

Now Kate was torn over whether to take the *Red Dawn* back to St. Louis to get more trade goods or stay with Rand. Or should she force him to come along? She was starting to see that there was really no way to force him

to get better, and already summer slipped away. She had
to put in motion her plans to spread the truth about the
Mandan tragedy, but going back to face Chouteau with a
bitter, crippled husband worried her. And then, one day in
early August, everyone came to them.

Swift Raven and Blue Wing alighted from a keelboat
and ran up the brow of the hill where Kate stood trading
with some Ioways and Omahas before the storehouse,
where Aunt Alice swept out the floor. Kate shouted and
ran to Blue Wing, her arms outspread. And then she
stopped to see her swollen middle.

"Blue Wing, a child, a child!" she cried, and hugged
her.

"Old Woman in the Moon did not turn from us," she
declared with a nod toward Swift Raven. "She sends to
us this son from Baby Hill! The first of the new Mandans!"

"Come up to the lodge!" Kate said, and told them all
about Rand's progress—or lack of it. She was gratified
they, at least, were touched by the sight of the sturdy
home she had made here. She ducked in to look for Rand,
then remembered Pete and Willy Nilly had carried him in
her rocking chair up the hill just behind the lodge. Rand
saw them coming and even smiled.

"You see, Rand, besides our own Mandan, here is a future for the tribe, however difficult things are for them!"
Kate told him when he stared at Blue Wing's middle, then
nodded at the proud Swift Raven.

"I envy you the chance to teach your child to walk, to
face that future," Rand told them, speaking in Mandan for
Swift Raven. In Rand's voice, the sound of the gutturals,
the long rhythmic words startled Kate at first. Tears
sprang to her eyes, for Rand had not shut those things
from his mind, and this language was another living heritage from those many lost.

"But I'm afraid my year-old daughter is walking better
than I ever will." Rand went on to quench Kate's flicker
of hope that this visit would lift his spirits. She felt suddenly furious with him. Would nothing light his dark
depths?

"But you must admit," she blurted before she could pull the words back, "Mandan tries harder than you!"

Her insult seemed not to faze him. "Tries harder, is stronger, Kate. That's because you bred and bore her without me around, because she's yours, just like this place here. You see, my friends, Kate has become the man of the family now, and she's done a damn fine job of it while I sit in this rocking chair and just—"

"Kate!" Aunt Alice called from down the hill. "The *Platte Warrior*'s putting in! And I see Cadet Chouteau aboard!"

Kate waved to Aunt Alice and turned back to Rand. Yes, bless Chouteau for once, she thought. Rand's face actually showed concern rather than just listlessness or bitterness right now. And so she would stake everything on this great risk.

"Blue Wing and Swift Raven," she said, "if you would be so kind as to stay and protect Rand, I'd appreciate it. Since he has given up his place as head of the household, I will have to face Chouteau alone." She saw Swift Raven, standing behind Rand, frown and begin to speak, but dear Blue Wing read things right to grip his wrist and shake her head at him.

"Kate!" Rand called as she walked down toward the river. "At least take Swift Raven with you or get the men down by the river first! Kate!"

For the first time since he'd been like this, Rand felt rich fury roar through him to drown his defeat. Chouteau dare not come here to their land! Was he going upriver to try to reestablish his graft, his cheating trade with the remnants of the Mandans? Swift Raven had said they were living now with the Hidatsas for protection and might even unite with the Arikaras, who had also been weakened by the Sioux and the smallpox. And he could not bear for Kate, however much she could outthink and outwork any man, to face that wily wolverine alone. Pete and Willy Nilly were swimming today in the Sky River, where he suddenly wished he'd been trying to get some strength back in his tingling but numb legs.

"Swift Raven, go with her, will you?"

"If she chief here now, I best do what she say," he answered, and would not budge.

Rand swore under his breath and hiked himself up by the arms of the chair to try to reach his crutches, which Pete had hung just out of his reach to spur him on. The rocking chair rolled, and he almost pitched forward.

"Just this once, I help," Blue Wing said, and handed him the crutches.

"Blue Wing, please, in case the bastard's brought others with intent to harm Kate, run down to get the men on the river," Rand ordered. She nodded and darted off.

With Swift Raven beside him, Rand propped his armpits in the crutches and swung his big body between them. With the hill, the grass, he fell twice. But he shoved Swift Raven's hands away and got up again, rushing now, sweating all over. He had a pistol in his inner coat pocket. Kate had stopped unloading it lately when he wasn't looking, and so he did not really contemplate using it on himself anymore. Besides, he would never do that to her, let her or one of the children see or find him shot, for they might blame themselves.

He should have told her he would not harm himself now. He should have told her how much he admired her, loved her, wanted her. Why hadn't he shared with her that with the tingling in his thighs, feeling—the ability even to grow stiff with longing for her—had returned, even when they argued? He had dreamed last night he danced wildly at O-Kee-Pa with her, then rutted with her the way the devil O-Kee-Hee-De wanted to with the hunter's wives. Why had he held all this inside when he could lose her now, lose everything she had built for them to that son of a bitch Chouteau?

Tears poured down his cheeks like sweat. Below him, on the bank, unarmed, hands on hips, Kate faced Chouteau alone.

"I should have known," Kate replied to Chouteau's explanation, "that you'd soon be trying to move your trade to other northern tribes. It's time to move on to others since you've decimated the Mandans in your pursuit of money and power."

"You'll not blame me for that—for the serum you had and lost! I only stopped to offer help, madame," the man insisted. "First, I have obtained new serum for the tribe, government-ordered. I even have a doctor aboard," he said boastfully.

She could have cried; she just shook her head. "Too late, thanks to your lackeys Blackwell and Marbois!"

"But both acted without my permission, I assure you, and both met unfortunate ends. Ah, speaking of that, here comes your poor, maimed husband."

Kate whirled. Her heart soared to see Rand swinging slowly down the hill with Swift Raven at his side. "He's not poor and not maimed, you deceitful wretch," she told Chouteau. She wanted to run to Rand, to throw herself in his arms, at least to tuck her hand in his, but she stood her ground between the men.

"Yes, at any rate"—Chouteau addressed Rand now— "I'd like to offer Major MacLeod—well, actually, I don't think it's 'major' anymore as despite the fact that General Clark is on *his* last legs, so to speak, your appointment as Mandan agent has been rescinded, MacLeod."

"An order signed by Stirling Mount no doubt," Rand replied. Kate thrilled to the steel-sharp tone of his voice.

"Fortunately Mrs. MacLeod's former fiancé is a great help to a man practically on his deathbed. But, MacLeod, I was going to say, I want to make an offer for you to return to my employ perhaps right here with this little trading post, if you'd like. Or I'll finance your trading company and—"

"You mean," Kate said, "you're making an underhanded deal like the one you made Clive once, or is this a public one to silence us? You dare to try to include us in your spider's web of unholy alliances?"

"Unholy? My dear madame, I really must protest—"

"She means *hellish*, Chouteau!" Rand interrupted. "You're a manipulator, a cheater, a liar—and a murderer."

Chouteau looked shocked, but he quickly recovered his characteristic aplomb. "Ah, I see you cannot be persuaded. Perhaps wisely, since I believe the Missouri River fur trade will soon play out. Perhaps an increased trade in buffalo tongues or robes—perhaps northern land for settlers will keep things going. At any rate I—"

"You and your ilk," Rand said in an explosive burst, "have nearly wiped out the beaver, and now you'll kill the buffalo for their tongues! And the Mandans mean less than that to you! Get off our land, you son of a bitch, and don't give me the chance to shoot you! And I swear to you, somehow, somewhere you will face the judgment of the Indians, and good Americans, even God for all you've done!"

"He says he's taking smallpox serum up the river, Rand," Kate told him.

"Of course," Rand said, drawing his pistol, "so President Jackson and his corridors of cronies can say they tried to help, that none of the massive murder of the Mandans was their fault. Get off our land, Chouteau, and never dirty this mudbank again!"

Kate gasped to see sun glint from lifted rifle barrels aboard the steamer. She and Rand glanced up to see a row of guns bristling along the railing. But from the trees walked Pete and Willy Nilly with their rifles at the ready. And when Blue Wing ran in with her skinning knife out, recognition of who she was obviously hit Chouteau, and he held up a staying hand to those behind him.

"Now, now," Chouteau said, his livid complexion blanching visibly, "let's not have a little war."

"Not now, but later a big one, Chouteau," Rand said. "We'll see you in Washington someday, we'll take you on in newspapers or . . . in art galleries," he added, and pulled Kate to him with one arm. One crutch dropped, he wobbled, but he stood leaning against her, standing with her.

Swift Raven spoke to Blue Wing, who translated for him. "Chouteau"—her voice rang out—"my husband, Swift Raven, say tell you he now chief of the Mandans, chief with Dark Water, this man here, once our Mandan agent. He say tell you Mandans only trade now with this woman, Prairie Wind, Kate MacLeod. He say never set one foot on Mandan land or you never go back to St. Louis, like you should go now."

Chouteau looked as if he would explode. Kate thought

for one moment he would argue, even give the order to fire, despite the weapons trained on him. But he turned and stalked up the gangplank. He muttered to a man who scampered up the sets of steps to the pilothouse. And without a word from Chouteau, his men quickly lowered their rifles.

When Kate glanced back to smile at Swift Raven, she saw why. The Ioways and Omahas, who had come to trade, had walked silently down the hill and stood, narrow-eyed, armed with guns and bows to back them up. She turned to Rand to hug him as the *Platte Warrior,* which had once been Clive's *Sally Kate,* backed out into the wide Missouri—and turned back downstream toward St. Louis.

"Let's take all our guests back up to our lodge—to our home," Rand said, and stooped to retrieve his fallen crutch. "Our home, when we're not up north, trading with The People and helping Swift Raven." Together he and Kate made their way up the hill with the Mandans, Omahas, and Ioways trailing behind.

The day after Blue Wing and Swift Raven set out north on a keelboat, Kate talked Rand into a swim in River of Sky. He left his crutches on the bank, then floated out until the clear, cool water was almost waist-deep. With Kate's help, he planted both feet, spread wide on the pebbly bottom and tried to get his balance. The current rippled against him, past him, but holding to her at first, then on his own despite the pain, he took one step, and another, buoyed by the water.

He found he could swim, even kick a little, though he moved through the water as slowly as a turtle. "It feels good," he admitted. "It's such a beautiful day."

She smiled at him. "And a beautiful place—*sinashush.*"

"*Sinashush,*" he said. "And my woman is much more beautiful than I have ever told her. Even in this cold water I must admit I'm having stirrings and certain longings. I will have to cut myself a love exploit stick from one of these trees so we can keep track of my recovery."

Kate was almost swept away by hope and joy. She went all gooseflesh in the water where her petticoat and bodice clung so coldly, however flushed she felt. "And I," she said as she looped her arms around his neck, "have always had certain longings."

"For me, I hope."

"Yes, to love you and be loved in return. To have a real partnership between us. And to be able to see things outside the city, to know and paint the different people in the world, despite the pain as well as pleasure there."

"We've had too much pain and not enough pleasure. My fault—"

"Don't say that!" she told him, covering his lips with her fingertips. "When something is your fault, someone will let you know. But some terrible things just aren't."

"You're right," he said with a decisive nod.

In the flow of river she held tightly to him. He lifted her in his arms, though they soon toppled over and splashed and laughed. But for one brief moment, held aloft, Kate had glanced down into the mirror of water, *a-wa-sa-ta*. And seen, smiling up, a grand portrait of her future, framed by free-flying clouds and clear prairie sky.

Author's Note

Exactly how the smallpox epidemic began at Fort Clark in 1837 was never established, except that it was probably brought in by steamboat, and some warriors may have stolen blankets infected with the disease. Smallpox is so contagious and virulent it can, and has, been spread that way. After it decimated the Mandans, the United States government rushed quantities of vaccine to Fort Clark. Yet because the Bureau of Indian Affairs knew full well that the Mandans were reduced to a fraction of their former size, no one was even named the new Mandan Indian agent.

The sad and shocking treatment of this hospitable tribe by the government and Chouteau's American Fur Company is true. However, I created the characters of Blackwell and Marbois, basing them on various Missouri River Indian agents and fur factors of that time. Mr. Laidlaw was a real person; his treatment of Fort Pierre employees is authentic. Cadet Chouteau (his name was Pierre but he was known as Cadet) himself was too central a character to create, so I represented him as closely as I could. (When the fur trade "played out," Chouteau went on to invest in other commodities and became a millionaire anew in New York City.) Chief Four Bears was a historical figure greatly admired by George Catlin and other visitors to Mitutanka; I have quoted from his actual final speech in Chapter Twenty.

Comments by other men who worked for Chouteau's American Fur Company also speak volumes about the crass, callous treatment of the Mandans and other tribes. Jacob Halsey, a Chouteau employee sent to Fort Clark after the epidemic, wrote: "[Loss to the company is] incal-

culable, as our most profitable Indians have died."
Another of Chouteau's factors, Kenneth MacKenzie of
Fort Union, complained, "Diseases introduced to the Indians by the whites have a tendency to make them mali-
cious." Later an Indian agent named Latta, who was sent
to the Three Tribes, to which the Mandans later belonged,
perhaps saw things more clearly: "The old American Fur
Company [was] the most corrupt institution ever tolerated
in our country."

In 1862 the Mandans formally united with the Hidatsa
and Arikara tribes, which had also been hit by the plague.
The Three Affiliated Tribes lived on the Fort Berthold
Reservation (Fort Berthold was a later fur fort) near the
present-day site of Newtown, North Dakota, where there
is also a Four Bears Memorial Park. Fort Clark was farther south on the Missouri, near present-day Center,
North Dakota, where there is now a Fort Clark State Historic Site. So once again, as they had been shoved northward from their settlements near the Heart River, the
Mandans moved farther from white civilization, though it
did them little good.

Tribal tragedies continued: By 1886 the Three Tribes
had lost 90 percent of the land once guaranteed to them;
when the Garrison Dam was built in 1956, a reservoir
flooded twenty-five percent more of their reservation
where farms, fields, and timber stood. Although there are
still settlements near there, many of The People moved
away at that time.

However, the proud Mandans still have a great victory
against incredible odds. As Roy Willard Meyer puts it in
his book *The Village Indians of the Upper Missouri,* "The
Three Tribes retained their language, traditions, and val-
ues ... [their] dignity and sense of identity."

As I researched background for this novel, I was able
to read about the times and places from many excellent
primary sources. These included fur factor Francis A.
Chardon's *Journal of Ft. Clark*; early Mandan visitor
Maximilian, Prince of Wied's *Travels in the Interior of
North America,* trans. H. E. Lloyd, ed. Reuben Thwaites;
and William Clark Kennerly's *Persimmon Hill.* Kennerly
was a nephew of General Clark's, and his book is a fine

remembrance of the grand old man and St. Louis of this era. Also of help was Donald Jackson's fascinating book *Voyages of the Steamboat "Yellow Stone."*

Other than the Sky River and Kate's River of Sky land, all landmarks and places along the Missouri River are authentic for that era. Today in some places the river itself has even changed its course, but my descriptions of river and bankside scenery are based on contemporary records of travelers, especially those of Maximilian. Even General Clark's maps were of help.

As alluded to in the story, Mandan is a challenging, difficult language to learn and pronounce. I took most of the Mandan words I used in this story from Maximilian's firsthand 1834 vocabulary, which he "wrote down with the help of several Mandans." However, I have occasionally simplified the very complex spelling needed to transcribe the words effectively.

I must note that rubbing frostbitten skin with snow, as Sam recommends to Kate for Blue Wing's treatment, is not good medical advice, although it was standard practice at that time among both Indians and whites.

I would like to thank the following people for their assistance and advice: my husband, Don Harper, who serves so ably and patiently as my business manager and proofreader; my wonderful agent, Margaret Ruley, whose continued support is priceless; the Dutton Signet people, especially my editor, Hilary Ross. Thanks to my St. Louis friend and fellow author Karyn Witmer-Gow for sharing information on historical places of interest in St. Louis. Also, Gary Bryant, at Firearms Unlimited in Naples, Florida, was extremely generous with advice about the single-shot Northwest guns and trade guns of the day.

Be sure to read
Karen Harper's
other wonderful
historical novels,
Circle of Gold
and
Wings of Morning,
also published by Signet.

Circle of Gold

When Rebecca Blake was orphaned, she was adopted by the industrious, well-educated Kentucky Shakers, and raised in their secretive, sexually repressed world. Little did she envision that one day a forbidden love would thrust her from her innocent life of denial into the lavish, sophisticated world of Victorian England's ruling class. This is Rebecca's story—of her courageous crusading for social reform ... her tumultuous marriage and the terrible misfortune that ended it ... and the passion and daring that returned her to her Kentucky roots and the childhood sweetheart she never forgot. Spanning two continents, this is the spellbinding saga of a beautiful and indomitable woman caught up in the surging tides of history and the crosscurrents of duty and desire.

Wings of Morning

Raised on the fiercely repressive Scottish isle of St. Kilda, feisty Abigail McQueen is both envied and scorned by the villagers for her independent ways. But nothing stops her from defying their primitive mores, which call for birthing practices that result in most newborns' dying of a mysterious disease. And when terrible tragedy claims both her husband and her baby, the shattered Abigail begins her relentless search for a cure.

It is the start of a journey that will take her from the wilds of Scotland to the lavish social whirl and sophistication of Victorian England, where she falls in love with a daring American sea captain, to a tropical island off Civil War-torn Florida. There, even with the war raging all around her, Abigail clings to her ideals, dreams, and desires.

Afire with the spirit and courage of an extraordinary heroine, this spellbinding romantic saga brims with the passion, tragedy, and authentic detail of history in the making.

"A provocative journey into
a splendidly realized world."
—Gay Courter,
author of *The Midwife's Advice*

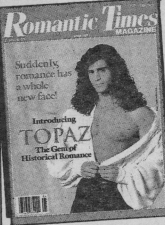
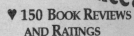